FORBIDDEN ISLAND

ALSO BY JEREMY ROBINSON

Standalone Novels

The Didymus Contingency
Raising The Past
Beneath
Antarktos Rising
Kronos
Refuge
Xom-B
Flood Rising
MirrorWorld
Apocalypse Machine
Unity
The Distance
Infinite
Forbidden Island

Nemesis Saga Novels

Island 731
Project Nemesis
Project Maigo
Project 731
Project Hyperion
Project Legion

SecondWorld Novels

SecondWorld
Nazi Hunter: Atlantis
(aka: I Am Cowboy)

The Antarktos Saga

The Last Hunter – Descent
The Last Hunter – Pursuit
The Last Hunter – Ascent
The Last Hunter – Lament
The Last Hunter – Onslaught
The Last Hunter – Collected Edition
The Last Valkyrie

The Jack Sigler/Chess Team Thrillers

Prime
Pulse
Instinct
Threshold
Ragnarok
Omega
Savage
Cannibal
Empire

Jack Sigler Continuum Novels

Guardian
Patriot
Centurion

Cerberus Group Novels

Herculean
Helios

Chesspocalypse Novellas

Callsign: King
Callsign: Queen
Callsign: Rook
Callsign: King 2 – Underworld
Callsign: Bishop
Callsign: Knight
Callsign: Deep Blue
Callsign: King 3 – Blackout

Chesspocalypse Novella Collected Editions

Callsign: King – The Brainstorm Trilogy
Callsign – Tripleshot
Callsign – Doubleshot

Horror Novels
(written as Jeremy Bishop)

Torment
The Sentinel
The Raven

Post-Apocalyptic Sci-Fi Novels

Hunger
Feast
Viking Tomorrow

Comics & Graphic Novels

Project Nemesis
Godzilla: Rage Across Time
Island 731

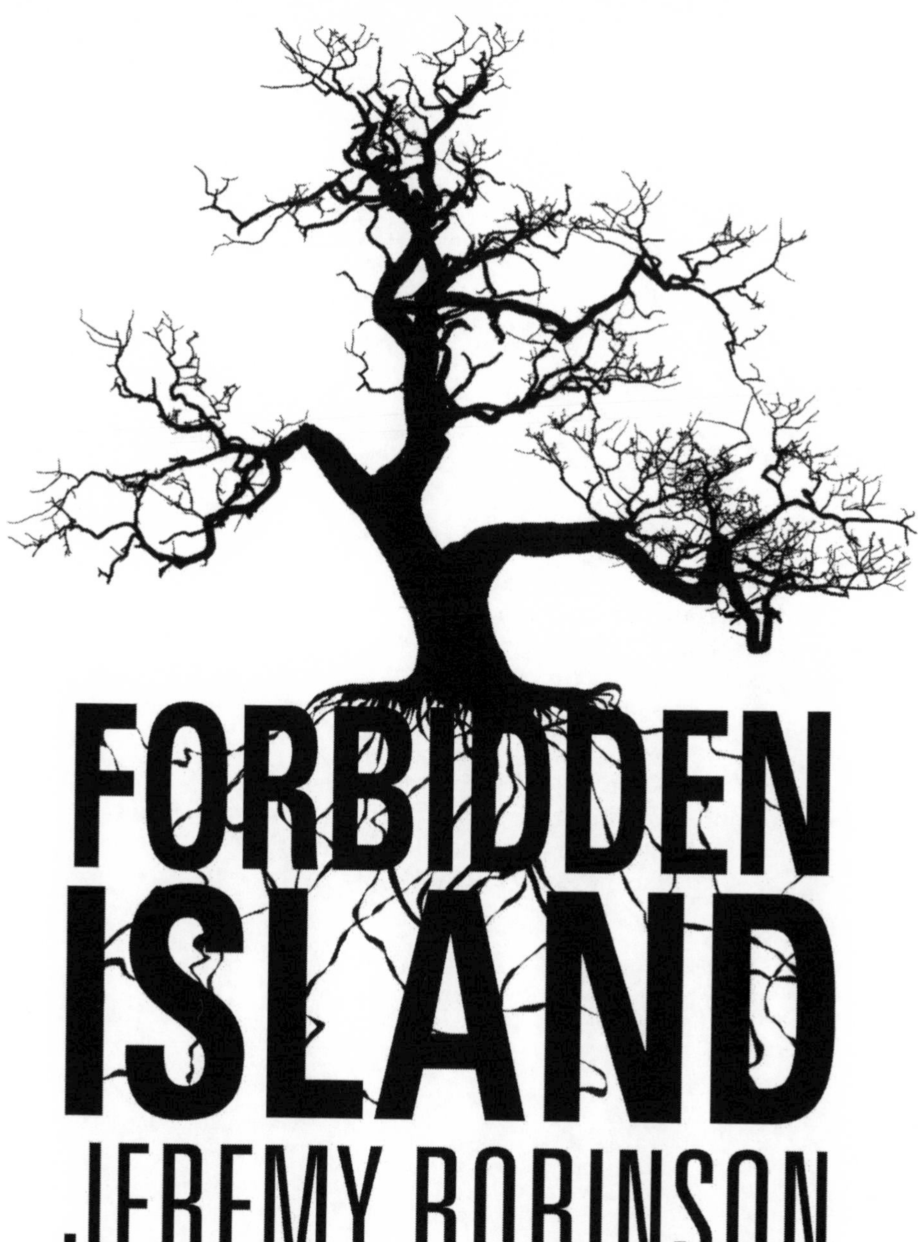
FORBIDDEN
ISLAND
JEREMY ROBINSON

BREAKNECK MEDIA

Visit Jeremy Robinson on the World Wide Web at:
www.bewareofmonsters.com.

For the RobinsonFest attendees.

May you never find yourself on the Forbidden Island.

PROLOGUE

North Sentinel Island, The Bay of Bengal, 1981

THE SETTING SUN made Mike Pastore nervous, not because he feared the coming darkness, but because the wild men preferred it.

The *Primrose*, a two-hundred-fifty-foot cargo ship out of Hong Kong, had run aground five days earlier, when a monsoon had heaved the ship upon the sharp reefs surrounding the island. Pummeled by relentless twenty foot waves, the vessel had been shoved to within a hundred feet of the sandy beach.

During the first two days, as the rains drifted toward India, the glowing sands looked empty and inviting; the lush jungle beyond promised shade and the thrill of exploration. If not for the still violent waves, the crew would have vacated the floundering vessel, and set up on dry land, to wait for rescue.

But on the third day, when the waves became manageable, *they* arrived.

Pastore had been on watch as the sun rose, a solitary guardian while the crew slept, ignorant to the danger. As one of three crewmembers who was not Chinese, he got 'shit duty' a third of the time.

A shiver ran through Pastore's body as he remembered the first native he'd seen. The man walked out of the jungle in a squat. His strange position, small stature and dark skin had convinced Pastore that he had discovered some kind of island-dwelling chimpanzee. Lured by intrigue, he had left the wheelhouse and stepped onto the starboard-side main deck, binoculars in hand. The memory was still fresh, and he didn't so much remember it as relive it in his mind.

The native wobbled across the shoreline, eyes on the ship. As soon as Pastore put the binoculars to his eyes and focused on the man, he'd stood to his full five-foot-tall height. By Pastore's normal standards, the man was far from intimidating, but the way he stared across the water, right at Pastore…

Save for a yellow band wrapped around the man's head, and another around his waist, the native was naked. Pastore watched the man, who remained rooted in the sand, for a full two minutes before raising his hand in greeting.

That was his first mistake.

His second was not immediately rousing the captain and crew—not because it would lead to tragedy, but because no one believed the tale of what he saw next.

The native man lifted his penis, spread his legs and stroked his genitals several times. While the man was clearly primitive, the gesture easily translated between ancient and modern cultures as something like, 'Fuck off.'

As the man gyrated, a woman emerged from the jungle shade, bow and arrows in hand. She wore a circlet of leaves around her head, and a beige band around her waist, from which a small pouch hung. Though her features, lost in the darkness of her skin, were hard to see, her appearance was that of a teenager. The subtle swell of her belly hinted at pregnancy.

The man took the long bow, nocked an even longer arrow, aimed high, and let it fly. Pastore ducked, clutching his head, as the featherless arrow fell short and *thunked* against the metal hull.

Upon collecting himself, Pastore looked up over the rail and found the man dancing, legs spread wide, bouncing back and forth, from foot to foot. When the man completed his display, the woman approached him from behind, wrapped her arms around his waist and took hold of his penis. At first, it appeared she was simply borrowing the man's member to repeat his rude gesture, but then the man grew excited.

What happened next kept Pastore from moving, or even thinking to wake his shipmates. The woman slipped around in front of her partner. Hands on knees, she leaned forward and stared out at Pastore as the man began to thrust. Looking through his binoculars, Pastore watched the pair copulate, their eyes, lacking any signs of pleasure, fixated on him.

And then, they were not alone. Six couples emerged from the jungle and began having sex, all eyes on Pastore. It was not an orgy. It wasn't even passionate. It was a defiant claim, the carnal act declaring, 'This belongs to us, not you.'

The couples finished without any fanfare or shouted orgasms. They simply retreated back into the jungle, disappearing into shadows, and breaking Pastore from his spell.

Pastore summoned captain and crew to the deck, but not a single native was seen for the remainder of the day, resulting in a strong rebuke. His crewmates believed his story to be the tired fantasy of a bored and lonely man. That night, as punishment, he was once again assigned an eight hour watch, starting at midnight.

It wasn't until 4am that he spotted signs of life again.

When he awakened the captain, he was met at first by near violence—being run aground and stranded by a monsoon had everyone on edge. But when the captain entered the wheelhouse and saw the orange glow of a dozen fires just inside the fringe of the jungle, he had gathered the rest of the crew himself.

They watched the small blazes flickering through the night, but detected nothing more. No chanting or tribal drums. No sounds of work being done. No smell of cooking meat. The fires, like the primal sex act, felt like a warning. A display of power. *Beware. We have fire.*

Two days had passed since the fires first appeared and with every passing hour, the natives had become more and more brazen. The crew had counted fifty nearly nude warriors patrolling the beaches, armed with bows and spears, but the shadows underneath the jungle canopy appeared to be composed of animated darkness, shifting not with the wind, but with a kind of living motion.

How many of them are there? Pastore wondered.

The warriors launched volleys of iron-tipped arrows, none of which found their mark. Pastore believed the men were simply trying to intimidate the crew while they constructed three small vessels. Once completed, the warriors would be able to reach the *Primrose* and her crew, who were armed with two axes, a small collection of knives, and a flare gun. They were outnumbered and outgunned.

The *Primrose*'s crew, like those of many cargo vessels, worked hard, but were more likely to spend a free day playing cards and drinking than exercising or taking part in any kind of hunt—unless it was for more liquor.

Not one of them had taken a life, and only a few had traded fists in a bar fight. If even a handful of the savages boarded the ship, the crew would be in grave danger.

With that knowledge, the captain sent a distress message, stating the situation as plainly as possible. "Wild men, estimate more than 50, carrying various homemade weapons, are making two or three wooden boats. Worrying they will board us at sunset. All crew members' lives not guaranteed."

The message had been sent out with the rising sun, which revealed three nearly completed vessels, each long enough to carry ten men. The fifty warriors stood naked and sentinel, watching the crew until the sun cleared the horizon. Then they retreated into the shadows, the captain believed, to rest before night returned.

And Pastore agreed. While the tribe was certainly active during the day, the nights had become more and more fervent. The campfires became bonfires. A strange, acrid smoke swept over the ship, carried by the ocean breeze. Men and women shouted in their strange tongue. The sounds of wood being cracked, carved, and bound filled the night. It made staying alert during the long watch easy, but it left Pastore beyond exhausted each morning.

The ship's deck was patrolled at all times. Thirty three crewmen, minus the captain, chief engineer, and chief mate had been divided into groups of ten, each taking an eight hour shift. Pastore remained on the night watch, but he'd been put in charge, and even better, he wasn't alone. But the terrified men with him still did little to ease his own fears.

What if the Captain is right?

What if they come tonight?

Pastore was a father of two sons, ages five and three. His wife, Amanda, was a hard woman to love at times, but he did. She put up with his long absences and was more faithful than any woman should be to a man of Pastore's obvious faults. On the surface, he was disheveled and portly. He preferred lite beer, cheap cigars, and the seedy bars in which those vices were normally enjoyed. But she somehow saw through all that, to the gentle man who adored his sons, worked hard to give them a home and a future, and always came home from a voyage with gifts.

He looked west, where the setting sun silhouetted the wheelhouse. Darkness would claim the sky within thirty minutes. His watch didn't begin for another four hours, but he found himself compelled to remain on deck, watching the beach for signs of life.

Aside from the three small boats, there was no sign of the wild men.

"Maybe they're not coming back?" a man named Stack asked. He wasn't on watch, either, but he had taken a break from gambling to give his pale skin some time in the sun, albeit dim. Or so he said. Pastore knew better. Like the other fifteen men on deck, Stack had come to assess the situation for himself, to determine if they would be attacked, and if so, perhaps take some time to plead with God for mercy, or perhaps for forgiveness.

Pastore would do neither. As one of the men with more to live for, he had volunteered to carry one of the two axes. And to see his family again, he would use it. There was no spear on this island that could stand up to its steel blade.

Pastore looked past a line of worried Chinese men and caught Stack's eye. "They're coming back."

"You an expert on the natives now? Just cause you seen them hump'n?" Stack sneered a bit. "Wasn't for you, we'd—"

"Shut it," Carson said. He was a big, bald, black man, whose skin was pale compared to the wild men. As the only real fighter on the ship and the recipient of the second axe, when he spoke, people listened. "Pastore didn't run us aground. That was the monsoon. And he surely didn't populate this island with savages. So unless you want to learn how they react to a man thrown overboard, I suggest you hush."

After that, no one spoke. Not because Carson had put the fear of God into them, but because the long shadows cast by the setting sun had come to life, ebbing and flowing as *something*, or several hundred *someones*, moved about.

Pastore waited for the first fire to be rekindled. But the island remained dark. As the sky turned purple, and then black, the island slipped into darkness. If not for the crashing of waves upon its shore, he would have believed the island had been plucked from the Earth.

As the night settled and the moon's sliver of light did little to change the situation, curiosity made way for fear. Everyone not on the early night watch retreated to the safety of the decks below, where even doors without locks might stymie primitives who had never seen such things.

But not Pastore. He stood by Carson's side, eyes trained toward the unseen island.

They stood there like that, waiting and listening, for hours.

But the world remained calm and silent.

The wild men weren't living up to the name bestowed on them by the captain.

As 4:00 am rolled around, with just over an hour before the sun's return, Pastore dared to hope that the natives had given up. Perhaps they had realized that the crew was stranded, no more capable of retreating from the island than they were willing to land on its unspoiled shores. All of the fired arrows and crude boat building could have simply been bravado, much like the strange sex act Pastore had witnessed: designed to repulse. Ancient psychological warfare.

Perhaps, he ventured further, *they were no threat at all.*

"Quiet," Carson said.

Pastore hadn't been talking, but he held his breath. He heard nothing aside from the rhythmic, now-calm surf, lapping against the hull below and the distant sands. A hushed conversation slipped through the night, coming from the bow, where three men, one of them Stack, stood watch. Pastore couldn't see them in the abject darkness, but he had stationed the men there. *Did they hear something, too?*

"What did you—"

"Shh!" Carson was visible as a subtle shadow, lit by the Milky Way's dull glow, but Pastore could see tension in the man's stance.

A sound like a bird, wings pumping, fluttered past.

They had observed a large number of bird species during the daylight hours, flitting between trees, chirping a variety of songs. But the small creatures had never left the canopy, and they had certainly never approached the ship.

It wasn't a bird, he realized. He'd heard the same sound just before that first warrior's arrow had struck the hull.

Pastore ducked down. "They're firing arrows!" His shout cut through the night and sent many more men running for cover, including Carson.

"You said they couldn't reach the deck from shore," the big man complained.

"They're not *on* the shore," Pastore said, breathing heavily, heart pounding. Their worst fears had been realized. The wild men were coming.

Another fluttering arrow flew past.

They're going to board the Primrose.

Kill us all.

Make trophies of our skulls, or eat us!

"Lights!" Carson shouted so loud that Pastore let out a yelp.

A moment later, the ship's extinguished deck lights blazed to life. Aside from lighting the ship and the water immediately around it, the lights did little else than reveal the crew to the islanders. So they had been turned off, giving both sides the cover of darkness, though only the wild men preferred it.

And if they had piloted their small ships through the surf, in the black of night, Pastore had no doubt they could see in the dark, too. Aside from the whites of their eyes, the wild men *were* the dark.

Carson gripped Pastore's arm hard enough to hurt. "We stand together. We fight together."

Pastore nodded, but he said nothing, mentally adding, *We die together.* He had much to live and fight for, but his heart lacked the same boldness, though he suspected Carson's bravery was little more than an act to maintain his reputation. Then the man stood, proving him wrong, and yanked Pastore up with him.

They looked over the starboard rail. Under the stark glow of the ship's light, the shallow waters should have shimmered back at them, revealing reef and fish. Instead, it was a wall of darkness, as though the ocean was still lost in shadow.

"What..." Pastore said, and then he saw a familiar set of eyes staring back at him. The warrior from the beach, now smiling. "It's them."

All at once, hundreds of heads turned upward, their white eyes glowing.

They didn't need the boats, Pastore realized. *They can swim.*

Movement drew his eyes toward the bow.

A wave of humanity was scaling the hull. Pastore's breath caught. There was no ladder there. He saw no rope. And yet, the wild men were making short work of the climb to the gunwales.

The men stationed at the bow saw it, too, and they began screaming for help. Help with what, Pastore wasn't sure, because each and every one of them retreated. Stack was among them, his voice several octaves higher than usual. "Inside! We can't stop them!"

Pastore couldn't argue. While defending the rail would have been easier than fighting on deck, there were far too many wild men. Without firearms, they would be overrun in minutes. Their only hope was to hide behind the ship's steel doors and pray for rescue.

With as many men rushing out from below decks to see what the uproar was about, their retreat became a mire of shoving, terrified men, who did far more harm to one another than the natives had throughout the entire week.

Pastore was the last man through the door. He turned and looked out over the aft deck. A flood of humanity rose up over the rail, launching arrows at the ship's lights. Shattering glass shimmered for a moment, and then disappeared as the wild men reclaimed the night.

With a shout of dread, Pastore slammed the metal door shut and locked it. The barrage of metal arrow heads striking the hull sounded like hammer blows, each one jarring, fraying the nerves, whittling down the souls of all who heard them. The natives would need a blow torch to carve through the thick metal, but it did little to calm his nerves.

The *Primrose*'s crew was now trapped.

Unholy, bestial roars, the scratching of claws, and the hammering of powerful fists assaulted the door through the remainder of the night. The attack continued without hesitation, rumbling every door. If there was a chink in the *Primrose*'s armor, the wild men would find it.

Hours later, after an unceasing assault, the attack on the doors stopped, only to be replaced by a repetitive booming *whump*, loud enough to shake the ship, a few minutes later.

Pastore's body, sick with adrenaline, shook as he pressed himself against the door, holding it against God knew what.

And then, a knock.

Three solid blows.

While the rumbling continued, there was a pause, and then another three knocks.

Pastore leaned away from the door.

"Don't move, man!" Stack shouted, looking far more wild-eyed than the wild men ever had.

"They're knocking," Pastore said. It was a simple argument, but one that everyone on the inside of that door understood: savages don't knock.

And then a voice, shouting from the far side, barely audible through the steel and over the loud thumping. "Hello, in there!"

English, Pastore realized. *Savages don't speak English!*

Pastore unlocked the door and then, while Stack protested, held back by Carson, he pulled the door open to see a bright blue sky. A large helicopter rested on deck behind a concerned man wearing a helmet, sunglasses, and a thick blond mustache.

"Can I ask what you all are doing?" The stranger glanced down. He pointed at the axe clutched in Pastore's hand.

"You didn't see them?" Pastore asked.

"See…who?"

"The wild men!" Stack shouted.

"Uh-huh. Heard you all were in a tight spot. Came out as soon as we could." The man looked out at the nearby beach. "Did a full circle around the island. Took a bunch of photos. Pretty place."

"But…" Pastore stepped outside, squinting in the sun, which had risen hours ago. There was no sign of the tribesmen. No arrows lying about. No scratch marks on the door. No boats on the beach. They had vanished just as stealthily as they had approached, leaving no trace.

As the *Primrose*'s stunned crew stepped out into the daylight again, they all agreed that the world wouldn't believe their story, just as they had not believed Pastore. It was bad enough to have run aground, but if they told a wild, unsubstantiated, tall tale about an army of savages laying siege to the ship, they would never work in shipping again.

It was agreed they would never discuss the strange events surrounding their brief visit to the island, and that the tale would be watered down to the captain's message. They had seen warriors. They had been building boats. But nothing more had come of it.

The crew was evacuated via the orange and white S-58T Sikorsky helicopter, over three trips. Pastore volunteered to be among the last to leave, along with Carson, the captain, and the mascot dog, who had wisely stayed in the wheelhouse for most of the week. As the helicopter made its final approach to take the last of them away, Pastore knew he would never see this island, or its inhabitants again, and that he would never truly understand what happened there.

He took one last look at the empty shoreline and dropped his axe to the deck. The island was a paradise, the likes of which men would travel the world to visit.

God help anyone that does, Pastore thought, as the helicopter rose safely into the sky. *Sentinel Island belongs to the Devil.*

1

The Present

"Mr. Baer?"

"I'm busy." Rowan Baer stood on the precipice of New Hampshire's Cathedral Ledge, admiring the view. The five-hundred-foot tall cliff provided stunning views of Echo Lake, picturesque North Conway, and the pine-clad mountains beyond. A moment ago, he had been alone with his thoughts, contemplating the choices he'd made, and their consequences. Life, he had concluded, was like a river, bending and shifting, following a path affected by outside forces with little deference to the human will. The woman standing behind him only solidified the point.

"I can see that," she said, her voice decorated by a slight Indian accent. "Though I didn't take you for the existential crisis type."

Despite his growing curiosity, Rowan refused to look back and acknowledge the woman's presence or her accurate assessment. He had hiked here in the darkness of early morning to watch the sun's first rays ignite the landscape, and hopefully something in his soul.

All it had done so far was cast shadows.

And now this. A woman who somehow knew his name stood behind him, course-correcting his life and usurping his intentions. *Do I know her?* He wondered, thinking back to what seemed like a lifetime ago, but was only twelve years. He'd grown up in North Conway and had no memory of someone with an Indian accent, who would have stood out in a state that was ninety-three percent white.

And anyone from the town who still remembered him would call him Rowan—or trouble. There hadn't been any going-away parties when he had joined the Army. Just quiet. Like before this woman showed up.

The chain link fence behind him rattled as the woman leaned against the far side. "Can you see the bottom?"

He could.

A hawk soared up from below, carried by warm air rising from the sun-baked rocks far below. Wings outstretched, it fixed its gaze on Rowan. The bird was likely indifferent to his presence at the local tourist attraction, but he felt mocked by its superior attitude. *You can't fly,* it taunted. *Can't hunt. Can't fight. So just jump.*

"Wait," the woman said.

Rowan reeled back as he realized he'd leaned a little further out over the edge. He stepped back and grasped the chain link fence, his arm the umbilical, the metal mesh a placenta, granting him life. What it didn't do was ease his pain. So he raised the bottle of Jack Daniels to his lips with his free hand. Just as the first pop of liquid fire touched his lips, the bottle was slapped free. He watched it spin out over the cliff, spiraling light brown liquor as it fell.

At first, he blamed the hawk, but it still hung in place, watching, scoffing. Then he turned to the woman. "You better have a—"

The woman standing on the far side of the fence was definitely not local. She wore matching bright red trousers and a tunic top, along with an orange scarf that flowed in the early morning breeze. She gave him a confident smile as he assessed her and found himself intrigued. His eyes lingered on the bindi painted on her forehead. The dot was usually red and signified marriage, but black? He pointed at it. "What does it mean? The color."

Her smile faded. "I suppose the same thing as your bottle."

He glanced back over the cliff. The bottle now lay somewhere at the bottom, shattered and unrecognizable.

Like my life.

"What do you want?" he asked.

"To hire you."

He laughed at that. A dishonorable discharge from the Army had made him a pariah to potential employers, at least in the fields at which he excelled. As an Army Ranger, he had served on the front lines in Afghanistan, and behind enemy lines in Syria. Now he served gasoline in the state's last remaining full-service gas station. The only people willing to hire someone with his record were into something shady, and while he had lost his way, he had not lost his moral compass.

"I'm afraid you came a long way for nothing," he said.

"The view is worth it." She leaned on the fence, watching the hawk, still riding the thermals. Then she gave the fence a pat, turned around, and started walking away. "Good luck, Mr. Baer."

He closed his eyes, summoning the strength of will to keep his mouth shut and avoid whatever trouble rode in this woman's wake.

I'm in control of my life, he thought. *I can decide where it leads, and when it ends. I don't need to be course-corrected. I don't need to follow the path of least resistance.*

He opened his eyes again, looking down at Echo Lake's sky blue water, and he saw the path of least resistance before him. Three steps, a few seconds fall, and life would lose all control of him. Or perhaps this was where it had been directing him all along.

"Wait," he said, and when the fiery colors of her outfit slipped deeper into the pine woods, he shouted, "Wait!"

"I'll be waiting in the car park," she replied. "If you can make it over that fence and down the path in the next ten minutes, without stumbling over the cliff, we'll talk. Otherwise, enjoy what remains of your day."

When she was no longer visible, Rowan looked down at the fence, his placenta turned adversary. He had leapt it with the ease of an arctic fox bounding into snow. But now, half a bottle later, he stood before a great wall.

"Shit." He took a deep breath, lifted his left foot into the chain link, and hoisted. His right leg came up fast. If he could straddle the top bar, he could slip over the top. It wouldn't be graceful, but it would be effective. The toe of his boot struck the top rail head on, jarring the fence and shaking his left foot free. The jolt wrenched his loose fingers away from the fence, and he spilled backward.

Life's river was pulling him over the falls once again, despite his best efforts.

This isn't my best effort, he thought as he fell.

I can do better.

Air coughed from his lungs as his back struck stone. He clenched his eyes, grimacing in pain as blood rushed to his head. *I didn't fall over the edge,* he thought with relief, and then he opened his eyes to an upside down view of his home town.

Rowan Baer hung his head over a five hundred foot drop, wondering how his life had come to this.

And then he decided to change it. What felt like a lifetime of hard work paid off as he leaned his torso up, using only his core body strength. Fingers bled as he raked them over craggy granite, pushing them into small cracks. That was when he saw his left foot, wedged under the chain link as he fell, flexing nearly to the point of setting him free. He reached out, caught hold of the placenta fence once more, and pulled himself away from the drop.

While catching his breath, he noticed the fence came to an end just ten feet away. *Not one of my finer moments*, he thought, *but still not the worst.* Then he pulled himself up and shimmied along the cliff's edge until he reached the last fence post and slipped around it, back onto safer ground.

The fifteen foot journey had taken up more of his ten minutes.

While the two mile long, mountainside trail he had followed to reach the cliff took thirty minutes at a slow pace, the few-hundred-foot-long path to the parking lot seemed far more arduous. He stumbled over stones, roots, and wooden steps. Chipmunks assaulted him with chittering squeals. Branches snapped as he wavered off course.

And then he saw it. The parking lot. A single, black SUV was parked there, its engine idling.

I made it, he thought, but then the brake lights flared.

They're leaving, he thought, and he broke into a run as the vehicle's wheels began to turn.

"Wait!" he shouted, waving a hand in the air. He didn't even know the woman's name. Would have no way to contact her. The reset button for his wayward life was about to drive away. So he pushed through the haze and ran faster still.

The SUV crossed the path's exit just as the woods disgorged Rowan into the parking lot. He judged his pace and the vehicle's, determining that he would have to slap its back window. What he didn't count on was being spotted. The SUV's brake lights flared again, but Rowan missed the warning and collided with the side window.

He opened his eyes to a pounding headache and a view of the sky. Then the woman stood above him, shaking her head as though thinking the same thing as Rowan: *This is what my life has come to.*

"Made it around the fence, did you?" she asked.

Something about the woman's casual acceptance of his shortcomings struck a chord, pulling a bark of laughter from deep within. "What's your name?"

"Sashi Batta. I work for the Indian Department of Cultural Services."

Rowan couldn't fathom what the Indian government needed him for, but he decided he wasn't in a position to ask, or care. "When do I start, Mrs. Batta?"

"Miss," she corrected. "And as soon as you peel yourself up off the pavement, and have a cup of coffee."

He reached a hand up, but she swatted it away. "Going to have to pull yourself up. That's the only way this works. And you're going to have to start thinking about lives other than your own. Can you do that?"

Rowan pushed himself up into a sitting position. His head pounded. "Maybe after that coffee."

"Good enough," she said, and then asked, "Is your passport up to date?"

"We going to see the world?"

She offered a sympathetic smile. "Not the nice parts."

2

TALIA MAYER COUNTED two intruders. A man and a woman. They had strayed from the rest of the expedition, which consisted of twenty-more men, many of them from already 'civilized' tribes that had joined modern society, wearing Reese's Pieces T-shirts while still sporting bones jutting from their pierced nostrils. They had once ruled the jungles, and now they served the wills of corporations exploiting the rainforest, or they were dependent on government subsidies for survival.

The outside world welcomed indigenous tribes with smiles and soda pop, but did little to improve their lives. In return for their jungle homes, they received tooth decay, clothing where none was preferable, and society-decimating plagues like the flu, for which they had no immunity or resistance.

Joining the outside world was a raw deal, and yet, a necessary one. As society progressed deeper into the jungle, tribes either stepped out of the stone age, or perished in it. Talia's job was to help with the transition, though her methods were unusual, if not frowned upon.

She watched the pair from above. They didn't talk, and they didn't mind the sweltering humidity—despite the sweat-soaked long-sleeved shirts, cargo pants, and boots both wore. The man led the way, carried a rifle over his shoulder, had a sidearm strapped to his hip, and wielded a machete, but Talia got a sense that the woman was in charge. It had been her idea to leave the expedition.

The man stopped and signaled to the woman to do the same.

Be smart, Talia thought. *Turn back.*

"Why are we stopping?" the woman asked, her brown skin, accent, and the black spot at the center of her forehead identifying her as Indian.

The man, a white American with the build and taut movements of a soldier, pointed to the sapling, bent and broken across the trail. "This is a fairly universal sign for 'no trespassing.'"

"Or what?" the woman asked, sounding appropriately nervous.

"I imagine the same thing as if you ignored a no trespassing sign in New Hampshire's backwoods, but with poison-tipped arrows instead of shotgun shells. We should go back."

Yes, Talia thought. Not many men who ventured this far into the Peruvian rainforest were smart enough to not only understand the Mashco-Piro people's warning signs, but to also obey them.

"I wish we could," the woman said. "But we go where we're paid to go, and do what we're paid to do."

Damnit. If the expedition had been scientific in nature, she might have convinced the Mashco-Piro to let these people pass through the territory unharmed. But the woman's words identified them as corporate shills, and though the Mashco-Piro couldn't speak English, they had no trouble recognizing greed. At best, these two worked for loggers or big oil, at worst, drug traffickers, though they didn't have that seedy vibe. These were high-class tribal rapists.

The man sheathed his machete and unslung his rifle, chambering a round, sealing his fate.

Talia tensed when she noticed the man hadn't moved.

His companion noticed, too. "Why aren't you moving?"

He placed a finger to his lips. His head craned in a slow circle, eyes darting about.

Talia slipped behind a branch, watching through a sliver in the canopy's cover. The woman was soft, but the man was dangerous.

The man slowly lifted the sapling and said, "After you."

"What about all the..." the woman raised her finger to her lips and then waved her hands at the jungle.

"They're out there," he said. "Only way to find out if they're going to kill us is to keep moving."

"That's not funny," the woman said and stepped past, but Talia knew the man hadn't meant it as a joke. She didn't think he was an expert in Amazonian tribes, but he had clearly spent some time in rough parts of the world where the code governing people's actions was less predictable. Once past the sapling the woman wisely stood aside and let the man take the lead again.

Talia waited for the pair to move on, staying still until she could no longer see or hear them. Then she moved through the branches, covering distance while descending to the forest floor, where she moved with relative ease. While the rainforest was lush with life, the thick canopy kept much from growing at ground level. She sprinted three hundred yards away from the path and then ran parallel to it, passing the intruders just minutes later without being seen or heard.

The fools would be lucky to leave with their lives, and that meant the Mashco-Piro's days were numbered. If a white man and a corporate woman were slain in the jungles, the Peruvian government would have no choice but to investigate, which would no doubt lead to a confrontation and the systematic dismantling of the tribe.

The Mashco-Piro's only hope was that they had been paying attention to everything she had taught them over the past year. If they kept their distance, showing themselves to be both willing to dialogue and avoiding overtly threatening gestures, the transition would be smooth. In the long run, the tribe would lose their identity, their ability to thrive, perhaps even to survive in the jungle, but they *would* survive. It wasn't ideal, but it was the reality faced by tribes on the jungle's shrinking fringe—and it was preferable to extermination.

She slipped behind the sweeping curl of a tall Ceiba tree's buttress root, just ten feet away from the worn path followed by the strangers. The five-foot-tall fan of wood snaked along the ground like a serpent, its coils protective rather than crushing. The spot was a favorite hiding place for Mashco-Piro children when they played 'hide and seek,' a game she had taught them, but it was large enough to accommodate a five foot five woman. It allowed her to watch the couple's approach, listen to the woman marvel at the tribe's manicured orchard of mango trees, and observe their intrusion on the Mashco-Piro village, just thirty feet beyond her hideaway.

The man entered the village with his rifle raised, eyes peering over the sights. He scanned back and forth, pausing at each of the fifteen huts, at the tapirs and monkeys abandoned mid-slaughter, and at the baskets of fruit and vat of poisonous curare, ready to coat the tribe's arrow heads. She had no doubt that those same arrows were already aimed at the man and woman, as warriors lurked in the shadows, while the women and children put their hide and seek skills to real world use.

The tribe's hunters were remarkable marksmen, but they weren't infallible, especially from a distance. If the first shot missed, she suspected the man's ability with that rifle would outclass the greatest Mashco-Piro warrior.

If the pair walked through the village and continued on their way, conflict might be avoided, but if they touched any of the tribe's limited resources, the warriors would protect their belongings. And rightfully so. In the outside world, lethal defense of one's material goods or property was legal. In America, it was celebrated. But if the Mashco-Piro acted in the same way, they would be branded rabid savages and hunted down.

Show them you're better than that, she willed the tribe. *Show restraint. Wait for them to leave.*

But they didn't.

The man and woman entered the center of the village, and after a quick inspection, they headed for one of the huts.

Talia's hut.

Her backpack was in plain sight, its red canvas easy to spot.

Shit.

The woman pointed to the backpack. "She's here."

Fuck.

The man and woman weren't here for the Mashco-Piro, they were here for her. But there was no way the tribe would know that, and since she had been accepted by them, her belongings were now theirs. If the man touched her backpack...

Talia moved through the forest with a silence taught to her by the Mashco-Piro women, who were just as at home in the jungle as the warriors were. She snuck through the village in a crouch, snatched an arrow from the vat of curare and closed in on her target.

The man crouched by the backpack, reached his hand out.

She couldn't hear the warriors drawing back their bows, but she felt certain they were. Her instinct was to shout, but in the Mashco-Piro culture, a shout of any kind meant distress. They didn't believe in battle cries or warnings. If she shouted at the man, he would die. If he touched the bag, he would die. So she did the only thing should could think of. She slipped up behind the woman, wrapped a hand around her mouth and placed the arrow tip an inch from her skin.

"Stand up and turn around," she growled. "Do it slowly, or you're going to die."

The man regarded her out of the corner of his eye. "Doctor Talia Mayer?"

"Put the rifle down," she said.

"Do you want me to stand up and turn around first, or put the—"

"Rifle first," Talia said. She was pleased when the man obliged her request, moving slowly. Hands raised, he turned to face her.

Talia stood behind the woman, but quickly noticed the man leaning to the side, looking her up and down. For the first time in nearly eight months, she felt naked. The Mashco-Piro wore no clothes. In the steaming jungles, clothing of any kind aside from a supply belt or sling was impractical, and things like insects were plucked away by communal grooming, usually before a meal.

"Talia Mayer?" the man asked again. "I heard you were unorthodox, but I didn't know you went native."

"What do you want?"

He pointed at the woman, still silenced by Talia's firm grip. "You're going to have to talk to the boss about that."

Talia slipped her hand from the woman's mouth to her throat.

"Rowan, behind you!" the woman said.

The man named Rowan started to turn, but stopped when he saw the dozen warriors who had silently snuck from the jungle. They had arrows and spears trained on him. His hands shifted downward. Talia wasn't sure how quick a draw the man was, but unless he was super-human, he'd be dead before he could squeeze off more than a few rounds.

"Don't," Talia said, pushing the arrow against the woman's throat.

"In my experience," Rowan said. "Anyone can threaten to take a life, but very few can actually follow through. Do you know which you are?"

"Move, and she dies," Talia said.

Rowan frowned. "I believe you."

"Talk fast," Talia said into the woman's ear.

"I—I'm here to hire you."

Talia had to fight not to laugh. It would just confuse the warriors. "I don't work for anyone, especially corporate—"

"We're not interested in the rain forest. *Our* interests lay on the far side of the planet."

Talia watched the encroaching warriors, who looked angry and confused. "Who do you work for? Talk fast."

"My name is Sashi Batta. Indian Department of Cultural Services."

"What the hell does the Indian government want with me?" Talia asked.

Rowan smiled. "That was my first question, too."

"I believe the clue to that question lies in who you are and what you do," the woman named Sashi said.

It wasn't a time for riddles, and Talia was about to explain as much when the answer came to her. "Sentinel Island."

Sashi nodded.

"Bullshit. The Sentinelese are protected."

Sashi shrugged. "Governments change, as do their priorities. Contact will be made, with or without your help. I would prefer the former."

Talia withdrew the arrow, relaxed her stance, and spoke to the warriors in their native Yine, explaining that the man and woman were part of a research team, that they meant no harm, and that she would escort them out of the jungle.

The warriors were reluctant, but trusted her. And that trust had been hard to come by. If Sashi turned out to be a fraud, she would witness savagery that would shock even the most violent Amazonian tribe, but still fall short of Sentinel Island's residents.

3

"I THOUGHT WE weren't visiting the nice parts of the world," Rowan said.

"Have you looked at the menu?" Sashi replied, eyes turned toward the English pub's front window.

"You're operating under the assumption that I'm averse to eating every part of an animal, fried, baked, or boiled." He waved a waiter over.

"W'can I get for you?" the surly Brit asked.

"Pint of—"

"Hey," Sashi growled.

"Shit," Rowan whispered, rubbing his eyes. "Glass of water."

"Ain't a lounge," the waiter said. "Buy something or get out."

"I'm beginning to see your point," Rowan said to Sashi, and then to the waiter, "How about some blood sausage?"

"You want chips with that?"

"You have French fries?"

"That's what chips are." The man shook his head as though he'd just learned the Queen was marrying Donald Trump. "Bloody yanks."

Rowan was tempted to slap the stink off the man's eyes, but he exerted the kind of self-control he was capable of while sober. "Then, yes."

The waiter turned and left.

Rowan leaned his elbows on the worn oak tabletop, still coated in a thin crust of peanut shells from whoever had imbibed there last. "If you bring me to a pub, a bar, or a packy again, I'm done."

She gave a sincere nod and said, "Sorry. I wasn't thinking. If it helps, I'm a vegetarian."

Rowan grinned. "Why do you think I ordered the sausage?"

Sashi half-smiled and turned her attention back to the front window, which provided a view of a single building that represented a moral code in stark contrast to the pub, known for its beer and sausage. "What's a packy?"

"Liquor store, if you're from New England." Rowan tried to relax, but the smells inside the pub had awakened his hunger, and worse, his thirst. It had been just a month since Sashi had found him. A month since his last drink atop Cathedral Ledge. He knew from experience that there would come a time, when each new day eased the craving a little bit more, but until that shift… "If he doesn't show soon, I'm going to have to wait outside."

Sashi said nothing. Just kept her eyes on the mosque across the street.

"So why this guy? If he's in hiding, I don't think he'll want to be found."

She didn't budge.

"Better yet, why Dr. Mayer? I get that she's gifted, and unusual, but she's also a little off, don't you think? I did some research. Her peers think she's a quack. Journals won't publish her."

Sashi glanced back. "Are you trying to make a point?"

"Just an observation," he said. "You're hiring broken people."

Again with the silent treatment.

"Have you even considered that Dr. Mayer, born and raised in Israel before heading to the States, might take exception to you hiring a Palestinian? Or vice versa?"

"You've been busy," she said. "Trying on diligence?"

"Would you prefer I put my drinker's pants back on? Because they're an easy fit."

She turned to face him, a sad sort of smile on her face. "Apologies. Diligence suits you."

"I won't be able to do my job if the people I'm trying to protect from external threats are a threat to each other."

"Understood, Mr. Baer."

"Rowan."

"Rowan, I think you underestimate the professionalism of the people we're hiring. Unlike you and me, they are classically trained and educated. They are accustomed to having their ideals, beliefs, and intellects challenged."

"Dr. Mayer held a poison arrow to your throat just two days ago."

"I wouldn't have used it."

Rowan tensed, but hid his surprise. Dr. Mayer might be a classically trained anthropologist, but she had also picked up some skills from the tribal people she'd spent a quarter of her life living among. Stealth was one of them.

He turned to look at her. The white blouse, blue silk scarf, and jeans she wore were a stark contrast to her choice of Amazonian garb—or lack thereof—but she somehow looked even more stunning. Her tan skin, almost black-brown eyes, and her dark hair hinted at the exotic, as though she had been raised in the jungle herself, which wasn't far from the truth.

"If we're going by first names now," Talia said, "I'm okay with that."

"How long have you been sitting there?" Sashi asked.

"Long enough to know Rowan thinks I'm broken." She stood from her booth and motioned for him to move over. Then she slid onto the cushionless bench beside him. "And that the man we're here to meet is actually over there." She pointed to the mosque. "And like with me, he has no idea we're coming."

The waiter returned with a glass of water and a plate of steaming ruddy sausage and rectangular fries. Talia's eyes lit up. "Is this—"

"Blood sausage," Rowan said.

Talia picked up a fork and knife. "Can I?"

"I ordered it to bother her." Rowan hitched his thumb toward Sashi, who cringed and looked back to the window. "Help yourself."

Talia cut a large piece off the end and popped it in her mouth. She appeared to melt as she chewed. "Oh. This, this is good."

It smelled good, too, but blood was not on Rowan's menu, cooked or not. His carnivorous instincts only went so far.

"After a year in the Amazon, you'd be willing to eat a lot worse, and it wouldn't taste nearly as good." She took another bite, oblivious to the grease running down her chin.

You can take the girl out of the jungle, but not the jungle out of the girl, Rowan thought, and he forgot to hide his smile.

"What?" she asked, carving into the heated up, intestine sealed, congealed blood.

He pointed to the sausage, made from pig's blood. "You're not a practicing..."

"Jew," Talia said. "It's not a derogatory word. And no. I was raised in a traditional Jewish home, but that's all it was, tradition."

"Like the song," Rowan said, getting a laugh out of Talia.

"Without the dancing." She finished off the first of two sausages.

Watching her eat had made Rowan hungry, despite how he felt about the meal, so he helped himself to the *French fries* while mentally flipping the waiter the bird.

"And what about our guy across the street?" Rowan asked. When Sashi didn't turn around or reply, he said, "Sashi, is he going to take exception to a Jew eating pork, or is he kosher?"

"Okay," Talia said, wiping her chin. "*That* is probably offensive. Don't say that again."

"There he is," Sashi said, pointing to a well-dressed man of Middle-Eastern descent, sporting a well-trimmed beard.

"What's his name?" Talia asked.

"Mahdi Barakat," Sashi said.

"Well, he doesn't dress the stereotype," Rowan said, reaching for another fry, when Sashi stood up and made for the door.

Rowan and Talia both froze, mid-bite.

"Is she?" Talia said.

"I think she is." Rowan dropped the fry and hurried after Sashi, who had already exited the pub and headed across the street. He heard Talia behind him, taking another hurried bite and then giving chase. The waiter was just starting to complain about their hasty departure when Rowan stepped into the street. He shouted for Sashi, but his voice was drowned out by a honking car stopped just a few feet short of his legs.

While the world pictured the British people as being polite, drivers in London had yet to support the view. He didn't give the vehicle or the driver a second look as he hurried across the street. By the time he reached the far sidewalk, Sashi was already inside the mosque. The building's façade looked pleasant enough, constructed from a mix of gold and red bricks. Twin minarets rose above the building, flanking a dome that rose above it all. He hurried up the steps, but paused when he heard voices behind him. Three men, also Middle-Eastern, approached him from behind.

Rowan had only ever seen men like this—wearing white robes and head scarfs—entering a mosque, through the scope of a sniper rifle. He'd seen them as potential enemies for so long that smiling and opening the door for them was a challenge. Given the looks on the men's faces as they entered, his discomfort wasn't hidden. He smiled and nodded to each, following them in and ignoring Talia's shouts as she pursued him across the street.

While the mosque's exterior was pleasant to look at, the interior was stunning. Columns, ornate tile work, and row upon row of carpets. Rowan felt like he'd been transported through time and space. And then he saw Sashi speaking to a petrified looking Mahdi Barakat, glancing nervously at the three men now walking past. Rowan looked at his watch. 11:50 am. Many more Muslim men would soon be coming through the doors to take part in the Dhuhr prayer time.

"You need to leave," he heard the man saying, and he approached with as kind a smile as he could muster. The smile didn't help. As soon as Rowan was spotted, the man began looking back and forth.

He's looking for exits, Rowan realized, and he raised his hands. "You're not in any kind of trouble."

The door opened. A handful of men entered, some dressed traditionally, some wearing suits, all looking at Rowan with distrust, at Sashi with confusion, and then at Mahdi with something like disappointment. Rowan hadn't been to church since he was a teenager, but he remembered the old Baptist congregation looking at him similarly when he'd attended services wearing ripped jeans and heavy metal band T-shirts.

"Hey!" It was Talia, looking irate. Her blue scarf was now wrapped over her head. She took Rowan by the arm and all but dragged him to Sashi and Mahdi. "Are you two stupid?"

Talia took Sashi's long, flowing scarf—white today—and wrapped it over her head. Then she pointed at Rowan, speaking in angry, but hushed tones. "You're an American with a buzzcut and the bug-up-your-ass posture of a soldier." She reeled around on Sashi. "And you are from India. Some of the men worshiping here could be from Pakistan…" She licked her thumb and scrubbed the black bindi from Sashi's forehead, "…and might take exception to your outward and disrespectful display of Hinduism."

"And you are a Jew," Mahdi said.

Talia eyes widened slightly. She pointed at Mahdi. "Okay, it sounds derogatory when he says it."

"We should go outside," Rowan said. Talia had made her point. Nothing good was going to come out of staying in the mosque. Not for them, and certainly not for Mahdi.

"Please," Mahdi said. "Quickly." He led the way out of the mosque and a block down the street before turning on Sashi. "Tell me, what is this about?"

"You're Mahdi Barakat," Sashi said. "The linguist."

Mahdi looked back and forth, alert for trouble. Another broken man. "What do you want?"

"To hire you," Sashi said.

"You could have rang."

Rowan noticed that Mahdi's accent was more British than Middle Eastern. He'd either spent a lot of time in this part of the world, or he was faking it.

"You're unlisted," Sashi pointed out, hands on her hips. "And we *both* know why."

The man blanched.

"Stop trying to intimidate him," Talia said, "and tell him where he'd be going. If he's any good at his job, he'll understand what that means. The risks and rewards, and the odds of anyone finding him there."

"Sentinel Island," Sashi said. "In the Bay of Bengal. As I mentioned in the mosque, I work for the Indian—"

"Yes," Mahdi said, but he wasn't looking at Sashi, he was looking over her shoulder, back toward the mosque. Rowan followed his gaze and saw five men, traditionally dressed, holding their ground on the sidewalk. Their faces were hidden by thick beards, but their eyes were predatory. "When do we leave?"

"Now," Rowan said, meeting Mahdi's eyes. "That's probably a good idea, right?"

Mahdi nodded. "Do you have a car?"

"Taxi," Sashi said.

"We'll take mine." Mahdi pushed a button on his car key fob. The black BMW beside them flashed its hazards, and the doors unlocked. As the five men hurried toward them, they piled into Mahdi's car, performed a quick three point turn resulting in angry honks and shouts, and sped away. Rowan looked through the rear window as they left the five men behind. They had narrowly avoided some kind of confrontation, but Rowan wasn't confident that Mahdi had made the right choice.

He *had* done his homework, and if everything he'd read about Sentinel Island was true, Mahdi would have been safer in England.

4

"AS FAR AS government housing goes," Rowan said, glancing back at the large villa that was built to look rustic, but was decked out with modern amenities including air conditioning, plush beds, and a jacuzzi tub, "this isn't half bad."

"You have no idea," Talia replied. She leaned against a towering Padauk tree just ten feet from the light blue waters of the Bay of Bengal, sipping a yellow drink with a pink umbrella in it.

Mahdi tried not to look at her, but he found his willpower lacking. She wore a short flower-print sarong around her waist that did little to conceal her legs, a tank top, and sunglasses. The restraint she'd shown in covering herself back in the mosque had been left behind in England.

"Enjoying the view?" Rowan asked.

When Mahdi realized the American was speaking to him, he flinched and averted his eyes to the water. "Uh, yes. Very beautiful."

Talia turned and smiled at him. "Better than the gray skies of London."

Rowan gave him a knowing smile and said, "Warmer, too. Why don't you shed some layers, Mahdi?"

While Rowan had made himself comfortable, wearing just shorts, Mahdi was still dressed in his slacks and button-down shirt from the previous day. The equatorial summer heat and humidity was getting to him, but the cargo shorts and T-shirt he'd been given did not meet his standards of what qualified for clothing. The bright orange color and logo made him think that the clothes had been pilfered from Rowan's suitcase. Since he had left London, with only the clothing he had on, he knew he should be thankful—more for the quick exit than for the clothing—but he felt more confused than anything.

Why did these people need his help? He was a linguist, as they pointed out, and a gifted one at that, but he had never been to India and he had little interest in tribal people. That they were willing to pluck him off the street in London and fly him several thousand miles without questioning him about the men who'd been following him was a source of concern. Then again, those men were looking for *him*, not the people with whom he now shared a beach.

He had kept to himself during the flight, listening to Talia regale Rowan and Sashi with stories of jungle life. She spoke of hunts, and drinks, and sexual activities that would enrage the men of his homeland. She was wild, like the places and people she visited. Untamed. Rowan was a casual man, and fairly lighthearted, but during quiet moments, Mahdi saw struggle in the man's eyes, and something darker. Sashi was nice enough, but kept an emotional distance, of which the other two seemed unaware. But this was to be expected of a government official. What wasn't to be expected was the speed and efficiency with which she had gathered her 'team.'

And for what?

Making contact with a tribe of natives locked on an island?

Talia's excitement over the prospect was earnest. She believed it to be the chance of a lifetime, so much so that she wasn't looking at the situation analytically, if she was even capable of doing so. Rowan was hired muscle. He didn't strike Mahdi as unintelligent, but he wasn't paid to ask questions.

And Mahdi? He didn't know what to ask until now, and Sashi had yet to arrive. They were being housed at the Sandal-Foot Resort, a collection of villas tucked into the jungle on the west coast of South Andaman Island, just twenty miles from the infamous North Sentinel Island.

"So what's your deal?" Rowan asked. "You seem like a nice enough guy, strong silent type, but you're hard to get a read on."

"There is not much to know," Mahdi said.

"Says the Pakistani linguist hiding in England."

Talia kicked sand at Rowan's legs. "Give him a break."

"Really? *You're* not curious?"

"The majority of Israelis and Palestinians co-exist peacefully, like...Red Sox and Yankees fans. Especially those of us in the sciences. Elevated minds prevail across all cultures."

Mahdi's smile was honest. He had not known what to expect from Talia, but he appreciated the respect she had shown at the mosque, and now for all of Palestine. At the same time, she might have been raised in Israel, but she had been educated in the U.S. and spent the majority of her adult life living in a hut or under the open sky. Her countrymen and women still in Israel might not share her liberal viewpoints.

Rowan raised a defiant finger. "First, when was the last time you spent ten minutes with both a Red Sox fan and a Yankees fan? Because: Not pretty." A second finger extended. "Second, my job is to keep you both safe. That includes from each other. Given the turbulent nature of your cultures, I think my line of questioning is fair." A third finger. "Third, would you mind moving a few feet away. As much as I'd like you closer, I can smell your drink."

Talia looked at her drink, frowned, and stepped into the sun-touched sand beyond the tall tree's shadow. "Sorry. I forgot."

"It's okay." He pointed at Mahdi. "I've got Mahdi to help me stay dry."

"Actually," Madhi said. "I could use a beer. But I will abstain in your presence."

"Well, now I really feel like a dick." Talia poured her drink into the sand.

Rowan watched the liquid fall, unconsciously licking his lips as the beach absorbed every drop. Then he turned to Mahdi, one eyebrow perched high on his forehead. "Wait, so you're..."

"Not Muslim, no."

Rowan appeared perplexed. "But..."

"Just as Talia is a Jew—"

"That was a little less derogatory sounding," Talia said with a wink.

"But is not Jewish, as in the religion."

"So I'm kicking it on the beach with a non-Jew Jew and a non-Muslim Muslim?"

Mahdi laughed. "Non-Muslim Arab. Or Palestinian." There were people in the world who might kill Rowan for his comment, many of them members of Mahdi's extended family, but he was not one of them. "And I am hanging with a white man who is..." Mahdi's joke stalled in his mouth. "Why are Americans not stereotyped by a single religion?"

"Because we're a little more diverse?" Rowan scratched his bare chest. "Arabs are pretty much Muslim, right?"

Mahdi shook his head. "Ten percent of Arabs are Christian."

"Huh," Rowan said. "Well, so far, one hundred percent of the Arabs I know can't tell a joke."

Mahdi laughed again.

Talia rolled her eyes. "The bromance begins."

"Bromance?" Mahdi asked, getting a rise out of both Talia and Rowan.

"We're already making progress," Rowan said. "Our linguist learned a new word."

Their laughter was cut short by a clearing throat.

Sashi approached them with a man in tow. While she wore the flowing colors of her homeland, he was dressed in a tailored business suit that must have retained heat like an oven. Despite the thick fabric and dark color, there wasn't a bead of sweat on the man's forehead. *A local*, Mahdi decided, *accustomed to the tropical environment.* Mahdi was fairly resistant to the adverse effects of dry heat, but his body didn't know how to handle humidity. He was relieved to see fresh, folded clothes in Sashi's hands.

She handed him a white, short sleeve, button-down shirt, a pair of pleated shorts, and leather boat shoes. "A little more your style?"

Mahdi accepted the clothing. "Yes, thank you."

"So these are the intrepid explorers," the newcomer said, his Indian accent far thicker than Sashi's. His perfect smile looked more expensive than his suit, and his perfectly styled gray hair defied the ocean breeze. "North Sentinel Island is not for the faint of heart."

"Everyone, this is Rattan Ambani." Sashi motioned to the man, who pressed his hands together and bowed like a Hollywood star receiving an award. "He owns the Sandal-Foot Resort. When he heard about our expedition, he graciously offered his assistance, providing us with villas to stay in, the use of the grounds, and not to mention a ship and a captain to take us to the island."

"The government hadn't already paid for lodging and transportation?" Mahdi asked.

"The Indian government is happy to accept the generosity of its citizens," she replied, her smile now forced. "And Mr. Ambani is one of our best."

"I must admit," Ambani said, "that I am somewhat infatuated with the Sentinelese people. I saw them once. When I was young and foolish. My friends and I took a yacht and anchored off the coast. The natives came out, of course, shooting arrows into the water, rudely gesturing."

"You're lucky to be alive," Talia said, arms crossed, looking unimpressed.

"Yes, yes," Ambani said. "I know that now. But we had heard the stories, of course. The bravado of youth propelled us to stupidity, but we knew well enough to leave before the sunset. I have not returned to the island, but I do occasionally wake upon hearing a noise, wondering if the Sentinelese finally decided to raid the mainland."

"They wouldn't be able to reach it," Talia said.

"Mmm." Ambani seemed to seriously consider this, and then his smile returned. "Regardless, I will sleep better knowing that the Sentinelese have been pacified."

"Pacified!" Talia looked ready to attack. Rowan was quick to his feet, blocking her path.

Ambani held his palms up. "What I mean to say, is that I will sleep better knowing peaceful contact has been made. That the Sentinelese transition into the modern world is without conflict. That is the nature of your expedition, is it not?" He motioned to Talia. "To bridge the ancient and modern worlds." Then to Mahdi. "To communicate as friends." Then to Rowan. "And make sure no one is killed in the process."

"You know a lot about us," Rowan noted.

Ambani placed a thick hand on Sashi's shoulder, with the weight of it, or perhaps her discomfort, forcing her arm lower. "Ms. Batta and I shared a delightful meal this afternoon. She was kind enough to reveal the details of your undertaking."

"Something she has yet to do with us," Mahdi said. He had questions that needed answering, and he preferred to get them from Sashi, rather than second-hand through a hotel tycoon, or from the other people who had been hastily hired for the job. He had requested details both on the way to the airport and on the plane, but Sashi had said they would be briefed after settling in. Other than a few scant bits of information about North Sentinel Island and the people who dwell there, he was mostly in the dark. Instinct told him to press for more, but when Sashi had revealed how much he would be paid for his services, he had refrained from asking any more questions. But that was yesterday. Today, far from home, he needed answers.

"My sincerest apologies," the businessman said. "I did not mean to step on toes. I am merely excited." He turned to Sashi. "I have prepared the conference room, as you directed. Would it be too much to ask if I could listen in on your presentation?"

"That would be fine," Sashi said to the man, before turning to the others and mouthing, 'Sorry.'

"I will see you all there," he said with a strange kind of fist pumping motion that Mahdi took to be a sign of victory. The man might be a tycoon, but he radiated the innocent excitement of a small boy. Mahdi couldn't decide whether or not he liked the paradoxical man, but he found himself shaking his head, along with the others, as the man strutted back toward the resort's main building.

"I am sorry," Sashi said, when the man was out of earshot. "Truly. Like all of you, I am merely doing the wishes of those who write my paychecks. Mr. Ambani has been generous, and kind, but he can be..."

"Ignorant," Talia said. There was no doubting how she felt about the man.

"Overbearing," Sashi said. "But we must endure him. At least while we are on his grounds, which after today, will only be at night." She clapped her hands. "Now then, I'm glad to see you all getting along, but it is time for the answers for which you have all so patiently waited, and to meet the rest of our team."

"Rest of our team?" Rowan asked. "How many people am I supposed to protect?"

"Our captain and the first officer, both of whom will remain on the ship at all times—"

Talia raised a hand. "Umm, I think pretty much everyone will remain on the ship at all times. Maybe with the exception of me, but that's only if I'm sure I won't be skewered the moment I step on shore. My methods might be unusual, but I'm still alive for a reason."

"Not that I want to shake hands with these people—" Mahdi began.

"Because that would be monumentally stupid as they have no cultural basis for hand shaking, and casual contact could transmit diseases for which they have no defense."

Mahdi sighed. Talia was an intriguing, but difficult woman. "It was a figure of speech."

She gave a nod. "Then the answer is, you'll shout from the boat, but probably mostly listen, and if you have something to say, I'll say it for you."

"We can discuss all this inside," Sashi said, walking backward and motioning for them to follow. "And we really should get started. There is a lot to go over, and I suggest an early bed time. We leave at first light."

Talia and Rowan followed. Mahdi walked behind them, listening as Talia joked, "I think I'd sleep better if Mr. Ambani was stuck on Sentinel Island, too."

Rowan made a faux pouty face and spoke with a horrible Indian accent. "Oh, but then I would definitely be dead."

Mahdi laughed again, considered a return to the running derogatory gag, but then the reality of his situation began to sink in. If spending a single night on Sentinel Island was a death sentence, why the hell were they going?

5

FROM THE DARK depths of the jungle to a plush conference room over the course of a week. While the path of Talia Mayer's life had been chaotic, she had only experienced such a dramatic transition once before, and she preferred not to talk or even think about that.

She hoped this experience would be better, though the soft chairs, tables piled with plates of cut tropical fruit, and the bitter-cold air conditioning were offending her sensibilities. Most of the world got along just fine, and were perfectly happy, without such excess. Despite growing up in a wealthy suburb of Tel Aviv, she didn't understand why modern man couldn't seem to live without absolute comfort at all times.

Every minute she stayed in the chilly room, she looked more forward to visiting North Sentinel Island. In her opinion, the Sentinelese lived the good life. From what she knew of them, their lifestyle wouldn't be that dissimilar to the Peruvian Mashco-Piro, with the exception of subsisting off the sea, rather than the jungle.

They deserved to maintain that life, as did the Mashco-Piro and nearly a hundred other tribes around the world who had yet to be tainted by first world envy. But that was not reality, and she accepted that. If the Indian government was set on making contact, then better it be through someone like her, than a stick-in-the-mud pencil pusher who carried a rifle for fear of the natives he was supposed to protect.

At the same time, she had never been hired by a government agency before. Her treks into the Amazon had been self-motivated and self-funded, due to a sizable inheritance. Thanks to her off-the-beaten-path lifestyle, most of that money still sat in her bank account, but when she needed to travel, bribe an official, or purchase medicine for a threatened people, she had the necessary resources. She had been beholden to no one, until now.

She sat between Rowan, who had a plate piled with fruit, and Mahdi, who hadn't stopped squeezing his fingers. Both men had been a surprise. She didn't know how well they would work in the field, but Rowan's easy-going sense of humor and Mahdi's straightforward intellect were helping her transition back into the modern world.

At the same time, they were both enigmas, whose presence here was just as odd as her own. They were a motley, unconventional crew. The Indian government either had very little experience with contacting the few remaining tribal peoples under their rule, or better—more traditional—options had not been available.

Of course, National Geographic had once attempted the traditional approach, and before the crew even reached the shore, the director's leg was skewered by an arrow. That expedition had come to a violent, bloody end before it had truly even begun. And few people had attempted contact since, and never with better results.

Sitting beside Mahdi was a man named Emmei, their ship's captain, who was tapping his hands on his knees and bopping his head to music only he could hear. He was descended from local Andamanese parents who had left the tribe and joined the modern world, working for the resort.

He physically resembled the Sentinelese people, but not overtly. His skin was a few shades lighter, and his facial features less pronounced. Thanks to a calorie-rich diet supplied by 'civilization', he also stood eight inches taller than Sentinelese men, whose stature had been reduced by millennia of living on an island with limited resources. Despite there being only twenty miles of ocean between the two islands, the two tribes had been separated for hundreds of generations. But the biggest diversion between the population was language. While many island tribes in the region could communicate, the Sentinelese spoke a language all their own.

Deciphering it would not be easy. She hoped Mahdi was up to the task.

Beside Emmei was Winston Rhett, a pudgy American documentary filmmaker. After a brief Google search on his phone, which would cease working a mile off shore, Rowan had determined the man had never actually released a movie. But that didn't seem all that important as he was documenting the expedition for the Indian government—not for mass consumption.

Sashi sat at the end of the single row of chairs, flipping through a binder full of notes. When the lights dimmed, she whispered to herself, stood, and headed for the podium at the front of the room.

Mr. Ambani hustled from the back of the space, where he had dimmed the lights, and sat down beside Rowan, eyes alight, radiating excitement.

Talia leaned back in her chair, arms crossed. She wasn't expecting to learn anything new. Rowan, on the other hand, opened a notebook, clicked a pen and prepared to take notes.

"I'm impressed," she whispered to him.

"I don't like to make mistakes." He smiled, but it wasn't genuine. In her experience, men who didn't like to make mistakes had usually made more than a few.

"Sorry for the delay. You've all been very patient, and I thank you for that." Sashi opened her binder, flipped through pages and picked up a small remote, clicking the button once. A rectangle of light blazed on a hanging video screen behind her. When Talia's eyes adjusted, she saw a projected photo of North Sentinel Island.

"This is where we will be spending the majority of our days," Sashi said. "North Sentinel Island. Though we will likely remain offshore, pending a breakthrough. I'm going to briefly cover what the public knows about the island, and then reveal a few things that are not widely known."

Sashi looked up and squinted at Mahdi, whose hand was raised. "There will be time for questions when I'm finished."

"Why are we here?" he asked.

"I'm getting to that."

"I believe you should lead with that," he said.

"I agree," Talia said. "I'm honestly still undecided about whether or not this is a good idea."

"What I meant is, why *us*?" Mahdi motioned to Talia and Rowan. "We couldn't have been your first choice."

"Also a good question," Talia said. Her respect for Mahdi was growing. He might not be adventurous, but he was intelligent *and* no-nonsense.

"You will get your answers," Sashi said. "But please, let me provide a little context." She looked at Talia. "Not everyone knows as much about the Sentinelese as you do, and even your knowledge is limited."

Mahdi crossed his legs and leaned back, acquiescing to Sashi's request.

Talia took Sashi's last comment as a challenge, but kept her mouth shut. She had studied North Sentinel Island while getting her master's degree, but that was years ago, and it was possible things had changed. After all, the government did seem to be in a hurry to make peaceful contact.

When no one else spoke, Sashi switched to the next slide. It showed a hazy photo of a naked black man on a pristine beach. The man had his arm cocked back, a spear ready to throw. "There are a handful of photos and two short videos of the Sentinelese people, none of them very high quality. We know they are small in stature, yet well built, with frizzy hair and very dark skin. They are a pre-Neolithic culture, wearing nothing aside from belts—for supply pouches—and occasionally decorative headbands. They are armed mostly with spears and bow and arrows, tipped with iron pillaged from shipwrecks and shipping containers that washed up on their beaches. They have also been seen wielding long shards of metal, mounted on wooden handles, like swords or short scythes."

That's new, Talia thought, but she didn't ask about it. The Sentinelese had access to pillaged iron for years. It wasn't surprising that they had figured out how to make new weapons from their finds. They wouldn't have the technology to forge the metal, but they could tie metal scraps to branches. Tribes like the Sentinelese survived by being creative and innovative in ways an American with a car, grocery store, bank account, and iPhone couldn't fathom.

"There have been a few well-documented encounters over the years." Sashi clicked to the next image, an aerial photo of a cargo ship floundering on the reefs around North Sentinel Island. "The first was in 1867, after a British surveyor working for the East India Company noticed a 'multitude of lights' on the island. The resulting expedition was driven away under a cloud of arrows, or so the men claimed. That same year, a merchant ship was stranded on the island, we now believe intent on enslaving its people. One hundred and six marooned men fended off attacks for several days before being rescued. We know there were casualties, but we do not have a concrete number. Perhaps the biggest offense against the Sentinelese people occurred in 1880, when an expedition led by Maurice Portman stormed and searched the island, finding paths. The tribe eluded them until Portman found and kidnapped an elderly couple and four children. The couple died and the children were returned, no doubt telling stories that solidified the Sentinelese view of the outside world for generations to come. There were several more brief landings during the British occupation of India, but all were met with violence and repelled.

"In more modern times, between 1967 and 1975, the Indian government sent exploratory parties to the island, hoping to make peaceful contact, much like we will be. But again, they were greeted violently and sent away.

In 1974, *National Geographic,* shooting the documentary 'Man in Search of Man', sent a group of anthropologists, with very different ideas from Talia, along with armed and armored policemen and a small film crew. Their efforts led to the director being shot in the thigh, and the expedition was called off."

"Their first mistake was leaving a plastic baby doll on the beach." Talia couldn't resist pointing out the stupidity of this gesture. "Can you imagine? Seeing a baby, unmoving and made of plastic? They have no concept of plastic, or of toys, or of white babies. It's no wonder they speared the thing and buried it in the sand."

"Thank you for the elaboration, Talia." Sashi nodded, and then she pointed at the cargo ship on screen. "This is the *Primrose.* She ran aground during a monsoon in 1981. The crew was stranded on the reef for a week and reported being shot at by fifty Sentinelese warriors. They believed they would be boarded. The crew was rescued by helicopter, but they were found locked inside the ship and in a state of near panic. Some of the survivors, now elderly, were recently questioned about the ordeal. They discussed previously unrevealed details. This recording is from a man named Harold Stack."

Sashi held up her phone and hit the play button in an audio app.

"They were everywhere," Stack said, his voice gravely with age.

"On the beach?" a male interviewer asked.

"On the deck. Everywhere. In the water. We ran. Just ran. They shot the lights out. Banged on the door all night. Trying to get in. It was… was… was…"

"Was what?"

"I—I'm not supposed to talk about it."

Sashi lowered the phone. "That was the last thing he said. He died two weeks later. We were able to speak with the helicopter pilot, who circled the island and took this photo. He didn't see the Sentinelese, or the boats the *Primrose* captain mentioned in his mayday message, or any arrows, spears, or other signs of attack. However, he did recall the exterior lights being broken, as one man cut his foot on a shard and bled in the chopper."

Sashi updated the image. It showed a small fishing boat washed up on the island's shore. "Now, as far as the public record goes, most modern contact ends there, with the exception of a single incident in 2006. There is a three mile exclusion zone around the island. Anyone found inside it faces heavy fines and jail time."

"But not us," Mahdi said.

Sashi seemed thrown by the comment, but then said, "Of course not. But in 2006, two men spent the day fishing off North Sentinel Island. That night, they dropped anchor and went to sleep. It is believed that the ship drifted to shore during the night when the anchor failed. The two men were slain. If you are squeamish, you might want to look away."

Talia noticed that no one looked away, and Mr. Ambani leaned forward, elbows on knees. The image updated to the slain bodies of two Indian men, their throats slit, their bodies covered in puncture wounds and their limbs broken at severe angles.

"That was not a defensive killing," Talia pointed out. "That was rage."

Sashi nodded, "And I'm sorry to say it is not an isolated incident."

The image changed, revealing two men and a woman lying in the back of a boat, similarly mutilated. Then again. A fishing vessel with four men slain. Then again, six young men, all dead, surrounded by empty beer cans, but not by a single arrow. Sashi moved to click the button again, but stopped. "There are, sadly, five more incidents that have been kept from the world. The total death toll is thirty-two."

"That's why we're going," Talia said.

"I don't understand," Mahdi said. He looked mortified, and rightfully so.

"If the Sentinelese have killed this many people, exclusion zone or not, they've been deemed a danger to modern society. People are always going to do stupid things—" She motioned to Mr. Ambani. "No offense." Though she meant offense, "—so the government needs to take action to either bring the Sentinelese into the modern world, or exterminate them."

Mahdi bristled. "I will take no part in the—"

"We're not here to exterminate them," Talia said. "We're their last chance at survival. If we can't make peaceful contact with the Sentinelese, their 65,000 year occupation of *their* island is going to come to an end."

6

ROWAN COULDN'T SLEEP. The past few days of travel and subsequent jetlag left his body exhausted, but the gears of his mind had discovered the secret of perpetual motion. He had prescription sleep aids, but it was already 3am. He'd need to be awake and alert in just three hours. He could manage that with little sleep and a lot of coffee, but not with Ambien swirling through his veins and dulling his mind. Normally, he'd find solace in the bottle, drinking enough to cloud his worries and make him sleepy without the hangover.

But that wasn't an option now. The contract he'd signed with Sashi, which also included a non-disclosure agreement, stipulated that he would be fired, without pay, if he so much as sipped an alcoholic drink. He'd signed the document before knowing they'd be staying at a resort fully stocked with every spirit known to man.

But he could manage it, he believed. He wasn't an alcoholic after all. He knew that opinion was a stereotypical alcoholic thing to believe, but he had gone years without a drink in between stints of heavy drinking. Those breaks were spurred on by circumstances, such as the moment Sashi had crossed his path.

The only reason I want a drink now, he thought, *is because of the stress.*

Protecting these folks from a tribal people with a history of deadly violence, was outside his wheelhouse. He was a skilled soldier. Deadly with a gun or a knife, but he had never been a mercenary before, let alone a bodyguard.

He looked up at the night sky, blazing with stars. Despite growing up in the woods of New Hampshire, the Milky Way appeared far brighter here. It reminded him of Afghanistan, a country in which he had seen beauty only at night. In the stars. Until those stars had become points of light descending from the sky, in the wrong place, killing the wrong people.

A warm breeze tickled his head. It made him wonder if he had a few strands of his hair longer than the rest. He had shaved it himself, so it was possible. He made a mental note to check, and continued his walk through the collection of villas that were the Sandal-Foot Resort. During the day, the villas looked well-constructed and modern. Everything rustic about them was an illusion, meant to make guests feel like they were roughing it. But at night, in the near total darkness, the villas looked like authentic jungle huts.

Rowan rounded a bend in the manicured path and stopped. Unlike the other villas, which were dark and quiet, the villa nearest the beach—Talia's—showed signs of life. The orange glow of firelight flickered in from between the cracks in the drawn, wooden blinds.

Mothlike instinct drew him toward the light, but as he walked nearer, he found himself becoming concerned. The huts didn't have fireplaces. It was far too hot here, all year long, to justify even a romantic flame. Candles seemed the likely culprit, but sleeping with lit candles in a villa built from wood, and covered by a faux grass roof was a recipe for human barbecue.

His pace quickened with his pulse. The amount of light seemed too bright for a candle or two. He didn't see or smell smoke, but if the blaze had just started... He slipped into a jog, ready to sound the alarm, when a shadow moved across the window, slow and unconcerned.

Talia was awake, and not screaming.

But what was she doing?

Feeling just a little bit like a creep, he slid toward the glowing window.

Talia was...different. There were moments when she seemed normal, usually when she was talking about the modern world, or the science behind her work. That was when her intellect took over, and she gave off the vibe of an adventurous, funny, and intelligent woman. Someone he might even be interested in. But sometimes...sometimes she had a look in her eyes. He didn't know how to describe it other than dangerous. Maybe it was because she had put a poison arrow tip against Sashi's neck when they had first met. First impressions and all that. He had written it off as a bluff, but who really knew what she had done while living with that Peruvian tribe? What she had told them was borderline scandalous. But what hadn't she told them?

He tried to steady his breath as he approached the window, but he couldn't help but feel like what he was doing was wrong. He'd been concerned at first, but if Talia was awake, and not panicking, then her villa wasn't on fire. Curiosity urged him on like a teenage boy, daring him to see what maybe he shouldn't.

Rowan stopped at the sound of Talia's voice. Was she speaking to someone? Was she not alone? He strained to hear, but could only make out one voice, and he couldn't understand a single word. She wasn't speaking English.

He straddled the shrub growing beneath the glowing window and leaned closer. Orange light filled his view. The villa, like his, was a single large room with an open concept bathroom, though the toilet had its own small closet-sized space with a door. Palm trees in a framed painting appeared to sway in the light cast by several flickering candles. The queen-sized bed was still made, an unpacked backpack lying atop its tropical colored quilt.

Motion snapped him rigid, breath held. A shadow danced across the wall, awkward, the motions rigid and insectoid.

The dance paused. The shadow grew larger, dancing once more as the candle flames shifted.

Talia strolled into view, her naked body seen in thin segmented lines.

Rowan's heart pounded, not because he was seeing Talia naked—he had already seen her naked—but because he knew he was now squarely in the wrong and needed to leave without being caught or his stint as a bodyguard would be short-lived.

He began to lift his leg up and over the shrub when he heard her voice again, the sound muffled through the window, but again, not English.

She wasn't speaking any language he knew.

One leg raised like a urinating dog, Rowan squinted through the blinds. Hints of red lines covered naked skin. Or was that the firelight playing tricks on his eyes?

A leaf rustled beneath his foot.

Talia's voice became a whisper. Her body stopped moving.

Rowan lifted his leg over the shrub.

Shit, shit, shit.

Talia's shadow grew larger, her heels thumping on the floor.

The unforgiving ground punished Rowan for his indiscretion as he dove and rolled out of view. Orange light blazed from the window as the blinds were drawn up. Rowan stayed motionless on the ground, watching Talia's candlelit shadow wobble on the footpath where he had stood just a moment before.

The shadow shrank as she retreated, and then the light dulled in stages. *She's blowing out the candles*, Rowan realized, scrambling to his feet. As soon as that last candle was out, and her eyes adjusted to the dark, she would be able to see more easily.

After a moment of indecision, he hurried past her villa toward the beach. Had he returned the way he'd come, she would have seen him leaving. As he walked, he thought, *I should have just knocked. Told her I saw the light and was concerned.* He would have left out peeking through her window, but could have told her the truth.

The way he'd handled it probably left her feeling vulnerable and afraid.

The sand squeaked beneath his feet. The ocean's waves lapped against the shore, far calmer than his pounding heart. He leaned down, hands on knees, and smiled. Then laughed. It had been a long time since his mischievous high-school years. How many motel rooms had he and his friends peered through while whittling down six packs?

Rowan shook his head. Fond memories often included drinking.

I'm not an alcoholic, he thought, and then he said it aloud, "I'm not an alcoholic."

A whispered, unintelligible reply, spun him around.

Dark trees blotted out a portion of the night sky. Nothing else.

The whisper came again, this time from the sea. He turned and saw only the moon's light shimmering over the waters.

What the hell…

Instinct drew a hand down to a sidearm that was not present. He was alone and unarmed on an island that, while not nearly as dangerous as Sentinel Island, still supported the Jarawa tribe, whose territory began just ten miles north of the resort. Sightings of the tribe were common as they sometimes entered civilization to pilfer supplies, food, and animals. Violence between the tribe and outsiders was at an all-time low, but that didn't mean it never happened.

Rowan crouched in the sand, trying to make as low a profile as possible. He was out in the open. An easy target. *What the hell am I doing here?* he thought. Despite being forced from the Army Rangers just six months previously, he was already soft. Out of practice. Distracted. Thirsty.

I'm going to get these people killed.

"Hey."

Rowan craned around, throwing a punch toward the voice.

His solid knuckles collided with ocean air, pulling him around and toppling him to his back.

"Hey!"

The figure standing above him was feminine, loose hair caught in the wind. The voice filtered through his fight or flight.

"Talia."

"The hell are you doing out here?"

"Couldn't sleep." It was the truth, but it came out like a lie.

"That's why you're having fist fights with the air?"

"Have you ever tried fighting the air?" he asked, heart rate slowing, thoughts clearing. "It's not easy."

"I would imagine not," she replied, and then, blunt as ever, "Have you been drinking?"

"As much as I would like to say yes, the answer is no."

She reached a hand down and helped him back to his feet. His face was just inches from hers when he stood. She leaned in, as though for a kiss, and then stopped. Sniffing.

"I told you the truth." he said.

"You did," she says. "But not all of it. Your aftershave is distinct. Why were you outside my villa?"

She wasn't smelling my breath. Busted.

"Look, I told you the truth. I couldn't sleep. I went for a walk."

"And then…"

"Saw the flickering light from your villa. I thought there might be a fire."

"So you peeked through the window." He was about to confirm this when she added, "And saw me."

"Not really," he said, on the defensive. "Not much. And not on purpose. I didn't know you'd be walking around naked at three in the morning."

"Okay, listen. You're a nice guy. We get along fine. But there are a few things you need to understand. First, I was getting ready for bed, and I sleep naked. As for why I was going to bed at 3am, I'm still on Peruvian time and trying to adjust. Second, you saw me naked in the jungle, which by the way, was uncomfortable not because of my nudity, but because of how you saw it. I lived with the Mashco-Piro for six months and didn't feel exposed until you saw me. That's not your fault, but it's true. And now, just because you saw me naked when I allowed it, does not mean I don't care if you see me naked when it's not my choice."

Rowan nearly defended himself. Had he been drinking, he would have. But the truth of her words sank in before he opened his mouth. When he did speak, it was a single word. "Sorry."

"Apology accepted."

"Really, just like that?" Rowan had expected a longer chewing out. His intent was innocent, but he knew it could be perceived horribly, which was why he had fled.

"Only because I believe you."

There was an edge to her words that was either habitual or a veiled threat. He didn't know which, but he decided he was safe because he had no intention of offending Talia, and he understood now that honesty, even when it was uncomfortable, would keep the two of them on the same page.

"Well," Talia said. "I'm not tired at all now. You?"

The adrenaline kicked into his system from the past few minutes made the idea of sleep laughable. "Not at all."

Talia sat in the sand. "Want to watch the sunrise?"

"That's in three hours," he said. "And on the other side of the island."

"Yeah, well, do you have anything better to do?"

She laid on her back, hands under her head. He could barely see her in the moonlight, but he thought she was smiling. "This place smells different, sounds different, and feels different on my skin, but this view doesn't change. No matter where you are in the world, the night sky is familiar."

He looked up and then sat down. She was right. And wrong. The further north or south you traveled in either hemisphere, the more the night sky changed. But in this part of the world, the stars above him were mostly the same as seen in the States.

He laid back in the sand, and without another word or touch shared between them, he enjoyed a peaceful night, forgetting his worries, his cravings, and his past. All that changed when the songbirds woke him up at dawn.

7

"ARE YOU OKAY?" Mahdi asked. He stood above Rowan Baer, whom he had found sleeping in the sand. The man had stirred at Mahdi's approach, looking up at the loud birds in the trees overhead, a frown on his face as he looked down at the sand beside him. These visible signs of life had been a relief. Rowan had appeared either unconscious or dead. Mahdi didn't know Rowan well, but everyone knew of his struggle. He made no effort to hide it, but also didn't fully admit it. That he had been hired to protect them was yet another odd choice for the Indian government. But Mahdi was safe and being paid well enough that he could remain so for a while longer. Perhaps he would even remain on the islands, stretching his money further than he could back in England.

He shook his head at the thought of returning to London. They had found him there. He didn't know how, but the men he had seen on the street did not look friendly. His two years in England had come to an end. He would have to find a new home.

"Fine," Rowan said, pushing himself up. He stretched his neck, touched his toes, and arched his back. A morning routine fit for a cat. "What time is it?"

"The boat is waiting," Mahdi said. "I was sent to look for you."

"Why didn't Talia…"

"She is sleeping, too," Mahdi said. "On the boat."

"How late am I?"

"We were to leave an hour ago."

Rowan grunted, mumbled something unintelligible, and then pointed down the beach. "Dock is that way?"

"Yes."

"I'll be there in ten minutes." He stumbled through the sand, headed back toward the villas.

Mahdi watched him leave, doubting whether or not Rowan would even be able to save himself. Self-destruction ran in Mahdi's family. He knew the warning signs. Rowan was an empty vessel. The course of his life would be determined by what eventually filled him, whether it be love, hate, nobility, or alcohol. Mahdi looked down at the flattened sand where Rowan, and someone else, had lain. If Rowan was spending time with Talia, a paradox, Rowan's future would likely be a tumultuous one.

Just do the job, collect the check, and find someplace quiet to live, Mahdi told himself. There was no need to worry about the affairs of the people with whom he'd been paired. His job was to stay on the boat and try to make sense of the Sentinelese language. That, he could do, and without fear of being speared or shot by an arrow.

Mahdi's boat shoes filled with sand as he walked along the beach, back toward the dock. He took them off and walked barefoot, the hot sand beneath his toes reminding him of a childhood cut short by bloodshed. And gunfire. And explosions.

"Did you find him?"

The shouted voice made Mahdi jump. He looked up to see Sashi standing in the waiting yacht, a hand raised, blocking her eyes from the morning sun. The ship named *Sea Tiger* was impressive, stretching a hundred feet in length with four decks of opulent living space. There was indoor and outdoor dining, a lavish galley, crew quarters, a gleaming white hull, and twin motors that could push them up to thirty knots, though they would not be traveling that fast.

Mahdi donned a pair of sunglasses and shouted back. "He will be with us shortly."

"Where was he?"

"Overslept." Mahdi didn't know Rowan, but still didn't want to cast a bad impression of the man.

Sashi, on the other hand, seemed determined to uncover Rowan's failures. "He wasn't in his villa. I checked."

"On the beach," Mahdi said, and then he raised a hand to stop her next question short. "He appeared to be sober and regretful for having fallen asleep."

A thumping of boots over wood pulled his attention to the long dock. Rowan was jogging toward the yacht and would beat Mahdi there. His clothes were changed, a thick backpack hung from his shoulders. In one hand he held a long case that looked like it should contain a musical instrument. In the other hand was a tall cup of coffee. The man had made up for his tardiness with military efficiency. Even stopped to help Mahdi up onto the raised dock.

"Sorry I'm late," he said to Sashi, while hoisting Mahdi up.

"Just don't do it again," Sashi said before turning to the wheelhouse above her. "Captain, we are all here!"

The engines turned over and coughed gray smoke.

A young woman with dark skin and very short hair stepped out of the wheelhouse and climbed down to the deck before leaping the rail onto the dock. She smiled at the two men. Mahdi was taken aback by the woman, who was not only agile, but dressed in a pair of white shorts and a pink bikini top. While he didn't believe in the tenets of Islam, he had grown up in a culture that preferred women to remain covered in public. And though he had lived in London for two years, there were not many nearly topless women walking the streets.

Rowan was far less distressed. "You must be the first officer." He extended his hand. "I'm Rowan."

The young woman, who was just shy of five feet tall, shook his hand and spoke with a thick and unique accent. "Chagara Do'ra. But most foreigners call me Chugy. I'm Emmei's niece."

Mahdi offered his hand. "Mahdi."

Her rough skin and firm grip spoke of a life far more physical than Mahdi's, and as he boarded the ship, Chugy untied the yacht's dock lines from the cleats. She flung the final line into the back of the boat, the engines revved, and the ship pulled away. Chugy leapt the three foot distance and vaulted the rail back onto the ship with a smile. She gave a thumbs up to Emmei in the wheelhouse, and he returned it with a chuckle.

Chugy's and Emmei's casual nature put him at ease. "Have you been to Sentinel Island before?"

Chugy's smile faded. "Only the very foolish or the very smart go to Sentinel Island. I'm not sure which we are yet."

"That was a 'no', by the way." Rowan clapped him on the shoulder and began stowing his gear.

The boat surged, stumbling Mahdi back into a bench at the stern.

Five minutes later, he was puking his breakfast into their wake.

While Mahdi had traveled extensively by train and plane, he had never been on a boat. The closest he'd come to experiencing the sensation was floating in the salty Dead Sea. At first, the gentle rise and fall of the ocean beneath the *Sea Tiger*'s hull had simply made him nervous. But now, carving across the open water, which had grown choppy, the rise and fall of each wave was unpredictable and occasionally violent.

The sea did not agree with him.

By the time the island was spotted on the horizon, an hour and a half later, the ocean and his stomach had calmed.

"There it is," Emmei declared, pointing over the wheel as the engines slowed and the boat sagged forward.

Mahdi climbed up into the wheelhouse to see for himself. The island was just a lump of land at the edge of the world.

"We are at the exclusion zone's boundary," Emmei said.

"You have permission to proceed," Sashi said. She was seated beside the captain, looking out at the island, something like apprehension on her face.

Motion turned Mahdi's eyes downward. Rowan stood on the forward deck with Chugy and Talia, who must have woken up and joined the crew while Mahdi was hanging over the stern rail. Both women were dressed for the weather, showing more skin than they covered. He couldn't hear what Rowan was saying, but everyone was smiling. He admired the man's casual ease and confidence. "I wonder which of them he will sleep with first," he said, and then he remembered who was standing beside him. He turned, wide-eyed to Emmei, intent on apologizing, but the man barked a laugh.

"I do not think he will have much luck with Chugy," Emmei said.

Mahdi was about to ask why when he saw the look of desire in Chugy's eyes, directed not at Rowan, but toward Talia. "Oh. Oh!"

It was at that moment that Mahdi knew that if the family he had left behind in Palestine ever found out about his time away from home, he would never be welcomed back. Had they known he would be working alongside an Israeli, an American soldier, and a lesbian, they would have preferred he stay at home to face those he had betrayed.

Am I selling my soul? he wondered, and he quickly decided that for such a thing to be possible, a soul had to exist, and Allah had to be real.

Am I dishonoring my family? My wife?

That was a question he could not answer, not because he did not know how his loved ones thought, but because he feared the guilt the answer would bring.

The engines surged again. Mahdi stood in the wheelhouse, watching the island grow larger. When the yacht began thumping through the waves again, his knees bent with the motion. His stomach remained still. *I can do this,* he thought, and then the engines slowed.

The sapphire ocean ahead faded to a halo of light turquoise surrounding the island. He pointed at the lighter water. "What is that?"

"The reef," Emmei said. "It extends out nearly a mile from the island in some locations, and there are only three breaks where a small vessel can safely reach the shore." He pointed to a line of darker blue, cutting through the halo. "There. That is where we will drop anchor."

"That's too far from shore to shout," Mahdi observed.

Emmei gave him an odd glance and then Sashi let out a quiet laugh. "I'm sorry to have misrepresented the situation, Mahdi. You will not be shouting from this boat." She patted the dash. "You will be shouting from the dinghy." She pointed to the small, twelve-foot-long craft being pulled behind them. It looked like a row boat with a motor.

Mahdi knew the small vessel well. He had stared at it for an hour while gagging.

It wasn't long before the *Sea Tiger* was anchored in a three-hundred-foot wide inlet between two beds of reef. Talia spurred everyone into action. While the rest of the crew grew noticeably quiet and serious, Talia seemed almost elated. Twenty minutes after anchoring, they were ready to go.

"I'm ready," came the gruff voice of Winston Rhett, the man hired to document their expedition. He carried a camera in one hand and dragged a net full of fresh coconuts in the other. He wore a loud Hawaiian shirt that looked near to bursting a button, cargo shorts, and a pair of sandals. His thinning, unkempt hair, caught by the wind, danced like an open flame. Mahdi had forgotten about the man, who must have been sleeping, or eating, until now. "Keep your panties on." He paused to look at Talia, and then Chugy. "Or not."

No one acknowledged the man, but Talia pointed at the coconuts. "As much as the Sentinelese like coconuts, we're not going to lead with gifts."

Winston looked incredulous. "Mr. Ambani insisted we give a gift—"

"Mr. Ambani owns a chain of hotels," Talia said. "He's not in charge."

Winston shot a look at Sashi, who simply shook her head.

"Every mission to reach the Sentinelese has begun with a gift, usually of coconuts, which do not grow on the island, but do occasionally wash up on shore. I'm sure the gift pleases them, but do you know how many of those expeditions—where white men brought coconuts, and tools, and candy, and dolls—" She rolled her eyes, "ended in success?"

Winston just stared at her.

"Not one," she said. "The coconuts stay, and if that's a problem, you can stay, too."

"He's coming," Sashi said. "Aren't you, Winston."

He dropped the net of coconuts where he stood and boarded the small boat from the aft dive deck. Chugy sat in the dinghy's aft, one hand on the engine, waiting to start it. She watched Winston sit, a frown on her face.

Mahdi followed, sitting next to the big man and wincing at his scent. Talia climbed aboard next, then stood, waiting for Rowan. He had the black case over his back, a sidearm holstered under his left arm, and he carried what looked like a clear, police riot shield. He climbed into the boat, ignoring the raised eyebrows from the others. Rowan sat and caught the boat line tossed to him by Sashi, who was remaining behind with Emmei.

Chugy piloted them away from the *Sea Tiger* and toward the shore, keeping them centered in the narrowing path of open water. Three hundred feet from shore, Talia signaled for the engine to be cut. The silence that followed was eerie until she picked up an oar and handed it to Mahdi. She gave a second to Winston, who complained. "Are you serious?"

"If you had never seen or heard a motor before, you might not understand that it is a man-made machine. This—" She slapped a hand against the wooden oar, "—they'll get."

"Don't we need them to hear us coming?" Rowan asked.

"They already know," Talia said. "They've been watching us since we first spotted the island."

It took fifteen minutes of inefficient rowing to get within fifty feet of the beach. If the Sentinelese didn't see the *Sea Tiger*, they certainly heard the wood-on-wood clunking from the oars striking the small boat's sides.

"Stop here," Talia said, standing at the front of the boat like the American paintings of George Washington crossing a river.

"Do you see something?" Mahdi asked.

"Shhh." Talia crouched, eyes squinted. Something about her body language became feral. "They're here."

Winston groaned. "I don't—"

A fluttering noise, like a fast approaching bird, filled the air. Mahdi saw a blur of motion before he was knocked back out of his seat. When he looked up, he saw Winston's loose neck skin quivering with fear, his eyes wide. In front of him stood Rowan, riot shield in hand, a long white scratch in its surface.

Talia lunged to the boat's port beam, nearly flinging herself in the water. When she came back up, she clutched a three foot long arrow in her hand. It was straight, featherless and tipped with a scooped triangle of iron. Talia glared at Winston. "You don't *what?*"

Winston shook his head. "Nothing."

"Good," Talia said. "Now back us up another twenty-five feet, and we'll see if the next arrow reaches us."

8

TALIA MAYER THOUGHT it was fitting that their expedition had nearly begun the same way National Geographic's had ended. She had watched the lone arrow sail over her head on a course that would have plunged the tip into Winston's thigh. She was disappointed it hadn't found its target—the man was disruptive and unnecessary—but Rowan was better at his job than she would have guessed, and that shield of his was an ingenious idea. Winston would have survived, but she doubted he would have had the fortitude to join them again after having a hole punched in his leg.

"How should we handle this?" Rowan asked, calm as ever, but focused in a way she had yet to see.

"We wait," Talia said. Meetings like this couldn't be rushed. The arrow was a blatant warning. It said, 'stay back or die.' She had no intention of staying back, but wouldn't push until the message changed.

"We should go the hell back," Winston said. His hands shook on his knees, which were bouncing up and down.

"You've never been shot at before?" Talia asked.

Winston looked like she'd just asked him if he was a tentacle-armed ape wearing MC Hammer pants singing, 'U Can't Touch This.' "What kind of question is that?"

"I'd say it was a prerequisite when choosing people to visit a tribe known for shooting arrows into people." Talia looked forward again, watching the island and the shadows beneath the tall trees lining the beach. "I'm pretty sure it's the only thing the rest of us have in common."

Winston scoffed. "How many of you have been shot at?" He looked from one face to the next, seeing only serious expressions.

"Even better," Talia said. "How many of us have been shot?"

She turned her leg over, revealing a straight scar. "It was just a graze, but the tip was poisoned. Took a month to recover." She slapped Rowan's knees. "Show him yours."

She had spotted the circular entry and exit wounds on the beach the previous day.

Rowan pulled his shirt collar down, revealing the scar in his trapezius. "Nine millimeter. If it had been a fifty cal, we wouldn't be talking right now."

"I have a scar," Chugy said from the back. She turned over and patted her butt. "Spear in my cheek. The Jarawa were not happy that my family left the tribe. They do not like us. Do you want to see it?"

"Please don't," Mahdi said, eyes closed and hand raised.

Chugy looked disappointed, but then gave Mahdi a playful shove. "Your turn then."

Mahdi frowned, but he didn't move.

"C'mon, now," Chugy said with another shove. "We're bonding."

Mahdi showed just a hint of a grin, but it slipped away when he began unbuttoning his shirt. He moved with slow, smooth motions, moving from one button to the next. Then he slipped the shirt off.

Talia looked him over, seeing nothing of interest, but Chugy gasped.

Mahdi turned around so the others could see. There were two long scars, knife wounds perhaps, and three round bullet scars. *No exit wounds,* Talia noted. He had to have had the bullets removed, and given the scars' placements, he was lucky to be alive.

"Five point five six millimeter," he said, turning back to look Talia in the eyes. "Fired by a Tavor TAR-21 assault rifle."

"Shit," Rowan said, understanding what that meant just as quickly as Talia did.

Like all Israeli women over the age of eighteen, she had spent two years in the Israeli Defense Force. It was how she escaped her past, and it had hardened her for the trials and tribulations that came from the life in the jungle that had followed her schooling in America. It also meant that she had trained with a TAR-21. Had shot it, and felt its deadly potential. She had never fired the weapon at a person, but she knew people who had. Perhaps even the person who had fired at Mahdi.

At his back, she thought. *He was running away.*

"I am sorry," she said.

He buttoned his shirt again. "It was not your fault."

It had been a long time since Talia had communicated with a Palestinian. For him to have been shot by an Israeli soldier, and not despise Israel and everyone born there, revealed an impressive strength of character that went beyond being an intellectual.

"Movement," Rowan said, voice hushed.

Heads ducked, but there were no arrows in the sky.

Not yet.

"Where?" Talia asked. Her eyes were keen and accustomed to spotting living things amidst a jungle's shadows. But she saw nothing other than towering trees, ground shrubs, and stationary shadows.

"Everywhere," he said. "Broaden your focus."

She had been peering at one individual location after another that looked like good hiding spots. She sat up and took in the island as a whole, letting her vision blur a little. Then she saw it. The shadows just inside the jungle moved as one, like a massive, living thing, but too slowly to notice when focused on a single spot. It almost looked like the dance of light caused by wind moving through trees, but the skies were calm and the trees still.

"I don't see anything," Winston said.

"Try looking through your camera," Talia grumbled. She had noticed that the man had yet to unzip his camera bag.

"I see them," Chugy whispered.

"Is this normal?" Rowan asked, looking back at Chugy. "Is this something the Jarawa do?"

With a slow shake of her head, Chugy said, "Nothing like this. The island looks alive."

Winston fumbled with his camera, hands shaking. He whispered curses to himself and searched for the power button. When he turned the camera on and looked through the viewfinder, he cursed again and removed the lens cap.

Talia shared a glance with Rowan, the message between them easy enough to understand: *Winston is not a filmmaker.*

Who he was and why he was really with them was a question for another time. Right now, they had visitors to attend to.

Mahdi pointed to the beach on the far right, where a sandy path curved up into the jungle. "There."

A lumpy black ball rolled toward the beach.

"Is that a rock?" Rowan asked.

"The Andaman Islands aren't volcanic, and the soil is deep. There aren't any rocks here that big, and they'd have no way to transport it." Talia lifted a pair of binoculars to her eyes. "It's not a rock. It's a man."

She handed the binoculars to Rowan, who looked toward the lone Sentinelese man, curled up in a ball, arms wrapped around his bent up legs. Every time his feet touched the path, he'd propel himself forward, rolling in a chaotic pattern, down toward the beach. He stopped upon reaching the deep sand, and began waddling, legs still bent, throwing arcs of sand over his head with each step.

Rowan lowered the binoculars and looked at Talia. "What. The Fuck?"

Though she could now clearly see the man on the beach, she took the binoculars back and continued watching. "Best guess, it's a kind of deimatic behavior.

"A what?" Winston asked.

"A threat display. Praying mantises raise their arms. Frilled lizards expand their hoods, making themselves look bigger. Cats raise their backs and hackles, and hiss."

"You are suggesting that these people behave…like animals?" Mahdi seemed uncomfortable with the idea.

"People *are* animals," Talia said. "A man in a bright yellow Lamborghini is no different than a male peacock flashing its bright feathers. He's saying, 'Look ladies, I'm successful and worth mating with.' Spend time in any bar, or a school, in any part of the world, and you'll see a dozen examples of threat displays. Some are subtle, but many are overt."

"I think the ol' stare down works the best," Rowan said with a grin. "Let the other guy try to imagine what you're thinking."

"But this…" Winston raised his camera toward the native scurrying across the beach, flinging sand all around. "This is…"

"Are you afraid?" Talia lowered the binoculars to look back at Winston. She was about ready to toss him overboard and let him swim back to the *Sea Tiger*. If it weren't for the tiger sharks that populated these waters, or the just-as-dangerous salt water crocodiles that occasionally killed a vacationing snorkeler, she might have actually done it.

"The fuck do you think?" Winston's finger pressed the zoom button, but the red light indicating that the camera was recording remained dark.

"Then it's effective." She turned back to the beach. The man had stopped his display and now sat in a squat, staring out at them. The man was unnerving in a way that Talia had never experienced before. While she had seen some strange things in the Amazon, she had never seen anything quite like this man. It was almost inhuman…which, she guessed, was the point. How many people would see such a thing and still decide to land on the island if given a choice?

Only the crazy, desperate, or very well paid. Aside from Winston, she believed most of the people in the dinghy were at least two of the three.

"Oh, gross," Winston said, looking through his camera. "Look what he's doing now."

The man had stood to his five foot height, lifting his penis and revealing his testicles. He gyrated his hips, thrusting himself at the boat.

Talia had read reports of this behavior, including even more lewd acts, performed on the beach in clear view of all watching. The Sentinelese were the masters of repulsing visitors, at first through their strange behavior, and then with violence, but often in tandem.

She stood in the prow of the boat, making herself a target, but also allowing herself to be seen.

"What are you doing?" Rowan asked, beginning to lift his shield.

"This is where everyone else has gone wrong," Talia said, and then she pointed to the man. "This isn't simply a warning, or a rude gesture. It's the beginning of a conversation." She looked back at Mahdi. "No offense, but your kind of linguistic skillset might not be much use, at least not until we're on the island."

"*On* the island?" Winston said. "No freaking way."

Talia noticed that he had yet to start recording, most likely because he didn't know where the record button was, and she wasn't about to tell him. She didn't need the rest of the world to see what happened next.

"How do we respond?" Rowan asked.

"The only way we can, which also happens to be the only way no one has ever tried." With that, Talia untied her bikini top and let it fall. Then she shimmied out of her shorts. While the rest of the crew either held their breath or gasped, she reenacted the man's gestures, sans the external genitalia.

9

"UMM." ROWAN STRUGGLED to find the right words to express his cocktail of confusion, surprise, and apprehension. He knew Talia was unconventional. Had already seen her naked, living among the Peruvian tribe. But the ease with which she made the decision to strip down and reveal herself to the Sentinelese, and everyone in the dinghy, struck him as unbalanced, especially given her opinions on Peeping Toms.

As Talia thrust her hips toward the lone Sentinelese man, who had stopped his own display to watch, the words Rowan was searching for finally came to him. "What are you doing?"

Talia slapped her hands on her chest and then thrust them out at the man like it was some kind of practiced dance, and maybe it was. Was this something she picked up from the Mashco-Piro? A kind of sign language that was common to all the Earth's ancient tribes?

He doubted it, but she *had* captured the man's undivided attention.

"We approach tribes like this in boats with loud motors, with modern weapons, wearing modern clothing, and giving gifts made from plastic and colored with bright primary colors, with made-in-China paint. Remote tribes have no frame of reference for these things."

She paused to thrust again and then said, "The result is that modern explorers are greeted in one of two ways."

"As gods," Mahdi said, his eyes diverted, a hand raised to help him resist temptation.

Moral traditions die hard, Rowan thought, *even if you're not a believer… or maybe Mahdi is just a better man than me.* Rowan was doing his best not to ogle, but Talia was a beautiful woman, her body toned from years of hard jungle living. As much as her strange behavior made him uncomfortable, the ease with which she employed her body intrigued him. A woman like her was probably wild in bed...when she wasn't talking to herself in strange languages.

Steer clear, he told himself. As exotic as Talia might be, he got the sense that she was also trouble. He looked up at her again. This was not the kind of woman you brought home to meet the parents, or even considered offering a ring to. She was...

"Devils," Chugy said. "Evil spirits. That is what my ancestors believed. Some of them still do. That is why my father and I are no longer welcome among them."

Talia ended her display with a final thrust and a slap of her hands on her hips. "The Sentinelese have seen giant ships wash up on their shores, and men wearing clothes created by technology we take for granted. They've seen helicopters descend from the sky, bending the jungle beneath them and pulling men to safety in the sky. These people's knowledge of the world is pre-neolithic. In the past sixty thousand years, life on the island hasn't changed. At all. But in the past forty years, they've encountered modern men who were either gods, or demons, and then had to make a choice between the two."

"I think their choice is pretty obvious," Rowan said, lifting his shield slightly as a second Sentinelese man stepped from the jungle, bow and arrow in hand.

"Our job...*my* job is to change that perception."

"How do you convince someone you're not a devil?" Rowan asked.

"Our skin and hair is different enough to cause concern, but strip away our modern covering and we at least look human." Talia remained standing in the bow, watching the two men on shore, making no move for her clothing.

"Fallibility," Mahdi said, eyes still diverted. "Gods and devils do not make human mistakes."

Rowan didn't like the sound of that. "If you're planning on taking an arrow to prove you're human, I'm not going to let that happen."

Talia gave a nod. "I'm unconventional, not suicidal. We're seventy-five feet out. The odds of them hitting me are—"

A fluttering sound was followed by a splash. Rowan turned fast enough to see the long arrow slide beneath the water, just two feet short of the dinghy.

"Good," Talia said. "But not great. In the past, people have responded to Sentinelese arrows in one of three ways: speeding away with a loud motor-powered boat, firing back with modern guns—" She tilted her head toward Rowan's black case. It contained an FN SCAR automatic rifle supplied by the expedition's government benefactors. "Or by calling in a helicopter to rescue them. All this teaches the Sentinelese is that their assessment is correct, and that they are powerful enough to defeat demons."

"So we need to respond…how?" Rowan asked.

"In kind," Chugy said, reaching for a long case running down the center of the boat. It was already in the boat when Rowan boarded and it was long enough to look like part of the hull. "They understand a human body, and they understand arrows."

Talia accepted the long case from Chugy, nodding her thanks to the woman who looked smitten by the attention. Inside the case was a long, unstrung, primitive bow. Lying beside it was a collection of arrows, not quite as long as the Sentinelese variety, and feathered at the back. These arrows would travel further with greater accuracy.

Rowan was beginning to understand Talia's methods. The bow and arrow were superior to the Sentinelese variety, but the technology used to create them was not beyond their limited body of knowledge. They might not have thought to steady their arrows with bird feathers, but they would recognize them. If Talia had brought a compound bow with metal shaft arrows and laser-cut hunting heads, it would have only reinforced the Sentinelese belief that the people visiting their island weren't people at all.

While Talia strung the bow, Rowan's eyes traveled down her body, noting not just her beauty, but a collection of thin scars greater in number than she had previously revealed, probably because most of them were on her butt. There was also a smudge of red on her leg. It looked like old blood, or…

"Hey," Talia said, looking down at him. "Try to stay on task."

Rowan reddened, but said nothing. Understanding who Talia was and predicting what she might do, was integral to his protecting her. Her naked body revealed more about her violent past than she had yet to verbally explain. Perhaps that was the real reason she didn't want him looking too closely.

When a Sentinelese arrow plunged into the water and struck the boat's hull, Rowan snapped his full attention away from Talia and lifted the shield. The way she stood in the prow would make shielding her difficult. He'd have to wrap it around her from behind, which could be awkward, or sit on the prow in front of her standing form, which could be even more awkward.

"We don't need that yet," Talia said, looping the bow string around the bent wood and letting it go taut. She took an arrow from the case, nocked it on the outside, drew it back and aimed toward the shore.

Rowan watched as the two Sentinelese men froze. The one with a bow, moments away from launching another arrow, lowered his aim.

"Are you seriously going to shoot one of them?" Winston asked.

"They've been shooting warning shots," Talia said. "I'm going to do the same. But better. The man with the bow; he's wearing a skull atop his head."

Winston shifted in his seat, camera raised and aimed at the man. "Geez, a skull? Are they cannibals?"

"That was the rumor Marco Polo spread," Chugy said, revealing that her knowledge of the Andamanese tribes extended far beyond local lore and tradition. "It kept the colonial English out for a long time. The human skulls and bones sometimes worn are those of ancestors, to absorb the dead's knowledge, wisdom, or social status."

Talia nodded. "Striking that symbol of power might get the message across."

Might, Rowan noted, imagining that it could also start a war…but if they failed, a war the Sentinelese could not win was in their future. It was a risk worth taking.

"Of course," Talia said. "If they hit one of us, then yes, I'll shoot one of them. Eye for an eye. That's how this works. It's an Old World rule of law that they should understand. But let's hope it doesn't come to that."

It won't, Rowan told himself, readying his shield and bracing for action. He'd tackle Talia into the sea if he had to.

"Have you ever had to shoot someone?" Mahdi asked, looking up, careful to keep his eyes on her head.

"Just once," Talia said, and she let the arrow fly.

The boat fell silent as the arrow arced up over the light blue water. Rowan raised the binoculars to his eyes and focused on the target just a moment before the projectile descended and shattered the skull atop the man's head.

Holy shit.

Of all the surprising things Rowan had experienced since stepping aboard the dinghy, Talia's skill with a homemade bow and arrow now topped the list. It was a marksman's shot, from an unsteady boat bobbing in gentle waves. He'd been hired to keep her safe, but now he doubted she needed protecting. She hadn't lived among forgotten tribes without being able to handle herself, and learning a few tricks.

The man with the bow lifted a hand to his head, feeling the remnants of the skull he'd been wearing. He then looked down at the shattered bits resting on the beach behind him. He shared a few words with the man who had rolled onto the beach. Then they turned away and walked back toward the protective jungle shade, casual, like not much had happened.

"That's it?" Winston lowered the non-recording camera.

"What more do you want?" Talia asked, stepping out of the prow and into her shorts. She dressed quickly, as though suddenly aware the crew could see her. "They sent a message. I replied. It's a dialogue."

"Then they're done talking?"

Talia tied her bikini top back in place. "For now. These things take time. Life out here doesn't move as fast as you're used to. We can wait. See if they come back. But I don't think we'll see them again for another day or two."

They waited for six hours, sharing a tube of sunscreen to avoid burning in the sun, and seeing no sign of the Sentinelese. Rowan kept his eyes on the tree line and his shield in hand all day long, but Talia was right, the Sentinelese were ghosts. Even the shadows had stopped moving.

But, Rowan thought, *that doesn't mean they're not watching.*

When the sun began its downward arc toward the horizon, they rowed a few hundred feet out and then let Chugy motor them the rest of the way. After a day in the sun, the *Sea Tiger* was a welcome sight, but even as they started the thirty-mile voyage to the Sandal-Foot Resort, Rowan couldn't shake the feeling of being watched.

10

*T*ODAY, MAHDI THOUGHT, *was a good day.*

He could never tell anyone that. His image was important to maintain. The very few people left in the world willing to help him would never understand. In fact, they would likely join the forces already seeking his life. Not just because he had joined a foolhardy expedition, or agreed to work with an American, an Indian, and a Jew, but because he had enjoyed it.

Every moment of it.

The sun and the sea. The unpredictable and intellectually stimulating company. The mysterious island and the people who populated it. Even, or perhaps especially, Talia's naked primitive display and the arrows being shot toward him. He had never witnessed anything like the day's events before. He felt seduced.

And conflicted. Though he didn't believe in any god, he felt the guilt of religious tradition and cultural bias. At the very least, he should distrust these people, if not loathe them and the countries they represented. But they had shown no such distrust toward him.

He knew that was, in part, because they didn't know his true past. But it still said a lot about who they were, and he owed them the same courtesy. Talia was still something of an enigma, either a genius anthropologist, or a woman who had lost part of her mind in the jungle. He had yet to decide, but she was kind and unpredictable in a way that made him anticipate the dawn.

First, he needed to sleep, which turned out to be difficult after the day they'd had. While the majority of the day had passed without further incident, the morning's encounter had awakened his mind. He'd spent so many years on the run, he hadn't had time to think about what had once been his passion. Could the Sentinelese be communicated with? Could he learn their language, or even just a few words of it? And if they really could save those people from government intervention, perhaps he could atone for past mistakes?

Mahdi sat in his bed. Compared to his shared apartment in London and his small home in Palestine, his villa at the resort was a mansion. The bed was plush and comfortable. The light felt easy on the eyes. The wood all around, and the way it smelled, made him feel connected to the world.

I'm not going back, he decided. No matter the outcome of this expedition, he was done with the modern world, its prejudices, and any hope that his old life and the few people in it who might welcome him back, could be regained. The only thing waiting for him was emotional and physical torment.

And them…

He looked at the room's phone. This was goodbye. Forever goodbye. He owed them an explanation, to remove all hope of his return. He could be mourned, as in death, but with the knowledge that he was someplace safe, without her, but alive. Then maybe she could move on. Find happiness again.

He picked up the phone, dialed nine numbers, hesitated, and then finished. The phone line clicked, rang twice, clicked again, rang three more times, and then she answered. It had been years since he had heard her voice. He felt both soothed and cast into a sandstorm.

"As-Salaam-Alaikem," she said. Then again, irritated. "As-Salaam-Alaikem."

"Wa-Alaikem-Salaam." The natural response slipped out. *I shouldn't have said anything*, he thought. *I'm putting her in danger.*

"Mahdi?" There was a squeak of hope in her voice that asked the unspoken questions: Is it over? Can you come home? Can you be my husband again?

He wished he could reply in the affirmative to all three questions, but there was only one reply he could give that would answer everything, let her know he wasn't coming home, and that might keep her from trouble. "Goodbye."

"Mahdi…"

He hung up the phone, eyes damp, and he still heard voices. He held his breath, not because he was afraid, but because he was hopeful. The pain of his previous life was now, and permanently, in the past. He could focus on the present once more, and it filled him with excitement. The tears dried and he wiped them away.

It was eleven o'clock, and they would be leaving early the next morning, but he didn't think he would sleep until he spoke to the others again. He needed to fully exorcise his excitement, which he had kept largely contained throughout the day, and all through their trip back and during the exquisite meal of local seafood prepared for them by the resort's master chef.

As the voices grew louder, Mahdi recognized them as the two people to whom he had no desire to speak: Winston Rhett and Rattan Ambani.

Winston's personality wasn't just abrasive; it was steeped in something filthy. Whether or not that had anything to do with their work, he had no idea, but of all the people he'd met thus far, he trusted the filmmaker the least. As for Mr. Ambani, his surface motivations appeared pure, but a man like that doesn't pursue anything that doesn't somehow benefit his own interests. Mahdi had known men like him, zealots of the self, disguised in cloaks of national, religious, or social interests.

Spurred by distrust, Mahdi decided to funnel his energy by spying on the two men. He turned out his villa's lights and slowly opened his window a crack. The two men were walking along the path between villas. Mahdi strained to hear what they were saying, but they were now whispering.

Though he couldn't hear the words, Winston's tone was unmistakable. He was irate. But what would the expedition's cameraman have to complain about to their resort host? While Mahdi might not like the man, he had provided them with excellent accommodations, food, and transport. *Perhaps Winston was provided a villa without air conditioning,* Mahdi wondered with a hint of a smile. The man was rather unkempt, yet he still managed to act like a prima donna. Whatever the cause, Mahdi's awakened thirst for adventure drew him to the door.

He watched the two men stroll past, their body language tense, Winston the far more animated of the two. What stood out most was their proximity to each other. These were not two men who had met just yesterday.

As Winston and Ambani walked around a bend in the path, heading toward the resort's conference center lobby, Mahdi slipped from his villa and carefully closed the door behind him. As he tip-toed in pursuit, his heart began to pound. He had been sneaky only once in his life before, and while that day had ended in tragedy, he couldn't help but smile now. Spying was fun.

He followed the pair to the resort's lobby, crouching behind a large leafed plant he couldn't identify. So much of this part of the world was new to him. The people, the landscape, the wildlife. Everything about it felt alive.

The two men paused by the lobby doors. Winston tried to open the door, but it was locked. He stepped aside while Ambani punched a numbered code into the key panel beside the door. While Winston's view of the keypad was blocked, purposefully, by Ambani, Mahdi could clearly see the old Indian man punch in four consecutive nines.

Ambani opened the door and stepped inside, leaving Winston to catch the door and follow.

They know each other well, Mahdi thought, *but they are not friends.*

When the two men had moved deeper inside the large building, Mahdi crept across the open courtyard separating the facility from the thicker jungle, where the villas had been built. He paused to look up at the night sky. Beauty surrounded him, made him reconsider what he was about to do. This life was good. Why risk aggravating their host?

Because I want to be free of myself.

Like Talia.

In that moment, he realized how he truly felt about Talia: inspired. She was free, more than he had ever imagined possible. He had no desire to strip naked and dance the way she had—certainly not in front of onlookers or a man with a camera—but he craved the freedom she represented. To go where he wanted, say what he thought, and to follow his instincts.

She would follow them.

He scurried to the door, checked over his shoulder for onlookers, and punched four nines into the keypad. The lock clicked. He pulled the door open, slipped inside, and eased the door closed behind him.

Inside, he could hear the men talking, no longer whispering. He crept closer to the conference room doors, which had been left open, listening to the conversation.

"This isn't that bad, still," Winston said.

Mahdi peeked around the door and saw Winston standing at a buffet table. Cut fruit from their dinner remained piled on a platter, the excess of luxury on full display.

Winston plucked a toothpick-speared pineapple chunk and put it in his mouth, mulling over the flavor as he chewed. "A little slimy, but still sweet."

"I did not hire you to assess the fruit plate, Mr. Rhett." Ambani stood still, hands clasped behind his back, a frown bent down in the same shape as his mustache.

"I told you, I'm doing my job."

"Not fast enough."

Winston picked up a plate and piled it with cut mango, papaya, sapota, jack fruit, pineapple, and banana. "I'm not the one you should be talking to. That bitch wouldn't let me take the coconuts, and I don't think she's going to. She thinks shaking her poontang around is going to smooth things over. Who knows, maybe if it works, if they welcome us onto the island, I can hand the coconuts over. But who knows how long that will take."

"They're not going to welcome anyone on the island," Ambani said. "They never have."

"Then you're shit out of luck, aren't you?"

Ambani took two long strides and swept a meaty arm through the air. Winston's plate of food burst upward, a colorful spiral of wet chunks. Winston watched the food fall, unfazed by the violence and the loss of his late night snack. "You are being paid well to do a job, and I expect you to do it."

Winston picked up another plate and began refilling it with fruit. "It will get done."

"How?"

"You said the Sentinelese are active at night, right? And Talia's going to figure that out. She's bat-shit, but she seems to know a lot. When she figures out that we need to spend a night anchored off the island, I'll bring the coconuts to the beach and dump them."

"They need to be found within twenty-four hours," Ambani said.

"I'll spray them before leaving them behind, but if the Sentinelese are as protective of their island as everyone seems to think, they'll find them first thing in the morning. Then we just need to wait for the island to go quiet."

Go quiet? Mahdi thought. He had no concrete idea about what these men were up to, but he knew it was not good—not for the expedition and certainly not for the Sentinelese, whom they'd been sent to help, not harm.

He took a slow step back, his mind already made up to tell the others what he'd heard.

"Of course," Winston said. "Everything would be a hell of a lot easier if I had some help."

"It is too much to ask of Sashi," Ambani said. "Even she has her limits."

"Sashi and her bleeding heart can stay on board the boat," Winston said.

"Then who?"

"I was thinking maybe the guy lurking just outside the door."

Mahdi's pulse hammered. *Is he talking about me?* It seemed unlikely as the man hadn't once glanced in his direction, but who else could he be talking about. Mahdi turned and ran, his bare feet quiet on the hallway rug. He reached the door and pushed. He nearly collided with the glass when the locked door didn't budge. He reached for the manual lock on the side of the door, but he was stopped by a hand on his shoulder.

He turned to find Winston, smiling at him, his gray eyes squinted through his thick glasses.

How had he caught up so fast? And without making a sound?

"Hi," Winston said. "Welcome to the team."

Mahdi felt a sharp pain in his arm, and then nothing at all.

He woke on time the next morning, his alarm chirping. He sat up in bed, confused, until he saw the manila folder resting on the room's small desk. Sitting beside the folder was a plate of fruit.

11

SOMETHING FELT OFF. Talia couldn't say what, but her instincts said to keep her head down, and they had yet to even reach the island. After the previous day's activity, she had slept well and woken with the sun, adjusted to the new time zone without a trace of jetlag. There was a time when such a dramatic shift in time might have left her with a migraine and seated beside a toilet for a day. Life in the jungle, unlike the day and night schedule followed by the agricultural modern world, was less rigid. She had learned to sleep when needed, and to stay awake for as long as a task—like hunting elusive prey—took to complete.

Seated at the *Sea Tiger's* luxury dining room table, crafted from a single slab of redwood, she observed the team. Rowan sat across from her, as far from the saloon as he could manage, eyes glued to a laptop that he occasionally chicken-pecked with his two index fingers. He occasionally glanced up, looking out the window at the rain falling in sheets and shaking his head.

No one was happy about working in the rain, on a boat, and most of them blamed her for the inconvenience. She had all but insisted that they return to North Sentinel Island, despite the inclement weather. It was important that the Sentinelese see them again, recognize the *Sea Tiger*, and grow accustomed to their presence.

It was bullshit. She enjoyed the rain. It cleansed the body and soul. Made her feel at peace.

Mahdi, the poor man, looked ill again. He clung to the saloon's bar, half-cheeking a stool. He looked ready to run to the head, as six foot swells heaved them up and down.

Winston sat beside him, beer clutched in his sausage fingers. He occasionally whispered to Mahdi, somehow making the man feel worse and then chuckling when Mahdi closed his eyes and lowered his head. Rowan had noticed as well, but when he caught Winston's eye to glare at him, the 'filmmaker' had raised his beer in a toast, forcing Rowan's gaze away.

She didn't know whether or not Rowan was truly an alcoholic, or just the kind of man who sometimes drowned his pain in alcohol. Either way, his stalwart resistance to imbibing was impressive, especially since they were surrounded by unique brews, pricey hard liquors, and fine wines while at the resort, and on the yacht. The only place truly free of temptation was the dinghy, which might be why Rowan had agreed to join her on a second trip to the island's fringe. That, or he was trying to sleep with her, though she didn't think so.

Chugy on the other hand... Her intentions broadcast every time they made eye contact. While the habits Talia had picked up in the jungle kept most men—and women—at arm's length, they only seemed to intrigue Chugy. It was cute, for now, but it could become a problem if Chugy decided to act on her desires. Not only was Chugy very young, she was also impressionable and vulnerable. Turning her down could lead to drama, and a distraction like that, in a place like this, could be deadly. So as Talia scanned the room, she avoided Chugy's eyes, watching her from the lounge that separated the dining room and the saloon, where she lay on a couch.

Sashi had been quiet all day. She seemed indifferent to whether or not they visited the island, and she had stayed in the wheelhouse with Emmei, who was his normal jovial self, despite the weather and the waves—and the dangers presented by both.

The engines reversed direction as they crested a wave. Everyone held on tight, fighting to not be sprawled on the floor. When the wave passed, the *Sea Tiger* was no longer moving. Talia swiveled around on the dining bench and looked out the rain-spattered window. North Sentinel Island was a mile off the port side.

"Ready?" Rowan asked, closing the laptop and stowing it in his olive drab satchel.

Talia smiled at Rowan. He wasn't genuinely enthusiastic, but she appreciated his willingness. Rowan could have easily usurped her desires. As the man in charge of safety, there were a dozen reasons he could have pulled the plug on visiting the island in the rain, but he didn't.

"I'm ready," Chugy said. The girl's sudden proximity made Talia flinch. Annoyance flared and she nearly chewed the girl out, but Rowan diffused the situation.

"Sorry, Chugy, but it's going to be just the two of us for now. Until the weather clears."

Chugy's disappointment morphed into a glower directed at Rowan. "Who will pilot the small boat?"

"I can handle it," Rowan said, staying calm, forcing a grin that almost looked natural. "The more people in the dinghy, the greater the risk of capsizing. In seas this rough, I can't risk more lives than necessary."

"Amen to that," Winston said, performing a mutilated sign of the cross. "Dominus imperium sancti and shit."

"Is it?" Chugy asked. "Necessary?"

"It's important that they see us again," Talia said.

"See *you,*" Chugy said to Talia.

Talia nodded. It wasn't necessarily true, but it certainly couldn't hurt, and it would let the Sentinelese know they weren't frightened by a little inclement weather. Establishing both their humanity, and their superiority—in a way that didn't frame them as gods or demons—could lead to a conversation not punctuated by arrows.

"Do you need me to come?" Mahdi asked, looking more nervous than sick.

"You're fine here," Winston said from the bar. "They won't be talking to anyone today."

Mahdi closed his eyes, sighed, and waited for Talia's reply.

"He's right," she said. "Sorry."

He gave a nod and said, "I'll be in my quarters if you need me," and then he took the stairs below deck.

As though synchronized, Sashi came down the stairs from the wheelhouse at the same time. "Anchor is dropped. We're a little further out than last time. Because of the waves. Emmei is worried about the reefs."

Rowan gave a nod and headed for the aft door.

"Are you sure about this?" Sashi asked. She sounded genuinely concerned. "The island will be here tomorrow. The storm might clear."

Talia had seen the weather reports. Most called for clear skies toward the late afternoon, but meteorology was as unreliable here as it was in most parts of the world. "We're in the tropics. The storm could be a monsoon by tomorrow. And if that happens…"

She let her words hang. They all knew what it meant. A monsoon could undo their expedition and put the Sentinelese at risk. They needed to do as much as they could, while they could, just in case the chance never returned. As she headed for the door, Talia couldn't help but feel pursued. Sashi's worry, Chugy's jealousy, Winston's abrasiveness, and Mahdi's discomfort followed her to the door, but it all stopped at the threshold, held back by the rain.

Rowan was already soaked through. He peeled his T-shirt off and joked, "Mind if I keep my shorts on? I mean, at least until I need to shake my junk at someone."

Talia laughed and stepped into the rain. Like Rowan, her instinct was to shed her clothing, but removing her bikini top and shorts with no anthropological reason would make the others uncomfortable—or interested.

"Hey, you two," Emmei called down from an open wheelhouse window. His booming voice cut through the hissing rain. "If you run into trouble, there is a flare gun in the first aid kit. We won't come to rescue you, but there are life preservers and we will know to watch the waters for your swimming return. If you are closer to shore, than the *Sea Tiger*...well, how you live or die is your choice. These seas, and the creatures that live in them, have killed as many people as the Sentinelese." He flashed a bright smile. "Happy hunting!"

Rowan raised two thumbs into the air, picked up his backpack and rifle case, and headed to the dive deck. As he began pulling the dinghy through the waves, Talia collected her gear and followed. Climbing into the boat was a challenge, and she nearly fell overboard when the dinghy dropped into a wave trough as she stepped in. Rowan's quick hands kept her upright, and saved her from looking like a fool.

Talia clung to the dinghy's bench and wrapped her legs under it. Rowan turned them toward the shore and gunned the engine. As they surged over waves, spending nearly as much time in the air as they did in the water, Talia heard a strange kind of bird call. When she looked for the source, she found Rowan, laughing, having the time of his life.

As they grew closer to the shore, Talia didn't bother telling Rowan to cut the engine. Rowing in these waves would be impossible. When they were within a hundred feet, she signaled for him to stop. The engine quieted, but didn't stop.

"Hold on!" Rowan shouted, and before she could tell him she already was, the dinghy made a hard turn to port. A wave caught them on the side, tipping the boat to a forty-degree angle. Talia leaned toward the wave, keeping them from going over. When it passed, she was about to unleash hell on Rowan when she noticed the boat was no longer rocking. She glanced over the side and saw the reef just three feet below. It was a risky move, but while six foot waves surged down the open channel, they broke against the coral a mile out, leaving the waters above the reef relatively calm. They glided over the shallows and into a deeper pool, where the water descended a good twenty feet.

Rowan killed the engine, dropped anchor and looked toward the island. Between sheets of rain and thrashing trees, there wasn't a whole lot to see. "So," he said, facing her again. "You want to tell me why we're really here?"

She didn't know how to answer. It was a simple question, but loaded with possible answers, all of them partly true.

"And I don't mean here," he said, motioning to the small boat. "I mean the island. The expedition."

She squinted at him, now not understanding the question at all. Their mission was clear: to make peaceful contact with the Sentinelese and bring them into the twenty-first century before they were exterminated for their crimes against idiots who should have known better.

"That's why you volunteered?" she asked. "To talk to me about why we're here?"

He stood from the engine and sat beside her so she didn't have to turn around, and they didn't have to shout over the rain. "I like Sashi well enough. In a way, she saved my life. But she's been distant since we came to the island. Uncomfortable around us, the way a commander is before sending men on a shit mission. We both know Winston isn't a filmmaker. I've been digging, but can't find anything about him online. That means we're either being lied to by Sashi, or he duped the Indian government. I thought Mahdi could be trusted, but he's withdrawn."

"I noticed," she said. He seemed sick on the boat, but wasn't his quiet, but confident self at breakfast. He seemed shaken.

"Emmei and Chugs are hired help. I doubt they know much, and I don't think they'd care, either. They're here for the money, nothing else." He smiled. "Well, almost nothing else."

She chuckled and ribbed him with her elbow. "And me?"

"Lady, you're certifiable, but I trust you."

She nodded. "What are you thinking?"

"That we're screwed."

Talia glanced up at Rowan, confused by his defeatism, but he wasn't looking at her. He was looking toward shore.

Not toward shore, she realized when she followed his gaze, *toward them.*

A long dugout canoe slipped through the water twenty feet away, a silent wraith, propelled by a lone Sentinelese man standing in the back, shoving a long pole against the reef. Four warriors sat in the front of the long canoe, armed with multi-pronged spears.

Rowan leaned toward his rifle case.

"Wait," Talia urged. "They're not hunting us."

One of the warriors thrust his spear into the ocean. When he lifted it from the water, a long arched fish was impaled on the end.

Talia and Rowan both looked over the side. The water below teamed with sea life.

"The storm is kicking up nutrients in the water," Talia said. "Drawing out the fish."

"Drawing out the Sentinelese," Rowan finished.

Talia opened her long case, revealing the bow and arrows she had brought. She chose an arrow with a long white line already attached, looping the loose end around her wrist.

"What are you doing?" Rowan asked.

"Relating," Talia said. "But doing it better."

"Shouldn't you, ahh, you know?" He pointed to her clothes.

He was right. It would be better if she was dressed, or not dressed, like one of them, but they had seen her—all of her—the day before. They knew she was human. "There isn't time."

As the five Sentinelese men moved past, spearing fish as they went, Talia stood, nocked an arrow, and aimed it at the sea. There were so many fish she didn't think it was possible to miss, but she didn't just need to catch a fish, she needed to do it better, and that meant bigger, or multiple fish in one shot. She was capable of both, but luck always played a part.

The Sentinelese men paused their own fishing efforts to watch. Talia followed a large, orange fish, waiting for it to cross paths with another. She loosed the arrow a moment before Rowan shouted, "Wait!"

But it was too late. The arrow punched through the ocean, and instead of striking the two orange fish, it slipped into the flank of a ten foot tiger shark, as it swam in front of her prey. The shark bolted. Talia watched in shock and then remembered she was tied to the line spiraling into the water. Rowan's wide eyes locked with hers, and then she was yanked off her feet and into the ocean, where predators now lurked, above and below.

12

ROWAN HAD BEEN trained to squelch things like shock and indecision. They were a good soldier's enemy. Most of the time. There were occasions when a little extra thought went a long way, especially when the mind was impaired. Alcohol and quick thinking were not good bedfellows.

But now, despite being as sober as an Amish funeral, Rowan went rigid with uncertainty.

Talia slipped away through the water like a torpedo, dragged by a tiger shark large enough to bite her in half. At the same time, there was a canoe full of Sentinelese warriors just twenty feet away, their spears now raised toward him. With his rifle still in the case, he wouldn't be able to retrieve it—and assemble it—without being impaled like a fish.

I should have brought my pistol, he thought, regretting that he'd left it locked up on the *Sea Tiger*. He hadn't wanted to get it wet, and never thought they would have a close encounter during a storm, a hundred feet from shore. But even with the pistol, he might only be able to shoot two of them before meeting the same fate as the fish they speared.

He looked down to the water, choppy, windswept, and rain-pelted. It was like looking through hammered glass. If not for Talia's hot pink bikini strap, he would have never seen her amidst the vibrant mix of fish and coral. She had to be ten feet down, twenty feet out, and still moving.

Why isn't she letting go? He wondered, and then he remembered how she'd wrapped the line around her arm. When the shark pulled, the line had tightened. She wouldn't be able to get free until the shark slowed down, and that wasn't likely to happen while there was an arrow embedded in its side…unless the wound was mortal, or the angered shark turned around to defend itself.

Even without the Sentinelese presence, there wouldn't be much he could do to help her. This wasn't a thriller novel. Jumping in with a knife clutched between his teeth would do little good since he couldn't outswim a shark.

Talia was on her own, and so was he.

The five Sentinelese men stared him down, unwavering, indifferent to the rain and Talia's disappearance. Rowan stepped to the side, distributing his weight more evenly, keeping the boat level. The men tracked him, but didn't move.

What are they doing?

The best he could come up with was they wanted to see how Talia's fate played out. If she could escape from, or maybe even kill, the shark, perhaps that would be their golden ticket to whatever screwed up chocolate factory the natives had hidden in the jungle.

During the thirty seconds it took for Talia to surface, the warriors didn't move. Then a loud gasp pulled their attention back to the water, thirty feet away, where Talia sucked in a breath before being pulled back under.

Well, he thought, *she's still alive, so that's something.*

And then the Sentinelese turned back to him, their eyes projecting more menace than their spear tips. Talia's appearance seemed to have shifted something. *But will they attack?*

A moment later, he had his answer: no. But when they started thrusting their genitals at him, he almost wished they would just kill him and be done with it. Seeing it from a distance was strange enough, but up close it was disturbing. When he'd first heard of the Sentinelese's more unusual tactics for repelling newcomers, he'd gotten a good laugh over it. But now, seeing it for himself, he wanted nothing more than to leave. But he couldn't leave Talia, not while she was still fighting for her life, and not without recovering her body if she didn't make it.

C'mon Talia, he thought. *Fight.*

Rowan winced at the sound of fwapping nut sacks. Then the thrusting turned to hopping, all five men perfectly balanced in the canoe. They waved their arms, snarled, hissed, slapped their hands, and then stopped. It was practiced. A routine of intimidation.

They stared at him again.

They're waiting, he thought, *but for what?*

What would Talia do?

Rowan knew the answer, but he didn't like it. Not at all. But he also thought he understood Talia's methods for the first time.

He glanced down at his shorts, then out toward the *Sea Tiger*. He could barely see the ship through the rain. Aside from the five men in the canoe, and Talia fighting for her life beneath the waves, he was unobserved.

Damnit, he thought, and he undid his belt. He dropped his shorts, and feeling very naked, considered his options. He thought about trying to repeat their routine, but didn't think that would be enough. Talia would mimic their behavior, but improve it. But how do you improve on genital thrusting?

Then it came to him. The Sentinelese had developed an advanced form of psychological warfare, able to repel visitors without wasting arrows. But when it came to intimidation through physical routine, nothing beat the ancient Māori war dance known in New Zealand as the 'haka.' A month-long training with New Zealand's Special Operations Forces had led to friendships and a competition where the NZSOF Kiwis showed off against the US Army Rangers, both sides performing the haka. While the Rangers were better on the real battlefield, no one could perform the haka like an honest to goodness New Zealander—man or woman. But Rowan had learned the routine, and though he didn't remember all of it now, he threw himself into the act with gusto.

With every slap of his chest, hiss, stomp, and tongue extension, he lost himself a little more to the dance. He didn't understand the words, but didn't think it mattered, the combination of gestures and shouts was easy enough to understand: *I will fuck you up*.

When the haka was finished, he unleashed a long hiss, tongue extended.

Then the civilized Rowan returned and he met the Sentinelese warriors' gaze, one at time. They appeared unmoved and unshaken, but then the man with the pole raised his hand and pointed out to sea. "Lazoaf." He shoved the pole against the coral below, and the canoe slid through the water headed back to shore.

Rowan watched them leave and then flinched when the water beside the boat erupted. Talia rose from the sea, her gasp for air sounding more like an ancient beast. Her arms clutched the side of the dinghy, her sudden weight throwing Rowan off balance. He caught himself on the side and then grasped Talia's arm, lifting her from the water and depositing her back on her seat.

Water-thinned blood coursed down her arm.

Rowan crouched, inspecting the arm. "Are you okay?"

Talia took a few more deep breaths and then looked at her arm. "It looks worse than it is."

"Were you bitten?"

"If I'd been bitten, it would be worse than it looks." She wiped her hand over the wound. "This was from coral. It's how I cut the line."

She looked around, indifferent to the still-bleeding wound. Stopped when she saw the Sentinelese men headed back to shore. "They *left?* What happened?"

Talia had been pulled into the sea by a tiger shark and nearly drowned, but not ten seconds after being pulled to safety, she was back on task. The woman was a force of nature.

"I, ahh, I did the haka."

Talia's eyes went wide. As an anthropologist with an interest in the world's tribal traditions, she would know the haka's origins. Knowing Talia, she probably had the chant memorized. "That…isn't a bad idea. What made you think of it?"

"They were doing their thing," he said, "You know…" He wiggled his index and ring fingers. "With their dangly bits."

"So you responded—"

"How I thought you might," he said. "It was the best I could come up with."

"And that's why you're…" She pointed a finger at his midsection. He looked down and was immediately consumed by embarrassment.

Rowan reached for his saturated shorts, but Talia caught his wrist. "Not yet." She turned back to shore where the five men had disembarked and were now dragging the craft into the trees. "What happened when you finished the haka?"

"They left," he said.

"They just left? Nothing else?"

"The man at the back, with the pole, he pointed out to sea and spoke a single word." Rowan shrugged. "Then they left."

"What did he say?"

"Lazlow…Laslome…Lazoaf. Something like that. Can I get dressed now?"

She hadn't let go of his arm. Looked back at the island. He couldn't see anyone now, but apparently, she did. "They're still watching. We can still send them a message."

"Another haka?" Rowan said.

"Something like that," she said, standing up.

Rowan looked to the shore, searching for any signs of the Sentinelese. When he turned back to Talia, her bikini top laid on the bench and she was sliding out of her shorts. "What...ahh..."

Talia stepped back and sat on the dinghy's prow, naked as Rowan. She lifted one leg onto the rail, her invitation unmistakable, to Rowan, or anyone watching from the island. "There are several reports of public sex acts between Sentinelese men and women, performed in front of visitors, on the beach. Those who were not deterred by the chanting or gesturing, lost their nerve upon witnessing the public sex. If we perform the act before they do, they'll know we're speaking their language, so to speak."

"And if I don't want to?" he asked, feeling hotter despite the whipping rains.

She shrugged. "Maybe nothing. But if you impressed them with the haka, maybe they'll think you're less of a man. Who knows. But...you want to." She pointed as his midsection again, and this time when he looked down, he saw indisputable evidence of his desire.

"So this is just part of the job then?" he asked.

She smiled, almost fiendishly. "Let's call it a perk."

He looked to the jungle. Saw nothing. Turned to the *Sea Tiger*, lost in a haze of rain. Then there was Talia, beautiful, naked, and willing, covered in rivulets of water, blood running down her arm, wild and exotic. He took a deep breath and caught a whiff of something fragrant, like flowery incense. A kind of primal energy came over him, perhaps from performing the haka, or simply from being naked in Talia's presence. He didn't know which, but as it increased, he no longer cared. He stepped across the small boat, leaned into Talia and let her envelop him.

13

MAHDI SNAPPED AWAKE. Confusion assaulted his tired mind. Visions of a fading dream danced in his memory, primal and chanting. And then, it was gone.

Where am I?

He sat up in bed, looking for the exit, and when he found it, he squinted at the frame's small size. Then he felt the world sway around him. His memory returned.

I'm in India...the Sea of Bengal...on a yacht.

He took a deep breath and let it out.

I'm hidden. I'm safe.

The yacht swayed again, and Mahdi's body compensated for the motion without a hint of nausea. Emmei had told him he would eventually get his sea legs. It was hard to believe while clutching a toilet in a cramped bathroom, which he learned was called 'the head' on a boat, but it seemed the captain had been right.

He headed for the door, feeling resilient for the first time since leaving the resort. And then the rest of his memory returned. The manila folder. The photos inside. The contact information. Winston knew everything about him, including how to reach the people who wanted him dead. One phone call, and the chase would begin anew, but this time, in India, Mahdi would have little resources and no friends to call on. If he didn't follow Winston's lead, wherever that might take him, his life was forfeit.

He felt ill again as he headed up the stairs. His past would haunt him forever. The questionable alliances of youth were hooked into the meat of his back, dragged along wherever he went, even to this remote island. He knew he couldn't escape them. Only death could free him. But he had hoped for a respite, a temporary freedom from fear. He'd felt the weight lift for a single day, despite the discomfort of being at sea. But that tenuous ceasefire of nerves had been ended by Winston and Ambani, whose motives he had yet to discern. All he really knew was that he had not been sought out because he was a skilled linguist. He was here because he was desperate, and easy to manipulate. To control. They were the very personality traits that had plummeted his life into chaos.

Hand on the rail, he paused to collect his thoughts, determining to walk the gray tightrope between right and wrong. He would do as Winston asked, so long as it did not pose a threat to the people on this boat. And if the crew was endangered...he would have to revisit his determination. If he didn't, and his friends-turned-enemies came for him in this place, his fate would be sealed.

The idea of it, of being killed after all this time, gave him a kind of peace, until he considered the beliefs he'd once clung to. Death might not free him from the tortures of life. It might just prolong them, indefinitely.

Infinitely.

He shook his head and continued up the narrow staircase. Now was not the time for a theological debate.

Halfway up the stairs, the sound of a small outboard motor reached his ears. He stepped into the saloon and found it empty. The lounge and dining room were also empty. He squinted at the late day sun beaming through the windows.

The storm had passed. The sun returned. Talia and Rowan were returning. Though he didn't understand their true purpose here, and now he knew he'd be doing no real work while on this expedition, he couldn't deny his curiosity had been piqued. The Sentinelese were an intriguing people, free from the emotional sludge of modern life. He envied them. Their freedom. Their lack of inhibition. While the rest of humanity had grown barriers between each other, the Sentinelese still lived as the very first humans had, without shame or religious restrictions.

Perhaps, if I could talk to them, they would allow me to stay?

He smiled at the thought as he walked through the dining room, headed for the aft deck. If there was one place on Earth the men desperate to take his life couldn't reach him, it was in the jungles of North Sentinel Island.

He patted his chest pocket, felt his sunglasses, and plucked them out. He put them on, happy to have his eyes, and the guilt he was sure they projected, hidden from the others. He stepped into the open-air aft deck and recoiled from the humidity left in the storm's wake. Then he saw Sashi, Chugy, and Winston, and he knew he had missed something while sleeping.

Winston looked bemused, Sashi uncomfortable, and Chugy was fuming. Emmei's voice fluttered down from the wheelhouse. The windows were closed, the captain happy in his air conditioning, but his boisterous laugh was still easy to hear. Chugy glared up at her uncle, and then, arms crossed, turned back to the arriving small boat.

Talia, standing in the prow of the dinghy, tossed the tow line onto the deck, and Chugy didn't make a move for it. Sashi and Winston looked confused by both the flaccid, dead snake of a line and Chugy's unwillingness to do her job. Though Mahdi had only seen the boat tied off once before, he bent down to pick up the line and climbed down onto the dive deck.

The small engine idled and then sputtered to a stop. Mahdi pulled the boat in close while Talia reached out to grab the deck and drag them alongside.

"Someone die while we were gone?" Talia asked.

"I was going to ask you the same," Mahdi said. "I just woke up."

Talia smiled and shook her head. "We've been gone six hours."

While the *Sea Tiger* crew seemed off, Talia seemed in a good enough mood. Rowan was smiling, too.

"I was tired," Mahdi said, and then he glanced back at the others. "Perhaps something happened during the storm? Something to the ship? But that doesn't explain—"

Emmei's muffled laughter reverberated from the wheelhouse.

"—that." Mahdi said.

Talia looked up at the others, whose expressions hadn't changed. When she made eye contact with Chugy, the young woman looked away, and Mahdi understood. Chugy had been scorned by Talia.

"Shit," Talia said, voice hushed, and then she turned to Rowan. "They saw."

Rowan's smile melted.

Mahdi's eyebrows rose slowly and out of sync. "Saw?"

"We had a breakthrough," Talia said. "With the Sentinelese. A conversation of sorts."

"They spoke to you?"

"Body language mostly," Talia said.

"And they spoke a single word," Rowan said. "Lasloaf or something. Hard to recall, though I'm pretty sure it meant 'get the frik out.'"

"Fascinating," Mahdi said. Without hearing more of the language, any attempt at translation or general understanding would be impossible. They could have just as easily been saying, 'How about this storm?' The Sentinelese language developed without outside influence for sixty thousand years. A question might not sound like a question. A single word could be loaded with context. And that could change with subtle inflections or even the volume at which it was spoken. "But I fail to see how this progress affected—"

"The conversation ended with a ritual of sorts," Talia said.

Mahdi nodded. The Sentinelese were known for their strange behavior, which to the outside world appeared rude and degenerate. "I understand…but I don't understand."

Rowan lifted his rifle case onto the dive deck. "We had sex."

"You had *what?*" Mahdi's fingers went slack on the line.

Talia grunted, holding the sideways boat to the deck on her own. "Little help."

Mahdi held on to the boat while Rowan moved more gear to the deck. "Sex. On the boat. Where the locals could see us. And apparently, everyone else."

"There is a history of the Sentinelese performing sex acts on the beach, in front of visitors. I wanted to beat them to it. Let them know we were trying to speak the same language."

Mahdi couldn't believe what he was hearing. Talia was unorthodox and brazen. And now she'd roped Rowan into her lurid anthropological mindset. "For all you know, the act of public sex is a declaration of war."

"As long as they understand it," Talia said, climbing out of the boat. "That's a start."

"Of a war," Mahdi countered.

"Sex in every culture, from civilized to primitive, is either an act of dominance or of love. We could have just as easily said, 'we come in peace.'"

"Or," Rowan said, "'We like to hump, too.'"

Mahdi laughed despite his discomfort with the subject matter.

"But the conversation at this point, is the important part. These people are under threat from the Indian government. We need to do whatever we can to initiate contact, no matter how uncomfortable it might be."

"I didn't think it was uncomfortable," Rowan said.

"You weren't sitting on the prow," Talia joked and took the line from Mahdi, whose face felt hot. She tied the boat off and let it drift away. "I'll brief the others, and if I need to, I'll talk to Chugy. Explain why it happened. Might help."

Talia picked up her gear and climbed aboard.

Rowan clapped Mahdi on the shoulder. "Don't worry, Mahdi, you're not alone. This is the strangest thing I've ever done, too."

Mahdi looked back out at the island. The day was clear. The distant beach empty. A shadow moved beneath the *Sea Tiger* and Mahdi remembered where he was. He climbed back aboard, and spent the next few hours watching unfolding dramas fit for American TV. Sashi was confounded by their behavior. Chugy was defiant and unwilling to listen, as though she'd had a relationship with Talia. Emmei didn't help matters by laughing at everything, including his niece's raw anger. When he could stand no more, Mahdi headed for the silence of the back deck. Sweltering was preferable to melodrama.

As the sun began to set, Winston joined Mahdi on the back deck. He lit a cigarette in silence, power-smoked it, and then flicked the butt into the sea. "Let's go." He tapped Mahdi's arm and nodded his head toward the door. "I want you to back me up, even if the others disagree."

"What are you going to propose?"

Winston glanced back. "Nothing you're going to like."

Goosebumps rose on Mahdi's arms as he followed Winston back into the cool dining room. Sashi, Rowan, Talia, and Emmei were seated at the table, snacking. Chugy was nowhere to be seen.

"I would like to get some night shots of the island," Winston blurted out. "I think we should spend the night."

"You'd have to know how to work that camera to get night shots," Rowan said.

Winston chuckled. "You think because the red light isn't on that I'm not recording? We both know that people are less inhibited when they think the camera is off." He smiled at Talia, who returned his gaze with poison darts from her eyes. "What do you think, Mahdi?"

"I, uh…"

Talia stepped forward, arms crossed. "Well, as much as I loathe to agree with a pig, you know, because I'm Jewish and all, I think staying overnight is a good idea. Given the minimal activity we've observed during the day, it's possible they're living a more nocturnal lifestyle. Unlike people in other parts of the world, there are no nighttime predators to worry about on the island."

"I agree," Mahdi managed to say.

"Great," Talia said, standing from the table. "I'm going to sleep. Wake me at midnight, or earlier if any activity is spotted."

Rowan stood next. "I'm going to do the same...in a separate bed... just so we're clear."

"They don't care," Talia said, disappearing below decks. Rowan followed a little sheepishly.

Mahdi wasn't sure about that. Chugy had made it clear that *she* cared. And while Mahdi believed Rowan, that they were going to sleep before a long night, he hoped the day's drama had come to an end. When Rowan closed the door behind him, he knew that it hadn't.

"Well, that's convenient," Winston said, and then to Emmei, "You brought the coconuts?"

"They are stowed with the life preservers," Emmei said.

"And the spray?" Winston asked.

Sashi opened a bag that lay on the floor by her feet. She pulled out a spray bottle that appeared to be some kind of Indian disinfectant.

"You are all...?" Mahdi was aghast that Winston had somehow convinced Sashi and Emmei to help him as well. But it wasn't Winston pulling the strings. Not really. It was Mr. Ambani, the resort tycoon. "What is in the bottle?"

"Take it." Sashi slid the bottle across the table. "Just do what you are told, like the rest of us, and everything will be fine."

Mahdi read between Sashi's words. She was telling him to comply, but also revealing that like him, she was being coerced, as was Emmei.

Winston headed for the door. "Mahdi, bring the spray. Emmei, fetch the coconuts. We'll go as soon as it's dark."

Mahdi chased after him and then remembered the spray. He ran back, plucked it from the table, and followed Winston back onto the aft deck. "Where are we going?"

"Perfect night for a beach visit, don't you think?" Winston stood on the dive deck, pulling in the dinghy. "Don't worry, I'll row."

14

"I HAVE EYES on the party," Corporal Rowan Baer said, peering through a pair of PVS-15 night vision goggles, allowing him to view the nighttime scene in hues of green. "One klick south of my position. Looks like a warehouse. Lots of movement. Over."

"Copy that, Starsky" came the crackling voice. "The Chief says there are friendly operators in the area. Please confirm party guests."

What I just did, Rowan thought.

His partner, Army Specialist Kyle Mohr, was shaking his head. "Next they'll have us taking classes so we can learn the difference between a clip and a magazine."

Rowan gave his M107 Barrett .50 caliber sniper rifle a pat. "Everyone knows we use clips."

Rowan toggled his throat mic. "Copy that. Confirming." He turned to a tap on his arm, took the brushed metal flask, and drank his fill of liquid courage. He had performed this task before, this dirty business of condemning men, women, and sometimes children, to death. He was good at his job, not only because he could infiltrate enemy lines, survive in the wild for weeks on end, and make it back out without anyone being the wiser, but because when it came time to pull the trigger, or in this case, aim a laser, he didn't hesitate.

That didn't make it easy. He wasn't a sociopath. He knew his actions got innocent people killed. Collateral damage was part of what it took to dismantle groups like the Taliban and ISIS, so he accepted the weight of it on his soul. The alcohol lightened the burden, for him and for Mohr.

After one last swig, he looked through the scrub brush concealing the sniper team. The magnified warehouse buzzed with green-hued activity. Men carried cases from the open doors to the back of black vans. It sure as hell looked suspicious. If those cases contained RPGs, AK-47s, or IED-making materials, they could do a hell of a lot of damage.

"Well," Mohr said, peering through the scope of his sniper rifle, "they're wearing towels on their heads."

They weren't all wearing Keffiyehs around their heads, but many of them were. It was hardly scientific evidence, but they'd made calls like this with less evidence. It wasn't like they could walk in, ask if the men were with ISIS and if they'd mind holding still while the Predator drone circling above launched a half dozen Hellfires down their throats.

"Works for me." Rowan toggled his mic. "Hutch, this is Starsky. Party is hopping. Say again, party is hopping. Permission to blow out the candles? Over."

"Copy that, Starsky. Permission granted. Over."

Rowan switched on the laser designator attached to his sniper rifle and looked down the scope, the bright green dot as clear to him as the North star above, but invisible to the men sneaking about in the dark. He moved the laser point to the center of the action, held it still, and called it in. "Candles are lit."

Rowan kept the laser on target and lifted the night vision goggles away from his eyes. In a moment, the view would be transformed into a fireball bright enough to blind anyone watching the scene with light-amplifying eyewear.

"What is that?" Mohr asked.

Rowan glanced at his partner, still wearing his night vision goggles. "Place is about to be lit. Lose the—"

"Shit," Mohr said. "I'm seeing ACHes with the towels now."

The ACH, or Advanced Combat Helmet, was a staple of the U.S. military, its distinct shape impossible to mix up with other helmets. Unless the men they were lasing were dealing in stolen U.S. military equipment, which was doubtful, they were looking at another ops group, likely jarheads.

Rowan toggled his mic. "Abort, abort, abort! Friendlies are in the kill zone!" He jerked his rifle to the side, shifting the laser sight guiding the incoming missiles.

The explosions rained down, fifty feet off target, but still close enough to kill. Shrapnel shredded some. Others were melted by the heat. Everyone else was shattered by the four shockwaves that wrenched joints apart, burst lungs, and stopped hearts.

Four seismic booms rolled past, dust swirling around, hot and chemical.

And then the screams began. Distant, from the few survivors. Beside him, Mohr, goggles still lowered, was blind. And in his ears, Hutch wanted answers.

"Hey."

Rowan sat up so fast, he nearly rolled out of bed. Sweat rolled down his forehead.

Talia took a step back, hands raised. "Whoa."

Rowan's breathing slowed as he remembered he was on board the *Sea Tiger*. He looked down. Saw his clenched fists, fight or flight reflexes ready for the first option. He forced his fingers to unravel, and felt his back loosen in tandem. "Sorry."

"Bad dream?"

"I wish," he said. "Hard to tell when it's a memory."

"I get it." She sat on the bed beside him. "Have some of those myself."

"Are you the villain in yours?"

He regretted saying it when he saw her frown. But then she put her hand on his back. Gentle. Caring. Honest. This was a side of Talia he had yet to see. All the fire extinguished. "We've all done bad things."

"I killed ten men."

The slow, smooth motion of her hand over his T-shirt came to a stop. "When you were a Ranger?"

He nodded.

"You must have known you would be asked to kill when you joined the Army."

"I don't lose sleep over enemy combatants." Rowan tried to purge the memory of that night from his thoughts, but failed. "I made a mistake. Ten Marines lost their lives because of it. And what did I get? A dishonorable discharge." He looked her in the eyes. "There was still alcohol in my blood when I returned to FOB. They *knew* me. Could have tested me. *Should* have. But didn't. Heads would have rolled. They chalked it up to human error, which is bad enough in the Rangers, and they sent me home."

Talia's hand began making slow circles again. "You don't believe yourself worthy of redemption? You could honor the loss of their lives by making something of yours."

"Doing this?" He motioned to the yacht around them.

"There are between one hundred and five hundred people living on North Sentinel Island. Right now, they are at risk of extermination. The Indian military might not land on the island with orders to shoot on sight, but I think we both know what will happen when arrows start flying."

"They'll respond with bullets," Rowan said.

"And any captured survivors will either die from disease within weeks or be 'integrated' into the modern world. Those few who make it, will likely commit suicide or take up a life of crime. The children who survive, and they're the only ones who really stand a chance, will be raised in orphanages and move through life alone, likely to suffer from depression and poverty. There is no happy ending for these people without us. The Sentinelese are going to be ripped out of paradise and subjected to a 'humane' genocide unless *we* help them. If we can break through and communicate, come to an understanding and broker a peace, they might even be allowed to remain on the island, like the Jarawa on Andaman."

"I was going to kill myself." The words came out before Rowan could filter them. His blunt confession stalled Talia's comforting rub once more.

She had no trouble switching gears back to his narrative. "Why didn't you?"

Rowan looked toward the ceiling. "Sashi. She found me on the edge of a cliff, bottle in hand. She gave me hope that there might be something more. That life might still have worth. I didn't really understand what that hope was, until now."

Talia leaned back, finger waggling back and forth from herself to Rowan, a frantic metronome. "You don't mean…us? Because I don't do relationships. Out there, on the dinghy, that was good, but—"

Rowan chuckled. "Not us."

Talia relaxed.

"What you said, about saving the Sentinelese, about redemption. I don't think I'll ever forgive myself for what I did, but…"

Thunk.

They froze at the sound of something solid bumping against the hull. Rowan slid across the tight quarters and peered through the small portal.

"What time is it?" Rowan asked.

"Eleven," Talia said.

In the moon's pale light he saw the dinghy slide past, a nervous Mahdi clumsily working the oars, Winston in the prow tossing a line to someone above as they moved toward the *Sea Tiger's* stern.

"What is it?" Talia whispered.

Rowan was about to answer when he saw netting resting on the small boat's aft bench, netting that had once held coconuts and now laid empty. Then the dinghy passed and Rowan's gaze shifted to the island. His eyes widened, and then compressed under the force of his furrowed brow. He leaped back from the window, retrieved his .45 caliber P320 Compact handgun from his backpack and stormed through the ship.

"What is it?" Talia asked, trying to keep up. "What did you see?"

Rowan didn't answer as he ran through the dining room and powered through the aft deck door. He stepped into the humid night air, catching Mahdi, Winston, and Emmei off guard. Fueled by his recent commitment to saving the Sentinelese, he raised the pistol toward Winston. "What did you do?"

He stalked toward the dive deck, aim unwavering, Winston's head framed by one of many bright orange fires raging on the island. "*What* did you do?"

Talia stumbled to a stop behind him. "Oh my god."

Rowan chambered a round and aimed again.

"Rowan," Talia said, but his name and her voice were lost in the fog of his rage.

"You have three seconds," Rowan said, aiming lower, toward Winston's leg. "Then you get a permanent limp." It was extreme, but Rowan wouldn't let Winston get away with whatever he'd done, not while the island burned.

15

TALIA SAW THE same thing as Rowan: Winston's indignant gaze, Mahdi's billboard guilt, and the island, glowing with the orange light of several flickering blazes, just behind the tree line. Her anger flared, and nearly vented as a string of curses, but then she saw what Rowan had missed. The flames were contained. Evenly spaced. The jungle, which had been rained on all day, was not burning.

"Rowan." Talia grabbed his arm as he stopped moving toward the two men now on the dive deck.

He shrugged from her grasp. Stabbed a finger toward the island. "You want this to go unanswered for?"

"It wasn't them," she said, voice lowered. The last thing she wanted to do was chide Rowan in front of the others. He had accepted her odd sort of anthropology like no one she'd met before. Even more surprising, he had taken part, improvising in a way that might have opened the doors to communication. He had his flaws, and like her, his demons, but in a very short amount of time, he had also become her friend. And since she didn't have many friends who wore more than a loin cloth, that was the most surprising thing of all.

He stopped and waited for an explanation.

"The fires are evenly spaced. The jungle is saturated. They could have set a fire with gasoline, but it would have gone out when the fuel was burned up."

"Then…"

She nodded. "The Sentinelese set those fires."

"Is it a message?" he asked, and he tucked the gun into the back of his shorts.

"Could be." She looked out at the seven bright spots. The orange light gave the jungle a hellish glow. It would be impossible to spot people amidst the dancing shadows, but they were there, doing God knew what, perhaps waiting for guests, or setting a trap. They had to know the *Sea Tiger* hadn't left, but were the fires for them, or part of a nightly ritual?

"How do we answer it?" he asked, his mind on the mission, once again revealing why they were becoming fast friends…with benefits.

"Short of setting the ship on fire, I'm not sure we can." She turned to Mahdi, who had boarded the *Sea Tiger* again, nervous and watching the fires burn. "When did they start?"

"On our way back," he said, and he clenched his eyes shut. Mahdi was conflicted, fighting his honest nature. "Five minutes ago."

"What were you doing?" she asked him.

"Fishing," Winston said.

Rowan leaned close to her and whispered. "The net."

She saw it immediately, bundled up in Winston's hand, the thin green lines unmistakable. She'd seen the netting before, holding fresh coconuts that she had specifically told him not to bring to the island. Winston handed the net to Emmei, who headed inside with a quick, "Excuse me."

Talia couldn't figure out the dynamic. Mahdi wasn't acting like himself, which told her he was recently recruited, and somehow against his will. Emmei seemed subservient to Winston, doing his bidding despite being the ship's captain. And then there was awkward, incompetent Winston, who normally came off as a little conniving, but now had a predator's glimmer in his eyes. The only thing she felt certain of was that the truth would not be uncovered through confrontation.

"I asked you not to give them the coconuts," she said, doing her best to sound mildly irritated instead of ready to castrate someone.

Winston gave a 'who gives a shit' shrug. "We were spreading good will."

"Is that what you were doing, Mahdi?" Rowan asked. "Spreading good will?"

"Seemed like a better idea than spreading our legs for all the world to—" Winston began.

Rowan stalked toward the man, fist clenched and pulled back.

"Rowan!" Talia stood between the men. As much as she would like to see the former Ranger drop Winston to the deck, it would result in his removal from the expedition, and she needed him to stay. With Mahdi's betrayal, he was the only person on the *Sea Tiger* she really trusted. "Don't."

Winston didn't flinch. He said nothing, either. Just stood his ground.

Mahdi looked about ready to jump overboard. "I am sorry. I was… pressured."

"Pressured." Winston chuckled as he stepped around Talia and headed for the door. "You all enjoy the bonfires. I'm going to get some shuteye. You can thank me in the morning when the natives are happy." He paused in the doorway. "Mahdi." He waited for Mahdi to look at him. "Keep on keepin' on, capisce?"

When Mahdi said nothing, Winston repeated himself using the tone of a too strict mother. "*Capisce?*"

Mahdi gave a nearly imperceptible nod.

"Good." Winston stepped inside and let the door close slowly behind him as his heavy feet thumped through the boat. When he was gone, Talia and Rowan both turned on Mahdi.

"What the hell, Mahdi?" Talia said.

The man shrunk. "I am sorry. I had no choice."

"Bullshit," Rowan said. "How long have you and Winston been friends? From the start? Before we picked you up in London?"

"I do not know the man," Mahdi said, growing angry. "I do not *like* the man. And I am *not* his friend."

"Not really our friend, either," Rowan said. "Are you?"

Mahdi said nothing, just kept his eyes on the water past the stern deck. The orange firelight's motion mixed with the undulating waves was entrancing.

Talia turned from the waves, trying a different tack than Rowan's. "You can trust us, Mahdi. Whatever he's done or threatened you with, we can help you."

When Mahdi looked up, she was surprised to see tears in his eyes. "I am helping *you*."

"How?" she asked.

"It is not important."

"It damn well is," Rowan said.

Talia put a calming hand on Rowan and leaned on the stern rail so she could see Mahdi's downturned face. "Are you helping them?" She pointed to the island.

Mahdi's face froze like a child self-aware enough to realize that anything he said would sound like a lie. His stillness spoke volumes. Winston's delivery of coconuts was not intended to be helpful. But what could it be, unless… "Did you leave anything aside from coconuts?"

Mahdi, still expressionless, whispered, "Just coconuts."

Talia was about to question him some more when emotion worked its way through the rigid muscles of his face, contorting from confusion to fear.

Rowan saw it, too. "What's wrong?"

"Down there," Mahdi said, eyes still on the water beside the ship. "There's something in the water."

Talia looked but saw only the fire light reflecting off the rippling waves. She was about to say as much when her nose picked up the smell of smoke, and something else. It was foreign, but at the same time it brought back memories of the marijuana and incense that permeated her college dorm.

"You smell that?" Rowan asked, watching the island. "Could that be part of the message? Could they communicate using fragrance? Like, what's it called? With animals?"

"Pheromones," Talia said, impressed with Rowan's theory, mostly because it wasn't really outlandish, and because she wasn't sure she'd have thought of it.

"Right, but with smoke? Is that a thing?"

She had no answer for that, but maybe Mahdi… He hadn't moved. Hadn't acknowledged the smell. His gaze remained fixated on the water behind the boat. She tried once again to spot anything other than darkness and orange light, but she saw nothing.

And then she did. A subtle shift of darkness and light.

Rowan saw it, too, flinching back. "The hell is that?"

The darkness slid past, a massive living thing that created no wake. Talia's heart, which remained steady while facing down angry tribes and wild animals, thumped with urgency. Fear like she hadn't felt since childhood began to prickle her arms.

And then she saw it for what it was, and she wished it had been a sea creature. "We're drifting!"

The shadow below was a patch of coral, darker than the surrounding sand, sliding harmlessly beneath them as the boat slipped through the water. That she could see it meant they were moving into the shallows, and that the coral wouldn't remain harmless for long.

Rowan launched himself up the stairs to the wheelhouse. "Check the anchor!"

Check the anchor? How am I supposed to do that?

The *Sea Tiger* had two anchors—one on each side of the bow. They were massive things dropped by controls in the wheelhouse, their chains and winches contained inside the ship's body. Despite not knowing enough about ships to evaluate the state of an anchor, she hurried around the port side of the yacht, one hand on the rail to keep from falling over. As she ran, she shouted to Mahdi just as Rowan had shouted to her. "Mahdi! Go get Emmei!" When he didn't move, she shouted again. "Mahdi!"

The linguist snapped from his trance, seemed to slowly comprehend the situation, and then headed for the dining room entrance.

Talia toppled deck chairs, shouting in pain as they whacked against her shins, and then she was at the bow, leaning over the rail, trying not to fall overboard.

Rowan's muffled voice boomed in the wheelhouse. She guessed the string of curses meant something had gone wrong. She heard a window open, and then his voice became clear. "No keys! What about the anchor?"

Talia strained to see over the side. The angled hull made it difficult. She could hear the anchor chain rattling and thumping against the hull. *That's not good,* she thought, and then she saw it. The chain hung in the water, dancing around. She moved to the other side and caught sight of the second chain, just as loose as the first, neither of them dragging weight.

"They're gone!" she shouted. "The anchors are gone!"

And then the *Sea Tiger* plowed into the reef.

Momentum carried Talia forward, up, and over the rail, and into the shadowy water below.

16

ROWAN STOOD DUMBFOUNDED for a three count. For the second time in less than twenty four hours he'd watched Talia sprawl over the side of a boat and into the sea. When his shock wore off, he charged out of the useless wheelhouse and vaulted down the steps to the main deck.

"Talia!" He leaned over the port beam as he ran, looking for motion in the water, but he saw no sign of her. No hint that she'd even fallen in.

Shouting rose up from inside the ship, angry and confused. He ignored them and hurried to the bow where Talia had stood before the ship ran aground. He leaned over the rail, but saw nothing in the water. What he did see was a loose anchor chain, and below it, a hole where coral had punched through the fiberglass hull. Water chugged in and out of the gap, but it didn't appear to be flooding the yacht, yet.

"What happened?" It was Mahdi, shouting to him from the aft deck.

"Talia fell overboard!" Rowan shouted, fighting his instinct to jump in after her. Without knowing where she was, leaping into water laced with sharp bundles of coral could be suicidal…and he'd left that part of him behind in New Hampshire.

Emmei stepped out from below decks with murder in his eyes, but when he saw Mahdi and Rowan searching over the side, he hurried to the wheelhouse, digging into his pocket. A moment later, flood lights all around the ship blazed to life. Talia had specifically said the ship should remain dark at night. The halogens would appear unnaturally bright from shore and could be misconstrued as supernatural. She was determined to have the Sentinelese view them as human and nothing more. Rowan understood and respected her position, but not when her life was at risk.

Shadows fled, giving way to clear water, white sands, multi colored coral and a rainbow star burst of fish fleeing the sudden illumination. But there was no Talia, and Rowan noted, no blood. In these waters, that was a good thing. But that didn't mean she hadn't been knocked unconscious. She could be beneath the yacht, or drifting further out to sea, beyond the light's reach, or—

"Somebody shut those fucking lights off!"

Rowan rushed to the starboard rail. Talia was twelve feet below, side-stroking toward the dive deck. When she saw him looking down at her, she repeated, "Shut the lights off!"

"Are you okay?" he asked.

"Damnit, Rowan!"

She was fine. He could see that for himself, and if he didn't do as she asked, he would be on the receiving end of all the hellish fury Talia could conjure up. And he had a feeling that could be significant. "Emmei," he shouted, heading for the wheelhouse stairs. "Turn off the lights."

He took the stairs two at a time, and entered the wheelhouse. It was a modern affair with computerized systems and plush accommodations. Emmei was on his hands and knees, looking under a console, whispering to himself.

"Where's the switch for the flood lights?" Rowan asked.

Emmei cursed, but didn't reply. The man was lost in his own dilemma. *Probably trying to keep us from sinking,* Rowan decided, and he looked for the light switch on his own. He found six outboard light switches on a well-labeled console and switched them all off with one swipe of his hand. The world outside the wheelhouse went dark again. Adjusted to the light, Rowan was suddenly blinded.

Emmei cursed again, this time in a language Rowan didn't recognize. There was a jangling of keys and then light. The small flashlight illuminated the source of Emmei's frustration; a bundle of wires hung beneath a torn-open console. All of them severed.

Emmei played the light over the rest of the wheelhouse. While much of it was intact and functional, a few screens had been shattered, and in places, the electronic innards had been exposed and pulled apart.

"We have been attacked," Emmei said.

"Looks more like sabotage," Rowan noted.

Emmei looked deeply troubled by this revelation. "Are we sinking?"

Rowan shook his head. "If we're taking on water, the coral we're wedged on is keeping us up. I think we'll stay above water until help arrives."

"There will be no help coming," Emmei said, angling the light at the first bundle of exposed and ruined wires. "This was communications. Radio. Satellite. Everything. I tell you, this is an attack."

The Sentinelese wouldn't have had any frame of reference for electronics, wireless communication, or even that the wheelhouse was what controlled the ship, let alone that they might understand how to operate the door. Nor did they have the capability to cut the chain-link anchor lines, a fact that Emmei had yet to ask about.

"Aren't you curious about why we ran aground?" Rowan asked.

Emmei shrugged. "Anchors failed. Happens in loose sand sometimes."

"In calm seas?" Rowan said. "Both anchors?"

"We are not the first to run aground here while anchored." Emmei paused at this, eyebrows furrowed. He stood and stepped around the wheel, pushing two buttons labeled 'Anchor 1' and 'Anchor 2'. Nothing happened.

"Don't bother," Rowan said. "The anchors are missing."

"*What?*" Emmei's honest shock propelled him from the wheelhouse.

Rowan followed him, but he wasn't interested in the anchors. He'd already seen the loose chains for himself. Back on the aft deck, he was relieved to see Mahdi helping Talia onto the dive deck.

"What's happening?" Sashi asked, emerging from below deck. Then she saw Talia, dripping wet and angry. "Is she okay?"

"It's not her I'm worried about," Rowan said. He searched the deck, but saw no sign of Winston or Chugy. "Are you good?" he shouted to Talia, who replied with a thumbs up. Then he turned to Sashi, said, "Stay with them," and headed inside.

Once the door was closed behind him, he slipped a hand around his back and drew his pistol. He didn't know what he expected to find, but he wanted to be prepared for anything. Someone had purposefully stranded them on a reef just offshore of the world's most deadly island, and he had a fairly good idea who.

After clearing the dining room, lounge, and saloon, he headed for the stairwell that led to the crew quarters. With every step he became more confused. Why would Winston or Chugy strand them here? It wouldn't be hard to figure out who was to blame, and if the situation became dangerous, they would share in that danger.

Or would they?

Rowan hurried, confident he would find the rest of the ship empty. It was difficult picturing Chugy working with Winston to sabotage the ship, but she had been upset earlier. Winston could have used that anger, turned her against the crew. But against her uncle?

He moved through the ship like a tornado, shoving open doors, scanning rooms and then moving on with military efficiency. He knew Winston's quarters were closer to the bow, but he didn't want to risk the man getting around him by skipping right to the end. After clearing every room except for Winston's, he paused by the door, switched the handgun's safety off, and slipped his finger around the trigger.

The door banged open. Rowan entered, gun raised and sweeping for targets, but he found no threat.

Though he *did* find Winston.

The man was sprawled in his bed, partially dressed and unconscious. Blood dripped from a fresh gash on his forehead.

Knowing he had the wrong man, Rowan checked for a pulse, felt a strong beat, and then moved on. It took him twenty seconds to run up through the decks and back into the open air. His sudden appearance startled Talia, Mahdi, Sashi, and Emmei, who were gathered on the aft deck, arguing amongst themselves.

"What happened?" Talia asked. "Where are the others?"

Rowan pushed past Mahdi, took one look over the deck and whirled around on Emmei. "Where is Chugy?"

Emmei looked confused and then worried. "I haven't seen her in hours. She was very upset by your..."

"Does your niece love you?" Rowan asked.

Worry shifted to anger. "Of course she—"

"Then why did she strand you at North Fucking Sentinel Island?" Rowan pointed out past the dive deck where the dinghy should have been tied up. The line was there, still tied to the cleat, but the boat was missing. The small craft would have been cramped, but could have taken them back to the resort.

"Chugy is missing?" Emmei started toward the door.

"Not missing," Rowan said. "Gone."

"What about Winston?" Sashi asked.

"Unconscious," Rowan said. "The wound on his head suggests he was struck. Probably by whoever took the dinghy, and since Chugy is the only one not here..."

"Could it be that you are wrong?" Mahdi asked.

"I'm not yet certain that you're not involved," Rowan said. Aside from the state of the ship, he had reason to distrust everyone except for Talia and Sashi.

Mahdi groaned. "I would never—"

"Rowan," Talia said. She hadn't spoken very loudly, but somehow managed to convey a black hole's worth of gravity to his name, stopping Mahdi mid-thought. Her eyes were on the dive deck and it took Rowan only a moment to spot the abnormality.

The dinghy was nowhere in sight, but the line tied to the cleat was pulled tight. Something was still attached. Had the dinghy been sunk? Rowan and Talia hopped over the rail, onto the dive deck. Rowan picked up the line and pulled. Whatever was attached was heavy, but not too heavy to reel in. He and Talia pulled together.

It's too light to be the boat, Rowan thought. The motor alone would have been heavier than whatever they were pulling in. And if the dinghy had sunk, there would have been debris littering the water. When they'd pulled in ten feet of line, he said, "Almost there."

And then the line snapped taut.

"It's stuck," Talia said, looking into the dark water. They could see the line streaking away into the water, but couldn't see the end in the night's limited light. "It's the coral."

Rowan felt a vibration on his fingers. Looked down at the line. Saw an inch slide back out of his hand. Then another. "It's not stuck." He crouched and tried to tie the reeled-in line to the cleat. Before he could loop it once, the line was yanked through his fingers. Friction-generated heat forced him to drop the line and watch it unspool until it snapped tight again. The rope cut a path through the water, surging back and forth as whatever was tied to the other end tried to swim away.

A distant grinding sound tickled Rowan's ears. It was followed by a vibration in his feet. And then, a realization. "It's pulling us off the reef."

"If that happens," Emmei said. "We will sink."

17

TALIA KNEW SHE was strange. Unconventional was the description most often used by colleagues she hadn't seen in years. But for all her eccentricities, she wasn't crazy. Risking your life was not the same as forfeiting it, a distinction Rowan understood for tragic reasons. If the boat sank, they would all die, either in the water, or on the shore. She slipped her folding knife from her pocket and snapped it open. Then she dropped down onto the dive deck and placed the razor sharp edge against the line.

"Wait," Rowan said, his hand on her forearm, his eyes on the water.

"I don't see anything." That wasn't entirely true. She could see the moon's bright reflection, the orange stripes created by the Sentinelese fires, and even the variations in brightness just beneath the water, revealing coral, sand, and stones. But she couldn't see anything worth waiting on.

The line snapped back and forth, yanked with enough violence to shift the boat again. Water lapped up over the dive deck, tickling Talia's toes.

"Smell," Rowan said, and she did, detecting the fragrant smoke rolling off the island first, and then something else. Something unmistakable.

Blood.

It was in the water.

"Chugy is missing," Rowan whispered, completing the picture. The young woman, Emmei's niece, might be tied to the line's end, a meal for whatever creature was thrashing beneath the water.

"If she's out there," Talia said, "she's already dead." She cut through the line with a quick swipe. The boat fell still. There was a single splash and then nothing.

The *Sea Tiger* fell silent until Emmei spoke. "Was it her?"

Talia should have guessed that the experienced captain would understand what had happened—that a large predator had attacked whatever was tied to the end of that line. With Chugy missing, her body was the most likely candidate.

"We can look in the morning," Rowan said.

"There will be nothing left by morning." Emmei's efficient truth stung. If Chugy was in the water, being eaten, her body would never be found. Then he squinted at Talia, Rowan, and Mahdi. "You three were on deck when we ran aground."

It wasn't a question.

"Yes, but—"

The captain focused on Talia. "*You* were in the water."

"I was knocked overboard."

Emmei turned to Sashi. Motioned toward Talia, Rowan, and Mahdi. "You said they would not be dangerous. That they could be—"

"Emmei," Sashi said, her voice raised. "This is *not* the time."

Talia felt like she'd walked into a lecture halfway through, trying to find the context in what was being said with no frame of reference.

Sashi is trying to say something without saying it.

Why did she tell Emmei she and Rowan would not be dangerous?

"My niece is missing," Emmei shouted. "Probably dead in the water. Winston is unconscious, or so he says." He pointed at Rowan, who watched the unfolding scene with a keen eye, his right hand inching toward the small of his back. "Or maybe Winston is dead, too. If they found—"

"Stop it!" Sashi shouted. "They are *not* murderers. They are good people. All of them. And I cannot say the same about everyone on this ship."

Is she talking about Emmei, or Winston? Talia wondered.

Emmei grimaced. "We are stranded within reach of the Sentinelese. Our communications have been sabotaged. The dinghy is missing, along with my niece, who would *not* abandon me. Someone on my yacht did all this, and the people you brought on board were the only ones on deck when all this happened."

"We were alone for just a few minutes," Rowan pointed out.

"And my bow was on that dinghy," Talia grumbled.

"We didn't have time to sabotage communications, cut the anchor chains, *and* set the dinghy loose. We were below deck until Mahdi and Winston returned." He looked at Emmei. "Where were you?" Then Sashi. "Where were both of you?"

No one spoke.

"And if we're being honest, Chugy was angry. She knows the ship well enough to sabotage the right systems, and she had the time. She could have done the work, slipped into the water, and taken the boat after Winston and Mahdi returned. She could have been tangled in the line and—"

"Enough," Emmei growled, but he didn't argue the points.

On the surface, it made sense, but it didn't feel right. And there was a glaring inconsistency. "If she was in the water, and left in the dinghy while we were on deck talking, who knocked out Winston?"

Talia, Rowan, and Mahdi looked at Emmei and Sashi.

Sashi was barely over five feet tall, and didn't look strong enough to knock a man out with a baseball bat. That left one suspect—the uncle of their other suspect—a conclusion that Rowan came to as well. He pulled the pistol out from behind his back and aimed it at Emmei.

"You see?" Emmei said to Sashi while thrusting his hands at Rowan. "This is the kind of people you brought on my ship."

Emmei's genuine outrage confused Talia. He was a ship captain at a small Andaman Island resort, not an Academy Award winning actor. No way he was faking such raw emotion. But someone had disabled the yacht and set the dinghy loose. Chugy still seemed like the most likely culprit, but Talia didn't think Emmei was involved. But could Chugy have done all that by herself?

Flickering orange drew her eyes back to the island. Were the Sentinelese watching them from the dancing shadows? Would they remain on shore, or attack the stranded *Sea Tiger*? If that happened, she had no illusions. Without a meaningful social breakthrough, the crew was in very real danger. Rowan was armed, but she doubted he'd brought enough ammunition to kill all the Sentinelese, and she wasn't about to let herself be a martyr for those who wanted to purge the island of its native inhabitants.

The idea of a purge became bottled in her mind, fermented for a moment, and then, when one of the fires on the island went dark, drained away. She watched the island, ignoring the others as they continued to argue and place blame.

A second fire, on the opposite end of the island, extinguished.

How did they coordinate that? she wondered. From her viewpoint in the water, she could see from one end of the island to the other, but anyone on the island would have their view blocked. The island sloped gently, but rose to four hundred feet at the core. That, and the towering trees covering every inch of land aside from the sand and coral, made it impossible for any kind of line-of-sight communication. She listened, but she heard no shouting voices. No drums, no horns, no noise at all.

A third fire went out and she realized they were perfectly timed. Synchronized. Practiced.

They've done this before.

Was it a message? Some form of communication meant for the *Sea Tiger's* crew? A warning? An invitation? Or perhaps it was a tribal ritual that had nothing to do with them, performed for so many generations that the timing was instinctual? Too many questions, and she doubted the answers would increase their odds of survival.

Another fire went out, right on time.

How are they putting the fires out so quickly? One moment they were blazing infernos lighting up a portion of the jungle's interior. The next, they were gone, no lingering flames or hint of hot embers.

"You can put that down."

Talia's attention swiveled away from the fires at the sound of Winston's voice. He stood in the doorway, a washcloth held to his bloody head. She wasn't sure how long he'd been there, listening, but apparently it was enough to know they were arguing about who wrecked the ship and bludgeoned him.

"I wasn't attacked," Winston said. "I was changing my clothes when we struck…whatever it was we struck. I remember falling, hitting my head, and that's it." He raised his chin toward Rowan. "Thanks, by the way, for leaving me to bleed all over myself."

"I had bigger problems on my mind," Rowan said. He didn't put the gun away, but lowered it. "Just be glad you fell on the bed. Floor wouldn't have been as kind."

Winston nodded. "Are we wrecked?" Winston asked.

"Run aground," Sashi said. "On the coral."

"Well that's just fucking grand." Winston hobbled to the rail. He'd put on a shirt before coming up, but hadn't bothered buttoning it, letting his prodigious belly bulge out. He turned from one person to the next, then asked, "Where's Chugy?"

"Not here," Rowan said.

Emmei shook his head, exasperated. "She is missing."

"Well then, there's your answer."

A shift of color drew Talia's eyes back to the island. There were only two fires left. A sudden sense of dread flowed through Talia's body, her ancient enemy resurfacing. "It's a countdown."

"What?" Winston asked, annoyed, and then to Rowan, "What is she talking about?"

"The fires are going out," she explained. "One every fifteen seconds. I think it's a countdown."

"A countdown?" Winston's injury had done nothing to dull his incredulity. "Do they even have a concept of time?"

"Every culture on Earth starting with the most primitive hominids had an understanding of time. Days. Seasons. The movements of the sun and moon. The Sentinelese might not have watches, but they probably have a better instinct for the rising and falling of the sun, and how it affects their lives, than we ever will."

A fire went out, shrinking down to nothing in seconds, leaving no trace behind.

"What happens when the last fire goes out?" Mahdi asked. "I know you don't know the answer, but since there is only one fire left, I thought it wise to discuss."

"In my experience," Winston said. "Countdowns never lead to anything good."

"Everyone inside," Rowan said. "Now."

Talia realized she and Rowan were still standing on the dive deck, water lapping at their feet. Hands on the aft rail, she vaulted herself back onto the yacht while Rowan pushed through the gate.

"You don't really think we're in danger?" Sashi asked, shuffling toward the door. "Out here? In the dark?"

"You're the one who showed us the photos," Rowan said. "You tell me."

Sashi had no response. She headed inside, followed by Emmei and Winston. When Mahdi stepped toward the door, Rowan stopped him. "The long case, in my room. Can you get it?"

Mahdi nodded. "Thank you for trusting me."

"It's not a compliment, I just trust him less." Rowan motioned toward Winston through the window. The big man had already taken a seat at the saloon, popping the top off a beer bottle.

Mahdi frowned, but didn't comment. He hurried inside, headed through the dining room, lounge, and saloon before disappearing below deck.

"And what are we going to do?" Talia asked.

"See what happens when the countdown reaches zero," Rowan said, looking back toward the island. After a moment he said, "I think it's been fifteen—"

The final bonfire flared, shrank, and then exploded with a brilliance that turned Talia's eyes away, and made her wonder if they had severely underestimated the Sentinelese. And then she heard them, whispering, the voices rising up from the dark water surrounding them.

18

"DO YOU HEAR that?" Talia asked.

Rowan was too busy watching the island to register Talia's question. The last bonfire had flared brightly, and then broken apart into seven smaller flames, fanning out across the island. *Torches,* he decided. *They're running with torches, fast, heading toward the sea.* When the orange lights reached the jungle's end, they went dark.

"Rowan," Talia hissed. "Do you hear them?"

His eyes snapped away from the island, registering the question, and he held his breath. He heard nothing unusual. "I don't—"

"Whispering," she said. "All around."

He was about to argue that she was hearing things when a sound, like a breeze, fluttered against his ears. The gentle swish separated into voices, each rising and falling with its own cadence, a song of hushed destruction. He couldn't make out any distinct words, but he also didn't speak the language.

Rowan raised his pistol and searched the boat. He saw nothing.

Are they all in the water? For a moment, he felt afraid for the natives. There was a predator in the water. Then he realized it could have been the Sentinelese pulling on the other side of that line, dragging the boat back into the water, attempting to sink it. He never did see the end of the line. For all he knew, a group of warriors could have been standing on coral, pulling them back as a group. They'd be impossible to see in the dark.

"Stay here," he said to Talia, motioning to the door. "Be ready to get inside and lock the door."

"Screw that," she said, flicking open her knife. Apparently, Talia's version of 'going native' included taking a life to defend herself. It made sense that she would be willing to kill—law of the jungle and all that—but it still caught him off guard.

He didn't bother arguing the point. Talia put an equal amount of resolve—all of it—into everything she decided to do. His boots thumped gently against the deck with each step. The sound was delicate, muted, but in the nighttime quiet, it announced his presence and direction like a drummer boy. He flicked the gun's safety off, wrapped a finger around the trigger, and leaned over the port rail.

Water. That was all there was.

The whispers fell silent.

"They're playing games with us," he said.

"Testing us," Talia replied, peering over the edge. "Seeing how we react." She looked back to the door through which the others had fled. "Perhaps determining which of us are warriors."

"Congratulations," Rowan said, with a smirk.

"Probably so they can target us first."

Rowan's frail smile shattered and fell away. He searched the water again. If the Sentinelese had been surrounding the ship and had just left, he should have still been able to see them. The moonlight was enough to see the surface by. The silhouettes of their heads, swimming bodies and canoes should have been easy to see. But he saw nothing. And heard nothing. "I'm not sure they were ever here."

"We both heard them."

He wanted to blame it on the wind, but there wasn't a breeze.

Motion drew Rowan's eyes down. A blur rose from below, surging quickly. When it broke the water, he saw a head, felt a rush of danger, and before considering the ramifications of his actions, pulled the trigger. There was a crack and a pop, hard and wet, all of it familiar.

"Rowan!" Talia shouted, shoving him to the side, stalling his second shot.

As he stumbled back, lowering his weapon, a dozen different scenarios flooded his mind. Instinct guided his reaction to what he perceived as an attack. But maybe it wasn't? Maybe it was a Sentinelese surfacing for a breath, or to say hello, or simply to frighten him. Maybe it was Chugy, returning to the boat after escaping the line, or returning from her sabotage of the anchors. The more he thought about it, the less confident he felt about his actions.

Talia looked over the edge with a frown.

If he had taken an innocent life, again, Rowan would be undone. His fingers loosened their grip on the handgun. His legs felt week. *Please don't let it be Chugy.*

"Well," Talia said, "You killed it."

It. Killed *it.* Rowan stepped to the rail and looked into the water. A single coconut bobbed in the water, white fluid leaking from a hole in its thick skin. *Thank God.*

When a second form rose from the depths, he took aim again, but held his fire, fighting his instincts. It was a second coconut. And then a third, and a forth. They rose from below, thumping against the hull, spinning in the small waves.

"I don't think they liked the coconuts," Talia said, smiling like she'd just watched her child take her first steps.

"You sound proud," he said.

She motioned to the coconuts with her knife. "They've sent us a very clear message."

"We don't like coconuts?"

"Probably closer to 'you can't buy our favor with coconuts.'"

"Or 'keep the coconuts, we prefer heads.'"

Talia laughed, but it sounded equal parts amused and nervous. "The point is, it's progress. They're communicating, and this message is far less confusing than the genital thrusting."

"But less fun." Rowan's joke felt hollow. Despite his enemy being a coconut, he couldn't shake the disturbing feeling those whispers had generated, and the fact that the Sentinelese could apparently swim great distances underwater, not to mention orchestrate a fairly dramatic pyrotechnic light show. They had underestimated the Sentinelese, as had everyone who had visited the island before them, which could help explain why so many people had been killed here.

Despite the coconut communication, and the Sentinelese sparing his life after performing the haka, he could not shake the feeling that the *Sea Tiger*'s crew would be the next victims attributed to the Sentinelese. *But we will be the last,* he thought. If the expedition failed, the Sentinelese were in trouble. If the expedition was murdered… He couldn't imagine many of the islanders surviving the government's response.

The door behind them slapped open. The sudden noise spun them around. Fearing the coconuts were a distraction, Rowan raised the pistol again, and when he saw a dark skinned man wielding an automatic weapon, he nearly pulled the trigger, this time out of trained habit rather than instinct. But he recognized the man, a moment before he put a bullet in his head.

"Shit, Mahdi." Rowan lowered the pistol. "I nearly shot you."

"I heard a shot," he said. "So I hurried."

Rowan motioned to the FN SCAR assault rifle procured for him by the Indian government. In full auto, the weapon was perfect for close quarters combat. In semi-auto, he could squeeze off single rounds. Using a scope, it was an effective alternative for a sniper rifle when shooting at targets at a distance of three to four hundred feet. The last time Rowan saw it, the weapon had been inside its case—disassembled. Rowan could assemble the weapon in twenty seconds. Mahdi was slower, but the weapon's assembly wasn't intuitive. He either had experience with an FN or weapons like it.

"You put that together?"

Mahdi looked down at the rifle, confused by the question, or feigning confusion. If Mahdi could assemble assault rifles, then the mysteries of his past and the men looking for him, might be less innocent than Rowan would prefer. Then again, Talia could probably assemble the weapon, too. And Mahdi was holding it all wrong.

Rowan tucked his handgun into the small of his back and reached for the FN. He was pleased when Mahdi handed it over, but his relief was wiped clean when Mahdi whispered, "Not me."

"Then who?" Rowan asked.

Mahdi looked over his shoulder, more worried about who was inside the ship than outside it.

"Winston," Talia guessed. "He's got something on you, doesn't he?"

"We need to tell the Sentinelese to not eat the coconuts," Mahdi said.

Talia's expression darkened. "What's wrong with the coconuts?"

Mahdi looked back again. He flinched when he saw Sashi, Emmei, and Winston emerge from below decks next to the saloon. Winston moved with one arm frozen behind him. Rowan recognized the stance. The man had a gun tucked into his pants.

When Mahdi didn't answer, Talia tried to step around him. "Fine. I'll ask him myself."

Rowan held her back. "He's armed."

Talia held up the knife. "So am I." She pointed at the rifle. "So are you."

"My job is still to keep this crew safe. A gun fight on a marooned yacht off the coast of North Sentinel Island is not the time and place for a violent confrontation over coconuts. There's a chance we will need him, and his gun, to survive. Until that's not a possibility, we play nice." He pointed a finger at Mahdi. "But you *will* tell us what's going on."

Mahdi glanced back again. The others were closing in, but moving cautiously. He whispered, "They sprayed the coconuts. I think with a virus. They are not here to help the Sentinelese. They are here to kill them."

"They?" Talia asked. "Who?"

Another glance. "Everyone."

19

MAHDI SHOVED HIS hands in his pockets and looked up at the stars.

"If you're trying to look casual," Rowan told him, "you're doing the opposite."

The door behind him opened and Sashi peeked out. "We heard a gunshot."

Mahdi removed his hands, wandered toward the dive deck and then remembered there might be Sentinelese warriors lurking in the water. He knew he looked nervous, but given the circumstances, nervous was appropriate.

"Rowan killed a coconut," Talia said, doing a much better job of acting casual. Even grinned convincingly.

Winston pushed his way past Emmei and Sashi, spilling the entire crew out on to the deck.

Rowan put the rifle's butt against his shoulder, ready but not raised. "It's still not safe out here. You should go back inside."

Mahdi wasn't sure who Rowan was preparing to shoot, but he decided agreeing with him would help keep bullets from flying. "I think that's a—"

Winston shot him a look and stormed to the port rail where Talia stood. "What coconut?"

Talia sneered at Winston's proximity, but the man didn't notice. He was looking down into the water, where a slew of coconuts bobbed.

"They didn't like your gift," Talia said. "Maybe you should take them back? Be a shame to waste all those good coconuts."

Winston gave her a squinty-eyed glare, like some kind of troll whose bridge was being stomped on by an obese billy goat. "Help yourself." He straightened up, watching the now dark island. "Did you see them? Were they carrying the coconuts?"

"We didn't see anyone," Rowan said.

"Where did the coconuts come from?" Emmei asked.

Rowan pointed at the water. "Beneath us. I shot the first one that surfaced. The rest came up pretty quickly after that."

Mahdi thought Winston might persist on his line of questioning, tipping the card that Mahdi had yet to fully explain to Rowan and Talia. If he did, it would allow them to question him directly without Mahdi risking exposure and Winston fulfilling his threat.

Winston huffed, looked at Sashi, and hitched a thumb toward Rowan. "This is the guy you hired to protect us? The great coconut killer."

Mahdi stood motionless, but his heartrate climbed faster as tension brewed. If there was a confrontation, he knew Sashi would have no part. He hadn't spoken to her alone, but he got the impression her innocence, like his, was motivated by self-preservation, or the preservation of loved ones. Emmei, on the other hand, worked for Ambani, and he would likely support Winston. And if that happened, Mahdi would have a choice to make, between what was safe, and what was right.

It was a choice he'd made once before, and he had been dogged by the results since. He wasn't sure he could do it again.

Luckily, Rowan was diplomatic when Talia couldn't be. "I think the danger has passed. Since there's nothing left to see tonight, I suggest we all head inside and try to get a little sleep. We can lock the doors, and I'll keep watch from the dining room."

Winston looked ready to rekindle the argument, but Sashi spoke up. "That sounds like a great idea."

"We can try to repair the radio in the morning," Emmei said. "Call for a rescue." He frowned. "And a search team."

As things calmed down, Mahdi found himself becoming exhausted. The night had been full of stress and treachery. He'd taken part in things that might haunt him for the rest of his life. Drawn to the bench lining the stern rail, he sat, head in his hands.

He had not prayed since he was a teenager, but thoughts of Allah trickled into his mind. If he was to be judged upon his death, he would surely be sent to the burning fires of Jahannam. As a man who had been raised in the teachings of Islam, and had turned his back on them, he'd been deemed an 'enemy of Islam.' Rather than being judged when Allah remade the world, he would be damned to hell at the moment of his death.

"Allah, spare my life," he said, and winced. It was a very Western way to pray. He raised his hands to his ears, said, "Allah…Akbar," and lowered his right hand to his navel. The motions felt wrong. Phony. Even if he got everything right, Allah would not hear him, because he didn't believe.

But then he heard a reply. The voice was fluid and strange. Decidedly not human.

He sat up straight, listening. He heard the conversation between the others, calmer now, but the words didn't make it past his ears.

Then he heard the voice again. From behind him. From the water.

His eyes opened slowly as he remembered where he was, where he was sitting, and what might be in the water. He turned around slowly, primed to dive away and raise the alarm. But he saw no one. Not a Sentinelese man, or Allah in human form. All he saw was water.

And no dive deck.

He stood up and leaned over the edge. The dive deck was submerged six inches beneath the surface, a foot when a wave rolled through on its way to shore. An almost musical gurgle rose up from below, carried by a string of bubbles.

Mahdi stood, snapped rigid by the realization that his judgment day might arrive sooner than later. He stepped back from the rail until he bumped into Rowan, who took one look at him and then raised the assault rifle toward the rear of the ship.

"What is it?" Rowan asked. "What did you see?"

Mahdi turned to Rowan. His voice came out with a squeak. "We're sinking."

The group moved toward the back of the ship to look for themselves, but the shift of all that weight toward the stern increased the subtle angle of the ship to the point where it could not be ignored.

"Back!" Emmei shouted. "All of you back!" He approached the stern alone, looking down into the water. He scratched his head. Took a step back. "We *are* sinking."

"That's pretty much what he just said," Rowan said, pointing to Mahdi. "Any idea of how long we have?"

Emmei shrugged. "Hours? It will be—"

A grinding noise interrupted. The yacht scraped over coral, the weight of the water flowing inside the ship pulling them off the reef.

"Perhaps less," Emmei said.

Rowan pointed at Emmei. "Life jackets and emergency gear." Then to Sashi. "Help him."

He turned to Mahdi next. "There are trash bags in the galley. Fill them with non-perishable food. Nothing that will be ruined by getting wet. When they're half full, bunch the top, inflate it like a balloon and tie it off. As much as you can get on deck."

"We will be missed," Winston said. "This is a six million dollar yacht. When we don't return on time, Ambani will send an army to look for it."

"You mean, look for *us,*" Talia said.

"If that's what you want to tell yourself." Winston shook his head as though he were speaking to a naïve child. "Either way, we won't have to spend more than twenty-four hours on the island."

On the island.

The words sank deep into Mahdi's chest. North Sentinel Island was one of the most dangerous places on the planet. Few people had ever felt its sands beneath their toes and lived to tell about it. And now they had to survive for a day, waiting for a possible rescue.

"Talia," Rowan said. "You can help me."

"And what about me, oh fearless leader?" Winston asked.

"You can stay on deck and keep watch with that nine millimeter tucked into your pants."

Winston grinned and pulled the weapon out. "How'd you know it was a nine mil?"

"Small and less effective," Rowan said with an honest grin. "It's what you're used to."

Mahdi was surprised when Winston guffawed, and then he was being herded inside the ship by Rowan. "Ten minutes. Then I want everyone back on deck."

"We might still have several hours," Emmei said. "Perhaps even into the daytime."

"We need to be off this boat, on shore, and settled in before the sun rises or everyone on that island will know exactly where we are. Our best chance at survival is to stay hidden until help arrives."

"And if we can't?" Sashi asked, squeezing her shaking hands together.

"We'll cross that bridge if we come to it," he said, and then the group dispersed, Emmei and Sashi headed toward the bow, and Rowan and Talia going below deck—leaving Mahdi alone in the dining room.

He headed past the saloon and through the door on the far side of the bar, entering the galley, in which he had yet to spend any time. He opened three cabinets before finding trash bags. Then he riffled through the galley cupboards and began removing armfuls of canned goods. Next he went to the fridge and took fresh fruits and vegetables. They were perishable, but would last several days and be unaffected by the water. He filled three bags halfway, blew them full of air, and tied them off as instructed. *It will work,* he thought. *The food will float.*

He believed Rowan an odd choice for security. Mahdi had a sordid past, but he was not in charge of keeping people safe. Then again, Rowan wasn't being used to hurt people. And Mahdi doubted the man would agree to such a thing. He returned to the cupboards, determined to fill at least one more bag.

"Hey."

Mahdi twisted around and sprawled to the floor, dropping two cans of pineapple juice. One cracked into his shin. The other rolled across the floor and stopped at Winston's boot.

"Pineapple juice? Don't tell me you're planning to open a resort here, too?"

"Sh-shouldn't you be keeping watch?" Mahdi asked.

"If the locals were going to attack tonight, they'd have done it already." Winston squatted down, strangely flexible for such a large man. "Here's the deal. Since you're kind of on the payroll now, you're safe. I think Mr. Ambani would like to keep you on in the future. A man of your particular...nationality can be intimidating, if you can learn how to stop acting like such a Nancy."

Mahdi did not know what a 'Nancy' was, but he inferred the term's meaning.

"The point is, I don't need to kill you. That's good news, right?" Winston waited. "Right?"

Mahdi nodded.

"The bad news is that those two—" Winston pointed to the sparkling clean white floor. "—need to die. On the island."

"But they don't know enough to—"

"It has nothing to do with what they know," Winston said. "They came here to die, and honestly, so did you. No one will mourn their deaths, or yours. No one will come kicking down doors, asking questions if they're never seen again. But their deaths will legitimize the use of deadly force, which may not even be necessary if enough of them handled those coconuts."

Winston gave Mahdi a pat on his shoulder. "If you hadn't been such a nosey nelly, the noose would still be around your neck. So, bravo for that, I guess. But now you need to help."

He held out an automatic switchblade. "All you need to do is push the button, see?" A three inch blade snapped out of the handle, the suddenness of it making Mahdi flinch. "Push the button again, and..." The blade retracted into the handle.

Winston pressed the blade into Mahdi's hand. "On the off chance their bodies are recovered, it needs to look like a local job. So no bullets. When the time comes, you act, or join the dead." He pointed at the fourth, partly filled trash bag. "If there isn't whisky in there when we get to the beach, I'll kill you first."

Mahdi sat still and silent. He didn't know how to respond. Winston's treachery was so blunt and without remorse. "Good talk," Winston said, tapping the barrel of his gun against Mahdi's head. Then he left.

Mahdi looked down at the knife in his hand and shook his head. He couldn't do it. Running for his life, he could do, but take a life to save his own?

Guilt swam its way up his throat, forming a knot. But he had already done that, hadn't he? With Winston, on the dinghy. He might not have plunged a knife in the Sentinelese, but if they died from a virus he helped transport to the island, that wasn't just murder, it was genocide.

Tears filled his eyes as the full weight of what he'd been part of began to gnaw on his soul. *I am a killer,* he realized, and when he heard footsteps rising from below, he wiped the tears from his eyes and slipped the knife into his pocket.

20

ROWAN FELT THE heft of his rifle, handgun, and the two weapons that belonged to him personally: a five inch Ka-Bar knife and a combat Tomahawk, as well as the black tactical uniform, sans the body armor, he'd changed into. The weapons and gear, along with the box of ammunition Talia carried, added fifty plus pounds to his weight. No way he'd be able to swim with it all, even with a life jacket. And he didn't expect the others to carry weapons over food, nor did he trust them to.

He stepped into the galley, followed by Talia. The cupboards and fridge had been ransacked. A box of trash bags was on the floor along with discarded open boxes of crackers and chips. Mahdi had apparently completed his job and moved to the deck.

The floor tilted as more water rushed through the unseen hole. A few cans of tomato sauce rolled out of the cabinets and across the floor. The ship's sinking would be faster than Emmei predicted, the rate of flooding increasing exponentially as the yacht dipped deeper into the water. They might have two hours, or thirty minutes. Either way, they needed to abandon ship ASAP.

He picked up the box of trash bags, wondering if they would be buoyant enough to carry his weapons, and keep them out of the salt water. He doubted it, but there weren't a lot of other options.

"I'm assuming you know how to use a handgun?" he asked.

"I won't kill the Sentinelese," Talia said.

"Not even in self-defense?"

"They're the ones defending themselves. We're the invaders."

"Have you considered that maybe the Sentinelese aren't just another noble tribe, defending their land from gods and devils? Maybe they're smarter than that, and are just a bunch of violent, rude assholes?"

"Sounds more like Winston," she said.

He held up the Sig Sauer handgun. "That's why I want you to take this when we reach the beach."

"Winston, I could shoot," she said with a smile, which faded when she realized he wasn't joking.

"One more question. Will you stop *me* from defending us?" Rowan needed her on his side. If she wanted him to fight for the crew's safety using only his balls and a haka dance, he would have no one left to trust.

After a few seconds of deliberation, she shook her head. "Do what you have to. I just can't."

"Sometimes not pulling the trigger is a good thing," he said, and he headed for the door. They moved through the empty saloon, lounge, and dining rooms, emerging onto the now visibly tilted aft deck.

Mahdi and Winston stood waiting, four trash bags blown up like balloons resting at their feet.

"Not a peep out here," Winston said. "Island's quiet."

"Maybe they went to sleep?" Mahdi asked.

"Some of them," Talia said. "They're vigilant, so it's likely some of the warriors sleep in shifts."

"Then they'll see us coming?" Mahdi asked.

"Chance we need to take," Rowan said.

They turned at the sound of footsteps. Sashi and Emmei approached from the port side. Sashi carried five bright orange life preservers looped around one arm, and a medical case in the other. Emmei held a large bundle of folded black material that Rowan instantly recognized as an inflatable raft. In the other hand, he carried a second large med kit.

Rowan pointed to the deflated raft. "Why didn't you tell me about that?"

"Forgot we had it," Emmei said. "Have never needed it."

"How big is it?" Mahdi asked.

Emmei shook his head. "Two people. Short range. The plastic oar was missing."

Rowan sized up what they had, how many people there were and where they had to go. "Lose the life vests."

"What?" Sashi looked mortified. "Why?"

"Some of us are already going to shine like beacons in the moonlight. Those vests are made to be easily seen.

"We won't all fit in the raft," she argued.

"Because none of us are going in the raft."

"You hired an idiot," Winston said to Sashi.

There wasn't time to screw around, so Rowan took the five life jackets from Sashi's arms and tossed them overboard.

"Hey!" Sashi shouted.

Rowan whirled around in time to see Winston stepping toward him. Stood his ground. "Have any of you made an incursion into enemy territory? Have any of you had to survive behind enemy lines for days, or weeks?"

No one answered. Talia might have done both while living in the forest, but she stayed quiet, letting the weight of his words have their desired effect.

Silence was compliance enough. Rowan looked at Sashi. At her clothes. "Do you own any clothes that aren't bright enough to melt a blind man's eyes?"

She frowned and shook her head. He'd seen enough of her hot-colored clothing to know she owned nothing subtle. He nearly made a joke about her being an easy target, but kept it to himself. The last thing he needed to do was scare people more. He needed them functional.

He pointed to the raft. "We'll load it with weapons and medical supplies. We can cover all that with the black trash bags. They'll float if they fall in, but let's try to keep the bright white med kits covered. We'll swim with the raft as a group. Two hands on the raft at all times, but let's keep our bodies low in the water. I'll stay in the back to hide my face." He turned to Winston, whose skin was equally pale. "You, too. It's not very far, and if the raft isn't supporting our full weight, it will carry us all to shore."

"And when we reach the beach?" Winston asked.

"We dig in."

"I thought we were going to hide," Sashi said.

"If we can, but it's a small island, and we don't know how many Sentinelese there are. Best case scenario, the boat sinks before sunrise and they assume we've left. But if they're looking for us…"

"They'll know every inch of the island," Talia said. "Every tree. Every branch. If something is out of place, they'll notice."

"Then we are without hope," Emmei said, and that right there was the kind of shit-thinking that got people killed. Despair was the soldier's first and worst enemy. It robbed the will to fight.

Thankfully, Talia had an answer to it. "In 1867, the merchant ship *Nineveh* wrecked on one of the reefs. The crew and passengers landed on

North Sentinel and camped on the beach. They held out for eleven days before being picked up by a Royal Navy rescue party."

"How many were there?" Emmei asked, and the way he asked made Rowan think he already knew the answer. He wasn't an anthropologist, but he grew up in a similar tribe on the neighboring Andaman Islands. He would know the island's history better than most. "How many people?"

Talia deflated a little. "One hundred and six."

"One hundred six people," Emmei said. "We are missing another hundred. But do you know how many survived?"

"All of them," Talia said with a trace of doubt.

"Western history prefers to forget its failings," Emmei said. "But we on the islands? We do not forget. When the Sentinelese killed, life got harder for the other tribes."

Rowan couldn't squelch his curiosity. "How many?"

"Fifty six."

Shit, Rowan thought, and he tried to keep the shock from his face. The death toll claimed by the Sentinelese was far more vast than he, and the rest of the world, had been led to believe. It seemed a miracle the island's population hadn't been wiped out long ago. If not for the protective ring of coral keeping ships at bay, he suspected they would have been. The dire twist on Talia's hopeful story changed little. They still had to reach the island before daybreak. With as much confidence as he could muster, he unslung the FN SCAR from his shoulder, gave it a pat, and said, "Well, they didn't have this, and they didn't have me. So let's get in the water, while we're still hard to see."

The sea was warm, but still cooler than the nighttime air. If not for the possibility of being skewered upon arrival, or eaten by a shark on the way, Rowan would have found the experience pleasant. He held the small raft steady while Talia and Mahdi loaded the weapons, emergency kits, and bags of food. Then he kicked away from the floundering *Sea Tiger* and waited as the others slipped into the sea one at a time. Mahdi was the least comfortable in the water, dog paddling to the raft and then clinging to it.

When everyone was in the water, holding on to the raft, Rowan said, "Kick slow. We're not in a rush."

"Speak for yourself," Winston said, eyes on the water.

"Sharks are attracted to fast movements," Emmei said. "Feet look like wounded fish. Slow is good."

"No splashing," Rowan said, "and until we're in a secure location, no talking. If you have to, whisper, and I mean like a mouse fart whisper."

Everyone nodded. Not a word. *Good,* Rowan thought, and then he pointed toward the shoreline with two fingers. Their slow progress through the water was both encouraging and agonizing. Rowan had seen battles, but he always knew who his enemies were and he had a good idea of from where they would attack. In the sea, at night, there was no way to know if a twelve-foot tiger shark was just biding its time, five inches from his feet. He found himself jerking his feet forward occasionally, and he heard Winston sighing out curses when their kicking feet touched.

The swim took them fifteen minutes, and everyone survived intact. Rowan recovered the FN SCAR from the raft and crawled onto the beach, the soft sand sticking to his wet body and clothes. He searched for any sign of the Sentinelese, saw no one, and then inspected the landscape. The sand around him was well traveled, covered with depressions created by Sentinelese feet. That was good. Their fresh footsteps wouldn't stand out in the loose, dry sand, and the waves would wipe away the depressions left in the wet sand.

A tangle of tall roots caught his attention. They formed a small bunker, sans the sand bags and reinforcements, from which they might be able to establish a defensive position. Assault rifle pressed against his shoulder, finger on the trigger, he stood slowly and made himself a target. When nothing happened, he hurried back to the others.

"There's a tangle of tree roots near the jungle," he whispered, his voice barely audible over the gently lapping waves. "We'll be concealed from anyone in the jungle, have clear line of sight down both ends of the beach, and can hide behind the roots if we see anyone coming. Everyone take as much as you can carry, without making noise. We'll move as a group. I want this done in one trip."

The supplies were divvied up, including the raft itself. He recovered his knife and tomahawk, and made sure Talia got the handgun and three spare magazines. Then they moved across the beach, and as quietly as possible, they loaded their supplies into the roughly ten-foot-square twist of roots. The trees fed by the long root system swayed high overhead, megalithic sentinels that had probably stood for hundreds, if not thousands of years.

Using hand gestures, Rowan got everyone digging and pushing sand against the roots, sealing gaps, and lowering their position. When they finished, he could sit up and have just his head showing.

Not bad, he thought. *Now we just need to survive until Rattan Ambani notices his pricey yacht hasn't returned, and sends help brave enough to evacuate us from the beach.*

Sashi stood and adjusted the raft, which lined the bottom of their bunker and held their supplies. She gave it two tugs, stood up straight to inspect her work and brushed the grit from her hands. He was about to whisper a harsh 'Sit. Down.' But it was already too late. When Sashi ducked down behind the protective wall of roots, she had an arrow protruding from her right shoulder.

Sashi fell to her knees, hand coming up to her shoulder, lungs sucking air. Rowan saw what was about to happen and lunged. He tackled Sashi into Mahdi's lap, hand clasped over her mouth. The impact lodged the scream in her throat. She stared at Rowan with wide eyes, breathing heavily through her nose.

"Not a word," Rowan hissed. "Not a damn sound. We don't want to wake up the entire island. Do you understand?"

Sashi's eyes darted back and forth, a panic driven search for danger.

Rowan clasped her cheeks in his hands. Forced her to look at him. "We can survive this, but you need to do what I say. Do you understand?"

Her breathing began to slow as their eye contact lingered, she absorbing confidence from him. She nodded.

Rowan looked up at Mahdi's surprised face, caught his eye, and gave him a look that he hoped transmitted the message, 'Keep her quiet.' When Mahdi nodded as well, Rowan slowly took his hand away from Sashi's mouth. When he was confident she wasn't going to scream, he gave her leg a pat and then moved back to the far side of their bunker, where Talia and Winston were peering through a gap in the root tangle.

"Just one of them," Winston whispered, his handgun clutched, finger on the trigger.

Rowan looked through the small opening. The silhouette of a single man snuck toward them, stepping silently through the sand. He held a bow, a three foot long arrow—like the one in Sashi's shoulder—already nocked and drawn back. The first person he saw would get an arrow in their body.

But he's not sure about what he saw, or who he might have shot, Rowan thought, *or he'd have already raised the alarm. There's still a chance.*

Rowan placed his hand on the man's pistol and eased it down. "We need to be quiet." Before Winston could argue, he added, "I'll take care of it. Just stay still and quiet."

He moved toward the jungle edge of their bunker and paused by Talia. "I'm sorry."

"Do what you need to," she said, though she didn't looked pleased by it. He wished this could be avoided, and prayed there was another solution. But he couldn't see it. All he really knew was that taking a Sentinelese life would probably negatively affect his relationship with Talia. And while the feelings between them were a far cry from love, her friendship felt like a beacon for him, guiding him away from the abyss into which he'd nearly leaped.

Without another whispered word, he placed the FN SCAR down beside Talia, trusting she would know to keep it away from Winston. Then he slid into the jungle where he was swallowed by darkness.

21

TALIA WATCHED ROWAN slip into the jungle without making a sound. She'd seen tribal warriors move with the same silent skill, and could manage it herself, but not while fully dressed in a tactical uniform. It was impressive. When he was gone, she turned her eyes back to the beach, watching the Sentinelese warrior's cautious approach.

He was fifty feet out, taking a step every few seconds. He moved in absolute silence, patiently stalking his prey. She glanced at Sashi, who had managed to stay silent, despite the obvious pain. No doubt, it was that silence that had confounded the man and led to his stealthy approach. She imagined his confusion. Had he hit his target? Had there even been a target? The night played tricks on the eyes, even to those who were accustomed to it.

Talia remained motionless, watching the man hunt them. When he was fifty feet away, she tensed. Where was Rowan?

At thirty feet, she began debating her resolve to not attack the Sentinelese. She had been in precarious situations before, and had always approached tribes as a pacifist, abiding by her rule to not let murder punctuate first contact.

She had been beaten, drugged, bound, and pursued, but most indigenous tribes stopped short of killing strangers. Once a dialogue was established, and her odd physical features—her olive skin tone, tan lines, long black hair, five-foot-eight height, and on occasion, the shape of her breasts which had been supported by a bra, defying gravity's relentless tug—were accepted as not supernatural, threats of violence ended.

But here, on Sentinel Island, violence marked the beginning, and often the end of every encounter. If this man spotted them, she doubted any of the techniques that worked so well with other tribal people would result in anything more than an arrow in her heart.

Doubt crept into her mind as steadily as the man crept through the sand. Would she let the man kill her? Her principles told her to, that her life's mission was to protect tribal people, not kill them, but what good was she if she was dead?

And it wouldn't be the first life she had taken. While she had never fought back against a new tribe, a year ago, during her time with the Mashco-Piro, they had been attacked by a nomadic rival tribe, trying to stake claims on Mashco-Piro territory. She didn't blame them. Their own territory had been logged, their people displaced. But she'd been accepted by the Mashco-Piro and called them her friends. So she fought to defend them and put an arrow in a man's leg. The wound was far from mortal, and the man escaped into the jungle, but the arrow had been poisoned. She never saw a body, but she knew the man was dead. No one survived curare.

She glanced down at her waist, at the leather pouch that resembled a modern fanny pack, and considered what was inside. When she'd recovered the pouch from her cabin, Rowan hadn't questioned it. No one had given it a second glance. But it contained power over life and death.

You brought it for a reason, she told herself. *You knew you might need it.*

Winston tensed, lifting his gun.

Rowan had yet to attack. The man was within twenty-five feet. A few more steps and he would be able to see over the wall of roots. A step or two later, he would be able to attack.

I can't do nothing, Talia decided. If violence was the language the Sentinelese spoke, perhaps it would also be the one they understood.

She placed a gentle hand on Winston's arm and shook her head.

He watched her, incredulous, while she opened the sealed pouch and removed three wooden straws, each one whittled down on one end and notched. She fitted them together, forming an eighteen inch blow gun. Then she removed a wooden case, popped it open, and removed one of twelve darts. The thin wooden spines were wrapped in tight twine on the back, and colored black on the tip, where they had been dipped in curare.

She carefully slipped a single dart into the blowgun, closed the case and returned it to the pouch. When she was finished, Winston was watching her with a mix of humor and doubt. She ignored him and leaned down, slipping the blowgun through the narrow gap and taking aim at the man, now just twenty feet away.

He slowed down, she realized. *Knows where we are, or at least suspects where his victim is hiding. He doesn't know we're all here. Doesn't know he'll die if he takes two more steps.*

She had to wait for him to get closer. Skilled warriors could effectively use a blowgun to kill small prey at a hundred feet, but to get that kind of range and power, you needed a four-foot-long blow gun and a more substantial dart, not to mention large lungs. Her eighteen inch gun and four inch dart needed close range to punch through skin and deliver poison to the bloodstream.

The man stepped closer.

Talia took a slow, deep breath through her nose.

The bow came up, the arrow angled down.

He can see someone.

She angled the blowgun up, aiming for the man's chest. It was an easy target and would quickly spread the poison throughout his bloodstream.

The warrior went rigid, a clear sign he was about to release the bowstring.

Talia closed her eyes, hoped she was making the right decision, and when she decided that self-defense, and the defense of others was justifiable, even against endangered people, she sent the full force of her lungs into the blow gun.

The dart puffed from the gun and was immediately followed by a wet thwack. Human flesh being poked by a dart should have been silent. Talia flinched at the sound, yanked the gun back and looked through the gap. The Sentinelese man was on the ground, but it wasn't a dart sticking out of him, it was a hatchet.

A second silhouette stood where the man had been, a hand raised to its neck.

"What..." Rowan managed to say before falling to his knees. Then to his side.

"Shit!" Talia said, standing in plain sight.

"What are you doing?" Mahdi asked. "Stay down!"

"I shot him," she said. "I shot Rowan."

"With a toy dart," Winston said.

"Poison dart," Talia said, scrambling out of the root bunker. "In the neck. It's going to hit him hard and fast."

Curare was a fast-acting poison, and while fatal, it didn't kill the victim outright. It worked by blocking impulse transmission between nerves and skeletal muscle. The result was involuntary muscle paralysis.

Victims couldn't move. Couldn't breathe. But smooth muscles, like the heart, continued to function. If a victim's breathing—human or animal—was supported for a few hours, until the poison wore off, a full recovery could be made. But in the wilds of the Amazon, most creatures poisoned by curare suffocated to death in minutes, which was exactly what was happening to Rowan.

His breaths were ragged and shallow, his eyes wide. He was fighting the poison, forcing air into and out of his lungs, but in a few seconds, it would be impossible.

She dropped to her knees by his side. "Hold on. Try to relax." It sounded stupid. He was drowning in the open air. And had no idea that she also carried the cure for curare poisoning. She dug into her pouch and removed a long metal container. Popped it open, revealing five small syringes, each one containing Pyridostigmine, a cholinesterase inhibitor that blocks the paralytic effect of curare.

In most cases, the victim would still need respiratory support, as the effects could take thirty minutes to kick in, but in those cases it was delivered long after paralysis set in, not seconds later. She yanked the stopper off the needle, found the dart in his neck, and plucked it out. Then she slid the needle into the same puncture wound and delivered the Pyridostigmine dosage.

She put her finger on his neck. His pulse was racing, but strong.

A final haggard breath wheezed out of him, and then nothing. His body went slack. His heart continued to pound, but it would no longer be delivering fresh oxygen from his lungs. "You'll be okay," she said. She tilted his head back and began performing mouth-to-mouth, filling his lungs with secondhand air, and enough oxygen to keep him alive until he could breathe on his own again.

She watched Rowan's chest rise as she blew in, and deflate when she stopped. After five blows she started to feel lightheaded. How long could she keep this up? *I need help,* she thought, and she glanced back toward the bunker. Winston stood in the bunker, his torso in plain sight, aiming the FN SCAR toward her.

Or was he? The angle was off slightly, aimed to her side where the Sentinelese man had fallen. Why would he be covering the man with a hatchet buried two inches into his spine?

Talia blew into Rowan's mouth again, and then looked. The Sentinelese man was missing. Her eyes flitted to Winston again; his aim had wandered behind her.

She tensed. Listened. Heard a swish of sand.

Talia dove to the side, clumsy.

She received a mouth full of sand, but avoided a swinging hatchet.

Spitting grit, she rolled over. The Sentinelese man, blood curtaining his legs as it poured down his back and around his thighs, stood above her, ready to swing again.

He should be dead. He should be dead!

The axe rose higher. She expected to hear a gunshot, but Winston held his fire.

Then the man swung, the blade sweeping down toward her hands raised in defense. The hatchet would take her hands, and then her life. But the downward arc never finished. The warrior's arm was caught.

Rowan stood beside the man, looking equal parts determined and ready to pass out. He yanked the smaller man's hand up and slipped the knife from the sheath on his belt and slipped it between the man's ribs, once, twice, three times, driving the man back with each blow.

When the Sentinelese warrior fell, Rowan went down with him. While the man lay still, Rowan rolled onto his back, his face red, straining. He gasped, sucking in a lung full of air like he'd just surfaced from a long free dive. After five deep breaths, he pushed himself into a seated position and said, "You poisoned me."

She crouched beside him. Felt his pulse. Strong and slower. "Wasn't aiming for you."

"Thought you wouldn't kill to survive," he said.

"Nobility is great until you're faced with a violent death." She shrugged. "I'm not perfect."

He smiled and pushed himself up. He searched the area, his eyes lingering on Winston, who still held the FN SCAR, but had lowered his aim. Then he pointed at the dead again man. "Arms or legs?"

"What?"

"We need to carry him to the bunker. Hide his body. Do you want his arms or legs?"

Talia moved to the man's head, bent down and picked up his arms. Working together, she and Rowan carried the man to the bunker and rolled him over the wall. After moving the supplies and the raft, they pushed the corpse into the ditch they had dug, covered him with a layer of sand and covered it all with the raft again. When they were done, Rowan made a quick trip back to the beach, brushed sand over every spot of blood and then returned to the protection of their alcove, which had already begun to smell like death.

Despite being groggy and overwhelmed with nausea from the curare and its antidote, Rowan spent the next half hour treating Sashi's wound. The med kits had everything he needed, including local anesthesia, which allowed him to remove the arrow, disinfect, stitch, and bandage the wound without any fear of Sashi shouting in pain. She thanked him when he finished, but his response was to shush her.

The next two hours passed in silence, everyone eagerly awaiting the sun. Talia knew they would be easier to spot in the day, but they would also be able to see. Fear of the unknown, especially in the world's still dark and mysterious places, was often far more poignant than a death you saw coming.

Still an hour from dawn, someone nudged her foot. She looked back and saw no limbs near hers, and no one looking. Rowan was watching one end of the beach. Mahdi and Winston watched the other. Emmei was sound asleep, and thankfully not a snorer. And Sashi was on her back, eyes on the star-filled sky, which had grown even more vivid as the moon slipped over the horizon.

Talia looked out at the beach again, but then felt another thump. She turned back and again saw nothing but the raft she rested on.

Then the sensation of being touched began to resolve.

The bump had come from below.

And then she saw it, the raft shaking, pushed up by something from beneath.

Pushed by the man they had buried.

The *dead* man they had buried.

22

EVERY MEMBER OF the expedition pushed away from the rumbling raft, forming a human crater with Allah-knew-what at the core. Mahdi had seen the man die violently—twice. That he could be moving defied not just logic, but the laws of physics and nature.

"What is happening?" he asked, the question coming out as something like a squeak.

"A burrowing animal?" Rowan guessed. "Attracted to the smell?"

Emmei, who had been startled awake, slid up and over the root bunker wall, more afraid of the dead Sentinelese man inside the bunker than the living outside of it. "There are no burrowing animals in the Andaman Islands large enough to move a body, or carnivorous enough to be interested in it. He is dead rising."

Dead rising.

While living in London, Mahdi became familiar with the West's zombie obsession. He had ascribed it to the Christian worldview, which proclaimed that the dead had risen and would again, though in a far less gruesome manner. The Muslim world held no such views. The deceased stayed in the ground. Even the great prophet Muhammad did not return the dead to life, and had remained in his grave after his death. He wouldn't have guessed Emmei had an interest in such things, but then, many cultures on Earth believed in the dead rising in one form or another. It's possible the Andaman Island tribes had their own views on the undead.

"If I'd poisoned him," Talia said, but let the comment hang. She hadn't poisoned the man. Rowan had stabbed him three times after burying a hatchet in his spine.

"He's dead," Mahdi said. "Something else is moving him."

"Put that away," Rowan said, pointing at the gun in Winston's hand, aimed at the raft.

Winston looked like he smelled something foul. "Fuck no."

"We might need the raft," Rowan argued. "And a single shot will wake up the entire island."

All eyes turned to Winston. The gun in his hand was more of a threat than whatever was moving the raft. "Fine," he muttered and lowered the weapon.

"We still need to stop it," Sashi said, clinging to the root wall, ready to throw herself over.

Rowan yanked the food bags out of the raft, inspecting them for holes. Then he removed the medkits. He slipped his assault rifle from his shoulder, straddled the raft, and raised the weapon's stock above his head. When the raft shook again, Rowan brought the weapon down, smashing the flat bottom where it had wobbled. There was no shriek of pain, though there was a wet crunch. Something organic had been crushed.

Rowan raised the weapon again. Waited. Just as he started lowering the rifle, something shifted on the opposite side of the shallow grave. He clubbed down again. Another crunch. "Must be more than one of them."

"Rats," Talia said. "Probably escaped from one of the shipwrecks. The *Nineveh*, or the *Primrose*. An invasive species like rats would flourish on an island like this."

"How's the saying go?" Rowan asked. "If you see one rat…"

Winston chuckled. "I think that's a myth."

Mahdi found himself relaxing. He could handle rats, and it appeared Rowan had solved their problem. Nothing stirred for a full minute. Then the group seemed to collectively remember they were marooned on North Sentinel Island, exposed on a beach. Rowan and Talia quickly reloaded the raft with the med kits and bags of food. Then everyone returned to their hiding spots. Even Emmei climbed back inside the walls, but his former sleepy demeanor was missing. He looked ready to spring away.

Mahdi slid down into the bunker, lowering his head below the root wall, but keeping his feet away from the raft. He felt silly, being afraid of a dead man, and two dead rats, but he wasn't the only one avoiding the raft. Only Talia seemed unfazed by the strange events. He didn't know a lot about her, but what little he did know spoke of a life on the fringe of civilization, where magic and spirits still explained what science had understood for millennia. To her, this might not even register as odd. She carried herself with an air of, 'just another day at the office,' but perhaps it was an act?

"Back to business," Rowan whispered once the group was settled. "No talking, no standing. The sun will be up in an hour and then we'll—"

There are moments in life that are so off, like witnessing the martyrdom of a friend turned suicide bomber, that the mind has trouble comprehending the sensory information being transmitted by the body. When Mahdi saw the trash bags of food arc into the air, followed by the med kits, and the life raft, he watched with a strange kind of detachment. It was as though a localized portion of the world suddenly reversed gravity.

It made no sense—not until the Sentinelese man buried beneath the sand sat up.

Whispered curses in four languages punctuated the bunker's immediate evacuation. Not remembering his frantic retreat, Mahdi found himself face down in the sand. When he pushed himself up, he knelt beside Emmei and Winston. Sashi, Talia, and Rowan were on the far side, all eyes on the man who had usurped their hiding place.

The Sentinelese man sat in his grave, coated in sand that had stuck to the blood that had drained from his chest and back.

"What the fuck?" Winston said, aiming his gun again. "What the fuck?"

This time Rowan didn't chide the man for raising his weapon. Instead, he joined him, aiming the FN SCAR at the man's head, panic in his eyes. The soldier had seen war, but never anything like this. Again, only Talia seemed unafraid, watching with squinted, suspicious eyes.

The Sentinelese man turned his head toward Mahdi, who scurried back until the man spoke. "Lazoaf."

Mahdi froze, staring into the black eyes.

"What did he say?" Talia asked, appearing startled for the first time. She picked up a handful of sand and pelted the back of the man's head. "Hey!"

The warrior's head snapped around with unnatural speed.

Talia flinched back, but stood her ground.

The man raised his hand toward her, bent and broken.

There were no rats…

"Lazoaf!" the man shouted.

Rowan snapped into action, drawing his knife and burying it in the top of the man's head. After the hard crunch and wet smack, Mahdi expected the man to fall.

He did not.

The man's body locked, transformed into a living statue. Rowan's hand came away from the knife, a disturbed look in his eyes.

"What?" Winston asked. "What do you see?"

"He's watching me," Rowan said. "Tracking me with his eyes."

Winston shook his head, lowering his aim and stepping back. "Not possible."

"Dead rising," Emmei said.

Emmei's superstitious beliefs seemed far less incredulous while looking at the still living man with a knife in his head, the man who had already been dead twice, who didn't cry out when his hands were broken. But it couldn't be possible. Couldn't be real.

"What does 'lazoaf' mean?" Rowan asked. "They said the same thing to me."

"I—I don't know," Mahdi said. It was a lie. He knew the word, but there was no way it shared the same meaning, even if it did make sense. There were 6500 languages spoken in the world, each with hundreds of thousands of words, all with their own unique sound. But with all that language, there were words that overlapped, combinations of sounds that even when spelled differently, or with entirely different alphabets, that sounded the same, but had different meanings.

The English word 'gift" means 'poison' in German, and they are both Latin languages. 'Kiss' in English means 'urine' in Swedish. Even the same word between two different cultures that both speak the same language can have different meanings. While in London, Mahdi learned that pants, braces, biscuits, and chaps all had very different meanings from the American English he had been taught.

That 'Lazoaf' sounded like a word Mahdi knew in one of the seven languages he spoke, was coincidence.

"What are you doing?" Sashi asked, and Mahdi noticed she was watching Rowan, who had lifted his hatchet.

"He's going to give our position away," Rowan said, hauling the hatchet back. "Dead or not, there is one way to make sure he can't talk."

But before Rowan could swing and decapitate the man, a wet slurp stopped him, and nearly stopped Mahdi's heart. The Sentinelese man's face moved, as though something underneath were fighting to come out, the skin going slack, and then flexing.

With a slick tear, a long horizontal triangle of flesh peeled back from the man's forehead. Pink goo stretched between the opening flesh and the muscly skull beneath, snapping as it spread open. A boney hook that twitched back and forth, tipped the end of the flesh.

Rowan's arms went slack. He stepped back out of the bunker, confidence obliterated.

Six more stripes of tapered flesh tore apart and slurped open. Gelatinous sinews stretched and oozed as the man's body began to tremble. The face beneath his face was muscle and bone; his eyes, free of eyelids, bulged.

Mahdi looked to the others, hoping to see some kind of understanding or recognition in their eyes, but he saw only his own fear reflected. Even Talia was unnerved, slowly stepping backward.

The muscles on the man's face twitched and contorted, becoming something less than human. The flesh beneath his bulbous eyes bulged, split, and snapped open, revealing a second set of eyes that looked at Mahdi while the first set remained locked on Rowan.

The jaw dropped open, lower than it should have been able to, and a high-pitched wail rose from its chest. The sound was followed by the report of a gun, echoing out over the sea, and through the jungle. The man's—the thing's—head thrashed back as the bullet Winston fired punched a neat hole in the front and a fleshy geyser from the back. The body fell back, still twitching.

When the ringing in Mahdi's ears faded, he heard the sound of feet running through sand. He looked up and found himself to be the last expedition member still standing beside the bunker. Rowan, Talia, and Sashi had fled in one direction, while Winston and Emmei ran the other way. Mahdi's instinct was to stay with Rowan and Talia, but when he looked back for them, they'd slipped into the night.

The body gurgled and spurred him into motion, sending him after Winston and Emmei, while every living person—if they *were* people—living on North Sentinel Island rose from their beds, and perhaps their graves.

23

ROWAN HAD RETREATED several times during his career as an Army Ranger, but each time the move had been strategic and well thought out, never once motivated by fear. But now, as he charged down the beach, wishing the shifting sand beneath his feet was pavement, he felt and comprehended little more than an all-consuming primal terror. He remembered this feeling from childhood, walking home from a friend's house at night, leaves blowing in the wind, his imagination chasing him, breathless, all the way home. But now, it wasn't his imagination looming behind him, and the leaves were a very real monster: a man turned thing, dead four times over and still moving.

The further he got from the Sentinelese man, the more his senses returned. He glanced back, saw Sashi and Talia on his heels, and the dead man slumped back in the sand, twitching but not chasing.

Fear subsided, giving way to training.

You're in the open, he told himself, *find cover.*

On North Sentinel Island, finding cover meant one thing: the jungle. The plan had been to avoid the jungle at all costs. The people living on the island would know the terrain, where every path led, and every hiding place. Their only chance was to think unconventionally. For a Sentinelese, who had no contact with the outside world, and zero military training, thinking like a soldier might be the kind of unconventional thing they needed to survive. He hoped so, because it was the best he could manage.

He wished there was another option, but since Winston pulled that trigger, their path had been set. The beach might even the playing field, but if the Sentinelese swarmed their position, and were as hard to kill as the freak show behind him, they'd be overwhelmed in seconds. And there was nowhere to hide on the beach.

A break in the foliage revealed a path that moved alongside the beach before bending away into the jungle. From the water, the path would be invisible.

Rowan stopped short of the path. Shoved a thick, leaf-laden branch up and said, "Here."

Talia slipped into the dense jungle without a word. She looked spooked, but like Rowan, she was guided by instincts that would help keep them alive. Sashi stopped, uncertain. She pointed at the path. "But there's a—"

"That's where they will be coming from," Rowan said, and he felt relieved when Sashi's protests ended there. For her to survive what little remained of the night, the following day, and perhaps a second night, she would have to do exactly what he said and when he said it, all without making a sound. It was a tall order for someone not trained in the grueling art of behind-enemy-lines survival, but Sashi wasn't a fool.

Not like Winston.

He'd all but doomed them the moment he pulled that trigger. The scream was loud, but it wouldn't have carried the same distance, and Rowan had been a half second away from using the hatchet to end things silently. If anyone died on this island, it was on Winston's head.

Rowan decided that if the expedition survived the island, and Winston managed to as well, the man would get a swift kick in the nuts. If people died, he'd get a lot worse. Rowan slipped into the jungle and gently lowered the branch back in place. Darkness swallowed him into a stomach composed of twisting roots and thick leaves.

"Can we just stay in here?" Sashi asked, a tremble in her voice.

"Too close to the path," Talia replied. "They'll smell us."

Rowan would have agreed with Sashi. They were well concealed and when people ran, they usually went as far from the scene of the crime as they could get. Staying relatively close might be the last place anyone would look for them. But the island scents would be intimately familiar to the Sentinelese. His body odor mixed with hints of deodorant and Sashi's fruity shampoo, both of which had survived their dip in the ocean, would be a fragrant beacon to any Sentinelese that passed by.

"And," Talia put a hand on Sashi's arm, "they'll see you. Take off your clothes."

"What?" Despite the night's horrors, Sashi looked scandalized. Indian culture was modest, and the only bits of skin Sashi had shown since he'd met her were her hands and face.

"You're dressed like a piece of fruit," Talia said, pointing out Sashi's maroon trousers, beige shirt, and orange scarf. "You can die brightly or let your skin hide you. What color is your underwear?"

"B-black," Sashi said.

"Well, then we'll match." Talia removed her shirt, revealing a black bikini top. Her shorts, which were black, remained on. Even if they weren't black, Rowan wasn't sure Talia would have gone full native, as the belt held her blowgun and darts and the handgun he'd given her, and the pocket held her folding knife.

Sashi glanced back at Rowan who made no effort to look away. "You can't be self-conscious while fighting for your life," he told her. "And I'm not taking off my clothes because my pale ass would shine like a lighthouse."

She smiled and shed her clothing, slowly at first, and then more quickly, not because she was resigned to the idea, but because Talia was waving her on. It wouldn't be long before the first Sentinelese showed up, and they needed to be gone when that happened. Sashi was very skinny, but she appeared to be in good shape. Stripped down to her very conservative black bra and underwear, she was uncomfortable, but she was already harder to see in the dark.

"Just pretend you're at the beach," he told her.

She motioned to her discarded clothing that Talia was covering with soil. "I wear that to the beach."

"Stay close," Talia said, and then she climbed over a tangle of roots. Rowan felt thrown for a moment. He'd assumed charge and then lost it, but this was Talia, who'd spent a good portion of her life living in jungles like this. If she could lead them to a good hiding spot, they could assess the situation there.

Sashi glanced toward him, probably wondering who was in charge, too. He gave a nod, and she followed after Talia.

They moved through the jungle for five slow minutes, stepping as quietly as possible, which was far too loud. Talia moved with the stealth of a jaguar, somehow always finding a root on which to walk. But Sashi stepped in all the wrong places, and Rowan's boots were merciless to the dried detritus on the forest floor. He was about to say something, when all at once, they moved in silence. It was as though the universe's audio had been muted.

"What happened?" Sashi asked, her voice loud in the strange silence.

Talia turned back, and Rowan noticed he could see her a little easier. He glanced up. The sky, barely visible through the trees, was purple. The sun was rising.

"Forest is clear," Talia whispered, looking down.

For as far as he could see, the jungle floor was free of undergrowth, fallen leaves, and dead tree branches. The thick canopy overhead explained the lack of small plants. They couldn't grow without sunlight. But the jungle looked like it had been swept clean, like a Disney World garden. 'Manicured' was the best word he could come up with for it.

"Nothing wasted," Talia said.

She was speaking to herself, but he understood well enough. Being trapped on an island, the Sentinelese had limited resources. Everything that fell from a tree would have a purpose, as food, shelter, weapons, or tools. It also made for quiet walking.

"Where are we going?" Sashi asked, and Rowan was beginning to wonder the same thing. Too far and they risked walking straight into a Sentinelese camp, or cutting through a trail.

"There." Talia pointed ahead. It wasn't so much a cave as it was a natural shelter formed by a partially toppled tree, the root system lifting up a rug of soil. It wasn't perfect, but it was better than—

Rowan ducked before he knew why, dropping to his stomach. Talia did as well, tugging Sashi down beside her. Then he saw them, two Sentinelese men, stark naked, walking casually and carrying on a conversation as though no gun shot had been fired, no tribe member murdered, and no search was underway.

They were either ignorant to the events on the beach, which seemed impossible, they were supremely confident in the expedition's eventual demise, which was entirely possible, or they knew something that Rowan didn't, which given the dead man's ability to self-resurrect, not to mention his blooming face and four eyes, was without doubt.

What the hell is this place? he wondered. He remained motionless until the men had passed. Then he crawled to the natural lean-to with Talia and Sashi. They moved to the back, pressing themselves into the roots and earth.

In the silence that followed, he heard a gentle breeze whispering in the leaves high above, and the distant thump of waves. The tide was coming in. "We can stay here. If a boat comes, we'll hear it."

Talia gave a nod and Sashi tried to make herself smaller.

As they settled in for a long stay, Rowan tried to analyze the night's events, but there was too much and he was too tired. It hadn't been long since the man on the beach split open and spoke, but it already felt like a bad dream, fading with each minute. Twenty minutes into their stay, all he could think about was how thirsty he was. If he didn't have bright white skin, he'd happily shed the black tactical gear. Not only did it weigh him down, but it kept him sweating, and with the sun on the rise, it would only get hotter and more humid. He might have to undress despite his bright skin or risk dehydration.

A tap on his cheek caught his breath inside his chest.

What was that?

The tap repeated, then tickled his cheek. Something was dripping on him. He leaned back and looked up. A gnarled, twisted root came to a stop above his face, a bead of moisture dangling from the tip. He opened his mouth and caught the drip. He looked at Talia, who was watching. "Water."

Her eyebrows raised. She was thirsty, too.

Talia opened her knife, slid closer, and cut the root, keeping her thumb over the end like she'd done this before. Then again, she probably had. Finding drinkable water was one of the biggest challenges for surviving in the wild, and in a jungle like this, some species of trees stored enough to drink. He had no idea what species of tree this was, but if it leaked water, he was going to drink it.

Rowan licked his lips as Talia positioned herself under the root. Then she moved her thumb and let the fluid trickle into her mouth. She put her thumb over the cut again, swished the liquid around in her mouth, and swallowed. "Water," she said. "Sweet, too."

Sashi drank next, and then Rowan, his thirst setting him on the root like a calf to an udder. They took turns until the tree had given all it could. As early morning sunlight snuck through the wind-massaged jungle canopy, Rowan started to feel good. Almost buzzed.

He was about to comment on it when a familiar smell reached his nose.

"They lit the fires again," Talia whispered. Her pupils were dilated, but maybe that was just because they were in the shade?

Sashi gave a strange sort of laugh and tossed some dirt. Being the smallest of them, and having drunk the most, if the root-water had intoxicating properties, it would affect her the most.

He was about to comment on the fires, and the water, when the relaxing effect of the tree's water was undone by the sound of screaming, and then gunfire. Was it possible that their flight through the jungle had been uneventful simply because the Sentinelese were chasing the others? He was about to ask when Talia muttered a curse and started crawling out from their hiding spot.

"What are you doing?" Sashi asked.

"If they die," Talia said, "the Sentinelese die."

Sashi was aghast. "You still want to *protect* these people? I'm not even sure they *are* people. And I don't think it will make a difference."

Talia squinted at her. "Why?"

Before Sashi could answer, more gunfire rocked the island. Whatever was happening, Winston was putting up a fight.

Before Rowan could weigh in, Talia stood and slid into the jungle, comfortable and stealthy. He moved to follow her, but Sashi stopped him. "We can't leave!"

"You should stay," he said. " We'll come back."

"What if you don't?"

"Follow the plan. When you hear a boat, hit the beach. If it's close, swim. If it's not, try to catch their attention. Maybe find your scarf and wave it around. But we'll be back."

Rowan didn't really believe it. Running into battle with the Sentinelese was probably a suicide mission. He'd much rather stay with Sashi, but Talia was his friend. He wouldn't let her face the enemy on her own. He slipped his hatchet from his belt, handed it to Sashi, and said, "Be quiet and careful, and you'll be okay."

Then he chased after Talia, finding it ironic that, after being kicked out of the Rangers, his life would still come to an end in battle. Had he been a Viking, he might look forward to what was coming, but he was just a guy from New Hampshire, and he was just starting to feel like life might still be worth living.

24

CONFLICT DEFINED HUMANITY, at the pinnacle of civilization and in the depths of the wild, where the concept of civility had yet to be considered. Talia knew this. Had experienced the dark nature of mankind for herself, as a child, as a teenager, in the military, and in forgotten jungles with ancient secrets. But she had never seen anything like she'd witnessed on the beach. North Sentinel Island wasn't just a dangerous place, it was sinister.

Talia had witnessed horrors through the lens of an anthropologist, analyzing the culture and history of a people, seeing how those things led to a path of violence. In that way, she could understand the acts of human sacrifice, cannibalism, and subjugation. But anthropology had nothing to say about men who were nearly impossible to kill, whose faces opened up, and who had four eyes.

She wasn't even sure genetics or evolution could explain it. The Sentinelese had evolved separately from the rest of mankind for sixty thousand years. Natural selection on the contained island had kept their stature small, the tallest of the men being five feet, and the women four foot five. From a distance, their appearance wasn't surprising at all. Even up close, she hadn't noticed anything unusual.

Not until the man came back to life the first time.

There was no evolutionary benefit to having a face that could split open, or a hidden set of eyes, and nothing on the planet could return from the dead. There were animals that could regenerate limbs, that could freeze solid, thaw out, and go about their business, but once a man was dead—from a severed spine, from a knife in the chest or the head—it was permanent, unless you were friends with Dr. Frankenstein or Jesus Christ.

But the inhumanity of the island's inhabitants didn't mean they didn't deserve to live in peace. It probably meant they would never be successfully integrated into the outside world, but exterminating them wasn't the solution. If anything, they should be protected because of their differences. Of course, that meant they'd be kidnapped, put in laboratories, and studied.

The future of the Sentinelese people was tenuous at best, but she would help them if she could…if they didn't murder her first.

Running through the forest should have been easy, but she found herself bumping into trees and stumbling over the tangles of roots that twisted across the ground like giant varicose veins. She'd crossed terrain like this before without any trouble, but her limbs seemed like they were on a timed delay. Her shoulder caught a tree as she ran past, the impact spinning her around. She dropped to her knees. Stopped the fall with her hands. Started laughing.

Am I high? she wondered, thinking about the sweet liquid they'd drunk from the tree. *I shouldn't have done that. I know better.*

She flinched when Rowan's boots stopped beside her. She looked up to find him smiling, too.

"You nailed that tree," he said.

She snorted and said, "I think that tree root water is psychotropic."

He tapped the side of his nose. "I'm not sure it was the tree juice."

Talia breathed deeply through her nose. The fragrant scent of smoke filled the air. It was subtle, but omnipresent.

"Islands like this have their own weather systems sometimes, right?"

She nodded. It wasn't uncommon for clouds to form over North Sentinel Island and nowhere else.

"So maybe they learned how to fishbowl the island."

"A collective buzz?"

He shrugged. "There's no Netflix here. No sports teams. No entertainment."

"And no inhibitions," Talia said. It made sense. Thanks to the coral reefs surrounding the island, food was abundant and easy to gather. As long as they had shelter and fresh water, what was to stop the Sentinelese from spending their days shagging and getting high? If that was true, aside from the starfish-face thing, North Sentinel Island was as close to a primal paradise as she'd ever seen.

But if that were true, why were the Sentinelese so violent? Had they evolved so far away from humanity that they viewed visitors as an entirely different species? The combination of modern technology, clothing, skin tones, and facial features, not to mention the strange gifts left by visitors, made that a possibility already. The just-beneath-the-surface physiological differences solidified the concept. How had they reacted upon seeing the undead man's face peel apart? How would the rest of the world react? With guns, needles, and eventually carpet bombs.

She couldn't tell the Sentinelese any of that. The best she could hope for was to prevent them from killing everyone and creating an international incident.

She lifted a hand. "Help me up."

Rowan pulled her up without any trouble.

"You don't seem to be as affected," she observed.

"Because I'm angry," he said. "I've been working hard to not feel like this. Don't appreciate not being able to escape it."

"Sorry," she said, but she spoke the word with a smile she couldn't control. "Let's keep moving."

"A little slower," he said, and he took the lead. She followed without a word, placing her feet where his had been, staying balanced, and as a result, making better time than she had been able to while running like a human pinball.

There hadn't been another gunshot, which was either a good thing, or a very bad thing.

After slowly climbing a slope and lying down at the top, they discovered the truth. Rowan lay down first, peeking over the top and then ducking down. He pressed a finger to his lips. The look on his face was so serious, she nearly giggled again, but she managed some self-control as she lowered herself and inched toward the crest.

The buzz faded some as she looked down on the scene below.

There were two Sentinelese men lying on their backs. One man, with a crescent of dotted scars on his forehead, had two holes in his chest. The other, wearing just a bright yellow cord around his waist, had been shot in the leg, his heart, and his head. Blood seeped into the cleared forest floor, which absorbed the liquid like a sponge. Three more men wielding spears stood around Winston, who was bleeding from a wound on the side of his head. He was on his knees, hands slack at his sides, a surprising lack of fear in his eyes.

"The fuck are you people?" Winston asked.

Talia didn't hear a 'who' or 'what' at the beginning of the question, but she would have liked to learn the answers to both as well.

The warriors ignored him, talking amongst themselves in a language Talia couldn't understand, and which sounded like nothing else she'd heard before…or like everything else she'd heard before. There were sounds reminiscent of Chinese, Swedish, German, English, and several African dialects, all of which were very different, but somehow blended into something fluid. Something new. Despite Winston's current predicament, she found herself smiling again.

The Sentinelese men kept their multi-pronged spears angled toward Winston, but they appeared to be discussing the bodies. They weren't agitated, or worried.

They're high, too, she thought. Chill with each other, but still capable of savage violence. But then, why was Winston still alive?

And where were Mahdi and Emmei?

The men became more animated, speaking and smiling down at the corpses. Talia didn't understand why at first, but then she saw it for herself. The two bodies were being absorbed by the earth. They weren't decomposing or splitting apart, they were simply sinking down, like the ground had gone soft. The dark earth wrapped around their bodies, sucking them downward until both men were gone.

Winston looked unnerved for the first time, shaking his head, and muttering to himself. At the same time, he was watching the men, never taking his eyes off them or their spears. He was waiting for the right moment. But for what? He was overweight and out of shape. What could he do against—

Winston moved so fast that neither Talia nor the Sentinelese men fully understood what was happening, until the wrenched-free spear was turned around and thrust into the chest of the man Winston had stolen it from.

The spear slipped out of the man's chest. He dropped to the ground in a lifeless heap. Winston stood, facing off against the two remaining Sentinelese men, who hadn't even flinched. They kept their spears raised, but made no effort to attack.

Winston stabbed his spear forward. "C'mon!" The blow was easily deflected by one of the warriors, while the other swiped his spear across Winston's chest. The prongs cut through fabric and skin, but nothing close to being a mortal wound. All it did was incite Winston further. He spun the spear in his hand, like he was testing the weight, getting a feel for how it moved. Then he attacked.

Three quick jabs failed to strike either Sentinelese man, but did drive them apart. Then Winston spun the weapon, and his body in a surprising display that nearly made Talia laugh. He looked equal parts dangerous and ridiculous, like a hippo doing ballet, like Disney should animate it and put it to classical music.

And then there was blood, spraying from a slice in one warrior's neck. The attack looked like it would miss, but as he withdrew the spear, Winston flicked in his wrist, putting a neat cut in the man's jugular. He spun, crouched, and swept the spear out again, this time drawing across the inside of the man's leg. The femoral artery.

More blood flowed.

The ground sucked it up. Thirsty for more.

Talia glanced at Rowan, who looked as stunned as she felt. He met her eyes, and she could see he was thinking the same thing. *Who the hell is Winston?* She pointed at the FN SCAR still over Rowan's back. He shook his head and mouthed, 'too loud.' Did he want Winston to die? Or did he think the bulbous man could survive on his own, without a gun, which would draw more of the Sentinelese to them?

The latter proved true as the last Sentinelese standing went on the attack. He struck with a wild flurry that was uncoordinated, but impossible to predict and block. Winston tried, but was driven back. Then the man stopped, held his ground and waited.

Was this how the Sentinelese fought? Did they take turns? Or was the man simply trying to confuse Winston? If Sentinelese warriors took turns attacking and defending, the man would fare about as well against Winston as the Red Coats had against New England's Minutemen.

Winston feigned an attack, forcing the man back. Then he threw the spear, aiming for the man's chest. The strike was blocked, but Winston hadn't stopped moving. He dove. Rolled across the ground. Came up with his recovered handgun, which he held like a pro. Pulled the trigger three times, two shots in the chest, one in the head.

Definitely not a filmmaker.

Winston stood, ejected the magazine and slapped in a new one without looking. He chambered a round and began tapping the bodies with his boot toe.

Rowan slid back behind the hill. Talia followed him. He used a series of hand motions that she thought must be some kind of Ranger hand speak. She didn't understand it all, but enough to know that they were leaving without Winston. She wanted to argue, to explain that if Winston, or any of them, died on the island, it could be justification to kill all the Sentinelese, which appeared to be more doable than their first encounter suggested. But the look in his eyes said he understood something that she didn't. At the very least, she would have him explain when they were out of earshot.

She climbed down a series of roots like a forty-five degree angled ladder, but she stopped short of the bottom. The smell of death cut through the subtle smoky fragrance that permeated the jungle. She heard, and then felt, footsteps.

She closed her eyes and pictured the island from above, their course south, into the jungle, and then east to find Winston. The sound approached from her left, from the north.

From the beach.

25

MAHDI WAS ALONE. Normally, he'd welcome the solitude. It meant he was safe. Unfound. But on this island, after the things he had witnessed, he would have welcomed company. Then again, company could mean a hunting party, or Winston, and he wasn't sure which was worse.

After fleeing the beach, and the hideous man who would not die, Winston and Emmei had followed chaotic paths, neither knowing where they were going, nor concerned with the other's direction. A moment of indecision, unsure of whom to follow, had left Mahdi alone in the dark. He had considered back-tracking to Rowan and Talia—they would have stayed together—but that meant passing the man on the beach, and risking contact with any Sentinelese summoned by the gunshot.

In the end, he chose to head in the general direction he'd last seen Emmei running. The man might not know the island, but the jungle's fauna would be familiar to him. If he'd spent much time living in the Andaman jungles, Sentinel Island might not be too dissimilar.

Twenty feet into the dense jungle, his plan had been consumed by darkness. So he found a tangle of roots and young-growth trees just ten feet from the beach, crawled inside and somehow fell asleep.

He was mortified when growling woke him to the morning sun. He spun in his hiding spot, searching for danger. When he found none, he remembered that he snored.

After a cautious emergence from his hiding spot, Mahdi searched the area, found two sets of footprints and followed the shallower of the two, hoping it would lead him to Emmei. Which of the two men was better suited to surviving the island was debatable. His distrust of Winston was not.

After just fifty feet, Emmei's trail became harder to follow. The forest cleared, leaving no opportunity for bent or broken branches. The cleared earth was tangled with roots. There was plenty of soil to walk on, but if you wanted to move through the jungle without leaving a print, it was possible, and Emmei seemed to be doing just that.

Mahdi scurried from tree to tree for what felt like an hour, heading in the direction the last foot print was headed. He spent a portion of the time moving, but the majority of it looking and listening. The jungle seemed quiet. They had seen birds from offshore, but he hadn't spotted any in the trees above or heard any morning songs.

He was about to give up on Emmei, and head toward the shore, when he found the trail again. It wasn't hard. Emmei had shed one shoe, and fifty feet beyond, the other.

Mahdi paused at the second shoe, considering Emmei's choice. Mahdi had slipped on a few roots, and he frequently heard the clunk of his shoes when he stepped. It made sense. Mahdi shed his shoes, collected Emmei's and buried them in the crook of a tree. He started out again and came across a trail of clothing. Emmei hadn't stopped at his shoes. Over a hundred feet, Mahdi found the man's pants, T-shirt, and then underwear.

Emmei wasn't young, nor short, and a first world resort diet had given him a round belly, but maybe he could pass as Sentinelese? Was that the man's hope? Mahdi doubted a close inspection would end in Emmei's favor, but maybe he could move through the jungle unmolested if he looked like one of them. Or perhaps he was hoping his dark skin would help him blend in?

Mahdi looked down at his own body. He'd shed his white shirt before abandoning the *Sea Tiger*. His skin was deeply tanned, far lighter than Emmei's, but his pleated khaki shorts would stand out. He knew what Talia would do. Rowan, too—and apparently Emmei. When evading a violent tribe trapped on an island, clothing wasn't optional, it was dangerous.

But the shame of nakedness was powerful, ingrained in the human psyche for about the same amount of time the Sentinelese had protected their island from outsiders. He opted to keep his shorts, but promised to shed them, and the purple underwear beneath, should it become prudent.

Now shoeless, Mahdi found moving through the jungle far easier, and quieter. He could hop from root to root, leaving no trail behind him. Emmei had been less careful after shedding his clothing, leaving an easy to follow path of bare feet. Mahdi thought he was overconfident in his ability to hide in plain sight, but at least Emmei seemed to have a plan, and a direction. His path never wavered. Never showed any sign of stopping.

Mahdi's only apprehension came from the fact that Emmei's path seemed to be headed inland, or at least across a portion of the island. So far, he'd been walking steadily uphill. The island, at its highest point was just four hundred feet above sea level. Mahdi estimated he was currently at about half that height, but surrounded by trees, with no clear view of the coast, there was no way to be sure.

A rich aroma filled the air. It was unlike anything Mahdi had smelled in Palestine or London. The closest comparison he could think of was Kew Gardens. The botanical gardens in London housed an astounding array of plant-life, smelling of earth, decay, flowers, and pollen. He'd left with a headache, and a sense of wonder. He'd felt something similar upon arriving at the Sandal-Foot Resort, but the smell there was dominated by the ocean. Here, there wasn't a hint of salt. Here, the air smelled of lush green life and organic decay that had been missing from the cleared jungle floor.

Mahdi slowed as Emmei's trail turned right, following a steeper grade that led to a wall of green. The canopy ahead thinned a little, allowing more light to reach the forest floor, resulting in a tangle of leafy plants, ferns, and vines. Steam hung in the air, alive with streaks of sun that shifted in time with bird songs as the wind picked up. The sudden magic and beauty of the place brought a tear to his eye and stumbled him back.

"I don't belong here," he whispered, voice shaky as a deep sense of the forbidden slipped through his pores and invaded his body. He felt like a child again, trespassing in his neighbor's yard, despite the signs, despite the warnings from his friends. He shouldn't have been there, and he had paid a long and hard price for his curiosity. He felt the same thing here, only magnified.

The shush of a body slipping through foliage snapped him from the past and sent him scrambling for cover behind a tightly bunched stand of trees that rose a hundred feet before branching out.

Standing still, breath held, he heard voices. The fluid sounds were casual, unconcerned. Maybe they didn't know? Maybe they hadn't heard the gunshot on the beach? That didn't seem likely. Then why weren't they agitated?

He listened to the syllables, the cadence of the language. There were brief snippets of recognition followed by sounds he could only describe as ancient. Whatever language it was, it resembled nothing else on the planet in that it sometimes resembled everything else on the planet.

A proto-language, he thought. *Something spoken by humanity's ancestors, something pre-Sumerian, and still spoken on North Sentinel.*

The idea was enough to tamp down his fear and reignite his curiosity. It could change the world of linguistics, and if the world's languages could be traced to a unified dialect, it could help bridge cultural divides. Not that he could ever publish on the subject, or take credit. The public attention would make him an easy target.

A pseudonym, he thought, and then he dismissed the hopeful thinking. A name without a face or a degree would be quickly disregarded. And he still needed to survive the island. When the voices faded, he leaned out from around the tree. The men who had passed through were gone, headed in the same direction Emmei had been going before veering right into the lush garden.

He spent a few minutes listening for more signs of life, heard nothing, and slipped from his hiding spot. There were now two sets of footprints, both barefoot, and two shallow troughs between them.

They're dragging someone, Mahdi thought, and as his body turned around to flee the area, he realized the person being dragged must be Emmei.

Leave him. Find the beach. Wait for help.

Mahdi took two steps and went rigid, a robot without power.

He had run away once before. Could still feel the sting of the scars in his back, the scars that were not from bullets, despite what he told the others. He didn't believe in an afterlife or eternal judgement, but he did believe in the sanctity of life, of helping people. Against his better judgment, or perhaps because of it, Mahdi turned around and snuck across the patchwork of roots, following the path left by two men dragging a third.

Ten minutes later, Mahdi found himself on the crest of a valley. He lowered himself to his stomach and slithered toward the edge. Blue light to his left drew his eyes. The valley was clear of trees. He wasn't sure how the Sentinelese, lacking modern tools, could clear so many trees, but they had. The valley formed a channel of earth leading toward the beach, where a thin layer of trees created a wall. Thanks to the tall trees growing on either side of the valley, their branches arching high overhead, the geographical feature would be invisible to satellite imagery. The deep shadow created by the canopy would hide it from the beach. Mahdi was confused by the odd valley until he reached the precipice and looked down.

The valley came to an abrupt end, like a scoop had been carved out of the earth, covered by a ceiling of roots, soil, and moss. At the center of the shallow cave was a smoldering fire pit, partially covered from either side by two large sheets of metal. *From the* Primrose, Mahdi thought. He'd read up on the ill-fated ship and he knew that it had been later dismantled and removed, but apparently not before the Sentinelese had raided it. He couldn't imagine how they freed the metal panels, removed them from the ship, and took them to shore. But here they were. Gouges in the ground showed where they could be pulled back to reveal the large fire pit, or slammed shut to snuff a blaze.

It explained some of the light show they'd seen the night before.

Movement in the cave. Mahdi held his breath while his eyes adjusted to the darkness. He could see movement within, but the Sentinelese were all but invisible in the shadows, as was Emmei. If this is where they brought him.

A gunshot echoed through the jungle, distant, behind him. His body tensed, teeth clenched. Two Sentinelese men burst from the cave, long bows and arrows in hand.

Before Mahdi could consider fleeing, they charged down the valley to where the sheer walls became gentle grades, and ran up.

Mahdi froze, hoping immobility would hide him. But the men never glanced in his direction. They slipped silently into the jungle without making a sound. Whoever fired that gun, probably Winston—had company coming, which meant there would be many more gunshots to come.

Mahdi knew from experience, both personal and generational, that violence escalated violence. The island would soon become a warzone, arrows against bullets. There was little doubt about who would survive. If the rest of the tribe was anything like the man on the beach, there was little hope for any of them. But until he knew that for sure, he'd try to survive, and do the right thing.

When he was sure the two warriors were gone, and the shadows below showed no signs of life, he crept to the sloped edge, slid down and headed for the shadows, surrounded by the fragrant scent of smoldering ashes.

26

ROWAN'S PLAN TO leave Winston behind evaporated the moment he felt the distinct vibration of footsteps in the roots beneath his feet. He couldn't see whatever was approaching, but he got the distinct impression that it wasn't small. Before they landed on the island, the largest living thing in the jungle should have been a five-foot-tall Sentinelese man. Since landing, Winston should have taken home the blue ribbon for girth. But it took a heavy foot to shake the ground. The vibration was subtle, pulsing through the network of roots.

He had no intention of making himself known to Winston, but from a tactical perspective, he wanted to see what was coming.

Know your enemy.

Talia crept to him, slid her face next to his. In a different setting their closeness would have been intimate: cheeks touching, warm breath on his ear. For a moment he became distracted by it, nearly aroused. But a fresh vibration returned the soldier to the battlefield.

What the hell is wrong with me? he thought, and then he focused.

"Wait here," he whispered.

"Not a chance," she replied, her hushed words tickling his ear.

"I just need to see—"

"We can't let him die."

Rowan closed his eyes. He didn't know how to explain.

Efficiently, he thought, as branches cracked and Winston said, "Step out, motherfucker."

"We were never here to save the Sentinelese," Rowan whispered. "We came to kill them. Well, not us. We're sacrificial lambs. The coconuts were for the Sentinelese. Infect them. Wipe them out. And then kill us, prove to the Indian government that any survivors needed to be dealt with harshly."

"Why? What's the angle?"

"Right now, doesn't matter," he said, "but I think we're the only ones out of the loop. And if Winston makes it off this island alive, we won't."

She leaned back, looked him in the eyes, her gaze intense. Then she nodded.

A gunshot made both of them flinch. It was followed by a string of curses the likes of which Rowan hadn't heard since Basic, the kind spoken by someone who knows they are without a doubt, seconds away from excruciating pain.

Rowan scaled the small hill again, Talia by his side, moving in tandem. She wasn't a soldier, but life in the jungle had given her similar instincts and skills. It made him appreciate her the same way she did him for being a willing participant in her aberrant anthropology. He still didn't understand *why* he had performed the haka, or had what was basically public sex—illegal in most of the world. Both were out of character, but maybe she just brought that out of him?

All thoughts of Talia fled his mind when he peeked up over the rise. On the far side stood Winston, pistol raised, angled up. He was backtracking, stumbling over roots, face coated in sweat. The cool and collected fighter they'd watched just a minute before had taken a back seat. He was caught in a fight-or-flight purgatory, unable to move in either direction.

When Rowan followed Winston's aim, he understood why.

A Sentinelese man, eight feet tall and stark naked, stalked toward Winston. He moved with the slow, steady gait of someone who had no fear of guns or their deadly potential. Winston had already fired once. The giant man wasn't ignorant of what the weapon could do, he just wasn't afraid of it.

No way Winston missed, Rowan thought. The man was a professional shooter. Overweight, sure, but not looking like a threat was part of what made him dangerous.

"How are you alive?" Winston asked, taking another step back.

Did Winston shoot this giant already? Rowan remembered the bullet holes in the dead and swallowed up warriors. The shots matched the wounds. So when did Winston kill this man? Had he been to the island before?

Rowan could only see the tall man's backside, but given the man's height, was sure he hadn't seen him before, from the boat or on the beach.

And then, with a slurp and a tear of flesh, he understood.

Folds of skin bloomed from the man's face. They snapped back, folding around the back side of his head, bony hooks digging deep, fastening the flesh in place.

This was the man from the beach.

The man they had killed four times over.

He'd been three feet shorter then.

Rowan had seen horrors during his life, had even been the cause of one of them, but he had no frame of reference for a thing like this. He glanced at Talia and saw that the woman who lived on the fringe, where the world was still mysterious and ancient, was just as confused.

Then the thing spoke, its voice fluttering through the air like a subwoofer dialed all the way up, pulsing through his chest. The words were unintelligible, but felt old. And angry.

The gun fired again, the bullet punching into a tree. The shot was wild, fired accidentally by shaking fingers, but it propelled Winston out of purgatory, into fight, followed quickly by flight. Winston lowered his aim, fired five times in rapid succession, each of the rounds striking the man-thing's left knee. The leg buckled. The monster dropped, but it wasn't stopped. Death only seemed to make it more and more horrible upon its return.

Winston did what Rowan and Talia should have done already; he ran. Rowan watched him barrel away, leaving an easy-to-follow trail of footprints in his wake. The giant would have no trouble tracking him.

The monstrous man grew still. His head cocked to the side.

It knows we're here, Rowan thought.

A third set of eyes, lodged in the skin wrapped around the back of the creature's head, snapped open. They stared at Rowan. The moment of eye contact felt like an electric shock.

Rowan toppled back, sprawling over roots until he reached the hill's base.

When he recovered, Talia was already there, yanking him up. "It saw us! Move!"

They sprinted. Within ten seconds, Rowan was lost, each towering tree looking like the rest. But Talia seemed to know where she was going, so he followed, happy to put as much distance between them and the monster as possible.

When Talia stopped, Rowan urged her on, but she shook her head and tapped her ear. *Listen.*

He paused, hands on knees, breathing deeply. Talia didn't seem winded. During his time in the Rangers, a run like that would have been a warm up. *I let myself go,* he thought, standing up straight, stretching a cramp. "I don't hear anything."

"We heard it walking," she said. "We'd hear it chasing us. I don't think this will be our last run. Better to save our energy."

"It could be," he said. "Our last run."

She squinted at him.

"We hit the beach, recover the raft, the food, whatever we can fit. Take our chances on the sea. Hell we could tie ourselves to a reef with gauze and wait for Ambani to send help."

"What about the others?"

"We'll take Sashi. It's a two man raft, but the two of you aren't that big. I don't trust the others, and they wouldn't fit. There's a good chance Winston has already come up with the same plan, so we shouldn't wait."

"What about Mahdi?"

"I…don't know. But I think Sashi does." He turned to start walking again, strident and determined. Paused. "I have no idea where we are."

Talia pointed. Managed a weak smile. "That way."

After a few minutes of cautious walking in silence, Rowan asked, "Have you noticed anything different about yourself?"

"What do you mean?"

"Your personality. Since arriving at the island?"

She mulled the question over. "Can you give me an example?"

He didn't really want to say it, but she was there for both events, and a participant in one. "Doing a naked haka ritual and having sex on a boat, bare ass to the world, isn't something I would normally do. And I'm easily distracted." He didn't say by what, but the hint of a smile she wore said she knew.

"Life in the jungle has a way of eroding inhibitions. Look at the Sentinelese."

"They've been living here for thousands of years," he said. "We've been on the island for less than a day, and the events in question took place before we ever set foot on the island."

She shrugged. "Taking off my clothes is par for the course for me."

"And the sex?"

She smiled. "That…was new." She fell silent again, brow furrowed, so he let her think. Another minute passed before she said, "Drinking from the tree was stupid. I would never have done that in the Amazon. There are ways to figure out if something will make you sick. Chugging from a tree nipple isn't one of them. What are you thinking?"

"That we should make sure *we're* thinking when we make decisions. Trust our instincts a little less. Question things a little more."

"Like should we have run from that…thing?"

"Hell no. Running was the right choice." He stared at the ground, lost himself in the twisting coils of roots until he saw the shape of an eye amidst them. He blinked. Looked up. "Any ideas about what we just saw?"

"I'm an anthropologist. I'm not even sure what scientific field that thing would fall under. Cryptozoology? Mythology? I'm not a slouch in those subjects. Part of my job is to understand ancient cultures and the myths that fuel them, but this… Well, it's not a myth. But visually?"

Rowan wiped his forehead dry with his shirt. The day was just getting started and it was already humid. In an hour, dressed in black, he'd be soaked through. But if they were lucky, they'd be sitting in a raft, out of reach from Winston, the Sentinelese, and the creature. A memory flitted through his mind, just out of reach. "It reminds me of something." He glanced behind them, half expecting to see the giant man or a Sentinelese hunting party closing in. All he saw were trees and shifting light. "I can't place it, but it feels…familiar somehow."

Rowan snapped forward again when Talia gripped his arm. The natural lean-to formed from tree roots and earth was straight ahead—and empty.

27

TALIA CROUCHED BENEATH the shelter where they'd left Sashi, while Rowan stood guard with his assault rifle. She saw no signs of struggle. No blood. "See anything?"

"No footprints aside from ours and Sashi's from earlier," Rowan said. "If someone took her, they did it without leaving a trace."

Talia heard the doubt in Rowan's voice, but she knew it was possible. She had seen similar feats of stealth and cunning. She climbed out from under the fallen tree. "Let's have a look around."

"And then?" Rowan asked.

"You know the answer," she said. "We survive."

She didn't like the idea of abandoning Sashi to the Sentinelese, but they couldn't wage war on the island, or the monster protecting it. If the Sentinelese had her, rescue would be impossible, even if they could locate her, which was unlikely. And if she had wandered off, she was a fool. Talia knew the opinion was harsh, but Sashi had hired them, brought them to this place, and very likely knew what they now suspected: that she and Rowan were human sacrifices to justify genocide.

She scanned the manicured jungle and saw nothing out of the ordinary…if she ignored that everything in sight was cleared of detritus and rot. The only thing aberrant about the perfectly clean forest was the tipped-over tree, its still-living branches leaning on its neighbor, leaving a gap in the canopy.

Talia looked up, expecting to see a bright blue sky. Instead, she saw a swirl of gray clouds. In the Amazon, the sky shifted from clear to thunderous storms almost every day. But in the Bay of Bengal, dark gray storm clouds could mean a monsoon, or worse: a typhoon. Either would put a damper on their plans to await rescue in the inflatable raft. "Hey," she said to Rowan, her face still turned up.

"That doesn't look—"

Talia glanced at Rowan. He was looking up, but not toward the sky. She followed his eye to the tipped-over tree and quickly saw the aberration. A hundred feet off the ground, Sashi was on the tilted tree trunk, legs spread wide, arms latched around the first set of branches.

"What is she doing up there?" Rowan asked.

Talia took a quick look around. They were still alone, or at least appeared to be. "Pretty sure the answer to that is self-explanatory. But I'll go ask her."

Talia began climbing the roots before Rowan could express the doubt wrinkling his forehead. The climb felt good until the scrape on her shoulder opened and sweat leaked in. The sting helped focus her. Reminded her that she needed to think, to temper her instincts.

"If she doesn't come down right away," Rowan said and let the thought hang. He didn't want to say the rest, but Talia understood. The sentence for loitering, and every other crime, on North Sentinel Island was death.

She watched him wipe his brow again, flicking the sweat away. "You should lose the clothing."

"In case you haven't noticed, I'm a white guy from New Hampshire."

"Good point, your body will be easier to hide when you pass out from dehydration." She started up the tree, making three quick lunges. She felt like she could scramble up the towering trunk, but she forced herself to take slow, deliberate movements. With confidence came a rhythm, and she made good time, reaching Sashi in two minutes.

Positioned beneath Sashi's buttocks, she pushed herself up, leaned as much as she dared and looked at the woman's face. Was she asleep? Unconscious? Dead? The rise and fall of her body with each breath was subtle, but present. Not dead.

Talia whispered, "Sashi." When the woman didn't stir, she tried again, louder, "*Sashi.*" She pulled herself closer, hovering over the woman's lower body. She placed a gentle hand on Sashi's lower back. Gave her a shake. "Sash—"

"No!" Sashi shouted, pushing herself up and into Talia. The back of her head struck Talia's cheek. The world tipped. Gravity took hold. At ninety degrees, Talia's legs wrapped around the tree. Squeezed. Her stomach clenched, the muscles stretching, some of them pinging loose. Her arched back groaned and vertebrae compressed, but the fall came to an end. The handgun tucked into the back of her shorts slipped out, bumped off the tree, and fell to the jungle floor. With a surge of anger, Talia leaned back up and gripped the tree just in time for Sashi to fall.

With one hand wedged in a crevice of bark, she used the other to hold onto Sashi while the woman slid down the trunk into Talia's lap.

"Let go! Get off me!"

"Sashi!" Talia shouted. "It's Talia!"

A flailed elbow caught Talia in the side of the head. Stars danced. There was only so much abuse Talia could take, but in the end, rage beat unconsciousness to the finish line. She felt a moment of pre-regret and then drove her fist into Sashi's temple. The strike was solid. It didn't render Sashi unconscious, but it had the same effect as a few shots of whisky, knocking the panic out of her.

Talia scraped her way back down the tree, one hand around Sashi's waist. Luckily, the tree bark wasn't that rough. If it had been, they'd have both been bloody when they reached the bottom. Instead, they were a bit raw, and would both have headaches, but they were otherwise unharmed.

At the base of the tree, still eight feet above the forest floor, Talia found Rowan dressed in black boxers, his belt strapped around his waist holding spare magazines for her gun, which he had recovered and holstered. He put the assault rifle on the ground and raised his hands. Talia tipped Sashi over. The woman mumbled a complaint, but hadn't fully regained her senses. Talia hung on to one of Sashi's arms, lowering her into Rowan's hands.

When Talia reached the ground, she found Rowan leaning over Sashi, patting the woman's face.

"Sashi, it's Rowan. Wake up."

She noted the wound in Sashi's shoulder. A puffy scab had formed. *That was fast,* she thought, and she placed her hand on it, expecting hot infected flesh. It was cool to the touch, but it got a reaction.

Sashi's eyes went wide in time with her mouth, but the scream that came out was muffled by Rowan's hand. He held it there while the shrill sound repeated. Sashi's eyes darted back and forth. Her breathing came at a rapid fire rhythm.

"You're safe," Rowan told her, and while it wasn't entirely true, there weren't any arrows flying at them. Yet. "Look at me. You're safe."

Sashi's breathing slowed. She focused on Rowan. There was a moment of confusion and then recognition. The panicked screaming melted into sobs of fear mixed with relief.

"Are you okay?" Rowan asked. "Can I move my hand?"

Sashi nodded and Rowan's hand came away.

"What happened?" he asked.

"I-I heard them coming."

"Heard who?" Talia asked.

"The Sentinelese. A lot of them. They were talking."

"Which way did they go?" Rowan asked.

Sashi looked around, found her bearings. When she pointed inland, Talia felt a surge of hope, but then Sashi spoke. "They came from over there." The gradual rise of the land led to a thick growth of trees fifty feet away. The jungle beyond was concealed, just as Sashi would have been from the approaching Sentinelese. "I heard them coming from all over. I didn't know where else to go." She looked up at the tilted over tree. "At the time it made sense. I wasn't afraid. But once I got up there…and they came out of the jungle."

A shiver ran through Sashi's body. "They were headed to the beach. The men had spears. The women carried woven baskets. But the children…"

Talia crouched down. They had yet to see any children on the island. "What about them?"

"They weren't walking," she said. "Not like people. They ran like animals. Like insects."

A flood of questions about the Sentinelese and their children entered Talia's mind, but she kept them to herself. Sashi was shaking again.

"Sounds like they were going fishing," Rowan said, and he shot Talia a quick look that said he didn't believe it either. If the Sentinelese were going fishing, it was for outsiders. Sashi had taken a big risk climbing the tree, but she had simultaneously evaded capture or death, and revealed a Sentinelese weakness—they didn't look up.

Why would they? Their primary food source was in the ocean, and the birds populating the upper reaches weren't big enough to feed anyone. Talia watched the treetops. Where were the birds? She couldn't hear them, either.

"My hatchet," Rowan said to Sashi. "Where is it?"

Sashi looked around, confused. "I—I don't know. I must have dropped it."

"Fantastic." Rowan looked at the empty shelter, and then the barren ground beneath the fallen tree. Shook his head and looked at Talia. "What do you want to do?"

Talia turned away from the treetops. "The whole island is surrounded by beach. The Sentinelese could be anywhere."

"Or they could be sitting with the raft, just waiting for us."

"What about the raft?" Sashi asked.

"We're getting off the island," Rowan said. "The three of us. We'll wait for a rescue at—"

The trees above swayed, the leaves rustling, as an invisible force moved through them. When the wind parted the branches, there was no sun or sky in sight, just dark clouds. Goosebumps dotted Talia's skin. The air had a chill in it. "If that opens up, we'll come back here. Until then, I think we need to be proactive. We've been lucky so far, but I don't think we can stay hidden forever."

When she believed the island was inhabited by normal human beings, she thought their chances of evading the Sentinelese were decent. Between her experiences in the world's jungles, and Rowan's as an Army Ranger, they weren't novices when it came to life and death situations. But after seeing that thing with the eyes… Every minute on the island felt a little closer to doom, but at the same time, it felt a little more like something else that made no sense at all—home. As much as she wanted to hit the water and never look back, she felt drawn inland. The war between instinct and logic never ended on North Sentinel.

"So we recon the beach," Rowan said. "If it's clear, we recover the raft and anything else that makes sense. If the storm passes or never builds, we take our chances on the sea."

Sashi climbed to her feet, brushing herself off. "And if the storm arrives?"

"We come back here." Rowan picked up his discarded clothing, bunched it up and tossed it into the crevice where the tipped-over tree's roots met the fertile earth. "Hide in the shadows. Use the raft to conceal our bodies. Wait out the storm. No help would come until it passed anyway."

Talia waggled a finger at the handgun Rowan had recovered. Opened her hand. He drew it, turned it around, and placed it in her hand. Then she pointed it at Sashi's head. "But first, you're going to tell us everything, and if I don't think you're telling the truth…" She chambered a round, letting the sound finish her thought.

28

THOUGH MOST OF the fire pit was covered by the two slabs of metal, Mahdi could feel heat radiating from below. Bright orange embers glowed, the heat sustained by the limited oxygen available through the two-inch-wide, six-foot-long gap. Wisps of smoke coiled upward before being swept away by the breeze, which was stronger in the valley. Air seemed to flow through the depression, cyclone through the scooped out hollow, and flow upward into the jungle above.

Something in the fire pit popped, issuing a geyser of black smoke. Mahdi watched it flow into the cave, and then seep back out from the ceiling, flowing up toward the treetops. His eyes lingered on the trees, swaying hard, revealing glimpses of gray sky. Living in London, Mahdi had grown accustomed to gloomy skies, but they rarely looked as dark and foreboding as what he saw overhead. The twisting clouds were energetic. Swirling. Compared to the storm he experienced at sea, this one looked angry.

Between the warm fire and the large cave, this would be the perfect place to ride out a storm, but the Sentinelese would know that, too, and they would likely return if it began to rain. Or would they? The previous day's downpour hadn't stopped them from fishing. Either way, he had no intention of lingering.

He paused after each step, trying to see deeper into the cave's recesses, but he never saw more than darkness. *Hurry up,* he told himself, feeling foolish. The Sentinelese who left could return at any time, and if there was someone in the cave, they already knew he was there. No one had shot him yet, so his odds were favorable.

"Emmei," he whispered as loud as he could.

He flinched and nearly ran when a groan replied. He couldn't see Emmei, which highlighted the possibility that they were not alone.

"Emmei, is that you?"

Another groan, but this one mixed with a muffled, "Yef."

Mahdi crept past the fire pit, chased by its heat, and slowed as he approached the broad cave entrance. Emmei's dark, naked form resolved as Mahdi stepped into the cave's shadow and his vision adjusted. He saw Emmei's large fear-filled eyes first, and then his naked body, bound at the ankles and wrists, a gag in his mouth.

Mahdi pulled the gag down below Emmei's chin. The man took several deep breaths, but said nothing. Then Mahdi tried tugging off the twine bindings around Emmei's ankles, but his shaking hands couldn't loosen them.

How can I free him? he thought, and then he remembered the automatic switchblade he'd been given. He took the knife out, snapped open the blade and began hacking through the fibrous bindings, which appeared to be woven from shredded plant material, bark, and leaves.

"Are you okay?" Mahdi asked, trying hard to not cut Emmei's skin.

Despite the gag's removal, Emmei just grunted.

"Why did you go inland?"

"Can't you feel it?" Emmei asked, his voice gravelly and slurred. "In your body. In your veins. Life. It's everywhere."

He sounds drunk, Mahdi thought. *Or high.*

Emmei reached out with his bound hands. Clutched onto Mahdi's wrist hard enough to hurt. "I want to go back. I'll take you with me."

"You won't be going anywhere if you don't let me free you," Mahdi said, glancing back over his shoulder.

Emmei released him, leaned back, and laughed.

The cave amplified the laugh and sent it booming out into the jungle. Mahdi cringed, but found himself smiling, too. His memories drifted back to the thick overgrown jungle from which Emmei had been dragged. What was in there that Emmei would risk his life to go back?

Perhaps I should go with him?

The knife cut through the bindings. Lost in thought, Mahdi didn't notice until he sliced through Emmei's ankle and blood began to flow. Mahdi snapped out of his thoughts and was about to apologize when he realized Emmei hadn't even felt the blade's sting.

Mahdi retracted the bloodstained blade back inside the handle. "We need to go."

"To the garden."

Mahdi almost disagreed with the man, but then realized deception might be the best course of action. Emmei either didn't notice or didn't care that his hands were still bound. The man wasn't thinking straight. "I know the way. You can follow me."

Mahdi stood and reached down to pull Emmei up by his wrist bindings, but he glanced back into the cave and froze. He saw the rear wall through adjusted eyes and forgot all about Emmei. He stepped deeper inside the cave, marveling at the intricacy. Black stone had been carved into a tangle of small sculpted bodies, all of them huddled and reaching out to what looked like an Egyptian obelisk, upon which two vertical words had been scrawled. It was a hellish statue.

The letters were faded and worn down, clearly ancient, but he thought he might be able to make them out if he got closer.

He tip-toed through the barren cave, Emmei looking on in silence, perhaps noticing the stone bodies and the obelisk for the first time.

The Sentinelese haven't been as isolated as the world believes, Mahdi thought. *At some point in history, they were visited by people who had a firm understanding of carving stone, perhaps as early as the Maurya Empire, or as late as the Chola Empire, who also had a strong naval tradition.* All he knew for sure was that the Sentinelese hadn't learned how to carve stone with such skill without outside help.

He paused. Other than sand, he hadn't seen any stone on the island. If such a large sample existed in this cave, there should be more. But North Sentinel wasn't a volcanic island. So where did such a large stone come from?

Before he could ponder the question further, he saw the text for what it was and gasped.

Emmei began laughing in response, and this time, Mahdi joined in. He couldn't help himself.

Mahdi read and spoke the language carved into the obelisk. Next to Arabic, it was the language of his youth. But what was it doing here? Of all the people who could have visited this island, why…and how…

The two words coalesced in his thoughts and he spoke them aloud, in English, for Emmei's benefit. "Flaming sword." He turned around. "Does that mean anything to you?"

Emmei stared back at him with wide eyes, but something was off.

He's not looking at me, Mahdi thought, and then he realized the man wasn't looking at the obelisk either. He was looking at the massive carving, his eyes darting from one end to the other. The mash of limbs and bodies was disturbing, but compared to a written message preserved through the ages, it was—

Emmei's lips trembled.

Mahdi turned around.

For a moment, he didn't see it, but then he noticed the statue again.

It had changed.

Discerning how was impossible. The tangle of limbs just looked different. Mahdi looked back at Emmei. "You saw what happened. What…"

The fear in Emmei's eyes spun Mahdi back around. This time the change was obvious. All thirty-something of the small heads, which had been partly concealed by stretching arms and legs, had craned around. The small faces, eyes closed, had chubby cheeks, tall foreheads, and close-cut hair. They looked at peace. Content little cherubs.

Mahdi backed away.

This isn't a carving.

It's children.

Emmei's laughter filled the chamber, rolling out into the jungle beyond where it was joined by a rumble of thunder.

Frantic, Mahdi turn to flee, but he tripped over Emmei and spilled to the ground. He scrambled back up, tugging on Emmei. "Let's go! Let's—"

The children's eyes opened, all of them, watching Mahdi with feline interest.

Emmei was a lost cause. The man's mind was gone. Mahdi knew he would regret the decision to leave the man behind for the rest of his life, but the length of his life was currently up for debate. Better to live with regrets and seek forgiveness, than die with his current list of regrets, which had yet to be forgiven.

The children began peeling apart from each other. Sticky skin stretched and separated, bodies once a solid thing coming apart, becoming individuals, their eyes fixed on Mahdi. The children were between three and four feet tall, with spindly arms and legs, skinny bodies, and not a shred of clothing. Despite clearly being alive, they still had the appearance of stone.

"I'm sorry," he said to Emmei, and scrambled out of the cave. He didn't pause as he rounded the fire pit, and he didn't look back until he reached the gentle slope where he could climb out of the valley.

The children moved down the wall, away from the obelisk, and toward Emmei, who shook with laughter that Mahdi now recognized as mania. Whatever the man had experienced in the island's interior had clearly broken his mind. *Could it have been worse than this?* he thought, and he decided *yes* when he remembered the peeled-open face of the man on the beach, and his second set of eyes.

It could be a lot worse.

And then it was.

The children lowered to the ground and moved on all fours, their arms and legs splayed wide, joints bent at ninety degree angles. They began shrieking at one another, the pitches varied, but all were ear piercing.

Is that a language? Are they communicating? It sounded closer to dolphin calls drizzled in terror fuel, but the way their movements became coordinated said that they were organizing.

Two of the larger children scrambled out of the cave. Their eyes were on Mahdi, and for a moment, he thought the chase had begun.

He was halfway up the incline when he looked back again. The two children, both boys, had stopped on either side of the fire pit. They grasped the large metal sheets, oblivious to their sizzling skin, and dragged them away.

Impossible.

Mahdi thought two grown men would have trouble moving the plates. *They must weigh hundreds of pounds each, and they're scalding hot.* The two boys made it look easy.

Wind barreled through the valley, propelled by the storm still forming above. The air struck the open pit. Embers flared bright orange, and small flames leaped up, but the blaze needed more fuel.

Emmei's laughter became a scream.

The Sentinelese children had found a fuel source for the furnace.

Emmei rose up over the short mob of bodies. They carried him like a crowd-surfing concert-goer. Though upright, their legs were still spread wide, each movement looking more insectoid than human. The *Sea Tiger*'s captain kicked and flailed, but the children never parted, never ceased his slow passage toward the waiting heat.

Emmei's heel connected with a little girl's head. The blow to her temple was hard enough to snap her neck to the side and spill her body to the ground. Then she was up on her feet again, no tears, no anguish in her eyes. She was indifferent to the pain, if she felt it at all, and to the fact that they were about to scorch a living man.

Mahdi fought the urge to go back, to help. It was suicide. Emmei's fate was sealed. Had been since he'd entered the lush interior. Mahdi's fate, on the other hand, was still undecided. He crawled to the top of the crest, prepared to run, but he stopped when Emmei's screaming reached a fever pitch.

They had him angled up, face first, over the open coals. Rising heat distorted the scene, but Mahdi could see that Emmei's mind had returned in time to experience this final moment. His screaming wound down to a high pitched hiss, and then sobs. "I'm sorry," he screamed to the sky. "I didn't know!"

And then the children released him.

Into the pit.

A spiral of flames burst high, consuming the body with a crackle of skin and fat. Emmei's body didn't move. Didn't scream. He fell into the blaze like any other log would, the smoke that once was a man, rising into the canopy.

The children, once again on all fours, fell silent, their faces somber, as though they had just carried out a serious chore and were awaiting their parents' approval.

Thunder growled from the sky.

Run, Mahdi thought, but he couldn't look away.

The children shifted their collective gaze from the fire to Mahdi.

Run!

They smiled. The line separating upper and lower lips stretched wide, and then too far, dividing their small faces horizontally, from ear to ear. When the children shrieked again, it was from open mouths as wide as their faces.

They weren't children at all.

Like the man on the beach, they were something else.

Finally, Mahdi ran, but as the shrieking rose up behind him, he knew it was too late.

29

"YOU'RE NOT GOING to shoot me." Sashi's feigned defiance wasn't fooling Rowan. She was terrified, not just of Talia or the gun she was holding, but of facing the island alone—again. While Rowan wouldn't condone shooting Sashi, if the truth didn't come out, she would be on her own. It was a death sentence, which was why he had no doubt she would talk.

Rowan scanned the area with his FN SCAR. When they first infiltrated the island, they were afraid to even whisper. Now they were standing out in the open, having a not-exactly-quiet conversation. Their inhibitions were still being affected, even if they weren't getting…naked. Rowan looked down at himself, and then the two women. Of the three of them, Talia, with her black bikini top and matching shorts was the most clothed.

The logic behind removing their clothing still made sense, but maybe their logic had been poisoned by instinct? *At least we're not naked,* he thought, feeling a dose of shame that he hadn't experienced while performing the haka, and what happened after.

Talia lowered the gun. "You're right. I won't shoot you. But I will leave you here."

"I'll follow you," Sashi said.

"You won't be able to keep up," Rowan added, knowing his lack of support would undo the last fragments of emotional mortar supporting Sashi's defiance. He liked Sashi, and she knew it. She *had* saved him. Pulled him from the edge of despair. But that salvation was only temporary. She had coaxed him away from the cliff to sacrifice him on the Devil's island. "The truth is the only thing that can keep you alive." He checked the jungle around them. "But keep your confession quiet."

Sashi wiped tears from her cheeks. She was in pain, and despite feeling compassion for her situation, Rowan kept his expression resolute and cold. Sashi's voice shook as she said, "If you promise to help me."

"Help you how?" Talia asked.

"I—I need you to kill someone."

"Not a chance," Rowan said.

"Is it Winston?" Talia asked. "Because if it's Winston..." A flash of surprise slipped through Talia's face. She was either surprised she felt so strongly or that she had said it aloud. Maybe both.

"That's my condition. If you want the truth, you need to free me from it." This time Sashi's defiance was genuine.

Given their circumstances, Rowan didn't see any option other than to agree. He wasn't swearing on a Bible, or signing a contract in blood. He didn't need to fulfil his promise. "Who am I killing, then?"

Sashi's eyes lit with hope. "You will?"

"If the secrets end," he said. "Now, who am I killing, and why?"

"Rattan Ambani," Sashi said.

"Ambani?" Talia said. "What does he have to do with the expedition? Other than the boat, and traitorous...crew. Huh..."

Rowan was surprised that neither he, nor Talia, had considered the hotel tycoon's involvement before. Emmei's and Chugy's actions were both suspect, and the pair worked for Ambani, not the Indian government.

"Very little of what you've been told about our expedition is the truth." Sashi cowered a little, as though expecting a beat down. But neither Talia or Rowan moved, or even spoke. The flood gates had been opened. All Sashi had to do was keep talking. Then she did. "We're not here to study, make contact with, or save the Sentinelese people."

"We're here to kill them," Talia said, struggling against grinding-teeth rage.

"How could the government condone—"

Sashi cut him off. "The Indian government doesn't even know we're here."

"Do you even work for the government?" Rowan asked.

She nodded. "Department of Cultural Services. That was the truth. Mr. Ambani approached me about the island. He wanted to initiate contact, to broker a peace with the Sentinelese, but we both knew such actions would be a death sentence for such a violent and protective people. I declined his proposal...and he turned to my husband, a real estate developer."

Rowan remembered the black bindi on Sashi's forehead, worn to express mourning of a husband's passing. "Your *dead* husband?"

"He's dead to me, but his heart is still beating. Ambani wants to develop North Sentinel Island. Make it an eco-resort. He intends to build a resort, but leave most of the island as is. He'll leave whatever villages exist and hire desperate Andamanese to act as Sentinelese, adding an air of danger to visitors' stays. 'A vacation to the past,' he called it. He'll make millions, but only if the island's current occupants either die, or deserve to."

"The vicious slaughter of two scientists and their American protection might justify it," Talia said, "If the coconuts failed to infect the island… What was on the coconuts?"

"I'm not sure," Sashi said. "Flu, I think."

"And when that didn't work?" Rowan asked. He knew the answer, but wanted Sashi to say it.

"You would be put in a position to be killed by the Sentinelese, or Winston would do it, and make it look like the Sentinelese had killed you."

"The string of murders you showed us at the resort weren't enough?" Rowan asked.

"Fakes," Talia said, and Sashi didn't argue. "I knew it was too much. The Sentinelese are protective, but they're not serial killers. Tribal people might seem savage to us, but they're guided by the same moral compass as the rest of us. The Sentinelese didn't want to kill us. They've given us more than one opportunity to leave."

"And the *Sea Tiger*?" Rowan asked. "Was stranding us here part of the plan?"

Sashi shook her head, twitchy and rapid fire. "Why would I ever set foot on this island?"

"All of this for a resort." Rowan raised his assault rifle, aimed it at Sashi. "Why shouldn't we leave you here?"

"My husband," she said.

"Your living husband," Rowan added.

"He made a deal with Ambani. The resort's contract will go to my husband, and along with it, a five percent ownership."

"All of this for *money?*" Talia asked, her rage barely contained. She was a woman of financial means, but clearly she had no love for wealth.

"Not for me," Sashi said. "I—I am here for my daughter. My presence legitimized the expedition. Without me—"

"He couldn't have hired us," Rowan said.

"And without my help…Ambani will marry my fifteen-year-old daughter."

"That can't be legal," Talia said.

"It's not." Sashi's head sank. "But that doesn't stop it from happening. Eighteen percent of Indian girls are married by age fifteen. I was one of them. I don't want that life for my daughter. If I could kill Ambani myself, I would. But to save my daughter I would do far worse."

"You'd let us be killed to save the people you love?" Rowan asked.

Sashi looked him in the eyes. "Yes."

Rowan lowered the rifle. "You're a better mother than mine."

"And mine," Talia added, the fury gone from her eyes.

Sashi's eyebrows rose. "You'll kill him, then?"

"He'd force himself on a fifteen year old girl, blackmail you into committing murder and genocide, and drag us across the world just to kill us? I've killed a lot of people, because I was ordered to, and others because I made a mistake, but I never had what I would call a 'good' reason to take a life. Yeah, I'm thinking I'll kill him. Who else is with him?"

"Winston," Sashi said. "He's a mercenary, and a sociopath. He's successful, I think, because people underestimate him. Emmei is simply well-paid and loyal to Ambani. Chugy, too."

"And Mahdi?" Talia asked.

"He was supposed to die with the two of you, but...he learned the truth."

"Why didn't he tell us?" Rowan asked.

"Mahdi is being hunted," Sashi said. "His brother-in-law is Hamas. Winston threatened to turn him over."

"He was going to sacrifice us to save himself." Rowan wasn't surprised. Very few people were willing to sacrifice themselves for other people, especially people they'd just met, but it was a far less noble motivation than Sashi's. If they saw Mahdi again, the reunion wouldn't be pleasant for the linguist.

Rowan wasn't thrilled with the answers, but he was satisfied that they knew the truth, and that Sashi wouldn't betray them. The emotion about her daughter's situation felt real. If he could help her, he would. "Time to go."

A relieved Sashi wiped fresh tears from her face and gave a nod. Talia took the lead. She moved like a stalking jaguar, silent and swift. Keeping up was a challenge, but without his boots, Rowan found himself able to move in complete silence.

Their return to the beach was uneventful. There was no evidence that the Sentinelese had passed through the area, and none of the tribe lingered on the sand, or in the choppy turquoise waters surrounding the island.

"They must have turned before reaching the beach," Sashi said.

"Mmm," Talia grunted and then stepped out into the sand. She scanned the beach in both directions, and then relaxed. "All clear."

When Rowan exited the wall of green and stood in the open once more, he noted Talia's attention was now on the sky. Looking out from the beach, everything appeared normal. The sky was blue. The ocean inviting and tropical. But above…dark storm clouds swirled. "Is that…normal?"

"The island has its own micro climate," Sashi said. "It's not unusual for clouds to form over the island while the rest of the sky is clear."

Talia pointed up. "But this?"

The black clouds swirled through the sky like an isolated hurricane. Lighting arced through the clouds, the thunder loud, shaking through Rowan's chest.

"It's extreme," Sashi said. "Yes."

Rowan started down the beach. They weren't far from the tree bark bunker, and they already knew the man they'd killed was no longer there. In fact, the more he thought about that thing, and its many eyes, the more willing he was to take his chances in a rubber raft, on the open ocean, during a lightning storm. His walk became a jog as he neared the bunker, but slowed when he saw a swath of destruction surrounding it. The first aid kits, food bags, and raft had been shredded and scattered about. Had the resurrected creature attacked in a fit of rage, or had the Sentinelese raided the stash? It was impossible to tell if anything had been taken.

"Shit," Talia said when she saw the deflated raft, shredded into strips.

Rowan made a quick mental leap from escaping the island to surviving it. He began scanning for any salvageable food or medical supplies. Talia joined him, discovering a can of chocolate pudding, but the search came to an abrupt end when Sashi stepped backward through the mess, toward the jungle, eyes on the ocean. Her eyes flicked down to Rowan's. "The water… they're in the water."

30

RUNNING WITHOUT A destination was never a good idea. The risk of overexertion, the temptation to push beyond limits or the possibility of rescue, and the danger of injury. Mahdi hated running. Thought it the fool's method of exercise. Hard on the knees and shins, and every other bone beneath the ribs. A cold, or rainy, or snowy day could prevent the run, and then what was the point of starting a routine? If Mother Nature could upend a resolution, it wasn't ever resolute. So, when he ran, it was on a treadmill, *Downton Abbey* on the screen, rain or shine. But still, he hated running.

Even more now. Because to stop was to die, most likely in a horrible way, just as Emmei had. Roasted alive. It was the kind of barbarism heard about in the Middle East, but seen far less than any American would believe. Wars sometimes claimed fewer lives than daily life in some U.S. cities. But he could call neither the extremists in his homeland, nor the gangs fighting over American streets, barbarous anymore. The Sentinelese had redefined the word.

Burned alive. Skin flaking in hot black sheets. Fat melting, spitting. The images were gruesome, but he allowed them to flood his mind, to blot out the exhaustion and adrenaline waging war for his mind and body. Slowing meant death. Running was all there was.

But running to where? There were no guideposts or obvious markers to help determine where on the island he was, or where he was heading. The Sentinelese might recognize every tree, but to him, they were all the same, sweeping high into the air, twisting trunks topped with billowing leaves, the mixture reminiscent of a lemon-lime soda commercial. All he knew was up, down, left, right, and forward. Back was not an option.

But then he stopped.

The jungle ahead was a wall of lush green. The boundary where life began and ended. It was where they captured Emmei, but it wasn't where they killed him. The question was, did he lose his mind because of what he had discovered on the other side? And if Mahdi was caught in some kind of sacred place, would he be dragged back out before he was barbequed?

Shrieking and the sound of small feet slapping rapid-fire over roots made up his mind for him. *I can be captured and killed here and now…or in there.* The difference seemed negligible, and if he lost his mind before being captured, perhaps that would be a mercy?

He shoved through the growth, pushing his way through branches. There were no thorns, but the foliage clung to him. 'Stay,' it told him, 'not that way.' But he persisted, and broke through. The jungle on the far side opened up, but looked nothing like the manicured ground surrounding the island. Where that was a family park, this was a lush tropical paradise. Cool humidity clung to his skin, easing the heat. Flowers tickled his nose, putting him at peace. *Lavender,* he realized, and then he saw the plant blooming nearby.

He felt both welcome and like a trespasser. But he was also desperate. He pushed onward, running through the lush terrain, sluicing through streams, crashing through long, hanging vines, and all the while, regaining his strength.

Ten minutes into his run, he got a second wind for the first time in his life.

I can make it, he thought. *If I just keep moving straight, I'll reach the ocean.*

And then what? Swim to freedom? He looked up at the sky, storm clouds swirling lower. *In that?*

I have to hide.

He wasn't a predator, he was prey, and if he couldn't outrun the monsters at his back, perhaps he could elude them the way prey animals around the world survived—underground. Digging a burrow wasn't an option. He'd only have time to carve out a foot-sized hole before they descended on him. But he also couldn't take refuge in a large cave. The Sentinelese would surely dwell within, and he'd already seen what kind of horrors lived in the darkness. *Something natural, something easily overlooked.*

Brush shook behind him, the leaves caught up in a frantic shimmy dance, the squeals growing louder. The child-things sounded more agitated now, more energetic, too.

I'm not supposed to be here. But what choice do I have?

Hope blossomed as he reached a stream flowing across his path. It was three feet deep, five wide, and framed by hanging grasses, roots, and fallen branches, which unlike the outer garden, had not been cleaned up. He slid into the water, bristled at the chill of it, and slogged downstream.

After a quick glance back to confirm that the short killers had yet to spot him, he lowered himself into the water. Roots scratched his skin as he slid against the shore, a carpet of hanging grasses enveloping him like a blanket, holding him, comforting him. Deep in his liquid cocoon, the water seemed to warm. With his face half submerged, he opened his mouth and drank. Cool water slid down his throat, easing him deeper into a sense of relief.

They're going to pass me by, he thought, and then he heard them splashing through the stream. He couldn't see them, but his imagination had no trouble conjuring images of the bent-legged, almost insectoid children with the wide and broad jaws.

The image had no effect. In fact, his memory flitted back to what they'd looked like before climbing away from the obelisk. Their large eyes. A smile dipped his lips beneath the water again. *Cute,* he thought, and then he fell asleep.

He woke to the sound of rain, hissing on the canopy leaves, dripping in the stream. He rolled, pulled in a mass of grass and coiled around it, content as he ever had been lying in bed with his wife, Yamina.

He felt guilty for feeling it, but the stream swept the emotion away.

"Comfortable?"

Mahdi's eyes blinked open. Nearly closed again. Then he saw Winston, in the water on the far side of the stream, his face poking out from behind a curtain of hanging grass and vines.

"You nearly got me killed," Winston said. "Leading them here."

"I didn't know you were here." Mahdi kept his voice to a whisper, while Winston seemed confident in their solitude. Mahdi had no idea how long he'd been sleeping, but if Winston had been awake the entire time, he'd have a much better situational awareness. And if he was talking loudly, perhaps they really were safe.

"Did you see it?"

"It?" Mahdi had seen a lot. *It* barely began to cover *them.*

"Eight foot tall. Four eyes in the front, two in the back, hopefully with a nasty limp. Best I can tell, it's the savage from the beach. The one I popped. But he's not dead. Again. And he's a might worse to look at now. Bastard chased me here. Hid from him the same way you did."

That the man from the beach was still alive wasn't really surprising, but it was disappointing. "That's not what was chasing me. They were a lot smaller."

"They?"

"Children."

"You were being chased by children?" Even on his side, hiding in a stream, and covered by greenery like a tucked-in child, Winston managed to sound condescending.

"They weren't children. Not really. They looked like children. At first. But they didn't move like children, and their faces..." A shiver ran through his body.

"What did they move like?"

"Crabs," Mahdi said. "Mouths like...like a manticore." The mythological creature was the only comparison he could come up with. That's not what the children were. They didn't have lion bodies. But they couldn't be human, either. Not fully human, anyway. Their ability to move along the ground, and the structure of their jaws, meant their genome had undergone dramatic changes since separating from the rest of humanity. But why? He saw no benefit to such adaptation, aside from being unnaturally frightening.

"So killer crab kids and a starfish face. Good news for you is that you can still get off this devil's asshole of an island. Just stay with me."

"And the others?"

"Let 'em die," he said. "It's why we brought them here. So what if it's Sashi instead of you. End result will be the same, though I'm going to recommend they just carpet bomb the place. Shit here is hard to kill."

"But her daughter..."

"Will marry a rich, fat, prick of a perv. What are the odds the man can even get it up still? Then he'll die. Maybe she'll kill him. And the keys to the castle will be hers. Hell, I might take the high hard one a few times to get that kind of payoff."

"Then you must have a way off the island?" Mahdi asked, hoping the man would be truthful. The idea of escape was tantalizing, but could he really walk away? Again? What scars would he be left with then?

Winston grinned, sideways and toothy. "Just stay close and do what I say, when I say it." He began to slide out from his hiding place.

"Can't we stay a while longer?" Mahdi asked. He wanted to go back to sleep. To return to his dreams, of which he could only remember soft white light and a deep voice. What was it saying?

"Flaming sword."

Winston paused, his face glowering. "What?"

"Flaming sword," Mahdi said. "It was written on an obelisk. The children were huddled around it before…" He grew less comfortable. Fear let him feel every prickle of detritus poking him.

Winston freed himself from the vines holding him against the damp wall of mud. He rolled into the stream, looking more like a fully clothed manatee than a man. "Before what?"

"Emmei is dead," Mahdi said. "They killed him."

"Huh." Winston pushed himself onto his knees, scanning the area, no fear in his eyes. "Just the two of us then."

"He died horribly," Mahdi said. "They cooked him in one of the—"

"Don't care."

"How can you not—"

"We weren't friends."

"You're not worried about being thrown in a fire?"

Winston held up his pistol. "Won't come to that."

"You can't kill them all with a gun," Mahdi pointed out.

"Near as I can tell, I can't kill a single one of them." Winston ejected the magazine, inspected the rounds and slapped it back into the grip. "These are for yours truly, and you, if you've got the balls. Not many better ways to go. Quick and painless. Pretty sure that's not how the Captain's life came to an end."

It wasn't. Not remotely. For most of his life, Mahdi had been afraid of guns. They were a part of life in Palestine, present during the hardest strife, and even the happiest of celebrations. To him, they represented what they were built to accomplish: death. But now…if there was time for a choice, he would welcome a bullet's salvation before being plunged into fire.

"You have a plan?" Mahdi asked.

"Streams lead to the ocean, right?"

"Or a lake."

"No lake on the satellite imagery."

"No streams, either."

Winston scrunched up his face and then glared. "Get your ass out of there."

Mahdi considered staying, but then thought better of it. Winston would either forcibly remove him or leave him, and Mahdi had no doubt he'd eventually be discovered. He lifted his vegetative blanket away and rolled into the river. The water was comfortable. Mahdi rolled onto his back, looking up at the swishing canopy, rain gathering into small fountains before falling to the ground, or the stream, gurgling music. A grin came over his face, or perhaps it had never left. If Ambani got his way and turned this island into a resort, no one would ever want to leave. He'd make a fortune.

His eyes lingered on the treetops, where yellow birds flitted through the swaying trees, their songs drowned out by the white noise hiss of falling water. The storm above was nearly black, but a spear of light shone through the clouds for a moment, its position parallel to the stream and definitely not where Winston intended to go.

Mahdi felt drawn toward the light, but his eyes were pulled toward movement. The tall, twisting tree trunks were covered in large, dark growths, like mushrooms. One of them had moved. Or perhaps falling water had splashed off the top. He watched for a moment, and then the calm instilled in him by the refreshing waters washed away.

All that remained, again, was fear.

"The children," Mahdi screamed. Winston turned toward him, impatient. "They never left."

The large man's eyes slowly turned upward, as the children uncoiled from their perches high above. They'd waited patiently for their prey to emerge, and instead of one target, they now had two.

Winston said nothing. Just started running downstream. Mahdi took one last look back toward the light cutting through the storm, felt drawn toward it, and then ran through the water in Winston's wake. The children unleashed themselves from the trees and plummeted to the ground, landing and then running on all fours.

31

THEY STOOD IN the water, covered by it, dark statues beneath the waves. Undulating waters gave them the illusion of life, but not one of the Sentinelese showed any signs of movement. Not the men, the women, or the children. But they had to be alive. Corpses couldn't stand upright, underwater, as waves rolled past overhead.

Rowan gave Talia's wrist a tap. "Take the lead. Keep Sashi with you."

"And go where?"

"Someplace we can get lost in. Or a choke point. If we need to fight, that's our only chance."

"My own personal Leonidas," Talia said. She was tense, but still smiling. The woman's feathers were hard to ruffle. Rowan tried to show the same level of bravery, but mostly he found himself not wanting, but craving a drink.

"Leonidas died," he pointed out.

"Then do better."

He smiled at that, but it quickly faded when a turtle shell of close-cut black hair rose through the waves. The Sentinelese man rose from the water as he walked toward shore, his face without emotion, his eyes locked on Talia. He stopped, waist deep, his skin goose-bumping as a chill wind swept down from the swirling sky. "Lazoaf."

Rowan looked from the man, to Talia. "Is he…is he talking to you?"

A slow nod. "I think so."

"That's the same thing he said before. What does it mean?"

She glanced at him. "Leave."

"You speak their language?" Sashi asked.

"They speak mine," she said. "It's Hebrew for 'leave.' But that doesn't mean that's what he's saying. In fact, it's impossible. He's communicating something, but it could be, 'give up, ' or 'die well,' or any number of things.

A gentle splashing drew their full attention back to the man, who was still waist deep in water, but now hissing and thrusting his midsection. Dozens of dark bodies beneath the waves shifted forward.

"Go," Rowan urged. "Slow until you hit the jungle. Then run like hell. Try to stay on the roots. Don't leave a path."

"How will you find us?" Sashi asked.

"I'll be right behind you. I just need to slow them down first, since they already know where we are." He flicked the assault rifle's safety switch off and looped a finger around the trigger.

"Don't kill them," Talia said.

"Really? Still?"

"I don't know what they are, but we're the ones in the wrong. We shouldn't be here. And it's not their fault that we are."

"I'll aim for their legs," he said, expecting a fight, but none came.

Talia took Sashi by the arm and led her toward the jungle's fringe. Rowan glanced back at the sound of shifting leaves, watched them slip out of sight, and then turned back to the Sentinelese rising from the water. The men carried bows and spears. The women held bundles of arrows. And the children…as they reached the shallows, they dropped down and walked on all fours, their arms and legs spread wide, like four-legged spiders.

He took a step back and then remembered the weapon in his hand. The FN SCAR fired up to 600 rounds per minute, which would have been great if the magazine wasn't limited to 20 rounds. He had two spare magazines—the rest were either gone, or buried under the mash of food and medical supplies. He could swap out the magazine in seconds, and he wouldn't have trouble emptying all three in sixty seconds. The problem was that no one could put that many bullets in this many people in sixty seconds. But in that same amount of time, the Sentinelese could rush him and overwhelm him without losing more than ten of their total number, which looked close to forty.

But maybe if he hit the right people, they would slow or stop their approach. All he needed to do was buy time for Talia and Sashi behind him. He hoped he'd be able to follow and rejoin them, but he wasn't counting on it. Lives had been lost because of his mistakes. This was a step in the right direction, but atoning for those mistakes would be a long path.

He looked down the sights, zeroing in on the first man out of the water, still gyrating as he walked through the now knee-deep water. Instinct pulled the gun's sights toward the man's chest—two rounds would put him down—but Talia's voice in his head tugged his aim toward the man's thigh. She was right. He didn't deserve this fate. None of them did.

Then again, they were also not exactly human…

So…

He eyed the children, moving faster than the adults, scurrying onto the sand on either side of him.

Out of time, he decided, and pulled the trigger.

The rifled barked out a bullet, punctuated by a lightning streak and a thunderclap.

A plume of red burst from the target's leg: blood and bits of flesh. Rowan had seen men take similar hits. Hardened soldiers. They all went down. No matter how tough you are, when a bullet turns the meat of your body into ground chuck, it stops you cold. You might get back up again, you might even run and fight through the pain. But when that bullet first carves a path through your body, you drop.

Unless, apparently, you're a Sentinelese warrior.

The man showed no reaction to being shot. No shout of pain. No flinch. And no limp as he continued toward shore, ever gyrating his genital warning…or superiority…or whatever the hell it was meant to communicate.

Rowan adjusted his aim, just slightly. Pulled the trigger again.

Red flesh and blood, combined with white bone fragments, popped from the back of the man's leg. Inability to feel or care about pain or not, remove a man's knee and he's going to drop. Blood soaked the sand as the man fell to one knee, but he still showed no hint of pain.

The rest of them kept on coming, their pace easy, but increasing with each step. By the time they reached the jungle, they'd be running. If the others didn't care enough about the warrior to stop and assist, perhaps there was another way. Rowan adjusted his aim. The gunshot shook the air, and his heart. One of the women dropped into the waves, her leg shattered.

Rowan felt horrible for shooting a woman. He was an old fashioned Yankee at heart. But neither the woman, nor the Sentinelese cared. They just kept on coming, their feet splashing through the shallows.

He adjusted his aim again. Same tactic, different target. The trigger slid, but not far enough to punch the round out of the barrel. Rowan pulled his finger away and lowered his aim away from the child. The kid was creepy as hell, scurrying toward him across the sand, looking more like an enraged, tailless Komodo dragon, but he was still a child.

"Shit," Rowan said as the Sentinelese broke into a run. He slid the rifle over his shoulder, sprinted toward the jungle and crashed through the brush. He'd been in situations like this before, bugging out as enemy combatants closed in. But there was always a chopper waiting to evac, his brothers by his side, and Apaches en route to clean up the mess. All he had now was the jungle ahead, which eventually ended as an identical beach on the island's far side, and a whole lot of 'nope' closing in from behind.

The jungle opened up. Rowan sprinted through it while trying to keep his feet out of the soft soil and on the firm roots. Talia and Sashi had done a good job hiding their escape route. He caught a glimpse of them ahead, cresting a hill toward the island's core. Then they were gone.

At the sound of shifting leaves behind him, Rowan altered course. He ran parallel to the beach, the forest floor clear of brush. The Sentinelese followed him, the silence of their pursuit somehow more horrifying than if they'd been hooting and banging on tribal drums. This was more primal, the way animals hunt, without fanfare. Just the chase, and death.

Sprinting warriors slipped in and out of his peripheral vision, running along the beach, separated from him by just ten feet of foliage. He angled inward, trying to distance himself from them while staying ahead of the angry mob behind him.

An arrow hummed past his head, a narrow miss. It struck a tree and dug deep. He zig-zagged back and forth, a frantic slalom run through the trees, exposing himself as little as possible. Spears and arrows fell around him, some coming close, most hitting trees. The Sentinelese were skilled hunters. He'd seen their aim. But they apparently had little practice with a moving target.

A *thunk* resounded from his back, the impact toppling him forward. He tucked and rolled. Just a moment before striking the ground, he realized it might have been the wrong move. But it was too late. His body rolled against the roots and the steel assault rifle, each impact like a baseball bat against his body. Momentum carried him forward and back to his feet, in pain, but still mobile. He glanced back and saw the women first, some gathering thrown spears, some tossing fresh projectiles toward him. They worked in shifts, gathering, running, throwing, running so that there was always something headed in his direction.

Then he saw the children, scurrying over the ground, each step silent and swift. He nearly tripped when the nearest of them opened its mouth and shrieked. It wasn't the sound that frightened him, though. It was the size of the open maw that resembled a pitbull's gaping jaws, but with large flat teeth. It wasn't exactly a predatory bite, but they looked powerful enough to crush bones.

Are any of the Sentinelese human?

He looked forward and found himself charging toward a line of Sentinelese warriors, drawing bow strings back. He cut a sharp right, and threw himself behind a tree just as a dozen arrows punched into it.

A fresh shriek lifted his eyes. The children were upon him.

Sorry Talia, he thought before twisting the rifle up and firing from the hip. It was the least accurate way to fire a weapon like the FN SCAR, but the broad-mouthed children were easy targets.

And then they weren't.

As the first bullet cut through the air, the lithe children bounded away in either direction. The bullets chewed into several women. Some ignored the wounds, but two, each of them struck in the head, dropped to the ground.

The nearest of the children, if that's even what they were, landed on a tree trunk, coiled its limbs, and sprang off, jaws open, fingers hooked.

Rowan tried to angle the rifle up, but the strap was tight around his back. He reached for his knife, knowing it would be too late.

The impact struck him hard, knocking the air from his lungs, but there was no gnashing of teeth or breaking of bones. He opened his eyes. The thing lay atop him like a sleeping child…with a blowgun dart in its neck.

He glanced up. Talia was behind the group of women, still closing in. She pointed inland, not making a sound, and then headed in that direction.

Rowan pushed to his feet, emptied the assault rifle's magazine, firing at the closest targets, and then ran in the direction Talia had fled, just as the Sentinelese men burst through the brush separating beach from jungle and took over the chase.

32

"WE NEED TO get out of the water." Mahdi lifted his leg from the stream's hummus-like bottom. Each step was a slog, slowing his desperate run to a flailing march.

"Banks are too steep here," Winston replied, somehow powering through the stream much faster. "Up ahead."

Thirty feet beyond Winston, the tall, overgrown banks dropped down to a small sandy clearing where a footpath entered the stream from one side and exited on the other. The open ground would make running from the children easier, but Mahdi was thirty feet behind Winston, and the gaping youth just ten behind him, and closing in. None of the children had entered the stream yet, but that was probably because they moved faster on land or, in some cases, in the trees. He could hear the little killers crashing through ferns and grasses lining the river, but he could see many more lunging from tree to tree, like oversized hairless squirrels.

Behind and around him, the children closed in.

"Winston!" he shouted.

The big man glanced back, looking more annoyed than worried, and raised his gun. Mahdi ducked as he ran, flinching at the sound of a gunshot. Then another and another. He heard two thumps on the bank and a splash behind him. Cool water struck his back, urging him onward.

Ten feet from the beach, a weight too heavy for the child's three-and-a-half-foot height, slammed into Mahdi's back. He shouted in surprise, but his voice was immediately drowned out by the clap of a gun. There was a loud hum, a wet thump, and then the weight was gone with a splash. Pain followed his freedom. He felt his ear, fingers tracing open flesh where his earlobe should have been. The salty sweat covering his fingers set the wound on fire. But there was no time to express the pain, or anger at Winston for nearly shooting him.

He could run with the pain. He had before.

It was louder back then.

Hotter. Drier. The kind of day that carried you into the next without leaving an impression. That was how it should have ended, but the moment he saw Aziz, backpack on his shoulder, sweat on his brow despite the moisture-wicking heat, he knew the day would haunt him. It had been chasing him ever since, just as the children did now, hungry and violent, seeking his destruction simply because he survived…and knew the truth.

Just as he did now. A part of it, at least. But knowing and understanding were not the same thing. He needed Talia for that, but their reunion with the rest of the expedition would likely end, or begin, in violence.

Winston followed the path left, putting distance between him and Mahdi once more. Mahdi understood the tactic. He had heard the joke about surviving a bear attack by outrunning your friend. If Mahdi fell to the children, Winston would be in the clear. At the same time, the man wasn't sadist enough to force it to happen. A quick shot to the leg would make Mahdi easy prey.

Then again, maybe the shot that took my ear was meant for something else?

Mahdi charged out of the river and became snarled in the overgrowth. He shook his leg to get free, but he was caught, and not by vegetation. Two thin branch-like arms reached out from the brush, twiggy fingers hooked around his calves, compressing the muscle.

Mahdi flinched back and fell, dragging the boy out with him.

The massive mouth spread into a smile—or was it a sneer?—and then snapped open, reaching for his ankle. One bite and he would be done. Mahdi had no doubt the powerful jaws and triple-sized molars could make short work of his ankle. Best case scenario, his ankle would be broken. Worst case, his foot would be chewed off. Both scenarios led to his inevitable death.

But there was still one option, and it didn't involve Winston. The man had run, just as Mahdi believed he would. While thrashing his leg, making it hard for the child to line up a solid bite, Mahdi dug the knife from his pocket and snapped out the blade.

"Allah forgive me," he said, but in his heart he believed no one was listening, and that his actions were justified. *They might not even be human,* he thought, and then he swung the blade down hard. The impact was harder than he'd expected. For a moment, he feared he had missed, but then he spotted the knife handle jutting from the boy's head.

He reached for the handle when the boy's eyes opened and looked directly at him. The boy began speaking, the words foreign to Mahdi's trained ears. But he didn't stir. Wounded, but not dead...with a knife in his skull.

Definitely not human.

The blade came free with a grinding slurp, the sound followed by a shriek.

Mahdi rolled to the side as an airborne child sailed past, fingers and toes splayed wide to grasp. The boy clung to a tree trunk, ready to spring out again, but Mahdi was already sprinting away, his legs pumping hard over smooth terrain.

"Winston!" he shouted, but he received no reply. The man had abandoned him.

It was justice, perhaps. He had abandoned a friend once, left him to face his end alone. Conscience held him back, and then morality propelled him. He was running then, as now, racing away from danger, in seek of help. He'd screamed back then, 'Bomb! Aziz has a bomb!' No one in the square had recognized Aziz, but Mahdi's pointed finger had made it easy to find the twenty-year old man with a too-heavy backpack.

Men rushed in. Palestinian men who longed for peace with Israel. A bomb in Israel meant retaliation. Warplanes. Missiles. Things that could not be defended against. Despite being childhood friends with Aziz, Mahdi had never understood his sister's attraction to the man. He was unpredictable. Violent on occasion. And too trusting. It made him an easy Hamas recruit, which was nothing special on its own. Everyone knew someone with ties to the radical group, but few of them ever really took action.

But Aziz was impressionable. Believed that virgins awaited him. That death would appease Allah. And there he was, headed for the gate, prepared to take Israeli lives.

But Aziz never got the chance. His thumb slipped off the dead man's trigger when two men tackled him. The C4 exploded, sending ball bearings meant for Jewish targets into the Palestinian men and women enjoying the very normal, too hot afternoon.

Mahdi was running away when the shrapnel had struck him down.

He was one of five survivors. Twenty-one others died. When questioned by the authorities, Mahdi had told the truth, and the resulting manhunt led to the deaths of several Hamas members. Those who escaped, or survived the raids were all told the same thing: Mahdi had betrayed them.

Mahdi had given up his wife and two children, moved to London, and as an illegal alien, he had worked menial jobs, his education of little help. He had been running ever since.

Was running still.

Winston's footprints on the path were easy to follow. The heavyset man's heels dug in deep. Mahdi slipped off the path, staying atop the tangle of roots. If the children were tracking them, let Winston be the bear's snack.

Voices slowed him down. Behind him, the children were out of sight, but low to the ground, or in the trees, they could be ten feet away and he'd never know.

He recognized Winston's voice. Angry. A warning.

Then Rowan's, defiant.

Run away, he thought. *Move around them, find the beach, and swim to a shallow reef.* But Rowan was a good man, tricked to this island. Mahdi couldn't run away from his demise like he had Aziz's.

Mahdi angled his run toward the voices, stumbling to a stop when he saw Rowan on his knees, fingers laced behind his head. Winston stood behind him, gun to the back of his head, execution style. The FN SCAR rifle was on the ground. Winston must have surprised Rowan.

"Stop," Mahdi said.

Winston gave his head a shake. "You and I both know we're not leaving until this asshole is dead."

Mahdi stepped around the scene, his eyes finding Rowan's. "Just so you know, there're about forty really pissed off Sentinelese about a minute behind me," Rowan said.

"We got problems of our own," Winston said, and he motioned Mahdi to step in front of Rowan.

"Pick up the rifle," Winston said.

Mahdi obeyed, hoisting the weapon over his shoulder. He knew how to use the rifle, but he didn't think he could angle it toward Winston without being seen, and then promptly shot. Winston was a lot of things, but slow and merciful were not two of them.

"Good. Now stab him."

"What?" Mahdi stepped back. Winston was serious. "Why?"

"You could just shoot me," Rowan said, pushing his head back, thumping the barrel of Winston's gun, a move that made the big man flinch and step back. "But you need my death to look legit. Like the Sentinelese killed me. Going to be hard to prove if you can't bring my body back."

"I'll carry you," Winston said. "Let you get gassy. Make a good flotation device."

Rowan grinned and Mahdi had no idea how he could manage such a thing, even if it was fake.

Winston glared at Mahdi. "Stab him with that pig sticker of yours, or I'll shoot you both."

Mahdi tried to think of a way out of stabbing Rowan, but he really only had one option. He reached into his pocket, drew the knife, the handle still slick with Sentinelese blood, and popped the spring-loaded blade. He stepped closer to Rowan, leaned his head down toward his ear, said, "Allah ,yaghfir li," while cutting through Rowan's flesh.

Rowan ground his teeth and hissed out each breath, but said nothing. Mahdi gave a goodbye nod and then thrust the knife into the center of Rowan's chest. He held the blade in place while Rowan shook and gasped. Then he withdrew the bloody knife and stepped back as Rowan fell to his knees, and then his side, his chest slick and red.

Winston laughed and clapped. "Oh my God, man, I didn't say kill him. Give him a limp. Slow him down. Let the natives finish him off. But God damn, maybe there is hope for you yet."

The sound of approaching feet alerted them to the presence of Rowan's pursuers, or perhaps their own. Probably both. Not needing to be told what to do, Mahdi charged down the path, Winston right behind him, no doubt ready to shoot him should the Sentinelese get too close.

He took one last look at Rowan, lying motionless on the ground, blood everywhere.

I am sorry, my friend.

And then he ran some more.

33

DEALING WITH FRUSTRATION was never Talia's strong suit. Living among tribal people, who were either competent, or dead, she rarely found herself annoyed by the people around her. If anything, they had to temper their frustration while she learned the language, customs, and culture of the people into whom she'd inserted herself. Since saving and leaving Rowan, she'd been running uphill and inland, but mostly she'd been waiting for Sashi.

The woman hadn't taken a break, but her run had slowed to a jog after five minutes, then to a brisk walk. Now it seemed that each step was an effort, pushing her hands down on her knees as they climbed up a steep grade.

A strong wind tore through the trees above, revealing storm clouds and a gap in the gray swirl where the sun still shone through. The clouds had begun to unleash their stored water, most of which found its way to the ground via a series of leaf networks, forming vertical streams. A spritz of rain fell through the opening.

Sashi paused in the wind, not so much buffered by it as reveling in the coolness of the breeze. They were both slick with sweat and clinging humidity, despite being scantily clad.

Talia enjoyed the breeze, and the brief rain shower, too, but there was no time to linger. "You need to move, or we're not going to make it."

"Make it *where?*" Sashi asked. She took the conversation as an excuse to stop and catch her breath.

"I meant, survive." Talia had no destination in mind other than being where the Sentinelese weren't, and where she'd motioned for Rowan to head. She had no idea if they'd be able to find each other on the island, or if he would escape the large hunting party pursuing him, but their odds of survival increased while he was with them. Not because he was the better survivalist or fighter, but because his skills balanced out hers. Together, both their odds of survival went up.

The same could not be said for Sashi. "I can't do it."

Sashi looked exhausted, wearing the face of a runner about to drop out of a race.

Talia took her hand. "Here." She pulled her to a large leaf that was the last stage in a stream of water trickling down the tree from far above. She angled the leaf toward Sashi. "Drink."

Though she looked unsure at first, Sashi gulped water, and then let it run over her face and neck before drinking more. Talia did the same, and stepped back. "Are you ready?"

"I don't know how far I can go," Sashi said. "I'm just slowing you down."

Talia could tell the woman wanted to suggest that Talia just leave her behind. It was the noble thing to say, maybe even the right thing to do. Had Sashi's collusion with Ambani and Winston been any less sympathetic, Talia would have already left her behind. But Sashi was as much a victim as the rest of them.

"Can you make it there?" Talia pointed toward the distant sunlight streaking down. She didn't have a good reason for heading to that part of the island. Maybe it was simply because the sun shone on it like a beacon. Really, it just felt right, like where they needed to be.

Sashi perked up a little. "I can."

Then they were off again, pushing upward through the cleared forest. Their pace improved, and even better, there was no sign of the Sentinelese. No trails. No footprints. No sounds. The only indication that the island was inhabited was the subtle smoky fragrance.

"I think they've lit the fires again," Sashi said.

Talia breathed deeply through her nose. Sashi was right. The smell wasn't lingering from the night before, it was growing stronger. Somewhere on the island, something was burning, despite the rain. "If you notice the smell get stronger than it is right now, say something. Means we're getting too close."

They rounded a large tree with spiraling curtains of roots, and paused. The jungle ahead was overgrown, dense, and alive. Unlike the cleared outer fringe of the island, the land ahead was like something out of a magical realm, where everything grew large and lush.

"It's a primeval forest," Talia said.

"What's that?"

"Old growth forest, untouched by man."

Sashi looked back at the jungle they'd come through. "Isn't that primeval forest, too?"

"The trees," Talia said, "but the Sentinelese have cleared and maintained the jungle floor. This...this is untouched. This is beautiful." She looked at a spiraling fern that came up to her waist. "Some of these plant species could be millions of years old, predating the Sentinelese."

Talia ran a hand over the fern, shaking a shower of water droplets to the ground below. Then she stepped forward, and in her mind, back in time. She forgot all about running as she strode through the underbrush, caressed by wet leaves. She turned all about, noting dozens of species she had never seen before. It was a botanist's dream come true.

Then she heard the birds. She looked for them, but saw nothing in the trees above. *Hiding from the rain,* she thought.

When the brush ahead shook, she ducked down to look, and she caught sight of something scurrying away. It was the first ground-dwelling animal she'd seen, aside from the Sentinelese, since arriving on the island. She thought it strange at first, but then decided it made sense. Any animal moving through the cleared forest floor would make easy prey.

That's why we should stay here, Talia thought. Hiding here was just a matter of ducking. She considered stopping, but decided to press on. There was more jungle to see. More wonders awaiting them.

And Rowan.

Talia's heart beat hard for a moment.

She'd forgotten about Rowan. "C'mon," she said, and she picked up the pace just a little.

The scent of smoke gave way to jasmine, and then she saw the orange flowers, curved like a voluptuous woman, hanging from a vine growing around several trees. Beads of water clung to the skirt-like petals, dripping down with sensuous slowness. Talia licked her lips. The place was intoxicating.

A giggle burped from Talia, expressing just a hint of the delight building in her chest. The sound staggered her to a stop. A flicker of logic and memory flared.

A single word came to mind: *inhibitions.*

The word was like a klaxon, warning of danger, waking her from the spell cast over her by the island's magic. What had started as a strange idea—that an island could affect a person's inhibitions—coalesced into certainty. She spun around, looking at the luscious plants and flowers. Aside from the trees, none of the plants looked familiar.

She considered the trees themselves, but she had seen no hint of pollen in the air. They had drunk from the root, but had begun losing their inhibitions before setting foot on the island.

She breathed deeply again and got lost for a moment. Jungle decay mixed with unseen fruits, flowering perfumes, and storm-born ozone infused her with a sense of peace—of lie-down-and-sleep. She wanted to give in to it, to be absorbed by the island itself, and become part of this world forever.

Then she detected something else.

Something that had always been there, on the island, and on the boat.

It's the smoke, she thought. *They're burning something. Altering our perceptions of reality, intoxicating us with mind altering agents.* In a jungle like this, there were probably dozens of plants that could confuse reality. It explained the lack of inhibitions and the inhuman things they had seen. Shared hallucinations weren't uncommon among drug users exposed to the same stimuli. And the Sentinelese would know that. Would have perfected the art. A man-like monster with six eyes could be a man wearing a mask. Back on the beach, they could have been simply mutilating a dead body they believed had returned from the dead.

Shit, she thought, and then again, *shit, shit, shit.*

Every decision they had made since stepping on the island was suspect. Everything they'd witnessed might not be real. Including this jungle. She and Rowan had been wrong. Maybe the Sentinelese were not sending out the smoke across the island for entertainment. Maybe it was psychochemical warfare. Talia searched the foliage and flowers for signs that she might not be seeing reality. For all she knew, she was tripping hard, but if it was an illusion caused by hallucinogens, she couldn't tell.

Treat it like it's real, she told herself, *but don't fall in love with the place.* If she could see the beauty and allure for what it was—the deadly call of a siren—then she might not forget the island's dangers. The Sentinelese might not be unkillable monsters, but treating them as such wouldn't hurt.

Guilt swirled in her gut. She was thinking about an untouched tribe, the kind that she had fought to defend.

But the Sentinelese weren't like other tribes. When an Amazonian people killed an invader, it was after much debate, and almost always after an attempted contact, or several warnings. Usually it was in self-defense. And if the trespassers fled, so be it. Conflict was avoided at all costs.

Here, invaders were hunted. Their minds altered. Death was a way of life.

Talia clenched her eyes shut. Even her fears were growing wild and out of control. She couldn't trust her thoughts.

Find Rowan, and get off the island. Nothing else matters.

"Sashi," she said, turning around to explain her revelations.

But Sashi was no longer there.

"Sashi?"

A swishing sound pulled her around again. Sashi slipped away through a curtain of ferns, thirty feet away, and disappeared.

Talia nearly shouted for her, but held back. Evading an enemy didn't work if you were shouting.

She charged ahead, arms raised, cutting through the ferns. Sashi had left a clear trail. All she needed to do was move faster.

The ferns parted into a less dense patch of jungle.

Ahead, there was sunlight.

And Sashi.

And the man with six eyes.

34

ROWAN OPENED HIS eyes, surprised to still be alive. Then he sat up, felt the hot lava pain in his chest, and reconsidered whether Mahdi sparing his life had been a gift or not. The sweet nothing of oblivion might have been better than the hellish island full of monstrous people, and the three inch slice over his sternum.

When Mahdi had obeyed Winston and snapped open the spring-loaded switchblade, Rowan was worried the man might actually kill him. When he said 'Allah, forgive me,' in Arabic, Rowan was positive. But it had been an elaborate and painful ruse that Rowan wasn't aware of until Mahdi thrust the blade into his chest…or pretended to. He had retracted the blade just as he shoved. Rowan didn't need to act hurt; Mahdi had cut open his chest, and shoved the knife handle against it. It wasn't as bad as being stabbed, but it hurt. A lot.

But Rowan understood. The cut, and the amount of blood flowing from it, had to look convincing, as did his death. He'd fallen, held his breath and kept his eyes open and frozen in shock. He'd seen dead men before. Those who died with their eyes open, their dead gaze unflinching, were nearly impossible to look at.

Even Winston couldn't manage it for more than a second, and the blood soaking Rowan's chest had been convincing enough.

Rowan listened to the two men running away. He was about to stand, and then he heard the Sentinelese rushing toward him. He stayed where he'd fallen, let the air out of his lungs, and stared at the sky. The rain-pelted canopy shifted in the wind, redirecting a stream of water. It fell fifty feet, landing atop Rowan's forehead. He wanted to move. Not blinking would be nearly impossible. But the Sentinelese arrived before he could turn his head.

Movement in his periphery tugged at his mind. It took a massive amount of concentration to not look, and show no emotion, and ignore the damn water drilling into his forehead and spritzing his eyes.

He heard the Sentinelese all around him. Most of them continued on, pursuing the two fleeing men. But several stopped to inspect his body. He saw them standing around him, but didn't look at anyone. He counted three men, two women, and an unknown number of the strange children.

One of the children gripped his shin and gave it a squeeze. The small hand felt far too strong. Rowan was worried the bone would snap, but he remained motionless. The child released him and then crawled up over his body.

Rain water blurred his vision of the canopy overhead.

Blink, his eyes screamed, but he remained rigid, his lungs starting to burn.

The child, a girl, he thought, crawled up over his stomach and hovered over his chest. Fingers tickled his skin, tracing lines back and forth. He could feel goosebumps rising on his legs.

Dead men don't get goosebumps, he thought. *If the Sentinelese notice…*

But the pain erased the goosebumps. The small fingers touched the wound on his chest. Pressed down. The pain was exquisite, pulsing fresh, warm blood over his body.

And still, he didn't move. Didn't blink. The tears in his eyes were concealed by the water beating against his forehead.

The child spoke and lifted her hand. Then she hopped away and continued in the direction Winston and Mahdi had fled. He heard several more children scurry after her.

Rowan didn't think the children were in charge, but the girl's assessment was trusted. After a few moments, the adults stepped over him and hurried into the woods.

Stay dead, he thought. *The Sentinelese are primitive, not stupid.*

After another minute, two warriors stepped out from behind the tree and followed after the others.

He waited another thirty seconds and then took a very slow breath. Fighting his body's urge to gasp, he breathed in another shallow breath.

Then he blinked, squeezing the water from his eyes.

When no attack came, he shifted his eyes to the sides. As far as he could see, he was alone. He sat up, clenching his jaw against the pain.

A flash of color drew his gaze down to the wound in his chest. An orange flower was stuck to him. He gripped the bottom, pulled, and nearly screamed. The child hadn't just probed his wound, she had inserted a flower stem into it.

Teeth grinding, he tugged the two inch stem out of his chest.

The large flower petals were elegant. The scent delicate and fruity. He was about to toss the flower aside when he noticed the flow of blood from the wound had stopped.

That's not possible, he thought. The wound was deep, and long. It wasn't fatal, but it should have required stitches. He had planned to cauterize the wound like a bona fide action hero. He stepped into the stream of water, letting it strike his chest. The wound stung, but no more blood flowed.

The wound wasn't healed. Far from it. But the blood had coagulated, forming a goopy scab.

He looked at the flower again. The tribe had to know of its healing properties.

They knew I was alive.

He couldn't think of a reason the Sentinelese would spare him. It seemed even more unlikely that they would also help heal him.

Why? he asked himself, and then he decided waiting around to find out was the wrong choice.

Cleaned of blood, but drenched in water and pain, Rowan drew his last remaining weapon—a knife—and headed inland. He wasn't sure he would be able to find Talia and Sashi, but he had to try.

Each step brought fresh waves of pain, but the further inland he walked, the less he noticed. His body didn't hurt any less, but his mind became preoccupied. A brew of flower scents, warm smoke, and electric storm filled the air. Each breath made him feel a little more alive.

Distant bird songs sifted through the trees whenever the rumbling thunder subsided. The storm's intensity was increasing, but it had yet to become dangerous. The trees protected him from the wind, rain, and lightning, while at the same time moving the jungle in a way that made it look alive.

He found himself wandering, eyes lifted toward the trees, and the occasional break that let him see the layers of twisting, dark clouds. Oblivious to the path ahead, he tripped over a root and careened forward. His fall was stopped by a tree, the side of his face mashing into the unmoving trunk. The knife fell from his hand.

Revived by the momentary adrenaline rush, Rowan shook his head and realized he'd been an easy target, distracted by the strange surroundings. *I'm tired,* he thought. But resting would be a mistake. If he fell asleep, which he could do in nearly any environment, he might not wake up. The Sentinelese had spared him once. He didn't want to test their mercy twice.

He bent down to recover the knife, and when he stood again, his vision tunneled. The tree held him upright until his vision returned.

Tired and hungry, he thought.

A scream snapped him back to full awareness.

That was Sashi.

He stepped away from the tree and turned toward the scream. A wall of thick jungle growth, not cleared by the Sentinelese, greeted him. When the scream repeated, he charged ahead. Branches lashed his arms. Leaves slapped his face. The ground, wet with water and coated with a layer of decay missing from the outside jungle, grew slick.

He ran, unable to see more than a few feet, until the ground fell out from under him. He toppled into a stream. The fall was cushioned by the three-foot-deep water, but he struck the bottom. Muck wrapped around him, tried to hold him down, but couldn't maintain its grip as he thrashed. When he resurfaced, he sheathed the knife again. It wouldn't do him any good if he lost it—or fell on it.

The grass lining the stream's edge was slick with water so he looped it around his hand, gripped it tight and pulled himself up.

His breath became ragged, each lungful desperate. But he pushed on, inhaling as much air as he could. And then, with a final slap from an elephant-ear-sized leaf, he stumbled out of the overgrowth and into a less dense portion of the jungle.

He saw Talia, twenty-five feet away, blowgun in hand. Between them was the monstrous man. He was taller now, despite standing with a hunch. More sinewy. His wounds, aside from the peeled open face, were healed. The bumps in his spine had grown out, jutting six inches from the back, the skin so tight it looked ready to tear.

What the fuck is that thing?

The eyes in the back of its head turned toward him, squinting with predatory interest.

Then a fourth set of eyes opened on its shoulder blades, watching him.

The eyes felt familiar. Tickled his memory. But he was too terrified to contemplate what he was seeing.

Talia puffed her cheeks and a dart flew from the blowgun. It struck the creature, right next to the two darts already embedded in its side. Rowan had felt the effects of just one dart. It seemed impossible that a man could resist the deadly toxin, but the thing was no longer a man, and maybe never was.

Rowan was about to draw his knife when Talia spotted him, reached behind her back and drew his pistol. Rather than firing it, she tossed it toward him. He reached up to catch the gun, but it hit his hand hard and bounced onto the muddy forest floor. He recovered the soiled gun, flicked the mud off and raised the barrel toward the creature just as Sashi screamed a third time.

Where is she? he thought, and then he saw for himself, as the monster lifted Sashi up by the throat, extended a finger and stabbed it into her chest.

35

"SLOW DOWN. SLOW down." Winston was out of breath, mouth wide, gulping air. The man's physical abilities were surprising, given his girth, but there was a limit. Mahdi was winded, too, but he could have carried on. Still wanted to. But he had little doubt that Winston could and would shoot him at the first sign of betrayal. Mahdi still carried the rifle, but Winston would be the quicker draw. Survival meant maintaining his deal with the Devil. For now.

"Your clothes are weighing you down," Mahdi said. Winston was the only member of the expedition not to shed his clothing. The man was cold, calculating, and ruthless, but he was also ashamed of his weight.

Winston looked down at his saturated shirt, then directed a glower toward Mahdi.

He'd rather die than expose himself. Mahdi pitied the man for a moment, but all the fat and stretchmarks in the world couldn't excuse Winston's actions. The man was just as much a monster as the Sentinelese. They deserved each other.

Winston leaned against a tree, gun in hand, hanging by his hip. His eyes were closed. A stream of water trickled from above, pelting his head.

Mahdi slid Rowan's rifle from his shoulder. He didn't know if Rowan was alive, but he did know he hadn't killed the man. It was a gamble, cutting Rowan's chest, hoping he would play along. But he couldn't kill him. Rowan was a good man. A protector, despite whatever past haunted him. And Mahdi would forfeit his own life before letting any more good men die.

Winston was *not* a good man.

Mahdi flicked the FN SCAR's safety switch off with a subtle click.

Winston didn't flinch.

Maybe I could *shoot him.*

He imagined the scene. The bullets punching into Winston's thick flesh. The blood. The screaming. The returned fire. The noise. Even if Mahdi survived, the Sentinelese would quickly find him.

Then again, who was to say they weren't about to leap from the trees and kill them both. They had done their best to evade the tribe, but there was no way to know if they'd been successful.

"If you kill me," Winston said, eyes still closed. "You'll die, too."

Mahdi pointed the rifle barrel toward the ground. "I wasn't—"

"You were thinking about it," he said with unwavering confidence. Reached up, tapped his ear. "The sound of a safety switch is often the last thing men in my line of work hear. So I listen for it."

Winston opened his eyes. Raised his pistol. "Now you…you're expendable. Just not yet." He stepped closer to Mahdi, reached a hand out and waggled his fingers.

Mahdi hesitated for just a moment. He didn't want Winston to have the rifle, but he could take it by force, and dying over it would serve no purpose. He frowned and handed the weapon over.

"Buck up, Mahd-man. Not everyone can be brave." Winston slung the rifle over his shoulder. "Of course, you're kind of a career chickenshit. Always running away. Hiding. Compromising your morals to survive. I can respect that, at least. It's the one thing we have in common. I used to be a 'good' man, too. Trying to do right by people. A real bleeding heart."

Winston pushed his chin out, motioning for Mahdi to start moving again. They struck out through the tangled jungle once more. The jungle grew thicker, greenery squeezing them in all around. The Sentinelese could be ten feet away and they'd never know.

Mahdi checked over his shoulder. Winston grinned at him. Beyond the big man was endless, wet green, spattered with colorful flowers. There were no signs of pursuit, but he had little doubt the tribe was back there, likely closing in. He turned forward and looked up without angling his head. The storm raged. Lightning flashed, strobing through the cracks in the canopy. Thunder shook the world. He watched the slices of sky until he saw it: a streak of yellow sunlight, beaming down toward the island.

Leading the way, Mahdi turned slightly inland when a tree blocked his path, and again while maneuvering through a field of tall ferns, and again, when climbing a hill. He adjusted their course until the streak of sun lay dead ahead, like magnetic north on a compass.

He didn't know why the sunlight called to him, but he couldn't resist it. Just seeing it gave him hope that his life wouldn't end on this island. But he also knew such a hope was foolish. Nearly everyone on the island wanted him dead. Even if he survived the island, there were people who would follow him to the ends of the Earth to exact their revenge, and silence what he knew forever. Death had been chasing him for years, and it seemed closer than ever.

But not in that light.

So he pressed on, walking in silence, until voices not belonging to him or Winston filled the air.

He stopped and listened. The voices were high pitched and relaxed. Women and children, he thought, but not like the children crawling along the jungle floor. These sounded younger. A cry cut through the air, calmed a moment later by a soothing voice.

Winston stood beside him.

"We should go around," Mahdi said, and he took a step to the right, hoping to circumvent whatever lay ahead and get back on course for the light.

Winston grasped his arm. "This is an opportunity."

"For what?"

"Shock and awe," he said. "A show of force."

"Have you forgotten the man at the beach?"

"The natives are freakshows. Hard to kill, but maybe that doesn't apply to the little ones. They'll get the message. Most people will give you a wide berth if they think you're capable of wiping out entire future generations."

"I believe you are capable of such a thing," Mahdi mumbled.

Winston grinned. "Even better."

Mahdi stumbled forward, driven by Winston's meaty shoving hand. Then the jungle growth cleared. Mahdi crashed through the brush, landed on his hands and knees, and announced their presence to the people in the clearing. His heart broke when he looked up.

Sixty feet away, fifteen Sentinelese woman, all of them barely four feet tall and naked, stared at him. Each and every one of them cared for a child. They were gathered around a fire, smaller than the one in which Emmei had met his end, but bright enough to cut through the shade cast by the storm and the jungle canopy.

The ground around them was like nothing else in the jungle. It was cobbled with pale, rounded stones that shouldn't exist on the island. The stones formed a spiraling pattern around the fire pit, which split off in three paths, winding their way through the partially cleared jungle, leading to a variety of simple huts.

It's the Sentinelese village, he thought, and then something at the edge of the cobbled fire pit caught his attention. One of the stones at the edge was partially exposed. And then he saw it for what it was. On an island without stones, the Sentinelese had used skulls—probably those of their ancestors—to create paths.

It was an ingenious use of their limited resources.

It was also horrifying.

Some of the women were nursing infants. Some of the toddlers hobbled to their mothers, just learning to walk. A few of the children were old enough to know that Mahdi didn't belong there, watching him with curiosity, and then worry as Winston stepped out of the jungle, assault rifle pressed to his shoulder.

"Don't do this," Mahdi pleaded.

"Shock and awe," Winston said. "There's no better way to say, 'fuck off.'"

"That's not what will happen," Mahdi said. He knew from personal history, and the long history of the Palestinian people, that killing to subdue a people never worked. As long as a Sentinelese drew breath, they would seek vengeance for the crime Winston was about to commit.

Mahdi threw himself at Winston, but the man was too fast. With a quick twist, he cracked the rifle stock into Mahdi's head, knocking him to the ground.

"I understand you had to try," Winston said. "After what you did to Rowan, I don't see Allah sparing any virgins on your behalf. Unless he was an infidel?" He shrugged. "Honestly, your religion is a mystery to me."

The rifle barked, firing a single round.

The few birds twittering in the canopy fell silent.

The Sentinelese women went rigid, and then one of them dropped to her knees, a baby wrapped in her arms, a hole in her forehead.

"No!" Mahdi shouted, and then to the Sentinelese women. "The baby!"

But none of the women moved, not even as the shot woman toppled forward.

An arm snapped out, arresting the woman's fall. But she hadn't been caught by one of the others. She'd caught herself, still holding her nursing child to her chest.

Blood dripped from the hole in her forehead. She turned her face up, looking at Winston. A red stream ran between her eyes, down the side of her nose, around her mouth and dripped from her chin, tapping on the ground with the rain.

Thunder shook the air.

The woman smiled, blood running into her mouth, between her teeth.

Winston fired again, striking the woman three more times. Her body bucked and snapped with each fresh hole, but she didn't fall, and didn't drop her child.

But the baby…it stopped feeding and turned its head toward Winston, adult anger in its eyes.

"Well, shit," Winston said, flicking the FN SCAR fire rate selector from semi-automatic to full automatic.

Run, Mahdi thought, but he wasn't sure to whom he was projecting the thought.

The angry baby let out a shriek and the small gathering sprang into action. The women holding babies flung them to the ground. The children dropped down, their legs bending like their older siblings. Even the infants went on the attack, catching themselves on the ground and scurrying toward Winston. The women leapt forward, charging alongside the youths, some of them running upright, some of them running on all fours, and still others picking up bows and arrows.

Behind them, the jungle shook, and several louder shrieks replied to the baby. The hunting party had been tracking them and was sandwiching them between the two inhuman forces.

Run! Mahdi thought again, and he knew exactly to whom he was thinking this time. He scrambled to his feet and ran as Winston opened fire, unleashing a fully automatic spray of gunfire toward the oncoming Sentinelese. Mahdi followed a perpendicular path between the two approaching sides.

He was nearly back in the jungle when something struck him. He toppled to the ground, flung himself around and looked at his arm, as pain burst from his forearm to his shoulder. A baby, no more than a year old, was latched on, just above the wrist. He shook his arm, but the baby clung on, its wide jaws compressing.

Winston's barrage chewed into the women and children, slowing their advance, but not stopping it. He sidestepped toward Mahdi as he fired, preparing to flee. But Mahdi wanted nothing to do with the man. He stood, baby still latched on, and ran into the jungle. Something in his wrist popped. Exquisite pain rose through his body and vented as a scream.

Propelled by pain and instinct, he slammed the baby into a tree as he passed. The impact sent another jolt of pain through his body, but also wrenched the child free. He felt a momentary pang of guilt for harming the child, but he saw it land on its hands and feet and turn toward him, blood dripping from its too-wide baby mouth.

He ran again, letting the jungle absorb him, striking out for the light once more.

Behind him, Winston shouted in surprise, no doubt encountering the infant for himself. There was a pop of gunfire that sounded more like Winston's pistol than the assault rifle, and then nothing.

The silence lasted for just a moment.

It was broken by the sounds of pursuit.

36

ROWAN PULLED THE trigger until the magazine was empty. He had no idea how many rounds he'd fired, but he knew that each and every one of them had struck the monstrous back. The creature had twitched with each impact. One of the long spines jutting from between its shoulders had shattered. One of the two eyes that had appeared on its back erupted with a geyser of white fluid. But the creature didn't falter, and it didn't remove its finger from Sashi's chest.

Instead, it craned its head to the side, staring at Sashi like it was trying to make sense of her. She screamed in its grip, but the sound came out as a raspy hiss, her airway constricted by the giant hand around her throat.

Talia fired two more darts, each having as little effect at the previous three.

"Put her down!" she screamed, but she didn't fire another dart. Instead, she returned the dart and the blow gun to the pouch on her belt, drew her knife and unfolded it. The blade wasn't large, and Talia didn't know how to fight with it, but she was ready and willing.

Rowan, on the other hand, had a five inch Ka-Bar knife sheathed on his hip, and countless hours of close-quarters combat training. He'd never been taught how to kill a twelve-foot-tall, all-seeing island demon before, but the basic concept—stab the shit out of your enemy—still applied. He didn't think it would put the creature down for good, but he hoped it would free Sashi.

Blade in hand, Rowan charged. Unlike Talia, he didn't announce the attack. He just moved. The eyes in the back of the creature's head, and the one eye still on its back, tracked him, but he had to hope the thing was more focused on Sashi, still in its grip, and on Talia, attacking from the front.

He was encouraged when Talia rolled beneath Sashi's dangling body, and assaulted the monster's legs. Rowan quickly realized he had been wrong about Talia. She knew how to use a knife, and where to strike. Her blade cut a deep gouge through one inner thigh and then the other. Two quick movements followed by gouts of blood, which flowed hard, and then stopped.

Talia raged at the quick healing beast, shouting and latching on to its leg, stabbing the blade in and twisting it, grinding the meat. For all her effort, the creature remained still, focused on Sashi, whose attempts to free herself were fading.

Rowan took stock of the situation as he closed the distance. The monster didn't respond to pain. It healed too fast to bleed out. Bullets to the head hadn't killed it in the past, and he didn't think he could kill it now.

He focused on the neck. *Too high,* he thought, and then he lowered his gaze to the spines jutting out from its back. They ended in bony nubs, each of them six inches long. Perfect handholds. He pictured himself leaping onto the thing, hoisting himself up in one quick move and then burying the large blade in the monster's spine, separating nerves and paralyzing its body. If it worked, he might even take the time to sever its head. *See if it can survive that.*

Seeing each of the steps he'd have to take, he followed his predetermined path, confident in his ability to follow through.

Then eight more sets of eyes opened on its back, some brown, some blue, some green, and some orange—all of them focused on him.

The great beast twisted, lifting Talia up under her arms, its long fingers wrapping around her body, puncturing her chest and side. She screamed through grinding teeth and began stabbing the arm.

The monster continued around faster than Rowan thought possible, and smashed Sashi's body into him. He tried to roll with the impact, but it was like being hit by a car. He slammed to the ground, covered in wet decomposition, and rolled ten feet before coming to a stunned stop.

He tried to stand, but his head spun and his body ached.

The many-eyed thing focused its attention on Talia, inspecting her the same way it had Sashi.

"Let them go," Rowan growled, dragging himself through the mud, reaching for the knife he'd dropped.

The creature spoke, its voice like the thunder rolling through the sky. "Lazoaf."

Rowan wrapped his fingers around the blade. Acting on instinct, with no plan in mind, he climbed to his feet and responded. "Fuck you."

Fourteen sets of eyes squinted at him, locking him in place.

Then the monster twisted again, throwing Talia toward him. Rowan dropped the knife and reached for her, but what was meant to be a heroic catch, turned into more of a collision. He might have braced *her* impact with the ground, but all that force was transferred to him, and it slapped him back into the mud, more dazed than before.

The creature faced him and lifted Sashi up, now holding her under her arms. Blood ran from the hole in her chest, a vertical river down her body, trickling from her toes. The monster spoke in a language he didn't recognize, but it still sounded Sentinelese. *Is it trying to tell me something?* The thought was quickly dismissed as the words repeated.

It's a chant, he thought. *A ritual.*

Then he shouted, "No!"

Sashi woke, her eyes going wide in time with her mouth. Had its words or his shout woken her from unconsciousness? The answer came when the creature turned her around, the thumb and index finger of its free hand poked into her back at the base of her spine.

"No," Rowan repeated, adrenaline surging him out of his stupor. "No, no, no!"

A tearing sound filled the air, followed by the briefest of screams from Sashi, then her life was torn away along with her spine, some of her ribs, and her skull, all in one quick and unbelievably powerful yank.

The man-turned-monster held its arms out wide, each hand gripping part of Sashi. On the right, her still-connected spine lolled back and forth, pulled by the skull, leaking fluid out of the sockets from which her two eyes hung. On the left, her spineless body lay deflated over the large fingers holding it. Blood and insides poured out like globs of melting ice cream.

Rowan shook as he pushed himself up. "Talia… *Talia.*"

She stirred, saw what had become of Sashi, and thrashed back. They scrambled through the mud as the creature stood watching.

Brush rattled behind them.

The Sentinelese are coming.

Rowan looked for his blade. It was out of reach, half buried in mud and crushed vegetation. Talia's was even further away.

Rowan tried to think of a way out, tried to think of a tactic that might make sense. But there was no last ditch effort and no Hail Mary play to make.

He stopped scrambling away from the monster and toward the approaching sound, determined to face his end without fear. The last time he'd been on the precipice of life and death, the bottle had fueled his bravery—or maybe it had been cowardice. This time, all that self-loathing and inner turmoil had been stripped away to reveal the man beneath. The man who could stand before death and—

The brush behind him parted.

It was Mahdi.

The stunned man looked up at the creature, and then down at Rowan and Talia.

The monster responded by dropping Sashi's body and twelve more sets of eyes opened up along the inside of its raised arms, and its chest. It flexed forward, stretching its back wide with a crack. The six inch spines grew out and flared to either side, the beginnings of wings with no skin stretched between them.

It bellowed at them from its peeled-open skeletal face, the eyes covering its body furrowed in anger.

Mahdi trembled, but stood his ground, and then reached out his hand. "Come! Let's go!"

Rowan took his hand and was pulled to his feet. Then he did the same for Talia.

The creature roared again, flexing once more. Fingers lengthened. Its body grew more massive. Ribs cracked and widened, giving it an emaciated, but muscular midsection. Veins twisted through its dark, tightening skin, twitching with each beat of its heart. The creature's feet swelled, as though absorbing water and nutrients from the Earth itself.

Mahdi grabbed Rowan's arm, and shoved him to the side. "Go, now! Hurry!"

The creature was twelve feet tall, its gait double that of a man. It could take an inhuman amount of punishment, and he doubted it would ever tire. Running away seemed like a waste of his limited energy—it would surely catch them—but all thoughts of a noble death retreated with the possibility of escape's return.

They hobbled toward the thicker jungle, running parallel to the monster. Its many eyes watched them go, slowly turning its body. It was either confused by Mahdi's sudden arrival and their subsequent flight, or it was simply giving them a head start.

It's toying with us, Rowan thought, and then he considered that they'd been toyed with since arriving on the island. They were outnumbered in enemy territory. If the Sentinelese had simply been defending their territory, the entire expedition would be dead already. That they weren't, meant that the Sentinelese were a sadistic bunch of primeval assholes.

As they entered the lush jungle, Rowan looked back one last time. The creature stood its ground, watching, but not moving. Not yet. Then he saw behind it, where the jungle was bathed in warm light. Rain water falling from the canopy above created a shroud, separating the muddy killing grounds from what looked like paradise. It tugged at his heart, and filled him with a desire that matched his dread. His run stalled.

We can't leave yet, he thought, and then a tangle of broad leaves bulged out and gave birth to a cannonball of flesh. Rowan was hit hard and sprawled to the ground. When he opened his eyes again, Winston lay partially atop him. The big man was soaked through, trembling, and full of uncommon fear. Then he saw Rowan. "You're alive?"

Winston got over his surprise quickly and pushed himself up. "Go! They're not far behind me." A growl spun him around and he caught sight of the creature, which had now taken a step toward them. "Oh, shit. Oh, fuck!" Then he was off and running, blazing an easy-to-follow path through the wet underbrush.

Talia dragged Rowan back to his feet again, and when he looked back at the seductive, sunlit foliage, she gave him a shove that started him moving once more.

The hiss of rain on the canopy grew louder, hiding the sounds of their flight, and their pursuers' chase. Continuous thunder drowned out everything else, including thought. They followed the path of least resistance, left in Winston's wake, until it faded. The man had regained his senses and disappeared.

Then they heard his voice as a whisper, despite the fact that he was shouting from ten feet away. "This way!" He slipped out of the jungle, waved them on, and then fled again.

Refocused, they paid special attention to the foliage, and where their feet fell. The Sentinelese would have no trouble following them here, but this was where the trail needed to end. Rowan went last, inspecting the path behind them, making sure that every leaf, twig, and flower appeared undisturbed. He did it for three hundred feet, and then bumped into Talia.

He turned to find her and Mahdi stopped before a wall of brown grass hanging over the side of a jungle mound, atop which stood several dead trees, the twisting vines covering them dried out and flowerless.

The grass parted slowly. Winston emerged from a small cave entrance. "They either don't know about this, or aren't allowed to come here. No one's been in this cave for a very long time."

Between crashes of thunder, Rowan heard slapping feet on the ground, and shouting voices. The Sentinelese hadn't given up. When he felt the earth rumble beneath his feet, without an accompaniment from the storm, he knew the creature hadn't given up, either.

"Inside!" he said, shoving Talia toward the entrance. She slithered inside, followed by Mahdi, and then Rowan. He and Winston lingered by the entrance, gently pulling the grass back into place. At the sound of approaching feet, they snapped their hands back and held their breath.

37

TALIA MOVED DEEPER into the cave, while Rowan, Mahdi, and Winston remained frozen by the grass covered entrance, where the shadows of the Sentinelese slid past, hunting them. She didn't want to be found as much as the others, but she didn't see the point in waiting around for it to happen. If they were discovered, they would die. Probably horribly.

She closed her eyes as memories of Sashi's separated body flashed into her mind. Nausea threatened to overtake her as shock and adrenaline began to wear off. She placed a hand against the cave wall for balance, expecting to feel cool, hard stone. But the wall was soft, wet, and held together by a delta of roots, millions of them, permeating the soil from above.

Eyes open again, and adjusted to the darkness, she saw patches of dull light streaking down from above. If not for the storm, the glow probably would have been bright enough to see clearly. With the thick clouds above blocking the sun, the illumination was dulled to a cool blue, dimmer than a child's nightlight.

Intrigued by the light, she stepped away from the dirt wall and moved deeper inside the cave. The wet cave floor, soft with layers of ancient decay, squelched beneath her bare feet. She looked back and saw a clear line of footprints. Winston was right. No one had been in this cave in a very long time, if ever. But she had a hard time believing the Sentinelese didn't know it existed.

So why aren't they searching it?

She stood beneath one of the light beams and looked up. Limp grass hung down from a hole between coils of roots, dripping water onto her forehead.

This isn't a cave at all, Talia realized, though she couldn't tell if the trees had grown up over an empty space like the aerial roots of Cambodia's banyan trees, or if erosion had removed the earth from beneath the growth.

The air grew cool as she walked deeper, chilling her skin. She wrapped her arms around her chest, feeling vastly underdressed, and not just because of the cold air. She felt shame creeping up on her.

Her forehead creased. She'd spent years of her life wearing little or nothing without a second thought. But here, in this dark place, surrounded by Sentinelese who knew no shame, she found herself questioning her life's choices.

Anger drowned out her guilt, freeing her mind.

That was when the pain came. She wasn't just cold. She was wounded. There were five holes in her body where the creature had gripped her. At the time, the pain hadn't been intense, and during their subsequent flight, she'd been distracted and numb. But here, in this chilled place, with her skin contracting and her mind clearing, her delayed anguish dropped her to her knees.

A sob rose in her throat, but she contained it and fell forward onto her hands. With the pain came memories. When the monster had held her, had pierced her body, her life flashed before her eyes. But the rapid-fire playback snagged on a single memory, the one she'd spent her whole life raging against and running from.

She saw him again. Her father. Dead for so long, his fortune funding her world travel and efforts to protect indigenous peoples, but still alive in her nightmares.

How many times had he come to her at night?

How many times had he whispered it was okay?

How many times had she thought about killing him?

She didn't know the answer to any of those questions. There was only one question about that time of her life she really could answer: how many times do you need to kill someone before they stop torturing you?

Once.

Tears flowed into the muck between her hands as she saw the image of her father above her, scissors in his neck, gagging on his own blood before falling to the floor.

It took five minutes for him to die.

It took Talia two days to leave the bed. And one more to call the police.

Shame returned anew. For being weak too long and strong too late. For being a killer. For being a victim.

When a hand touched her shoulder, she spun around, slapped the hand off her, and raised a fist. She nearly let out a battle cry and finished the attack when she saw Rowan's wide eyes.

He raised a finger to his lips and whispered, "They've moved on, but who knows how far. Are you okay?"

She motioned to the wounds pocking her body. They hurt, but no longer bled. "I have holes in me."

"Not what I was asking."

She turned away, let the water trickling from above splash against her face, and stepped deeper into the cave. "I don't like it here."

"It's oppressive," he said.

"Not all of it, though. The island." She looked him in the eyes. "The light."

"You felt it, too?"

"I'm not sure what I felt."

"You felt at home," Mahdi said, joining them. "Like it was where you were meant to be."

"Yeah," Rowan said. "That. You saw it, too?"

Mahdi nodded. "I think we should avoid it. Like an oasis, it can only lead to death."

"What on this shithole island doesn't lead to death?" Winston asked, leaving thick boot prints atop their collection of barefoot impressions.

Talia had a lot to say to the big man, but she contained the words and violent acts inspired by his presence. He was her enemy, but he was also the Sentinelese's enemy, and right now the larger their tribe, the better their odds of survival.

"You didn't see it?" Rowan asked. He was tense, but he hadn't vented his anger toward the man who had arranged their deaths, either.

"The mystical beam of sunlight? Eye of the storm? Yeah, I saw it, but it didn't make me want to stay. Didn't feel like home. What I want to know is what the fuck that thing is."

"It's going to make building a resort difficult," Mahdi said.

Winston chuckled, and hitched a thumb toward Mahdi. "Can you believe this guy? He's really starting to grow a pair."

Mahdi glowered, but said nothing.

"You knew nothing about all this before coming here?" Rowan asked Winston.

He replied, "As much as she knew." He nodded his head toward Talia. "Maybe less. Half of the presentation you were shown was bullshit. Sashi put it together. She could paint a grim image, that one."

The disrespect he was showing toward a woman they had just seen dismantled swelled Talia with rage. She jabbed a finger at him, but he spoke first. "Before you get all self-righteous, you should know Sashi was a fraud. Did she try to sell you on a sob story about her daughter? That she was impoverished. Or kidnapped. Or—"

"Given in marriage to Ambani," Rowan said.

Winston laughed again. "That's a new one. His taste runs young, but Sashi never had a daughter. Or a husband. She's been lying to you from the start."

"So have you," Mahdi said.

"I'm a professional. I'm doing a job. I don't get my jollies from it. But Sashi, she—"

"Enough," Talia said, and when Winston looked in her eyes, he understood the threat. She might not be able to kill him, but she'd have help, and if they failed, the Sentinelese would likely hear the struggle and finish the job.

He raised his hands, still smiling, and said, "Mercy. We're all in this blender together, and we need to find a way out together."

Talia pursed her lips and turned toward the dark depths of the cave, where something twisted and old filled the space. She looked back when Rowan spoke.

"No good plan exists outside of intel. So let's pool what we know."

"They're hard as fuck to kill," Winston said.

"The big one?" Rowan asked.

"All of them," Mahdi said. "The others don't change, but they don't die, either."

"And all of them are dangerous," Winston said.

"Even newborns," Mahdi said, and when Rowan looked incredulous, he added more. "They can run like animals. And their mouths…" He lifted his left forearm into the light streaming from above. An eight inch wide rainbow of tooth-shaped bruises dotted his skin. "An infant did this. Broke my wrist."

"Doesn't look broken," Talia said, forcing herself to rejoin the conversation.

Mahdi twisted his hand around. "People heal faster here." He pointed at Talia. "You stopped bleeding without applying pressure. Without a bandage. In the rain." He turned to Rowan. "I am sorry for what I did."

Rowan shook his head. "You saved my life."

"That was sneaky," Winston said.

Rowan glowered, but kept his focus on Mahdi. Traced his fingers over the wound on his chest. It was covered in a rubbery looking patch of skin. "And you're right. But I'm pretty sure we can still die. Sashi isn't coming back."

"They burned Emmei."

Talia wasn't fond of Emmei. He had betrayed them, too. But burned alive… It was a horrible way to die. She wouldn't wish it on her enemies. Not even Winston.

Mahdi's eyes went wide. "There was an obelisk. The children were huddled around it. I thought they were all a statue but…" He closed his eyes. "There were words carved into the stone."

Talia perked up, forgetting the pain and carnage for a moment. "Words? Could you read them?"

"You could have, too," Mahdi said. "Herev lohetet."

"What language is that?" Rowan asked and then looked to Talia. "What does that mean?"

Rowan's voice sounded distant. Talia had faced the mysteries of the ancient world on more than one occasion. She knew there were things that would never be explained or understood. But this island… The Sentinelese and their monster defender were bad enough, but 'herev lohetet?' Here? It made no sense. It made less than no sense.

Rowan's impatience raised his voice to a dangerous volume. "Someone tell me—"

"It's Hebrew," Talia said. "It means 'Flaming Sword.'"

"Hebrew?" Winston scoffed. "That's not possible."

"After what we have seen on this island," Mahdi said, "I think it is safe to say that *anything* is possible."

Rowan's face shifted slowly into shock, like a stop-motion video of sand dunes forming. "What?" Talia asked him.

Rowan blinked, and then he surveyed the cave like he could see through the walls to the island around them. "I know where we are."

38

ROWAN HAD NEVER had such an expectant audience, not since he'd dressed up as Cher in high school and lip synched *Shoop Shoop Song*. But there were no teenage friends groping his balloon breasts, just three very desperate people, all of whom wore varying degrees of 'don't bullshit me' on their faces.

Part of him hoped his theory *was* bullshit. If it wasn't he didn't think they'd ever make it off the island, especially not after knowing the truth.

"I shouldn't tell you," he said. "He can't let you leave if you know. Because the world shouldn't know."

"Shouldn't know what?" Talia asked. "And who is *he?*"

"And what do you mean by *let* us leave?" Winston added.

Rowan held his ground and his tongue. He'd been trained to withstand torture, he could take a grilling from three people, only one of whom probably knew how to torture a person.

"It is unlikely we will survive as it is," Mahdi said. "It's safe to assume that neither Emmei, nor Sashi, nor Chugy, knew what you do. And yet, they have all perished."

Mahdi's cool logic worked its way past his defenses better than any torture could. He was right about the others. They'd all died not knowing the truth. And maybe it *wasn't* the truth, but it felt right. If the revelation of where they were—where they *really* were—brought them peace in death, who was he to hold that back?

He raised his hands, signaling his willingness to talk, and closed his eyes. He dug through his memory, back to a childhood spent in church. He'd been obsessed with the Bible's wilder stories. Noah's ark. Jonah's whale. The Nephilim. The burning bush. His conservative parents didn't let him watch cartoons, or even read secular fiction, so these were the stories that had fueled his childhood imagination. But there was one that had always captured his younger self's attention, because like Atlantis—which he had learned about at school—it was still out there, waiting to be rediscovered.

But not without consequences.

Eyes closed, Rowan did his best to recite the passage in question, pulling it from his distant memory. "After he drove the man out…he placed on the east side of the Garden of Eden cherubim…

Mahdi gasped. "And a *flaming sword* flashing back and forth…"

"To guard the way to the tree of life," Talia finished.

"You all go to Sunday School together?" Winston asked. "Or did I miss a party on the yacht where you all drank the Kool-Aid?"

"The story of Eden is shared by Jewish, Muslim, and Christian traditions. While Islam rejects the concept of original sin, the major elements are mostly the same."

"I get the Garden comparison," Winston said, "but I haven't seen a flaming sword flitting about."

"They've been chasing us the whole time," Mahdi said.

Talia nodded, but her brow was furrowed in thought. "Not everything in the Bible, the Koran, or the Torah, is meant to be taken literally."

"The flaming sword isn't a description of a physical thing." Rowan hadn't even pieced this part of the puzzle together, but it fell into place. "Capital F. Capital S. Flaming Sword is the tribe's name."

Winston's sarcastic smile lingered, but had faded some. "So they're what? Not human?"

"Very not human," Mahdi added.

"So what, angels? Demons?"

"Neither." It was a guess, but Rowan couldn't picture demons protecting Eden, and he knew which of the Sentinelese was an angel. "The Cherubim are angels. The Flaming Sword is something else."

"Cherubs are the little chubby things, right?" Winston asked. "Heart bows and little wings."

Talia laughed. "The Cherubim are mentioned several times in the Old Testament. They're most well known for being atop the Ark of the Covenant. But they're only described once."

When it came to freakish monstrosities in the Bible, the Nephilim, Jonah's whale, and Job's Leviathan had nothing on the Cherubim. Only the horrors of Revelation compared. Rowan tried to recall the verses, but found his memory faltering. So he paraphrased. "They were human in form, each with four faces and four wings. Hooved feet. Like a calf. They had human hands under their wings. The four faces were human, lion, ox, and eagle. Two of their wings spread out wide, and two covered their bodies. The creatures looked like burning coals…" Thunder crashed overhead, muffled by the jungle, and the cave ceiling, but strong enough to shake the ground. "Lightning flashed out of it."

"You think that thing…" Winston pointed toward the exit. "…that ugly fucker out there…is an angel?"

"A Cherub," Rowan said.

"I haven't seen more than one face," Winston said.

"You're still thinking literally," Talia said. "We need to think about what the lion, ox, and eagle stood for at the time."

"And," Rowan said, "it's changing."

The others fell quiet. The description wasn't a perfect match, but it was far closer now than it had been when they'd first encountered and killed the man on the beach. If Rowan was right, the Cherub had been slowly revealing itself to them. But why? Why not just kill them?

"Lazoaf." Rowan focused on Mahdi. "You recognized the word. What does it mean?"

"'Leave,'" Talia said. "In Hebrew."

"Ain't this going to ruffle feathers," Winston said. "When we tell the world Hebrew is the language of choice at the Garden of fucking Eden."

"Perhaps they were using a language two of us knew, but would also recognize as out of place, and time. Plenty of English-speaking people have been shipwrecked here. Had they spoken English, we would have assumed they had captured someone and learned the language."

"So *God* is trying to warn us away?" A silent chuckle jiggled through Winston's body.

"Or the Cherubim." Rowan felt ridiculous saying it. Angels? Eden? Monster-people protectors of mankind's birthplace? But he couldn't deny it made a crazy kind of sense. "What about the healing?" He touched the squishy scab over the slice in his chest. "How do you explain this?"

"The tree," Mahdi said, his voice full of wonder.

"There are lots of trees on the island," Winston said.

Rowan understood. "The tree of life. In the story of Eden, Adam and Eve ate from the Tree of Knowledge of Good and Evil. The Flaming Sword and Cherubim were left behind, after mankind was evicted from the garden, to protect the Tree of Life."

"So the first tree did what, made us killers and ashamed to be naked?" Winston looked at Talia. "Which didn't really work on all of us."

"It introduced sin," Rowan said. "So they say."

"And the Tree of Life?"

"Immortality," Mahdi said. "Eating from both would make a human God-like."

Winston perked up. "And you think the tree is where? In that light?"

Rowan felt like a veil had been lifted. Could that be why they felt drawn to the light? If any of this was rooted in reality, as insane as it seemed, could there really be a Tree of Life? Should they be running toward the light instead of away from it? The idea was seductive, but could they even make it there? Had the Cherub been giving them opportunities to leave? "I suppose it might not be a literal tree. Or even literal fruit. But maybe—"

"It's all bullshit." Talia stood, her back to them, arms crossed, staring into the cave's darkness, where barely visible twisting vines hung. "This isn't Eden. The Flaming Sword isn't a tribe. And that ugly asshole isn't an angel."

The three men waited in silence. Even Winston had been caught up in the idea of life everlasting, and he didn't look thrilled by Talia's rebuttal.

"I've lived with tribes like this before. I've seen their rituals. I've communed with spirits. I've seen things…I've felt things, that you wouldn't believe. But none of it was real. The tribal people didn't have the scientific knowledge to understand their experiences, but I did then, and still do now. And I've been on enough trips to know when my mind is being screwed with."

"Trips?" Mahdi asked. "How does travel—"

"Drug trips," Rowan says. "She's saying that all of this is…" He turned to Talia. "What? A hallucination?"

"I haven't taken any drugs," Winston said. "And I sure as shit would know if I'd been roofied."

"It's the smoke," Talia said. "Every time we've seen or experienced something strange, the smoke has been present. Even in the rain. That fragrant smell is ever present."

Not down here, Rowan thought. If Talia was right, perhaps that's why the cave felt so oppressive. Maybe they were coming down from a high now that they were free of the smoke? Their bodies could be craving more. It also explained the lack of inhibitions, and why he was now feeling a little too naked in his underwear. The fading effects were triggering his shame.

"But we're all seeing the same thing," Mahdi asked.

"Only you saw the Flaming Sword text," Talia pointed out. "And it just happened to be a text you could read."

"Emmei saw—"

"Emmei is dead," Talia said. "We don't know what he saw."

"And the Cherub?" Rowan asked. He didn't see how they could all see something like that. "Is it a mass hallucination?"

"When people are hallucinating, they're in a very impressionable state. The Cherub could simply be a Sentinelese man in costume."

"But his height?" Mahdi said.

"Stilts," Talia said. "The eyes could be painted. The point is, we could be seeing what they want us to see. They've had more than enough time to perfect the technique. We can't trust anything we see. The Sentinelese are just people, but if we're smelling that smoke, they'll be whatever they, and our cultural understanding of what we're seeing, tells us they are."

She pointed from Mahdi, to Rowan, and then to herself. "All three of us were brought up being taught the Eden story. It's not a big mental leap for our imaginations to make the connection. You might have even consciously thought of this place as 'an Eden.'"

Rowan raised his hand, feeling a little ashamed for connecting these same dots earlier, and for presenting the Eden theory at all. "I did."

It had all felt so right, and it made sense of what they'd experienced, even if it didn't make sense to the modern mind. The part of him that still enjoyed those old Bible stories wanted the island to be Eden, but grown-up Rowan, free from the smoke's hallucinogenic effects, knew it wasn't. "What about the healing?"

Talia shrugged. "Maybe the smoke has a coagulant effect? Our bodies are covered in the stuff. It's in our blood. It could be dulling the pain, too. I might be on the scientific fringe, but I still believe in science, and all of this can be explained without jumping on the supernatural short bus."

"Okay, I've heard enough," Winston said. "Never thought the jungle queen would be the rational one, but here we are. How about we get back to forming a plan?"

"Already have one, but you're not going to like it." Talia frowned. "None of us will."

39

WHILE THE OTHERS argued about when to leave the cave, Mahdi stepped deeper into it. Winston's large, wet shirt had been torn into four lengths of fabric. Talia's plan was simple. The wet cloth would protect them from the smoke's hallucinogenic properties and allow them to see the Sentinelese for who they really were. If they could do that, and make it to the beach, perhaps they could survive. It wasn't really a plan. More of a tactic. But everyone agreed it was better than waiting to rot in the cave.

Winston had been reluctant to give up his shirt, but he couldn't deny it made sense. When he removed the shirt, it became clear that it wasn't his fat belly, long stretch marks, or copious amount of hair for which he was ashamed. It was the tattoo covering the large canvas that was his back: a Viking shield maiden with angel wings, riding a griffin. Not only did the image mix mythologies, but also amazing artistic skill with poor taste. Aside from her shield, the woman was naked and in the throes of passion, one hand lowered to her crotch. Everyone agreed that when they made their escape, Winston would go last, so the image on his back wouldn't distract those behind him.

Mahdi squinted into the darkness. The light streaming down through the root gaps overhead wasn't quite enough to see by. He waited for his eyes to adjust and moved deeper. The others were fifty feet behind him, but it felt like he was stepping through a portal to another world.

The air chilled, sending a shiver through his body.

A deep sense of wrongness burrowed into his gut.

It's just a cave, he told himself, and then he stopped. A withered, twisted tree stood before him. It grew up into the ceiling, its coiled, witch-finger branches merging with the roots system above. The blackened tree wasn't just dead. It radiated death.

But it was just a tree. He crouched by its trunk. It looked burned. He reached out and touched his finger to the bark. Part of him expected an electric shock or a supernatural explosion, but it was just the charred remains of some ancient fire. Free of the smoke's effects, old trees were just old trees.

There were footprints at the base of the tree. Two sets. One larger than the other. The ground was as dry as the tree here. The prints were old. He followed them around the tree, but stopped short of pursuing them deeper into the hollow.

"Mahdi," Talia whispered. She stood beneath the beams of dull light, easy to see. "Where are you?"

"Here," he replied, moving back the way he'd come. "There is a tree."

"Great," Talia said. "A tree on an island covered in trees. Good job."

He smiled at her sarcasm. "This tree is special."

"We decided to leave before dark," she said. "That means now."

"If Ambani isn't already looking for us, we'll need to survive the night. That will be easier if we're hard to see." Mahdi held out his finger, revealing the streak of ash.

Talia looked around Mahdi, eyed the tree, and then snapped her fingers at Rowan and Winston, who were hovering near the entrance. The two men appeared to be getting along fine. Neither had lingered on the fact that Winston had planned, and tried, to kill them all, and Mahdi was thankful for that, because he had played a part. They were professionals. Survivors. But Mahdi had little doubt that once they were free of the island, one of the two men would kill the other…and then perhaps Mahdi.

As Rowan and Winston approached, Mahdi returned to the tree and snapped off several branches. They were dry and brittle despite the moisture in the air, the tree's charcoal form resistant to decay. He returned with four large chunks and handed them out. "For your skin."

"I don't think the natives have any concept of racism," Winston said, "But they might not appreciate us going all black face."

Mahdi replied, "It's to—"

"I know what it's for, Mahd-man." Winston began rubbing the charcoal on his arm. "It was a joke."

Ten minutes later, they were all coated in a layer of dry black.

"Won't this just wash off in the rain?" Rowan asked, looking down at himself.

"Charcoal stains skin," Talia said. "You'll need a lot of soap and water to get it off, and even then, you'll probably have to wait for your outer skin layers to be replaced before you return to your pasty white self again."

Rowan's smile came and went with the quickness of the lightning flashing overhead, sending strobes of light through the holes in the ceiling. "Let's go."

They headed toward the overgrown entrance, wet cloths tied around their mouths and noses. Rowan and Winston were both unarmed, and both insisted they could manage. Talia had her blowgun and two remaining darts. And Mahdi carried the spring-loaded knife, still stained with Rowan's blood. It wasn't an impressive arsenal, but it would have to be enough.

When Rowan parted the grass, revealing the jungle beyond, they all knew it wasn't nearly enough.

Instead of seeing a green jungle, all they could see were Sentinelese. Women stood beside their grown children, holding the babies, some of whom were nursing. The women with free hands held arrows. Then there were the men, wielding bows, arrows, and spears, all of them thrusting their genitals. The air was clouded with swirling smoke, lit like a dance party by the flashing lightning cutting through the canopy gaps.

They knew we were here, Mahdi thought. *They've just been waiting for us.*

Rowan let the grass fall back in place and turned around, shock in his eyes. "Shit."

"On the plus side," Winston said, "with all that smoke, they've got to be tripping balls."

"High or sober, we can't fight our way past all of them," Rowan said.

"We've got them bottlenecked," Winston said. "Let them come to us. We'll take them out, one at a time as they come in."

"There had to be more than a hundred of them out there." Talia inserted one of her last two darts into her blowgun. "I think they'll stop sending people in, and maybe you haven't noticed, but they've been waiting, and still are waiting, for us to come out. They're primitive, not stupid."

"Maybe the cave is sacred or something?" Winston asked.

"Or..." Talia's struggle to remain calm was etched on her face. "They're just *not stupid.*"

While they argued, Mahdi wandered back into the cave. He inspected the roots overhead. He might be able to cut through the roots with the knife, but it would take a long time, maybe days, and he'd only be able to reach them if he was standing on someone's shoulders. He turned to the darkness beyond, where the charred tree remained locked in time. *Maybe there is another way out,* he thought, and then he spoke the words aloud.

"What?" Talia asked, still standing guard by the entrance with Rowan and Winston.

"Maybe there is another way out." He pointed into the darkness. "There are footprints by the tree. Old footprints. They head in the opposite direction."

"For all we know they died at the back of the cave," Winston said. "If we leave the bottleneck, there won't be anything to stop all of them from coming in."

"Except that they're not even trying," Rowan said.

Winston threw up his hands. "That could change."

"There are no footprints approaching the tree from this side of the cave," Mahdi pointed out. "They come and go from the other end."

Talia struck out for the tree. "Good enough for me."

Mahdi followed.

"Have fun with the bottleneck idea," Rowan said and fell in line.

Talia paused by the tree to inspect the barely visible footprints. She crouch-walked like an ape, finding the approaching path, and then the path leading away. "A man and a woman. They walked in. Hurried out, like they were afraid."

"Probably because this is a nightmare tree," Winston said, stepping beneath the branches. "Now let's find out where the footprints lead before they try to bum-rush us."

Talia led the way, crouched down, hands gliding over the footprints. She stopped when it was nearly too dark to see her. She reached out to Rowan. "Take my hand. We're operating blind from here out." She looked back to Mahdi and Winston. "Same to both of you."

Mahdi took Rowan's hand and reached back for Winston, who said, "Kinky," and then held on.

They moved through the darkness, squatting low like a centipede. There were no sounds of pursuit, but Mahdi wasn't sure there would be. He could feel the footprints beneath him as they moved. They felt chaotic and confused, the spread between them widening as the people's hurried walk had become a run.

Mahdi bumped into Rowan, who had stopped, and was then bowled over by Winston.

"Shh," Talia whispered. "Up ahead."

The faintest spear of light cut through the air ahead of them, in part because it was small, but also because the light outside was already dull. How much time had passed in the dark? How long before the sunrise?

They moved slower at first, and then as a patchwork of small holes appeared directly ahead, they hurried. Able to see again, they separated and approached a thin, but overgrown wall of roots, too congested to squeeze through.

"The roots must have grown over the entrance after these people left," Rowan said.

"Unless the cave wasn't here at all." Talia tugged on the roots. "They're dead."

Mahdi held his knife out. "We can cut through."

"Will take too long." Winston stood up. Gripped the roots in his hands. Gave them a pull. "I can get us through. But it's going to be loud."

A rumble of thunder peeled across the sky above.

"Just time it right," Rowan said, peeking through the gaps. "I don't see anyone out there, but we're going to have to run like hell. We're only a few hundred feet from the Sentinelese, and they could have patrols."

Winston leaned forward, a football defenseman waiting for the snap. "Just tell me when."

Lighting flashed.

"Now!" Rowan said.

Winston charged and threw himself at the wall of roots. Thunder thumped through the sky, merging with the crack of old wood and the wet splat of Winston landing in mud on the far side. What it failed to conceal was his shout of surprise when the muddy ground, gravity, and a steep grade conspired to propel him downhill.

"Let's go!" Rowan said, tightening his facemask. He slid down the hill after Winston.

Talia and Mahdi exited together, glancing downhill. It was just a fifteen foot drop before the angle became gentle. A layer of smoke lay below, held down by the storm's wind and humidity. They fixed their masks, slid down together and were helped up by the two soot-and-mud-covered men at the bottom.

The smoke was thick enough to sting Mahdi's eyes, but he had yet to smell it through the saturated fabric.

"Just keep moving downhill and we'll reach the ocean."

A shadow in the corner of Mahdi's eye tugged his attention, back and up. He stumbled back and would have fallen if not for Rowan's quick hands.

"Mahdi, watch your—"

"I don't think the masks are working." Mahdi's gaze remained locked on the hilltop from which they'd emerged. The others followed his eyes and tensed as one.

Standing above the ragged hole torn by Winston, was the Cherub, watching them through dozens of unblinking eyes, each of them making eye contact with one of the four of them. Its massive body, both muscular and emaciated, twitched with energy. The broad chest swelled with each deep breath, hissing out between clenched teeth, louder than the rain. The spines on its back spread wide, like an insect threat display. Loose skin hung from the spines, like molting flesh, but Mahdi suspected it would soon be stretched wide, granting the creature the ability to fly.

It's not real, he told himself. *It's a hallucination.*

And then the Sentinelese joined the monster, standing on either side of it, adding their own unblinking eyes to the power of the creature's. They were real. All of them.

An infant shrieked, its mouth wide, revealing teeth where there should have been none. The mother cupped her baby in one hand, cocked it back and then let it fly, shrieking all the way.

"Run!" Rowan shouted, and it was the Sentinelese who obeyed first. Arrows and spears flew, while warriors, women, children, and babies either ran or were thrown toward them. Behind them all, the Cherub raised its arms to the sky, where lightning cut through the clouds, and even more children scurried down the trees.

40

TEN SECONDS AFTER shouting, 'Run,' Rowan was frustrated by his inability to do so. His slowness wasn't from a lack of effort, or a shortage of heart-pounding adrenaline. It was caused by the thick jungle, which seemed in league with the Sentinelese. Branches scratched his arms. Large leaves obscured his view and slapped his face. Twisting roots stumbled him. Pain was progress's price, but he was willing to pay it. To tarry was death.

"I thought these things were going to protect us from the smoke," Winston complained, pulling the fabric away from his face while barreling through a short palm, uprooting it.

"We're soaking wet," Talia said. She was leading the group now, moving in and around the foliage rather than charging through it. "It's sticking to our bodies. Whatever the active chemical is, it's breaking through the skin barrier to reach the bloodstream. Short of a biohazard suit, nothing can be done about it." She ducked under a low hanging branch that Winston crashed through a moment later.

"I fail to see," Mahdi said between heavy breaths, as he brought up the rear, "how any of this matters. Just go!"

Mahdi's urging was punctuated by a three foot arrow that punched through a large leaf and *thunked* into a tree just a foot away from Rowan's head. He grabbed the arrow as he ran by, hoping to pull it free. But the long shaft broke, leaving the arrowhead—a potential weapon—buried in the wood.

The jungle around them filled with the sounds of shot and thrown projectiles, small scurrying feet and the sound of a hundred people chasing them down, not to mention the rain-created white noise and the boom of thunder.

Of all the ways Rowan had pictured his death, something like this was not on the list. Until being banished from the Rangers, he had always imagined dying in battle, like an ancient Norseman. But those images usually involved a more desolate landscape of the Middle East, not a tropical jungle, and not at the hands of an ungodly, mind-bending, primitive tribe.

For a time, he'd become obsessed with his own death. He'd planned and plotted it out, the time of day, what he would have for breakfast, even the trajectory of his brief flight before the end.

Now, he knew the best way to honor those whose lives were ended by his mistake, was to live well and do right by people. He didn't want to die, and he'd do his damnedest to make sure the people under his protection weren't killed, too. He'd failed with Sashi, but he was determined to safeguard Talia and Mahdi.

Winston, on the other hand, was on his own. And Rowan carried no guilt about Emmei's or even Chugy's demise. Sashi might have been part of the conspiracy, and she might have even been a liar like Winston said, but she had been under his care at the time. He could have fought harder.

A spear fell in front of him, narrowly missing Talia's leg. This time he would fight harder.

He snatched the spear from the ground. One of its many barbed tips fell off, but that did nothing to reduce the weapon's lethality. "Keep going," he shouted. "I'll slow them down!"

Talia stopped. "Rowan."

"Just go!" Rowan turned to face their pursuers. "I'll find you at the beach."

Respecting his desire to protect them, she gave a sad nod and resumed her course, falling in line beside Mahdi, Winston now in the lead.

Strike and move, Rowan told himself. He wasn't planning on making some kind of last stand. He just wanted to give the others some breathing room, and Talia some time to find someplace to hide. Rowan could fight, but in the jungle, Talia's instincts and experience would keep them alive long term, or at least until help arrived.

The jungle separated and gave birth to a black, fast moving blur. Rowan jabbed with the spear, felt a moment of resistance, and then the many prongs, designed for snagging fish, slipped through the belly of his attacker. The impact knocked Rowan back. To keep from falling, he planted the back of the long spear against the ground. It jerked to a stop, and kept him upright. The sudden jolt also plunged the spear further into his attacker—a woman.

She was four feet tall and couldn't have been more than eighteen. Despite the spear in her gut, she glared at him.

It's not real, he thought, fighting a mix of guilt and revolt. Guilt for spearing a young woman, and revolt because despite the way she stared at him, he knew she was really dead. At the very least, she was dying, painfully. No one could have such a single-minded focus on their target. Not the toughest Ranger. Not the Sentinelese.

Unless it's the smoke, he thought, wondering if her clouded mind could even feel pain, or the life leaking out of her.

The jungle parted again. This time it was a male warrior, bow in hand, arrow drawn back. He focused on Rowan, and then ran headlong into the woman's backside. The impact shoved the spear through the woman's back and into the man's abdomen. He slumped over her, and Rowan thought them both doomed. But then the man stood, still impaled, and drew the bowstring back.

Fighting a skewered man felt wrong. It was far from chivalrous. But they were far from civilization, and even further removed from such romantic views of battle. Rowan planted one foot and kicked with the other. The woman's chest flexed and cracked, but the rest of the strike's energy propelled her and the man back. The arrow fired into the trees.

The couple fell back, while Rowan tugged on the spear. Slick with blood, the weapon slipped free of the two Sentinelese, but was missing all but the central tip. The rest of the pronged spear tips remained in the pair, binding them together on the ground where they tried to pry themselves apart, despite mortal wounds.

Rowan turned to run, but he was struck in the back. He feared it was a spear or arrow that hit him and knocked him into a tree, but either would have punched through his body, and there was nothing protruding from his chest. That was when a second wave of pain exploded from his shoulder.

He reached up without looking, grabbed hold of something fleshy and yanked. When it came free, several layers of skin went with it. Raising the spear, Rowan turned to strike his newest attacker, but he stopped when he saw the infant rolling on the ground.

Mortified, he took a step toward the writhing child, but stopped when its eyes snapped up at him, filled with very adult loathing.

He stumbled back. *It's a hallucination,* he told himself, but the blood and tooth marks in his shoulder were real. It was impossible to tell what was real and what was the world's worst trip, but he didn't want any part of either.

The baby flipped onto its hands and feet.

"Don't," Rowan implored, his heart breaking. Even if this wasn't real, he would be haunted by this for the rest of his life. "Stop!"

But the little Sentinelese child didn't stop. It lunged, fingers hooked, wide jaws open, arcing toward his neck. A strong bite, a severed artery, and it would all be over. But Rowan couldn't kill it, whatever it really was—a trained monkey, perhaps—so he swung with the spear and batted it to the ground.

He didn't wait to see if it recovered, or if the speared couple freed themselves. He'd seen enough, and he could hear the rest of the tribe approaching like a rush of wind.

The trail left by Talia was nearly impossible to find, but Winston had left a path of destruction in his wake. Rowan picked up speed as he moved through the cleared trail, but he was no longer alone. He caught sight of a man with a bow and a woman with arrows behind him on his left, and a lone warrior carrying a bow, ahead of him on his right.

The man on the right had no arrows, so he focused on the left pair, and just in time. The man took an arrow from the woman, nocked it as he ran, and quickly fired.

Rowan dived and rolled. The hard roots on the jungle floor were merciless to his bare back, but preferable to an arrow. He heard the projectile soar above him and strike something hard. He was back on his feet as quickly as he'd left them, and continued running.

As he turned to look back at the couple once more, he caught sight of the man on the right, who now had an arrow nocked. *Where did that come from?* The man on the left did, too.

Rowan juked like a football player, feigning in one direction and then moving in the other. The arrow fired from behind missed, the arrow fired from ahead slipped through the soft flesh of his side, moving so fast that the entire three-foot, featherless length, slipped in the front of him, and right out the back.

He shouted in pain, but kept moving. That was when he saw the man in the lead slow down, yank the arrow that had missed him from a tree trunk and nock it.

He's using the missed arrows, Rowan realized, *and is a better shot than the warrior behind me.*

Rowan lobbed his spear toward the man and broke left.

The warrior abandoned his shot to avoid the spear.

With a layer of jungle between them, Rowan stopped hard, turned and swung. He couldn't see the approaching bow and arrow team, but he could hear them. The chop struck the man's throat, lifting him off the ground and flipping him backward. The woman emerged behind him and was airborne. Her fingers grasped Rowan's head, nails digging into skin, while her legs wrapped around his waist.

They went down together. As the woman dug trenches into Rowan's scalp, he used their momentum to lift his legs, wrap them around her head and yank her in the opposite direction. As she fell back, Rowan sat up, snagged one of her dropped arrows and plunged it through her shoulder and into the ground.

He rolled away, clutching more arrows, and stole the bow before the gasping warrior could recover. He nocked an arrow, drew the bow string back and let it fly toward the sound of slapping feet.

The second bowman stumbled through the brush, hands wrapped around the arrow jutting from the center of his chest. He fell to his knees, and Rowan felt relieved by the look of impending death in the man's eyes.

Then the warrior gripped the arrow and pulled it free. As blood oozed from the wound, he didn't fall forward and die. Instead, he turned to look at Rowan and began standing again. Rowan fired a second arrow into the man and then ran.

He made it twenty feet before realizing he was no longer being pursued by the Sentinelese; he was running among them. He could only see bits and pieces of dark skin between the branches and brush, but they were there. And when a shadow moved past him on the ground, he knew they were above him, too.

At least the jungle is hiding me, he thought, angling his trajectory so that he was still moving downhill and toward the coast, but on a path that would separate him from the Sentinelese.

Just as the sounds of running, climbing, and clawing fell behind him, he burst through a stand of ferns and into the manicured jungle. The sudden lack of vegetative resistance spilled him forward. He rolled back to his feet, keeping a grip on the bow and two arrows he'd commandeered, but when he heard nothing behind him, he paused to look back.

The Sentinelese were there, too, stopped like him, and staring right back.

He took three slow steps back, and then sprinted away.

Out in the open, running over cleared ground and roots, he could no longer hear the Sentinelese chasing him, but he could feel their presence growing, could sense the doom closing in.

Just get to the ocean, he thought, *and then swim...swim until you reach India.*

A shadow fell over him again, and this time, when he looked up, he knew that no amount of swimming would help. The Cherub, wings fully formed, framed by lightning, flew over the canopy.

It's not real. It's not real. He repeated the mental mantra over and over, but each time it felt like a lie. They had stepped on land forbidden to mankind, and now they were going to pay the price.

41

DESPITE THE MANICURED jungle being blanketed in hallucinogenic smog, Talia could see the beach ahead, or rather, the light of day reflecting off its sands. She glanced up. The rain still pelted the wind-swirled canopy. Thunder and lightning ruled the sky like Thor had grown weary of Valhalla and migrated to the Midgardian tropics. But ahead, there was sunlight, carved up by the tall trees, painting the forest floor in long streaks of light and dark.

She ran in the dark whenever possible, but the course ahead was winding.

The slap of feet and boots pursued her, but they belonged to Winston and Mahdi. She hadn't looked back at the two men, but both were loud, and their pace unwavering. At their current speed, the trio would reach the sand in a minute. Then, a swim.

She was winded, and she was sure the less fit men behind her would be, too. Drowning was a possibility, but many of the reefs created shallows that could let them catch their breath…perhaps just long enough for a swimming Sentinelese to catch up…or a shark to sense them, or a salt water croc to take a bite. The ocean wasn't much better than the island, but if they got free of the smoke, they would, at the very least, be able to discern reality from drug-induced hallucination.

Beyond the footfalls of the two men behind her was a more gentle tapping. At first, she wrote it off as large drops of rainwater falling from the leaves overhead, but the regularity of them, and the fact that she could only hear them behind her, conjured pictures of tiny Sentinelese children and babies, scurrying over the forest floor.

And the sound was steadily growing louder.

But was it real?

Children couldn't run like insects. Babies couldn't leap between trees or survive being thrown like living grenades. There was no biological benefit for having mouths that wide. Natural selection didn't create children whose jaws seemed able to unhinge, an ability that seemed to be lost in adulthood. None of it made sense, unless it wasn't real.

But the creatures had made physical contact. Had left wounds on all of them. So while there might not be any ancient killer angel on the island, something had pierced her sides. The Cherub had to be a large Sentinelese man, or perhaps a few of them acting together. And the children... Animals wearing masks. A species of Macaque. They weren't known to live on the island, but they did populate other islands in the Sea of Bengal. And who was to say what species lived on the island, aside from the Sentinelese? In the past 60,000 years, not a single biologist had set foot on the island.

Real or not, whatever was chasing her would kill them all if they were caught. Sashi might not have been torn apart by an ancient protector of some fabled land, but she was dead. So was Emmei. All notions of protecting the Sentinelese at the cost of her own life had faded. The Sentinelese didn't need her help. A platoon of Special Ops soldiers wouldn't be able to take the island. And Ambani, if he tried again, would never succeed, especially without the Indian government's genuine support.

A shout from behind flinched her back to the course ahead. Just thirty seconds more and there would be sand beneath her feet. She nearly kept going when she realized the shout had come from Mahdi.

She spun around just as Winston barreled past, no concern for the man in trouble.

Mahdi stumbled forward, thrashing with each step, fighting a baby clinging to his back. The small thing—not a real baby—had a fist full of Mahdi's hair, and its other hand hooked into his shoulder. Its broad mouth was open, lowering to clamp down on Mahdi's neck.

Talia opened the case holding her blow darts. Muscle memory allowed her to act without taking her eyes off the creature. Despite Mahdi's bucking, the large teeth lowered toward his neck. There was no time to load the blow gun, and she'd never be able to hit the moving target. So she gripped the dart in her hand and charged.

"Mahdi, get down!"

He saw her coming through wide, wet eyes and obeyed, dropping to the ground. The sudden shift in direction flipped the baby onto its back, but it didn't let go, and the flip didn't erase the anger from its eyes.

Talia stepped over the child and hesitated for just a moment. She thought, *It's not a baby*, and then she poked the dart, and its deadly poison, into the thing's neck. The wheezing started immediately. Its small fingers released Mahdi and scratched at its chest. The sight of it broke Talia's heart.

Did I just kill a child?

"Look out!" Mahdi shouted.

Talia turned in time to see a second child, this one older, leap over Mahdi's supine body, arms and legs splayed wide, ready to wrap around her. Instinct guided her hand back down to her last remaining dart. She pulled it free and jabbed.

The boy struck her head on, wrapping around her and taking her down to the ground. The grip of his legs was crushing. His fingers raked across her back, unleashing rivulets of warm blood. Then he sat up and wheezed, eyes going wide before turning back to Talia with a 'how dare you' expression.

Tan hands slipped under the boy's armpits and hoisted. He came away, his body loose. Rather than throw him to the side, Mahdi demonstrated the kind of man he was by lowering the boy to the ground, bracing his head in his hand.

"They're coming," he said. He spoke the words in a calm, matter-of-fact way that reflected none of the panic he should have been feeling. The Sentinelese were closing in, but there weren't nearly as many of them as Talia had expected.

Movement pulled her eyes to the right. Rowan ran through the forest, still heading toward the beach, but angled away from their position. The majority of the Sentinelese tribe charged behind him, a wave of inhumanity. Lightning flashed, casting a large moving shadow on the forest floor, but when she looked up, the canopy had shifted once more, filling the green ceiling's gaps.

Mahdi took her arm and pulled her up. Gave her a shove. "Run!"

Talia obeyed, watching Rowan as she moved, until he slipped from view. Then she focused on saving her own life again and made for the beach. Fifty feet from the glowing wall of brush that separated jungle from beach, an arrow flew past. Then another, and another. The shots were wild, made while running.

Spears flew next, joining the arrows. The sudden hail of projectiles felt off. It felt desperate, like they knew the chase would soon end. Talia agreed, but she saw the impending outcome as victorious for the Sentinelese. They could bide their time. Save their ammo. Spearing a swimming human would be infinitely easier than skewering the small fish they caught on a daily basis.

So why the hurry?

She heard the answer ahead.

A motor. A *boat* motor. It sounded small, and familiar.

"Is that…" Mahdi said. He didn't need to finish the question. They both knew what it was.

"The dinghy," Talia replied, rushing toward the wall of brush, looking for a weak spot. When she spotted a gap between two shrubs, she pointed and shouted. "There!"

Mahdi took the lead, aiming for the clearing.

The sun's brightness was diffused by the vast amount of white smoke in the air, but it was still powerful enough to make her squint after a day spent in the island's storm-and-canopy-dimmed interior.

Two steps past the green wall separating them from the beach, a spear flew over Talia's shoulder. By the time she had opened her mouth to shout a warning, it had plunged into Mahdi's calf.

He screamed and staggered forward, but didn't hit the ground. Not right away. Talia barreled into him from behind and tackled him through the foliage. They landed in soft sand, which kept Talia from sustaining injury, but it did nothing to sooth the bleeding hole in Mahdi's leg.

The spear, now lying between Talia and Mahdi, had been jarred free during the fall, its bloody tip coated in sand. She snatched it up, and held it toward the jungle, waiting to jab the first Sentinelese to leap out.

But the predatory tribe chasing them down had gone silent, and invisible, no doubt hunting from the shadows like they preferred. Talia scanned the beach in both directions. Aside from rivers of smoke, streaming out of the jungle and rolling out over the water, the sands were empty. Behind her, Winston stood in knee deep water, waving his hands like a wounded bird. Beyond him was the dinghy, racing toward shore, carrying six passengers, two of whom she recognized: Rattan Ambani and Chugy.

At this point, she didn't care who was in the dinghy. If the Devil himself was steering the boat, instead of Chugy, she'd hop on board.

A trickle of rain on her back drew her eyes up. The storm had formed over the island, a swirling, angry cyclone, but the sea beyond it was bathed in the late day sun's light. Above, thin clouds spun around the island, the rain here closer to a mist. The sky behind her was dark and furious, raging with lightning. And while the wind pushed tendrils of smoke out of the jungle, the ocean was calm and unaffected. And in the ocean, anchored beyond the reefs, was another yacht, just as gleaming white and spectacular as the *Sea Tiger* had been.

"Can you walk?" she asked Mahdi.

He grunted and pushed himself up in a hopping stand, the toes of one foot pressed into the sand to keep him from toppling over. Blood coursed down the wounded leg, clumping in the sand. He was in pain, but he looked ready to get the hell off the island.

That was, until he turned toward the approaching boat.

"Ya Ibn el Sharmouta!" Mahdi said, hop-walking *back* toward the jungle.

Talia had no idea what Mahdi was doing, but she understood, 'Son of a bitch,' in a dozen languages, and the look on his face didn't require any language skills. Mahdi was more afraid of the people on the boat than he was of the Sentinelese.

She caught him by the arm. "What are you doing?"

"They are Hamas," he whispered.

Talia focused on the boat anew. The four men standing behind Ambani had the look of killers and the AK-47s over their shoulders to match. As an Israeli woman on Ambani's hit list, she didn't think her odds of surviving their rescue was any better than Mahdi's.

"They're here to kill you?" she asked.

"They will torture me first. Find out who I told about them. Punish my indiscretions. Then they will kill me."

"No," Talia said. "They won't."

Mahdi looked her in the eyes, desperate but interested. "Why not?"

"Because we'll fight." She looked down at the spear in her hands, and then pointed to Mahdi's shorts pocket where the automatic knife's shape could be seen. He dug into the pocket, snapped open the blade, and gave a nod that was more forced than confident.

But then he spoke the truth they both knew. "It won't be enough."

Four AK-47s would make short work of them, even if Talia managed to impale one of the men from a distance. Then there were Chugy and Ambani, who might both be armed. And Winston. His loyalties would shift to whomever would help him get off the island. And since Ambani wanted them all dead…

"I could kill you right now," she said to Winston, who was unarmed.

He looked back over his shoulder, arms still raised, but no longer waving as the boat approached. "I'm aware. But then they'll gun you down for sure. Or we could see what happens when I tell Ambani the island, and his resort plans, are a bust."

"Those four men are Hamas," she said. "They're here to kill Mahdi."

"Sucks for you, Mahd-man."

"And I'm Israeli."

"Right," he said. "Sooo…"

"Help us kill the men," Talia said. "When they let you on the boat."

Winston lowered his hands, furrowed his brow, and then said. "Nah." A smile. "Neither of you are worth risking a bullet."

Talia tensed, raising the spear.

"Throw that and both of you die. Keep your mouth shut and maybe I won't tell them where you're from." Winston chuckled. "Toss in a beej later and maybe I'll convince Ambani to let you walk."

Talia looked back at the quiet jungle.

Where are you?

If the Sentinelese attacked, the chaos might give them a chance. At the same time, they would probably be two of the first targets. They had both frustrated the Sentinelese's efforts to kill them, and had acted violently toward the tribe. Whether or not they had actually killed anyone was up for debate, but they were still well established enemies.

And yet, they were still alive, and a known threat. The Sentinelese acted most violently toward unknown threats.

That's why they stopped, she realized. *They heard the boat, too. They must be reassessing the situation, deciding who to attack first. Or waiting for the small boat's crew to fall under the smoke's hallucinogenic spell.*

We need to make ourselves less of a threat.

Talia dropped the spear.

"What are you doing?" Mahdi asked.

"The knife," Talia said, motioning to the ground with her head while unbuttoning her shorts. "Drop it. And your clothes."

42

SHAME.

In a strange kind of way, shame had no place on North Sentinel Island. The natives felt none, and the mind-bending haze billowing from the many fire pits reduced inhibitions and feelings of guilt, humiliation, and remorse. Evidence of that was clear at every stage of the expedition's journey, but for Mahdi, it was only now reaching a pinnacle.

He stood, awkwardly balanced on his injured leg and stark naked, discarded clothing still around his ankles. He was in full view of two women, neither of whom were his wife—the only woman to see him in such a state since he had been a child. And then there were the six men, one on the beach, five in the boat. He glanced back at the jungle, and when no spear punched through his chest, he wondered how many men, women, and children were seeing his nakedness.

He knew the act of public nudity was shameful. He, like everyone else on the planet—aside from tribes like the Sentinelese—had been taught that basic truth from an early age. But now, standing in clear sight of men who would mock his nakedness, and others who would behead him for it, he felt...nothing. The stigma of nudity had abandoned him.

Mahdi laughed, and a similarly naked Talia shot him a questioning look.

"I feel no shame," he explained.

She eyed him up and down. Gave a wry smile. "Have nothing to be ashamed of."

He marveled at her casual humor. He might not be ashamed, and the smoke's effect had allowed him a laugh, but he was still terrified: of what lurked in the jungle behind him, and of the men accompanying Ambani.

The scrape of boat on sand pulled his attention forward. The dinghy had arrived. Chugy leaped out first, machete in hand. She stormed toward

Winston while the four Middle Eastern men slipped into the knee deep waters, assault rifles aimed toward the jungle.

They're here for me, Mahdi thought, *but they've been warned about the Sentinelese.* He wondered how they had found him. He hadn't given Ambani a reason to summon them. He couldn't have known how things played out on the island. And why risk getting involved with Hamas?

Mahdi closed his eyes. Shook his head.

The phone call.

Hamas was a terrorist organization, but they were well connected. It wouldn't be impossible for them to trace a call, and they had likely been monitoring his family's home, perhaps tracking every call, waiting for his moment of weakness. And when it came, it led them to Ambani, who would gladly trade Mahdi's life to avoid conflict with terrorists.

They are here because of me, he thought, *but they don't know where 'here' is. If they knew the true extent of this island's horrors, they would have never left the yacht.* He tried not to grin.

"Where is he?" Chugy asked. "Where is my uncle?"

"Ask him." Winston tilted his head toward Mahdi, redirecting Chugy's fury.

She charged up the beach, oblivious to the jungle's dangers. Full of rage, it wasn't until she closed to within ten feet that she noticed Mahdi and Talia were naked. Her curiosity was short-lived, replaced once more by fury. "Where is Emmei?"

"Dead," Mahdi said, and he flinched at the bluntness of his answer. A lack of inhibitions didn't just affect the way people dressed, it also loosened the tongue. "The Sentinelese. They—"

"Lies," she said.

"They burned him," Mahdi said, and despite the mind-altering smoke, he regretted revealing the detail, in part because it was harsh, but also because it stoked Chugy's anger into madness.

"Lies!" she screamed, tears in her eyes. She raised the machete, the blade poised to strike Mahdi between the neck and shoulder.

Three gunshots sounded, freezing everyone in place.

"Leave him." The voice was heavily accented with Arabic, and familiar to Mahdi. It was Baseer, the man who had recruited Aziz. Most of his face was covered by a thick beard, sunglasses, and head wrap, but the scar on his cheek, which carved a line through his beard, was distinct.

Chugy snarled, but backed off a few steps, lowering the machete.

While the Hamas men maintained a watch, Winston approached the dinghy, whispering with Ambani. Mahdi tried to hear the conversation, but over the rumbles of thunder behind him, and the hammering of his heart, it was impossible.

"You bring shame to your family. To your wife and your child." Baseer said, looking Mahdi up and down. He turned toward Talia and spat. "And with a Jew no less."

Ambani must have told them about who else was on the island, which could also explain the AK-47s. They weren't just for the Sentinelese, they were for Rowan. But the former U.S. Army Ranger was nowhere to be found, and even if he showed up, he had no weapons.

"You are the murderer of innocents," Mahdi replied. "Your actions bring death and destruction to our people, and to my family. My conscience is clear. The only shame to be found here, is with you. Hamas believes it is fighting for the people of Palestine, or even worse, the will of Allah, but most of Palestine does not want you, and the true followers of Islam do not support you. I am an atheist, and yet, I am a better Muslim than you."

Mahdi had never spoken such words. It felt simultaneously wrong, and liberating. While many in Palestine shared his point of view, fear of reprisal from the violent vast majority kept them quiet. Whether it was the smoke, or the knowledge that he was going to die no matter what he said, Mahdi could no longer hold back the truth. And this way, Baseer was sure to forgo the torture and simply put a bullet in his head—a notion confirmed a moment later when the Hamas leader raised the barrel of his rifle toward Mahdi's temple and shouted in high-pitched Arabic, "Allah, drape this infidel in your fiery wrath for all eternity and steep the criminal Jew in boiling—"

The prayer was cut short by a confused, gurgling choke.

Baseer had an arrow in his neck, angled in such a way that it had missed his arteries and spine. His breathing became ragged and panicked, but he was not dying, nor would he, as long as the arrow remained lodged in place. He dropped the AK-47, which was still strapped over his head and shoulder, and he raised his hands to the arrow, feeling both ends, his eyes widening as he began to comprehend what had happened.

"Mahdi!" Talia said. "We need to mimic the Sentinelese threat display!" She was already thrusting her hips toward the newcomers, but would it really fool the Sentinelese? Would they see them as less of a threat? Or would that require something more?

Before Baseer could stumble back, Mahdi grasped the end of the three-foot-long, featherless arrow and yanked it back. Blood sprayed from the hole in the front when the man screamed. Rather than counter the attack, Baseer held his hands over the twin wounds, front and back. He could do nothing to stop Mahdi from kicking his chest.

Pain lanced up Mahdi's injured leg when he kicked, but it was Baseer who fell back into the sand, gasping and choking.

"I will not back down again!" Mahdi shouted at him, hopping in the sand, trying to stay upright while venting. "I will not run away anymore!"

A spear arced past and struck Baseer's chest, pinning him to the sand. The man's panic came to an abrupt stop, his dead eyes staring up at the storm.

The remaining Hamas men opened fire, peppering the jungle with rapid-fire bullets. When the fusillade came to an abrupt stop and the three men ejected their spent magazines to reload, arrows fluttered through the air.

One man took an arrow in the eye and dropped like a tree. Mahdi watched the man splash back into the ocean, but his attention shifted quickly toward the dinghy, sliding backward. Winston was pushing the boat out of the sand while Ambani ducked behind the shield Rowan had left on the dinghy.

An arrow slipped through the muscle of another Hamas man's thigh, but he stayed upright and resumed his barrage, this time sweeping across the jungle.

"Down!" Mahdi shouted, tackling Talia to the sand as bullets buzzed past, shredding leaves and branches.

While the men emptied their magazines again, Chugy dove into the water, slid up behind the now waist deep Winston and climbed over his body to leap back into the boat.

This time, when the two Hamas men reloaded, they crouched, making themselves smaller targets, and they kept their eyes on the jungle. When the arrows flew once more, they sprang into action, battle tested and unafraid. Yet only one of them was fortunate enough to avoid being impaled. The other took three arrows, the first two in his gut, and the second in his open mouth as he prepared to scream. None of the shots were instantly fatal, and as his last remaining compatriot finished swapping magazines, he twitched on the sand.

The final Hamas man opened fire once more, but reduced his firing rate to three round bursts. He wasn't firing at any one target. He was simply covering his retreat toward the boat…that he had yet to realize was abandoning him. He turned to where the boat had been, saw where it was, and then quickly adjusted his aim.

Ambani screamed in surprise, as bullets punched holes in the shield. Chugy dove lower into the boat before she could lower the engine. Winston, still not in the boat, ducked beneath the water's surface.

The man continued firing as he waded toward the boat, shouting, "Tawaqquf!" He stopped in knee deep water when a spear struck his back. He wavered for a moment, and then bumbled around, confused by what he was feeling. It was explained to him a moment later when a second spear pierced his chest. He looked down at it, eyebrows rising in understanding. Then he collapsed to the water.

Arrows and spears flew from the jungle, splashing down around the boat and ricocheting off the still functional shield, which Ambani now held in the middle of the dinghy. "Start the motor!" he shouted at Chugy, who was already yanking the starter cord.

Chugy yanked on the cord, but rather than finishing the pull, she toppled back and nearly fell overboard when Winston heaved himself up. But the small craft was no match for his girth and it nearly capsized.

"Get off!" Chugy shouted, kicking Winston in the face.

While she took hold of the starter cord once more, Ambani drew a sidearm and pointed it at Winston, who ducked under the water once more. He fired three shots. Winston slid beneath the boat.

An arrow struck Ambani's extended arm, forcing him to release the weapon, and duck back behind the cover of his shield.

The motor growled to life and spat smoke.

It was drowned out by a roar.

43

BRIGHT LIGHT BECKONED Rowan onward, so he ran toward it despite his unwavering belief that his life would soon come to an end. Whether or not he made it to the beach, or into the ocean, escape was no longer in the cards for him.

And he was okay with that.

Better than okay.

If the others survived because of his sacrifice, he would be pleased with his death. Maybe even his life. Mistakes had been made, but they couldn't define him any longer.

Since being found by Sashi, he had overcome the bottle's temptations, and had fought to protect people once more. It felt good. It felt right. It had been a long time since his life had reflected either quality.

His only regret was that he wouldn't live long enough to do more, to make his life really matter. But perhaps Talia and Mahdi would? He would never know, but he could give them a chance.

He weaved through the jungle, following a chaotic course, hoping to drag out the chase, knowing it would end in the light. *At least I'll see the sun one last time,* he thought, as an arrow thumped into a tree behind his head.

The Sentinelese were closing the distance, following a straight path despite Rowan's zigzag. They knew the island, its terrain, and where it would direct him. Rather than chasing Rowan, they were simply heading toward the pursuit's end.

Clutching the stolen bow and two arrows, he adjusted course again, this time heading straight ahead. If he was going to fight to the end, he wanted to see the men, women…and children, who would do him in.

The light ahead grew into a wall of brilliant white. The sunlit smoke was nearly blinding from inside the shaded jungle depths. But then he crashed through the brush and spilled out onto the sand. The sun-bathed blue sky lay just beyond the island's reefs. But above, the storm still raged, pouring rain and lightning down on the island. A stationary hurricane.

It's not possible, he thought, watching the storm. *But neither is hallucinating an entire storm.*

Smoke snaked from the jungle all around him, flowing over the beach and out to sea like the gaseous tentacles of some giant monster.

Rain pelted his shirtless body, whipped by the wind. *This is real. The sand. The storm. The Sentinelese.*

Focus on what is real, he told himself. *Focus on it, and fight it.*

He pushed himself up, nocked one of the two arrows and drew the bowstring back.

A moment later, a warrior leapt out of the jungle, clearing the brush and holding a spear, ready to throw.

Rowan adjusted his aim and let the arrow fly.

The airborne man was struck in the chest. The impact unfurled his body and flipped him backward. He landed in the sand with a wet slap.

The second Sentinelese to leave the jungle was a baby. Like the man, it sailed through the air. Unlike the man, there was no way it had leaped so high. It had been thrown.

Rowan aimed his second, and last, arrow at the infant-turned-projectile and he couldn't bring himself to fire.

It's not real, he told himself, knowing it was a half-truth. Something had been thrown at him, but it wasn't a human child.

He shouted in frustration, unable to fire, and he swung the bow instead. The wood struck the small body, deflecting its course into the shallows, where it thrashed about. A woman followed the child, likely the one who'd thrown it. Rather than leaping, she quickly found herself lying on her belly beside her stricken comrade, Rowan's arrow in her chest.

Neither were dead, but they weren't exactly mobile, either.

Stay down, Rowan willed them, and then he grasped the arrow sticking out of the man. He placed the arrow on the bowstring and had to fire it immediately as a quiet warrior charged from the side. The man took the arrow in the chest, spun, and fell.

Not one of the fallen Sentinelese had shouted in pain, or shown any kind of emotion at being shot. They'd been physically incapacitated, but they seemed to possess no fear of death.

Because they can't die, he thought, and he followed it up with another. *Bullshit. If they get up, it's because the first shot wasn't a kill shot, or because the smoke is making me see them get up.*

Three men and two women emerged from the jungle as a group. They looked about, taking in their fallen tribesmen. He thought they might attack with a little more caution, but he was wrong.

The five Sentinelese charged together. Rowan reached for an arrow, hoping to pluck it from the second man's body, but there was no time. He deflected a spear strike with the bow and struck out. He hit someone hard, but had no idea whom he'd struck or if it had any affect. Blows came from all directions, some of them blunt—fists and feet. Other were sharp—arrows and spears.

He focused on the weapons, evading their points, even if it meant taking a hit. A spear slipped past his side, under his arm. He clamped down on it, spun into it and threw a punch, connecting hard. A woman fell to the side, already rolling to her feet, but she'd let go of the weapon.

Rowan spun with the spear tip extended straight out from his armpit, which for the Sentinelese, was face level. Two men ducked back. The third took the multi-pronged tip in the face, falling away with three spines lodged in his cheek.

Without looking, Rowan kicked out behind him. His foot struck something soft—a stomach—and the 'oof' that followed it could not be held back. As the woman fell to her knees behind him, Rowan pressed the attack on the three men.

Using a combination of Ranger and Kung-Fu training offered to all U.S. Special Forces, Rowan spun, struck, and jabbed with the spear, like it was a bo-staff. The warriors who stood their ground were struck or impaled until they fell back, giving him a wide berth. He'd wounded all five of them, their blood soaking into the already wet sand. But they still lived.

He extended the spear tip and pointed it at each of the five attackers, his back to the ocean.

I can take them, he thought. *They're not used to people fighting back, especially people who know* how *to fight back.*

But then the three arrow-wounded Sentinelese stood. The two men and one woman were bleeding, but still mobile.

Not possible, he thought again.

One of them had been shot in the chest. As near as Rowan could tell, he'd been shot in the heart. No amount of blood-congealing smoke could save a man from a wound like that.

He's still on the ground.

He's not real.

Rowan made a mental note of the Sentinelese he believed were dead and then focused on the rest.

That was when the rest of the tribe arrived. They slipped out of the jungle, casual, like they were out for a stroll. First, there were just a few of them, and then what looked like the entire tribe. They hung back near the jungle, watching, unconcerned about the possibility of him attacking them. Some of them sat down to watch. Women collected their infants, scrambling on the shoreline, and began nursing.

His death was to be a spectacle.

"C'mon," Rowan growled. "Let's give them a show."

Gunshots rang out to his left. He turned toward the sound, looking down the beach, but the sand curved away. He didn't know who was shooting, but he had little doubt the confrontation involved Mahdi and Talia.

He wanted to help them, but he was under no illusions of rushing to the rescue. His life ended here. If they survived the island, it would be without him.

"C'mon!" he shouted, jabbing the spear, but the Sentinelese maintained their distance.

Why aren't they attacking?

He knew they weren't afraid. The Sentinelese didn't run from fights. And they didn't shirk from violence, or from attacking first.

They're either waiting for me to make the first move, which would leave me wide open to a counter attack, or...

Rowan spun around, spear raised in defense.

He saw a dark blur, felt an impact on the raised spear and then one on his chest. When he regained his senses, he found himself lying on his back in the sand. The spear had been cleaved in two. When he looked up, a lone Sentinelese woman strode from the water, naked, beautiful, and holding his combat hatchet.

Since the others weren't attacking, he assumed this was meant to be single combat. He rolled backward and onto his feet, clutching the two sides of the spear, hoping the Sentinelese wouldn't simply skewer him from behind.

Lightning ripped through the sky above and he couldn't help but look. The streak branched out in all directions, filling the dark clouds with purple light and silhouetting a large, winged shape.

It's not there, he told himself, and he focused on the approaching woman. *But she is.*

He took a sideways fighting stance, plotting his moves. Block with the left, strike with the right. Two quick moves. One clean strike. It would drop the woman and clear a path to the ocean. While she still fell to the ground, he would make for the waters and then swim. The plan ended there, but at least it was a plan.

The woman appeared to size him up, too, looking him over through squinted eyes. She stopped out of range. Didn't flinch when a barrage of automatic gunfire tore through the air.

He tried to match her disinterest in the unseen battle, but struggled to not glance toward the sounds.

A moment later, the blast of gunfire repeated, and this time his ears picked up on the distinct sound and rhythm. He'd heard it in training, but most often when it was directed toward him.

Those are AK-47s.

The knowledge did him little good, but the distraction nearly cost him his life. When the woman stepped toward him, he almost didn't notice. By the time he did, she was within striking distance.

Instinct shouted at him to strike. Follow through with the plan. But the woman had not attacked. Instead, she'd stopped short.

The pair held their ground, neither moving, nor attacking.

When the woman finally moved, Rowan flinched back, but it wasn't necessary. She moved with a calm steadiness, lifting the combat hatchet toward him. Then she spun the weapon around in her hand, holding the handle out toward him.

"Lazoaf," she said.

"Lazoaf?" Rowan responded, the tone of his voice adding a 'for real' that even the Sentinelese understood.

The woman grinned. Extended the hatchet a little further.

Rowan reached out slowly, expecting betrayal and was somewhat shocked when he was allowed to reclaim his weapon. *Do they want me to die with my own weapon? Is this some kind of cultural thing? Honoring me as a warrior?*

He couldn't think of anything else that made sense…aside from the truth.

Lazoaf.

Leave.

They're letting me go.

"Why?" he asked.

She stepped closer, raised a finger, and poked it against the still tender, but partially healed wound on his chest. "*Geula.*"

Her extended finger traced a path around them, indicating the Sentinelese tribe. "Herev lohetet." Then she poked Rowan again and said, "Herev lohetet. Geula."

She nodded like he understood and then stepped back.

The Sentinelese to his left parted, clearing a path down the beach, toward the sounds of gunfire.

Hatchet in hand, he nodded his gratitude and then sprinted away, hoping he wasn't too late to help Talia and Mahdi.

While running, he glanced at the sky and saw nothing but clouds.

It's not real, he thought, clutching the hatchet, knowing what he could do with it. *But I am.*

44

A LEVIATHAN ROSE up beside the boat, white like the great whale, but decorated with an outlandish, brightly colored tattoo. Winston had swum beneath the boat and shoved off the ocean floor. He gripped the dinghy's side, once again trying to pull himself in.

Once again, he failed.

An unprepared Ambani was catapulted into the ocean though.

Chugy managed to stay in the boat, clinging to the outboard motor's throttle handle. When gravity pulled Winston back into the water, she drew a knife and leaped after him, venting her anger with a shrill battle cry.

Winston ducked beneath the water, allowing the airborne woman to sail past and splash down in waist deep water. Chugy surfaced first, knife clutched, teeth bared. She grunted and screamed as she looked for a fight. When she didn't see Winston, she turned toward the shore, looking first to the jungle and then toward Talia and Mahdi.

Talia recognized the look in Chugy's eyes. She'd seen it before, reflected in a mirror the night her father died. The news of Emmei's death had lit the fuse, but the men who had come to kill Mahdi had turned the long fuse into a short one, which had just run out. She was looking for a target now, and found it when she looked at Mahdi.

"You killed him, didn't you!" Chugy waded toward shore, the knife blade pointed at Mahdi.

They were far from defenseless. Talia's spear and Mahdi's knife still lay at their feet. An AK-47 lay not far away. It was strapped to Baseer's body, but it wouldn't take long to free.

The problem was, if either of them picked up a weapon, they might make themselves a target for the Sentinelese.

Then again, the barrage of arrows and spears had come to a stop. The Sentinelese had no doubt realized the island's invaders were fighting amongst themselves. Perhaps they were content to let their enemies kill each other. Or maybe they were watching for sport. The Sentinelese and their customs were impossible to understand. The smoke still pouring out onto the sand, clouding air and minds alike, made every observation she had made dubious. She had no more real information about who the Sentinelese were and how they lived than when she had first arrived.

That's not true, she thought. *I know that they are masters of psychochemical warfare.*

Beyond that, why the Sentinelese did anything was anyone's guess.

The water behind Chugy bulged. She was so focused on Mahdi that she didn't hear the water sluicing off Winston's broad body. Talia nearly shouted a warning, but her mouth clamped shut when she saw Ambani's lost pistol in Winston's hand. Had she warned Chugy and Winston survived the ensuing fight, he would turn the gun on Mahdi and her.

Mahdi, however, lacked her cold logic. Despite Chugy's clear intent to plunge a knife into his heart, Mahdi pointed and shouted over a drum roll of thunder. "Behind you!"

Chugy's face twisted with confusion. Why would the man she intended to kill warn her of danger? Was it a ruse? She must have heard Winston as she pondered these questions, because she snapped around, swinging the blade in a wide arc. As she followed through, twisting around, a thin red line appeared on Winston's belly. Beads of blood formed along the line, but nothing more.

The big man barely noticed the scratch and kept his wits as he dismantled his adversary. A quick pistol whip to the side of Chugy's head stunned her. He caught her by the wrist as she stumbled, and gave it a twist. With a crack of bone and a shout of pain, the knife fell from her hand.

Winston yanked Chugy's injured arm behind her back, keeping his hand on her wrist, the pain making her compliant. He raised his gun hand toward the jungle and then toward Mahdi. "I was thinking about letting you live, Mahd-man. But that? After everything we've been through together? That hurt."

Using Chugy as a human shield, Winston moved back onto the beach, his feet buried in sand. He glanced up as lightning filled the sky, smiling and then confused. He scanned the clouds and then faced Talia. "Fucking island. Plays with your God damn mind."

Talia said nothing. Made no move. Hoped the Sentinelese would press the attack once more, but they remained silent and hidden.

"My offer still stands," Winston said. "You can leave, right now, with me."

Talia knew she should stay quiet, maybe even feign interest, lower his defenses and then strike. But he wouldn't believe it, and she couldn't bring herself to not reply honestly. "I'd rather take my chances with the locals."

"Ouch," Winston said with a grin. "That hurts." He leaned in close to Chugy's ear. "How 'bout you, Chugs? Willing to switch teams for a ride off this island?"

Chugy let out a primal shout and thrust her head back, connecting with Winston's nose. She spun, throwing an elbow, but fell short when two gunshots dropped her to the sand. She dragged herself a few feet away from Winston and then fell still.

Talia took a step forward, but stopped when Winston raised the gun toward her. All of Winston's vile humor was missing from his face. That two women would rather die than trade sex with him for freedom had scratched off a scab he pretended didn't exist.

"You can all fucking die here, then." His finger began compressing the trigger as purple light filled the sky. Wanting to see something beautiful before she died, rather than Winston, Talia looked up. Streaks of light cut through the sky overhead, the strobing flashes revealing rain drops…and something else.

Something large.

With wings.

Then the light coalesced into a single streak that flashed downward, toward the beach.

Toward Winston.

Thunder and gunshot merged. The sound ripped through the air with soul-torn-from-body violence.

Hot white light exploded from the beach, launching glowing orbs of hot sand.

Talia closed her eyes and crouched. Her body was pelted with steaming debris, burning her skin.

She flinched when hands clutched her shoulders. "Are you all right?"

Mahdi.

She opened her eyes, confused by the pain in her head. Mahdi was crouched beside her, concern painted on his face. He put a gentle hand under her chin and turned her head. "Looks like a graze."

"A graze?"

"You were shot," Mahdi said.

She felt warmth spreading over her scalp. Blood flowing. *Shot, but not dead.* Her head pulsed with pain. *A concussion for sure.*

"Winston?" she asked, struggling to stand.

"I don't think he will—" Mahdi's assurances were cut short by a groan.

"Ugh... Fucking hell," Winston said. Steam rose from his red and boiled skin. The lightning had struck him, but had not killed him. He tried to take a step, but remained locked in place. Dazed, he looked down. Winston's confusion at what he saw matched Talia's.

But then she understood. The lightning had turned the beach sand, which his feet had been buried in, to glass that had been quickly cooled by the rain. Winston was locked in place, and would never leave the island.

Confusion became desperation became rage. He raised the pistol, which had been fused to his hand, toward Mahdi. "I'm not going to—"

A loud crack silenced Winston and snapped his head to the side. His body went slack and tried to fall forward, but his joints and the solid glass around his feet kept his dead body upright. The hatchet buried in the side of his head looked familiar, and the skill with which it had been thrown was unmistakable. Talia traced the weapon's path backward, knowing who she would see.

Rowan ran toward her, blood mixed with water dripping from his arms and legs. He'd been through hell, but he was still alive, and still fighting to keep them alive as well. "We need to go. Now."

"No shit," she said, blinking past the dazed feeling starting to overtake her, and hobbling toward the sea.

The surge of a boat motor drew her eyes up.

Ambani was in the dinghy, twisting the throttle and turning the boat back out to sea. He had no parting words. Didn't even glance back.

"We can swim," Rowan said, but she knew the yacht would be gone long before they reached it. She stumbled to a stop, feeling hopeless and defeated. Before she could fall to her knees, something massive fell from the sky.

It landed into the ocean with a colossal splash. The sound of shattering wood and fiberglass exploded into the air as the boat's back end shot up and launched Ambani into the sea once more.

"That was real." Rowan looked at her. "That was real, right?"

"The boat is destroyed," Mahdi said. "Of that we can be sure."

"But how?" Talia asked. They were all wondering the same thing. If the boat was real, and it was destroyed, how had it happened?

The answer rose from the water, spread its fleshy wings wide and opened what looked like a hundred sets of eyes. Lightning flashed overhead, reflected in the many eyes, all of which looked at the man clutched in the Cherub's hand—Ambani.

The twelve-foot-tall, hunched monster took three long strides into the shallows. The many eyes flitted to Rowan, and Mahdi, and Talia. Her insides quivered when it looked at her, but the glare didn't last long. The eyes shifted back to the unconscious Ambani. And then the long fingers coiled inward, punching holes into the resort tycoon's body and waking him up.

"Is that real?" Rowan asked.

The Cherub lifted up Ambani's screaming and writhing form up. Its tight black skin stretched over its long slender muscles and thick bones. The rib cage looked close to bursting. The bony, peeled-open face turned up to watch Ambani, along with its many multi-colored eyes, all of them furious. Then it spoke. A single, rumbling word. "NIDON."

Talia recognized the word. *Condemned.*

The five long fingers buried in Ambani's flesh slurped out. The man shouted in pain, but looked relieved.

Relief shifted quickly to horror as the giant clutched him tightly enough to snap bones and crush organs. Blood oozed from his mouth alongside a gurgling, short-lived scream. Then Ambani was cast aside, his flung body colliding with Winston, whose knees snapped forward. Both men crashed to the sand-turned-glass.

The many eyes shifted again, and this time remained locked on the three remaining invaders.

This is why the Sentinelese didn't attack. They knew the Cherub was coming. They knew what we have been denying since we first saw it.

"It's real," she said.

Rowan gave a nod. "It's real. It's all real."

"Then there is no hope for us," Talia said, the throb in her head growing more intense as her heart rate increased.

"There is," Mahdi said. He bent down, retrieved his knife and Talia's spear, and added. "Go. Both of you. To the yacht. Now! Go!" Then he charged the Cherub, which seemed as surprised by his reckless action as Talia and Rowan.

She wanted to stop him. To save him. But there was nothing they could do aside from run into death's grip alongside him, or abide by the soon-to-be dead man's wishes, and survive.

"Let's go!" Rowan said, helping her run into the sea, angling away from the Cherub.

Mahdi threw the spear, plunging it into the creature's side. There were no illusions about him being able to slay the beast. He was simply buying them time. If they could get in the water, get lost in the waves, and swim under them, perhaps they could reach the yacht. Beyond the island's borders, maybe the Cherub would let them live?

"This isn't going to work," she said, slowing.

Rowan tugged on her, still fighting. "Just keep moving."

Mahdi shouted as he swung his small knife, stabbing the creature's thigh. He stabbed twice more before being picked up.

Waist deep in water, Talia felt her foot strike something solid. They were wading through the dinghy's remains. She looked down and saw a distorted, but familiar shape, and stopped.

"What are you doing?" Rowan asked, and he tried to pull her deeper.

Mahdi screamed. He was held aloft, just as Ambani had been before being crushed, the Cherub's fingers buried in his body. Talia had undergone the same thing. Remembered the vision of her past.

It set me free, she realized. *It was judging me.*

But she had no idea what secrets were in Mahdi's past, or what the verdict would be.

It can't simply be judging between good and evil. That's not it's job. It's a protector. It needs to know if we'll keep the island's secrets.

She had decided to do as much before setting foot on the island, but would Mahdi? She wouldn't take that risk.

She pulled free of Rowan's grasp and plunged beneath the waves. When she came back up a moment later, she had her recovered long bow and three arrows, the first one already nocked and being drawn back. As Mahdi's cry of pain became shrill, she unleashed the arrow.

It sang through the air and punched through the back of the Cherub's head. Its body went rigid, but did not fall.

She fired again, the second arrow finding its mark just a few inches to the side of the first.

The Cherub turned its head, its eyes drifting toward Talia as she drew the bowstring back once more. The rest of the creature's eyes moved from Mahdi to her.

"Talia..." Rowan's voice was full of warning and regret, but he didn't abandon her.

She fired the third arrow, striking the creature's head once more. The eyes in its head closed like a mother losing her patience, but struggling to remain in control. Then the rest of the eyes followed suit. The Cherub twisted one way, and then the other, flinging Mahdi free. He toppled through the air, crashing into the water twenty feet away, where he sank beneath the surface.

Rowan swam to him and lifted him up, feeling for a pulse. "Alive."

Talia smiled and then her vision faded. She saw Rowan dragging Mahdi toward her, and then nothing.

She remembered water. And floating.

She was stretched and pulled, arms aching. And then weight returned. She was lying on something hard and flat.

A floor.

Her eyes opened. Rowan lay beside her, gasping for air, slowing. Easing. Looking back.

They were on the yacht. Mahdi lay on Rowan's far side, chest rising and falling. They were alive.

"How?" she asked.

"I'm a good swimmer," Rowan replied with a weak smile.

"I meant, why? Why are we alive?"

"*Geula.*"

"Where did you hear that?"

"What does it mean?"

"Redemption."

His smile grew. "That's what I thought."

"Where did you—"

"A Sentinelese woman. Before she gave me my hatchet and let me go. And after declaring me Herev Lohetet."

Talia's eyebrows rose until the shifting skin moved the wound atop her head. "Flaming Sword? You?"

"All of us, actually. I think. We'd be dead otherwise, right?"

"If it was real," Mahdi groaned, lying still.

Talia tried to comprehend everything she was being told and everything they had experienced. Her modern mind told her none of it was real. That they had simply seen visions. But visions couldn't kill people, destroy boats, or pick her up. She'd been in the Cherub's hands. Felt its fingers around her. Inside her. But drugs could have a profound effect on the human mind. Unreality could feel real. They could have spent half their time on the island tripping hard, believing they were fighting monsters while the Sentinelese put on a puppet show.

But her heart…her heart said something else.

"Real or not, the island needs to be protected from the world."

Rowan laughed. "It's the world that needs protecting from the island."

Talia smiled. It was the truest thing she'd ever heard in her life. It was also the last thing she heard before passing out again.

EPILOGUE

"HEY STARSKY, THE raft is floating," Talia said, her voice calm.

"Copy that, Jungle Princess," Rowan said over the secure channel while steering the commandeered Sandal-Foot Resort yacht. While he hadn't spent a lot of time behind the wheel of a boat, and certainly not a hundred-foot-long pleasure ship, it handled like a dream despite the rough seas. "En route."

Despite the seriousness of what they were attempting, Rowan was smiling. He hadn't realized how much he had missed this. The code names. The adrenaline rush of sneaking through the dark of night.

"Madman, what's your status?"

"Standing by," Mahdi replied. He wasn't fond of the codenames, but he understood the need for them. If they were to accomplish their goal, secrecy was paramount. He had chosen Madman, not in honor of Winston's nickname for him, but to reflect the kind of man the island had made him—the kind of man willing to rush toward danger, rather than away from it. He was a new man. It helped that they had used Talia's money and connections to sneak his family out of Palestine.

"Try to look nice," Rowan said.

"When do I not look nice?"

"It's a bunch of white rich kids from the U.S. You're from the Middle East. And have an accent."

Talia's voice laughed over the radio.

"I will smile," Mahdi said. "But they do not have a choice. Am I right?"

"In a few seconds they won't," Talia said. There was a pause and then a distant whump.

Rowan cut the engine and coasted to the blinking dive flag. He looked out of the wheelhouse window and watched Mahdi pulling Talia from the ocean, dressed in a wetsuit and carrying a small detonator. She hurried across the deck and climbed the stairs to the wheelhouse, stepping inside and closing the door behind her.

"Worked as planned." She clicked the detonator button a few times. "Charge went off in time with hitting the reef. They'll be going down fast."

It was a similar plan to the one they believed Chugy had implemented on Ambani's behalf. The plan was to strand them on the beach, leaving Winston to kill the duped trio, and survive the night for a morning pickup. They'd found evidence as much in Ambani's office at the Sandal-Foot Resort, which Talia had bought at auction following his 'death at sea.' The yacht had been part of the package deal, and the resort was now their home.

As Talia began shedding the wetsuit, the distress call came right on schedule.

"Mayday, mayday, this is uhh, shit, what's the name of our boat?"

"I don't know, man. It's a rental."

"Fuck. Uhh, we've hit a reef outside North Sentinel Island. We're taking on water."

Just take your finger off the damn button, Rowan thought.

"Can anyone hear me? Uhh, over."

The unsecured radio crackled and Rowan depressed the call button. "Copy that, son. I'm not far. Heading your way now. How many should I expect to pick up? Over."

"Eight," the kid replied. "Over."

"Eight," Rowan said to Talia, no longer transmitting. "Eight kids."

"Eight idiots," Talia said. Over the past three months, she had worked hard to educate the resorts scattered throughout the Andaman Islands, about the Sentinelese and the dangers they presented to their guests… with certain details withheld. Despite the warnings, there were still people willing to venture to the island with the desire for a cheap thrill, with the chance of discovery, or just from plain carelessness.

"What are you all doing out here?" Rowan asked over the radio.

"We're YouTubers," the kid said. "Thought it would be fun. You know, get video of some naked tribe people. I heard they boink on the beach. Uhh, over."

"Like I said." Talia peeled the wetsuit leggings off, standing in just her bikini. "Idiots."

Rowan throttled forward again, heading directly toward where the small boat had anchored before Talia had cut the line. He turned on the flood lights, illuminating the stranded and quickly sinking boat. Eight young men and women stood in the back, waving their arms.

"We see you!" the kid shouted through the radio. "We see you!"

"No shit," Rowan said to Talia, rolling his eyes. "Maybe we *should* leave them."

"Aww, Starsky, if you can find redemption, maybe there's hope for them, too." She kissed him gently, a promise of things to come…in the privacy of their villa. While they had come to the conclusion that much of what they had experienced on the island was real, they still believed the smoke, or perhaps the island itself, altered the way people thought. Lowered inhibitions. Returned people to a state of not caring about such things, the way that life was meant to be, or so Talia said. But the bond forged during the trials experienced on the island was real, as was the attraction between them. It had simply become less…public.

A small outboard motor roared to life. Then the dinghy, driven by Mahdi, cut through the water, clearing the reefs with no trouble. The petrified teens boarded quickly and without hesitation. Within minutes, Mahdi was on his way back.

As they neared the yacht, Rowan killed the flood lights. In the dark, not one of the kids saw Mahdi put on a sharp-toothed clown mask. "Ready?"

Talia smiled and handed him a werewolf mask. Her mask was human, but the face was melting. "This is my favorite part."

As Rowan put on his mask, Talia assembled her new blowgun and took out eight darts, each tipped with a psychotropic concoction of her own creation. Combined with the horrific masks, the kids were guaranteed to have the worst nights of their lives.

But they would survive.

In the morning, they would awaken on a beach, not far from their own resort, clearly intoxicated and missing a rented boat. The ensuing trouble would ensure they never returned to North Sentinel Island, and would land them on a shit-list shared between the area's resorts, a list that had been started by the Sandal-Foot Resort's new owners. A list that already had thirty-five names on it.

Thirty-five people who had been spared the tortures of stumbling upon forbidden land.

Who had unknowingly avoided judgment by an ancient tribe tasked by a higher power to protect the island, and their monstrous Cherub.

Who had been saved by the newest members of the Flaming Sword… all of whom vowed to never set foot on the island again, so help them God, and of whom they had all begun to reshape their opinions. Mahdi attended a mosque with his family. Talia had found a synagogue, and was reconnecting with her roots. And Rowan attended a small church, started by missionaries and run by Andaman tribespeople.

While the differences between the religions spurred lively discussions, the story of Eden bound the three together, and as the *Nigahl*—the Redeemed—they worked day and night to protect the secret with which they had been allowed to live, and to prevent the outside world from stumbling upon it.

When the last of the eight kids' pupils dilated and they were all laid back in a drug induced stupor, Rowan dropped anchor, jumped onto the aft deck and turned their night into a living hell.

As the teens screamed at horrors he couldn't see, experiencing wild trips on their own and as a group, he couldn't help but wonder if the same thing had been done to them. There was no denying that Emmei, Sashi, Chugy, Winston, and Ambani existed, but had they died?

When these kids woke on the beach the following morning, they might all recall their rescuers being murdered, or becoming monsters, or being murdered *by* monsters. Perhaps the true nature of Ambani's expedition was to simply pass on the torch from one team of protectors to another.

It was a nice theory.

Helped him sleep at night.

But every time he saw the island, and felt all those eyes staring back, he knew the truth: that normal life on planet Earth was separated from the supernatural by a thin veil, which they had crossed through and crawled back out of, bearing fresh scars and a new mission.

It had been real. All of it. And now Talia, Mahdi, and he stood watch, attempting to keep the two worlds apart. So far, they had succeeded, but he knew they would eventually miss someone. And if the story of Eden was true, what other ancient stories, beasts, and locations were real? He'd been studying the Old Testament with Talia and Mahdi in relation to their new job, pondering ancient mysteries and creatures.

Despite all their time, energy, and resources, there were two questions that had remained unanswerable: *If the supernatural is real, who is safeguarding it from the world and who is keeping the world safe from* it?

And then there was another question. No one had asked it aloud, but he believed all of them were thinking it. To give it voice would be to invite temptation, and eventual doom.

His mind flitted back to the island, past the sand, through the manicured jungle, and deep inside the overgrown garden, back to the yellow-lit paradise none of them had reached. That was where their journey had ended, and the question began:

What is in that yellow light, and how can I reach it?

A NOTE FROM JEREMY

I don't normally write about what is real and what is not real in my novels, but I feel like it might be necessary this time. Let's start with what is real. North Sentinel Island exists, as do the Sentinelese who populate it. They really do greet visitors with violence, and other strange behaviors, like sex acts on the beach. Some of the violent encounters detailed by Ambani are fabrications, but many are not, and some, like the actual wrecking of the *Primrose* have been slightly altered. Basically, the Sentinelese really are an island-dwelling tribe that has never had meaningful or positive contact with the outside world, living at a stone age technological level.

Now, as for Eden, its existence falls into the category of belief. But the details of that place, as detailed in the Bible are mostly accurate in the story. The Tree of the Knowledge of Good and Evil (a long name for a tree) was the tree from which Eve plucked the forbidden fruit and then shared it with Adam. 'That wasn't in the novel,' you say. Ahh, but it was! Remember the dead tree in the cave, with the footprints casually approaching and then running away? Mystery solved. The second tree is the Tree of Life (a much more concise name), which is guarded by Cherubim (plural!) wielding a flaming sword. Now, this is where I took some artistic license, both with the Cherubim's monstrous appearance, and with making the flaming sword a tribe. Other than that, there is no reason the island, an actual paradise untouched by the outside world for 60,000 years, couldn't be Eden—the location of which is never revealed in the Bible.

Whatever the truth is, I suggest not visiting the island to find out for yourself. Whether the Sentinelese really are a tribe of people guarding the Tree of Life, or simply a primitive island-dwelling people, you'll likely never leave alive.

Though this is one of my freakiest novels (and that's saying a lot), I hope you enjoyed the ride! If so, and you'd like to see more books like this (or maybe a movie deal for it…oooh) then help spread the word! The best thing you can do to help this, or any novel, is by posting a review on Amazon, and if you have the time or inclination, on Goodreads and other bookselling sites. Every single one makes a difference and helps Amazon determine which books it will recommend to other readers. Facebook posts, Tweets and good old-fashioned word of mouth is great too.

Thanks for taking the journey down this rabbit hole of doom with me, and I hope you'll come back for the next!

—Jeremy Robinson

ACKNOWLEDGMENTS

Going to keep it short and sweet this time. There are a cadre of people upon whom I rely to support my writing efforts and bring you the best novels possible. Kane Gilmour, my amazing editor whose dedication to the stories sometimes surpasses my own. Hilaree Robinson, and my three amigos, Aquila, Solomon, and Norah, you continue to inspire me…though not for stories like this one, because, weird. Roger Brodeur, your continued support and proofreading is always welcome. For Hebrew translations and phonetic transliterations, I need to thank Kati Takacs, Edward G. Talbot, Aaron Brenner, and Bhil Heath. Any errors that remain are my own. And to Lyn Askew, Julie Cummings Carter, Elizabeth Cooper, Dustin Dreyling, Jamie Lynn Goodyear, Dee Haddrill, Becki Tapia Laurent, Sharon Ruffy, Jeff Sexton, and Kelly Tyler, my dedicated special ops team of proofreaders, you guys rock and helped make this book shine.

—Jeremy

ABOUT THE AUTHOR

Jeremy Robinson is the international bestselling author of sixty novels and novellas, including *Apocalypse Machine, Island 731*, and *SecondWorld*, as well as the Jack Sigler thriller series and *Project Nemesis*, the highest selling, original (non-licensed) kaiju novel of all time. He's known for mixing elements of science, history and mythology, which has earned him the #1 spot in Science Fiction and Action-Adventure, and secured him as the top creature feature author. Many of his novels have been adapted into comic books, optioned for film and TV, and translated into thirteen languages. He lives in New Hampshire with his wife and three children.
Visit him at www.bewareofmonsters.com.